PRAISE FOR A VERY TYPICAL FAMILY

"I loved this. I couldn't put it down. Engrossing, satisfying. The minute I turned the last page, I messaged three friends to tell them they had to grab it. It's that good!"

—KJ Dell'Antonia, *New York Times* bestselling author of *The Chicken Sisters*

"By turns mordantly funny and deeply moving, *A Very Typical Family* is an emotional gut punch of a story about the often-fraught relationships we have with the people we loved first and fiercest: our siblings. Godfrey's redemption-seeking narrator is one of the most endearing eccentrics to grace the page since *Eleanor Oliphant Is Completely Fine* and *The Cactus*. If you like characters who march to their own beats—and who doesn't— you'll love this rich and compelling story."

—Ashley Winstead, author of *The Last Housewife*

"With wit and a big heart, *A Very Typical Family* gracefully tackles one messy family's rocky path back to one another. Godfrey has crafted a trio of siblings that readers will fall for on their journey of finding the courage to reach across the distances we create. Clever, sharply written, and at once darkly funny and tender, Godfrey's debut captures what it means to come home in every sense."

—Holly James, author of *Nothing But the Truth*

"At times lighthearted, at times gut-wrenching, *A Very Typical Family* is a touching exploration of what it means to forgive others and forgive ourselves. With a quirky protagonist and affecting characters, Godfrey has crafted a moving, memorable novel."

—Syed M. Masood, author of *The Bad Muslim Discount*

"Darkly humorous and deeply emotional, *A Very Typical Family* is a timeless story of hope and forgiveness. With rich imagery of Santa Cruz, Sierra Godfrey paints a vivid portrait of coastal California in this impressive debut novel."

—Kristin Rockaway, author of *Smart Girl Summer*

A VERY TYPICAL FAMILY

A Novel

SIERRA GODFREY

Please be advised, this novel depicts scenes of domestic violence and abuse.

For helpful resources, please refer to the back matter of the book.

Published by Sourcebooks Landmark, an imprint of Sourcebooks
P.O. Box 4410, Naperville, Illinois 60567-4410
(630) 961-3900
sourcebooks.com

Library of Congress Cataloging-in-Publication Data

Names: Godfrey, Sierra, author.
Title: A very typical family / Sierra Godfrey.
Description: Naperville, Illinois : Sourcebooks Landmark, [2022]
Identifiers: LCCN 2021056043 (print) | LCCN 2021056044 (ebook) | (hardcover) | (epub)
Subjects: LCSH: Estranged families--Fiction. | LCGFT: Domestic fiction. |
  Novels.
Classification: LCC PS3607.O3254 V47 2022 (print) | LCC PS3607.O3254
  (ebook) | DDC 813/.6--dc23/eng/20220118
LC record available at https://lccn.loc.gov/2021056043
LC ebook record available at https://lccn.loc.gov/2021056044

Printed and bound in the United States of America.
MA 10 9 8 7 6 5 4 3 2 1

To my boys: Ken, Matthew, and Tim.

CHAPTER 1

Natalie Walker was in danger of being late to work on what was possibly the biggest day of her career. First there was the previously undiscovered stain on the cardigan-blouse ensemble that was her power wear. She wasn't sure of the stain's origin but suspected spaghetti sauce from two nights ago when she had attempted to cook. It was too late to change, and dabbing at it only seemed to make it worse. Then she knocked over the jar housing a tiger swallowtail butterfly that served as a subject for sketching that she kept on the windowsill in the bathroom, sending the poor thing, wings blurring, skittering under the radiator. It survived.

She was almost out of the apartment when the mail carrier shoved a wad of mail through the flap in the door. Natalie would normally leave the letters on the mat, but the wedge of envelopes stuck in the flap. She pulled at the stack, falling backward as they released, sending the mail splaying all over the floor around her. There were a worrying number of bills—and one other envelope. It was addressed to her from a law office in her hometown. The sender was someone with "Esquire" after their name, which she knew meant lawyer, and that was undoubtedly bad if it was coming all the way from Santa Cruz, California.

"Good news never comes in a letter, Penguin," she told her cat, who sat licking his nether regions and caring not at all that his owner was getting ominous letters from lawyers.

She checked her watch and did what any normal person who'd gotten their brother and sister sent to prison would do: shoved the letter in the bottom of her bag, where it was safely out of sight, and dashed for the train.

Once on the train and trundling toward Boston safely on schedule, she let herself relax. Time to mentally practice the speech she hoped she would be giving at the company meeting. Public speaking was a little like what she imagined a swim through piranha-infested waters would be like: scary, unnecessary, and possibly fatal. *I am delighted to accept this position,* she would start. *I can't wait to carry us all into the next ten years.* No, that needed work. Something less vague.

After a decade of working for a small architectural firm where she wrote dossiers on the historic houses they restored, today she could be promoted to director. She had paid her dues, and the CEO often consulted with her about upcoming projects. It was time to put that to work by managing the office, overseeing their projects, and charting the future of Argo & Pock Architecture. As the director, her photo would finally make it onto the website's "About Us" page.

It was with an extra bounce in her step that she entered the building and made her way to the elevator bank. Even the ping as she arrived on their floor sounded brighter than usual.

"Hey, Natalie!" Katrina, one of the architects, beamed at her as she hurried by. "Today's the big day, huh?"

Natalie grinned in response. She didn't want to say anything, because she didn't know for sure about the promotion, but honestly, they all knew.

Her phone chimed with a break-a-leg text from her best friend and roommate, Teensy, as she headed for her desk. Natalie had to admit, she felt pretty good.

She dropped her bag on her desk and saw her friend Nina walk by. Nina was Natalie's afternoon latte pal and also the small company's human resources representative. It was Nina who had told Natalie several weeks ago over steaming cups of chai that the director position was up for grabs. Natalie wanted to chat with her about the meeting, but Nina had already disappeared down the hall.

"Morning, you." Paul slung a casual arm over the top of Natalie's cubicle wall and handed her a small bouquet of flowers.

"What's this for?" Natalie couldn't help smiling, pleased at his thoughtfulness. Paul was one of Argo & Pock's newest employees and also Natalie's boyfriend and Teensy's older brother. She hoped he wouldn't mind too much that she would be his boss in a little over thirty minutes.

"'Cause you're you."

"Aw." She wanted to hug him, but they tried to keep things professional at the office.

"See you at the meeting." He blew her a kiss and moved away, making her do a little inner squeal all over again that she'd passed his resume to Ann Argo, the CEO. That Paul had an architecture degree and was freshly back from living in Germany, where he'd worked on structural engineering projects, had made him a shoo-in for a job here. She dumped the dead flowers from her vase into the trash and put the new ones in their place behind a thick report detailing the Federalist-style roof molding of a renovation on Acorn Street—one of those wonderful old buildings that helped make her fall in love with Boston, and one of her favorite projects too.

Natalie's nerves prevented any meaningful work from getting done, so she opened her trusty sketchbook and filled in the fur on a drawing of a fox she was working on. She loved sketching animals and bugs and the calm concentration it brought. Ann was less thrilled with the amount of time the sketches took, but she had never denied the usefulness of having a project historian on staff who could draw.

"It's time," Natalie whispered to herself. Her stomach did a flip. The rustling of people standing and gathering filled the office. She made her way to the large conference room and sat next to Paul, trying to make it look like a casual choice.

"All set?" he whispered.

"Yep." She grinned, and he gave her hand a discreet squeeze. Things were going so well between them. How great that he could be here with her to witness her big moment. Not for the first time, she thought about how it would be to marry him. Teensy, who already felt like family, would become her actual sister instead of only her friend. They would have family barbecues and take big trips to the Cape in the summer. She would finally have a family again, and everything would be perfect.

Once everyone was seated, Ann addressed the group. "I really appreciate you all gathering. As you might have guessed, we have some big news about the direction of the company. The past few years have seen our work and staff grow at a huge rate. As you know, we've expanded to other major cities and states." She glanced at Daniel Pock, her co-CEO, who had recently opened the Chicago office and had flown in for this momentous occasion. "We're now pursuing Atlanta, Philadelphia, and Seattle as potential markets. We've taken on new investors, which means we can not only restore historic buildings but also buy properties, restore them, and sell them at profit."

A murmur of excitement rippled through the group. They all knew about Argo & Pock's expansion plans, but it was still exciting to hear about all the progress they'd made.

"And so, as I focus with Daniel on considering the new locations, it has become clear to me that we need someone to head things up here in Boston. Someone who is capable and knowledgeable, who not only gets the nuances of old homes but also understands the importance of building relationships with the community and city councils as we restore them. Someone who wants to grow Argo & Pock as much as I do."

Natalie's heart pounded. Ann may as well have looked up *Natalie* in the dictionary and read the description.

"We've decided to promote from within. This person will report to me and enable our staff, which was six people ten years ago and is now nearly thirty, to keep us on our growth trajectory. In five years, we expect to be a team of nearly two hundred with offices on both coasts and in between. I know this person is capable of helping us focus our efforts and achieve this growth."

Clapping erupted around her, but Natalie sat on her hands to stop them from shaking. She was one of the original employees. The only others remaining were Ann and Daniel, Argo and Pock themselves. This was it. "And so, with that, I have chosen someone with experience, a fresh vision, and extensive education, someone who only recently joined our team but who has shown himself to be hugely capable in that short time..."

Natalie blinked. *Him*self?

"Please join me in extending my deepest congratulations to Paul Sorenson, our new unit director for Boston!"

A rush of clapping, hesitant at first, then gathering steam, filled the room. Paul stood from where he sat next to Natalie and looked both humble and pleased. Natalie watched in shock, unable to care that other people were checking her face for a reaction.

Paul strode to the front of the room to join Ann. "I'm so grateful and honored..." His mouth moved and made sounds, but Natalie didn't hear the words. Had he known? Had he been told ahead of time he was getting it?

She kept her head straight and eyes ahead, keeping herself tightly under control as a wave of humiliation rolled over her. Tears began to march into her sinuses, but she did not allow them to come near her ducts to see the light of day. She would not cry. She'd done it before at work, like when an irate city planning member had screamed at her for including a home's supposed ghost in her report, or when a historical society board had berated her for not including a long family history in a document. She did not want her coworkers, particularly Ann, to be reminded of her past failure to keep her emotions in check. Was that one of the reasons a man, new to the company, had been given her promotion? Oh God.

Somehow, she made it through the rest of the meeting, during which Paul blathered on about what a great honor it was and how he hoped to apply everything he'd learned in Germany to Argo & Pock's work. Finally, it was over and she could bolt back to her desk. She pretended to check on her jar of pill bugs, wishing she'd finished the sketch of their segments before they'd died en masse, but her mind was focused on the betrayal.

Paul. Not her. Paul.

She fixed a bright, fake smile on her face for the rest of the day and avoided Paul, who also seemed to be very busy all of a sudden. Either he was avoiding her or he was busy signing promotion paperwork or moving into the corner office she'd dreamed of being hers. When Nina came by, looking wretched, Natalie avoided eye contact with her.

"I'm sorry I didn't tell you," Nina whispered.

Natalie shook her head. "You couldn't. It's your job to stay mum."

"I'll tell you everything from now on."

"Nina. It's all right." Ann had seen fit to choose Paul. Her decision had been made. It was too late.

"I'll refuse to sign off on the paperwork," Nina tried.

Natalie thanked her and waved her away. No sympathy—she'd cry for sure. She held it together until she was on the train home and then let loose, covering her wet face with her hands. Natalie had put in more hours and was more qualified than anyone. Ann had even *told* her to lean in! Meanwhile, Paul had sailed in using Natalie as a foothold, with his supposed fresh vision and other nonsense. How on earth could he give a fresh vision to a company he'd been at for only three months?

She would quit. This was it. The last straw.

Well, she wouldn't quit. Rent was due in a week, and she needed that paycheck. But she would update her resume. Start looking for a new job.

She didn't hear from that traitor until she was on the train, when he sent her a single text: Please, let's talk. Ha! So he could tell her he was sorry that she'd thought she was getting the promotion when it was him all along? No, thank you.

Five months she'd been seeing him, sleeping with him, talking with him, making plans. It had gone so well. Teensy had been trying to get Natalie and her brother to meet-cute for years. When no cute had been met, Teensy had turned to what she called "manufactured opportunities," such as tricking them into the garage and locking the door when they were all over at her parents' house for dinner, an alarming event that Natalie and Paul had ended up laughing about—and which had led to a date. And he'd been looking for a job at the time. Since Paul had a degree in architecture and Natalie worked in building preservation, it had seemed natural to hand Paul's resume to Ann and say good things about him so he'd get the job.

He'd certainly gotten one.

The worst part was, he'd been the best boyfriend she'd ever had. At first, she had been drawn to him because he was the sophisticated, enigmatic older brother. And then he'd been nothing but sweet and attentive during their months together. She'd been happy with him.

When she finally got home, Natalie was ready to collapse. She made some calming tea but sensed this would be inadequate. A chocolate assist was definitely in order. She dug into the very back of the freezer for the good chocolate ice cream. Desperate times.

Although she resisted it, her mind replayed the moment of Ann's announcement. Paul had been so smooth, running up to the front of the room and talking about taking Argo & Pock in all kinds of new directions (it was only the Boston office, for chrissake!) while introducing process-centric alignments or some other nonsense. He did have that professional sheen to him, and it was true that he was more experienced. He'd never mentioned wanting the position, though, not even when she'd shyly shared that she hoped to get it.

Her phone buzzed with yet another text from Paul. She couldn't face him right now. She shoved her phone down into the bottom of her bag, where her fingers scraped an envelope.

The letter. She had forgotten all about it.

She pulled it out and stared at it again. There was no way it was good news. It was probably something awful from a lawyer, telling her she was dead to her family—and she already knew that. Should she open it now, when things were already crap, or later when things were better, thereby turning them back to crap?

The sound of the key in the front door decided it for her. She shoved the letter back in her bag and sat up, preparing herself for the aural onslaught of Teensy. Natalie loved her dearly but sometimes appreciated the quiet moments before Teensy—an extrovert who loved to talk—arrived home. Her best friend's talkative nature wasn't a bad thing, and of course Natalie wasn't perfect either. Teensy loudly and frequently voiced disgust over Natalie's specimen jars and general messes. And she objected at all times to Penguin, who likewise did not carry much of an opinion of Teensy.

"Well? Are we celebrating?" Teensy yelled, throwing her keys on the table and shrugging off her enormous bag in one fluid movement. Penguin leaped off Natalie's legs and skittered down the hall, a streak of black fur with white patches. "You got the promotion, right? I was think-ing we should get celebratory drinks at McKearney's!"

Natalie took a deep breath but couldn't muster enthusiasm.

"What?" Teensy said, her grin disappearing. "What's going on there, on your face? What happened?"

"I didn't get it."

Teensy visibly deflated, her tall frame dramatically sagging. "What do you mean, you didn't get it? You're the most qualified person there!"

"Apparently not."

"I can't believe this. Have they totally lost their minds? Ah, okay, this is terrible news, but let's go to McKearney's anyway, and instead of celebration drinks we'll have Fuck Them All drinks, okay?"

"No, Teense, I don't—"

"And Paul! Paul will help. I'll call him."

"Stop." Natalie sat up fully. "Paul's the one who got it. Paul. Your brother. He got the promotion."

Teensy stared at her, eyes two wide circles of surprise.

"Yes," Natalie said. "The job *I* got him. He just took my promotion."

Teensy sank next to her on the sofa. "But he wouldn't do that to you."

"But he did."

"Oh, Nat." Teensy leaned her head against Natalie's much smaller shoulder. "We're going to need Sadness and Wallowing Drinks instead."

Natalie didn't feel like going out, but McKearney's and Teensy would probably cheer her up. "All right. One drink." It would be more than one, but that was probably what she needed.

Teensy gave a thumbs-up and shouted, "Good. You'll see. You'll feel better getting off the couch."

Without a single thought for the letter, Natalie got ready to go out. She would forget that Paul was her new boss. Forget that she should have gotten the promotion. Natalie was very good at forgetting things she didn't want to remember. She'd spent fifteen years honing this skill. She was a master at it.

CHAPTER 2

Teensy chattered nonstop in the car to McKearney's, telling Natalie about a man she'd met in the bodega near work. He was five foot three, she said, but charming in a way that made their height difference nonexistent.

"Listen, I'm the first to say that a differential like that would be nearly impossible," Teensy said, entirely too loudly for the small space, "but he was so smooth! Everything he said made me feel at ease. He made me laugh. He made me feel fantastic. You know what I mean, when someone makes you feel good about yourself simply by being them?"

"I do know."

"He's so...I don't know...inspiring. He had this sense of joy about him," Teensy said, swinging the car into a parking spot.

Natalie's older brother, Jake, was like that. Or had been fifteen years ago, when she'd last seen him. Even a walk down the street with him was be fun. Natalie allowed herself the luxury of picturing her brother, with the requisite pang that followed. Admitting that she missed him or her sister, Lynn, was strictly off-limits. It was bad enough with Teensy and Paul and their great sibling relationship always in her face.

"He sounds amazing." Natalie worked hard to inject enthusiastic support into her voice. If it weren't for Teensy in all her loudness, Natalie didn't know where she'd be right now. They had formed a firm friendship back when Natalie had stepped into their shared college dorm room in Boston alone, with no one to see her off or kiss her goodbye. No weepy parental drop-off or lingering too long in the dorms for her. Her mother hadn't even driven her to the airport in San Francisco. Teensy had taken hold of her immediately, giving Natalie somewhere to go for Thanksgiving and winter breaks and, even better, summers.

Natalie tripped getting out of the car and landed poorly on her ankle.

"This is what I need right now," she muttered, waiting out the bloom of pain.

"You're having such a shit day." Teensy held her arm as she hobbled into the bar. She abruptly stopped in front of Natalie, making her whimper in pain. "You know what? Let's not go in. Bad move. Sorry."

"Why?" Natalie tried to look around Teensy's large frame, but Teensy moved to prevent her. "Is a skanky ex-boyfriend in there?"

"Let's just go." Teensy tried to push Natalie back out the door.

But Natalie saw him. It was hard not to. Besides being taller than almost anyone else in the bar, including his sister, which was a feat, Paul's blond head was a beacon in the crowded bar. Talk about height differentials: next to the Teensy and Paul, Natalie's small, curvy frame, straight dark hair, and olive complexion from a Greek great-grandmother on her father's side made for a striking difference. She and her sister, Lynn, had both inherited these features, although Lynn probably hated that she and

Natalie shared any resemblance to one another. Natalie wouldn't know, because Lynn had cut her out of her life.

Oh no. Paul was waving at them.

"He's seen us," Natalie said. "Let's get it over with."

"Are you sure?" Teensy asked, looking anxious.

This had to be done sooner or later. "It's fine." They lurched over to his table.

Paul at least had the grace to look a little chagrined. "Hey. I was hoping you'd both be here. Nat, you ran off today at work. Why are you walking like that? Is your foot okay?"

"Rolled my ankle." Natalie lowered herself into the seat next to him. He frowned, as though her rolled ankle was an inconvenience to him.

"I was hoping we could have talked before you left."

"I had a lot of work to do," she said, shrugging. "Super busy."

"You left early," he pointed out.

"See how nice it is that we're all here," Teensy babbled.

"It is!" Paul brightened, looking pleased. "Did you hear my work news?"

"Ah," Teensy said, looking nervously between them. "Mm-hmm, you got the director position. Congrats. You know what? You kids talk. I'll get drinks!" She jumped up and headed for the bar.

"Congratulations on the promotion." Natalie did her very best not to choke on the words.

"Thanks." Paul nudged her shoulder, as though this intimacy would erase the fact that she'd wanted the job. "It's the first time I've been excited about a job in a long time. And I have you to thank."

"What?"

"You got me the job to begin with."

"Oh. Yes." She looked at her hands to hide the emotions clouding her face so he wouldn't see the hurt in her eyes. That drink Teensy was getting her couldn't come fast enough.

"Listen, I know you wanted the position," Paul said. "You're probably disappointed, and I feel terrible about that. I trust Ann had a very difficult decision to make. But this opens up possibilities for us both."

Natalie gaped at him, unable to think of a single possibility in her favor. Maybe she was being awful. Was she being awful? Jealousy was never good, even when it was entirely warranted.

"Natalie, listen." He had that earnest look on his face that he got when he talked about work. "I'm here for you. We're a team."

On one hand, she appreciated that he'd picked up on her tension. That was solid boyfriend behavior, there. And she liked him a lot. On the other, she needed to decide whether him being her boss warranted breaking up with him.

"I'm disappointed," she admitted. "I need a little time to get over it."

For a moment, he looked like a pouty child with a pushed-out bottom lip. "I wanted to talk to you about what happens now. This position is going to let me put roots here. I've decided to buy a condo downtown, and I hope you can stay with me often. I mean, I'm talking about you moving in. I'd really like it, and I think we're ready. There will be no weirdness because I'm your boss, I promise."

Natalie closed her eyes. She wished she were one of those people who could process things faster. It might take her a day, or a year, or ten. Look at what had happened with her brother and sister—that had been fifteen years ago, and she still wasn't over it. She was slow to react and change, that was the problem. A known flaw. Like the ugly fact that she was thirty-two years old, but her salary was more like that of a twenty-two-year-old, and she was unable to afford rent on her own. She had really needed that promotion and the raise, and if that wasn't happening, what was her plan B? There wasn't one, of course. She swallowed, feeling a little sick at just realizing that now. If she held very, very still, like a deer hiding from a predator, maybe this bad news would go away.

"Because," he continued, talking fast now, as though he knew her attention was slipping, "I know we aren't that far into things, but I think we're good. I *know* we're good. I care for you. I'm on the way to loving you. So what do you say? Yes? It's a huge place, massive windows. View of the harbor. It'd be much better than you sharing a place with my sister."

The image was lovely. She would have liked to pick a place with him, but she'd mentioned a few weeks ago how much she would like a home with huge windows in it. He'd be paying the mortgage, so she guessed he could choose the place—even as a slight drop in her stomach suggested that him making all the decisions was not exactly how she had envisioned her life with a partner. Living with Paul, the first person in a very long time whom she was serious about, was a solid step on the path to the life she wanted, where the hurt and grief of having siblings and a mother who hated you would fade away.

"Let me think about it," she said. As soon as the words were out of her mouth, she knew they were wrong. What, was she supposed to kiss him goodbye each morning and hand him a homemade lunch while he went off to her job? "We'll talk later, okay? I have to go." She got out of her chair, wobbling on her dumb ankle, and limped toward the bar.

"I am totally committed," Paul called after her.

"Need to bounce," she hissed at an obviously worried Teensy, who hovered at the bar, cringing. "Now."

"You got it." Teensy put down the drinks she was carrying and steered her out of the bar.

Teensy kindly said nothing on the ride home. It was only a five-minute drive, but it took that long for reality to hit Natalie: she might be losing her carefully constructed future. She imagined going into work, where it was one thing when you were dating a coworker and another thing altogether when you were sleeping with the boss. Worst-case scenario, he would expect to screw in the supply closet, which was a secret fantasy of his that he had not dared act on before, and she would resent his face. She would have to quit, or he would fire her—and then what? She had no idea what she was going to do.

— — —

Natalie called in sick to work the next morning. Penguin kept her company in bed, and together they scrolled through awful daytime television. It was better than going in and facing her humiliation in being passed over for the promotion they all thought she was getting.

Teensy was home too, as it was her morning off from the family counseling practice where she worked. She bashed around the kitchen, frying eggs and singing, which made Natalie burrow deeper into the bedcovers. Sometime around midmorning, Teensy burst into her room holding up Natalie's bag. "Your phone keeps going off in this thing." She dropped the bag on the floor next to the bed.

"Thanks." Natalie didn't move. Her finger hovered over the TV remote. Penguin flicked his tail in irritation at the forced pause in their show.

Teensy narrowed her eyes. "You going to wallow all day?"

"That's my plan."

"Do you want some counseling?"

"You know I don't."

Teensy rolled her eyes and left.

Natalie leaned out of bed for her bag, upsetting a jar of crickets on her bedside table that had been both subjects for drawing and sustenance for her small green anole lizard named Patrick. The jar lid remained intact, luckily. (Teensy would never let her hear the end of it if crickets spilled out onto the floor—not after the last debacle involving praying mantis eggs that had hatched ahead of schedule.) She pulled out her phone to see four missed calls and six texts from Paul and two calls from Ann. She put the phone on silent and threw it back in the bag, where her eyes landed on the unopened letter again.

She pulled it out, weighing it in her hand as though it were made of lead. May as well get whatever it was over with. She slid a thumbnail under the flap of the envelope and pulled out a single sheet.

Dear Ms. Walker,

I am the administrator overseeing the trust set up by your mother, Patricia Louise Walker.

I offer my condolences on her recent passing. She died on May 22, and while every attempt was made by her partner, Buck Howard, to notify Patricia's children, he did not have your contact information.

Natalie stopped reading, arrested by a smack of shock. Her mother had died more than two months ago, and she was only now hearing about it?

Patricia established a trust some years ago, placing the title of the historic Victorian at 325 Oak Street in it and listing her three children as beneficiaries. You are each to receive a third ownership in the property. My role is to assume fiduciary responsibility for managing the trust assets and to carry out the purposes of the trust.

Ownership of the house where she'd grown up—the massive mansion her great-grandparents had built in Santa Cruz with stunning cupolas, a tower, and intricate gingerbread trim? Her eyes went back to the letter to learn more, even as she struggled to process what she was reading.

Patricia left conditions for the fulfillment of the trust. All three of her children must come to the property within three months of the date of this letter in order to inherit. If any one of you does not appear within that time, the property will be donated to the Santa Cruz Historical Society. The house is currently unoccupied.

Natalie looked up, eyes wide. That mansion was a block from West Cliff Drive, the city's most picturesque street, the ocean only a short walk from the front door. It was worth millions of dollars now, easily. The house was listed as a historical property because her great-grandfather had been some biggie in diamond mining and had sunk most of his fortune into the house, only to die shortly after construction was completed. His son, Natalie's grandfather, had not been keen on remembering his father's colonialist sins, but the house remained written up in local history books regardless. That house was one of the reasons Natalie liked writing histories of properties at Argo & Pock.

It was impossible that she and Lynn and Jake could all be there together, though. Her mother knew the siblings hadn't spoken to each other for fifteen years. Was this her idea of a sick joke?

As trustee, I will determine whether the requirements of the trust have been met. Please contact me at your earliest convenience with your intentions.

Yours sincerely,
Jorge Garcia, Attorney,
specializing in family trusts

Natalie realized the paper in her hands was shaking. She had the urge to put the letter down, take a long nap, and forget the whole thing. She wondered what her mother had died of. It had been four years since they'd last talked. A lot could have happened. She thought of the old house with its three floors and seven cozy bedrooms, the two living rooms, the formal dining room with charming built-in cabinets, and the library full of unread stories. The smell of furniture polish and old wood and the sound of ancient creaking floorboards. And it would all go to the Santa Cruz Historical Society. Unbelievable.

Natalie dug her phone out of the bag and dialed the number on the letter even as alarm bells went off in her head, warning her to wait, calm down, and think things through. She could not, though. She needed more information.

A receptionist picked up, and once Natalie identified herself, she was put through.

A rich, grainy voice came on the line. "Jorge Garcia."

She took a deep breath. "This is Natalie Walker. I'm calling because I received a letter from you about my mother, Patricia—"

"Ah, yes. Patricia Walker's estate. You have my condolences on your mother's passing."

Natalie swallowed. There. It was real. Her mother was gone. Complex, spaghetti-like feelings overwhelmed her, and she didn't know what to feel first. Sadness? Regret? Indifference? What was the right thing to feel when your mother had stopped speaking to you years ago?

"Thank you. I'm only surprised it took her this long to kick it." The words were out of Natalie's mouth before she had time to consider them, and she regretted them immediately. It wasn't what she wanted to say, or suggest, and it wasn't as though her mother had been particularly old. Clearly, bitterness was the first emotion Natalie would feel. "I didn't mean it like that."

"I'm sure you didn't," the lawyer said in a tone that was too kind, too empathetic.

He was going to think she was a callous ass who didn't care about her mother dying. It was so, so much more complicated than that.

"It's a lot to take in," she said.

"Of course."

"How—how did she die?" Natalie held her breath. She had not considered any of her family dying before.

"Ovarian cancer, I'm afraid," the lawyer said. "Her partner, Buck, assured me her passing was peaceful."

Natalie still could not breathe. The idea of Buck at her mom's side was wrapped up in memories she'd buried so deep down it would take a backhoe to dig them up. "And…did she have treatment?"

"I don't have that information. I'm sorry."

She pressed a fingertip to her temple as though that would help bring clarity. "And are you sure I'm an heir?"

"Your mother was quite clear that all three of her children were to be beneficiaries equally, provided you all return within three months."

Natalie shivered. Fifteen years had passed since the arrest, or That Night, as Natalie thought of it. She hadn't spoken to her brother or sister since. Tension-filled phone calls to her mother over the years had devolved into total estrangement. Shortly after Natalie had arrived in Boston for college, her mother had told her, "I can't choose between my children. I can't."

Natalie had asked, "Do you want me to give you space?" even though she was three thousand miles away and as far as space went, her mother had it.

Patricia had been silent for a long time and then said, "Yes. I need some time."

Natalie had wanted to ask how much time. Days? Weeks? Years? "I get it. I'll be home at Christmas."

Her mother had not replied, and Natalie, who hated long, tense silences, had finally asked, "What?" though she was pretty sure she knew what. "You don't want me to fly home, do you."

"I think it's better if we play it by ear," Patricia had said, confirming Natalie's fear.

For a while after that, Natalie would call occasionally to ask how things were. Patricia would say, "I'm working through it." Natalie always felt that was a ridiculous answer. It was a way of putting her off, like the time Patricia had left them on their own for several weeks after their dad had died when Natalie was ten, Lynn thirteen, and Jake fourteen because she needed to "work through things." Natalie realized now that her mother had been having some kind of breakdown, but kid Natalie had only known that her mother had gone away, Lynn was the one making mac and cheese for dinner, and Jake was making sure they all got home safely from school.

Before Natalie had stopped calling her mother at all, four years ago, Natalie would say, "It would be good to see you. We could talk." She had hated herself for sounding so vulnerable, so emotionally needy, but this was her mom. Surely Patricia would respond.

Patricia had only said, "At some point."

The last time Natalie had seen Lynn and Jake, they were being led away in handcuffs and wearing orange prison clothes after their sentencing. Natalie had written to them in prison, but Jake's letters had returned to her unopened with RETURN TO SENDER stamped on them, whereas Lynn had responded with long diatribes about how selfish Natalie was. Natalie had spirited this away into the Hole of Not Caring (along with being unable to sustain a decent relationship—until Paul—and not advancing in her job) and had done a passably good job at hiding from herself that the estrangement didn't hurt at all, as though she didn't feel like she'd been stabbed in the gut.

Natalie took a shuddering breath as she gripped the phone to her ear. "And…do they know she died? Lynn and Jake?"

"I don't know," Mr. Garcia said. "I have sent them both similar letters as yours. You were the first to call."

Natalie knew exactly where Jake was, of course, because she had Googled him often over the years. She knew all about how he'd gotten an education—a doctorate—after getting out of prison and was now a big shot scientist at the University of California Santa Cruz's Long Marine Lab. His faculty web page for the Department of Ecology and

Evolutionary Biology had him listed as the "principal investigator at the Walker Lab." Not only was the lab named for him, but he was also the author of numerous publications on the migration patterns and nesting behavior of Monterey Bay cormorants and sandpipers, with recent research focusing on bird intelligence. Last she'd checked, Dr. Walker (she could not imagine calling her brother Dr. Walker) was leading a seabird research team. That her druggie brother, Jake, had become a smarty-pants professor of birds was something she was secretly enormously proud of—from afar.

Lynn, however, had no online footprint. "Where, um, is Lynn?"

"The address I have for her is in Brooklyn, New York."

Natalie had no idea Lynn was in New York. It was shockingly close to Boston, compared to California. She wondered what her sister did there.

"And I have to be at the house in order to inherit it?" she asked.

"That's correct," Mr. Garcia said. "Along with your siblings."

"That's not going to be possible. We don't—we don't speak. Can you consider this my agreement?"

He chuckled, as though she were being facetious. "I am here to oversee the terms of your mother's trust, Miss Walker. Please let me know when you think you'll be in Santa Cruz next."

"But that might not be for years." If ever.

"The terms of the trust are clear."

She huffed out a disbelieving breath. "So you're going to give the house to the historical society?" They had to be drooling over the prospect, if they knew.

"As I said—"

"Yes," she interrupted. "I get it. Thank you for your time."

"I hope to see you soon."

After she ended the call, Natalie pictured the house: her grandfather's wall-to-wall books in the library, covering all sorts of enticing subjects; the little turret room on the third floor; and of course the ornate living room, where everything had gone wrong—where Lynn had challenged her not to call the police, and where Natalie had, without breaking eye contact, called them anyway.

It was hard to imagine the house being uncared for. The house had always felt as though it had a personality. The kids in the neighborhood loved to say it was haunted. It wasn't, sadly. It was the kind of old house Argo & Pock would do an incredible job with: a historic Victorian with every gingerbready detail possible. Natalie stared into space, feeling the strangeness of using the rusty brain muscle that thought about that part of her life. All right, so none of her family wanted to talk to her, but she had always assumed someone would tell her if her mother was sick or near death. Her mother had not been old—she had been in her fifties. Natalie could not picture her as frail or ill, and she wasn't sure how or what to feel.

No. There were reasons no one had told her anything. She could never go back to the house or to Santa Cruz. There was certainly no way the three of them could get there within three months. Her verbal agreement from the East Coast would have to be enough.

She searched on her phone for Jake, even though she did it every few months. Nothing had changed on his website to indicate he wasn't still in Santa Cruz. Mr. Garcia had said Lynn was in New York. She tried to picture her sister with a Joe Pesci accent and found that she no longer remembered the sound of her sister's voice. She searched for Lynn again, but as with previous times, she found nothing.

Natalie ached to see them.

But there was no way. She would not be able to get the time off work. And there was Penguin to think of. It could not be done.

"Right?" she asked the cat, but he looked away.

Her phone pinged with an incoming text. She checked it to see one from Nina.

Are u ok??? Ann is trying to get hold of u!! Call her!!

Natalie sighed and quickly typed back, I'm ok, before dialing Ann's number.

"Where are you?" The CEO's voice was clipped, the way it got when she was annoyed.

"Stomach flu."

"It seems as though you're playing hooky because you have sour grapes over Paul's promotion."

Natalie cringed. "What? No."

"Don't bullshit me, Natalie."

Natalie tried to think of what to say that didn't admit she was absolutely fermenting her sour grapes into wine. "Okay, fine. I thought I would get that promotion."

"I can certainly understand that." Ann's tone softened. "You've been with us a long time."

Natalie nodded even though Ann couldn't see it.

"You know, you do great work for us," Ann said. "And you draw exceptionally well. You're always putting those sketches into the reports. Have you thought about doing more of that?"

"I draw, yes, but that's not my professional goal," Natalie said. This wasn't totally true. Her secret dream was to be a scientific illustrator, but she had no training. It was a little late in life to switch over to something that she had no education or experience in.

"Listen," Ann said. "Let's—let's find a solution to the emotions here. I know you and Paul are together. I don't want a weird atmosphere in the office because of this. Why don't you take some time off? Think about what you want."

Ann was not known for offering her employees time off for thinking. And Natalie had already used all her vacation time for the year. "Are you firing me?"

"Not at all. I'm saying that I can see this is a big pill to swallow, and I want success for everyone. Take a week or two and cool off, and then let's see where we are."

This sounded worrisome, but Natalie glanced at the letter lying on the bed. "Actually…I did receive a letter about my mother in California. She died and left the family house to me and my brother and sister, and I need to be there to inherit."

"Well. I'm sorry to hear that. You can go to California. I'll extend whatever vacation time you have."

"I have none."

"Take the two weeks, Natalie." And there it was: the fanged edge to Ann's tone that Natalie knew so well. Ann ended the call.

There was no denying that space from Paul could help right now. Natalie ran a hand down Penguin's length and leaned back against the pillows. It seemed ludicrous that she would return to Santa Cruz after all this time. The East Coast was her home now.

Then the realization that she would have to get on a plane hit her. No way. Could not. She had a break-out-in-hives fear of flying. And rightly so. "I can't fly. It can't be done."

Penguin looked at her with his soulful yellow eyes that suggested that if she went, she would need a chaperone, and that chaperone might as well be him.

"Nat!" Teensy called from the kitchen. "You want lunch?"

Natalie climbed out of bed and went out to the living room–kitchen area.

"It lives," Teensy said. She unpacked a plastic bag of sandwich bread, giving Penguin a nudge away from her feet.

"I called Ann."

Teensy's brows knitted together. "Did she fire you for playing hooky today?"

"No. Not exactly. She suggested that I take some time off."

"Uh-oh." Teensy's eyes went wide. "Why?"

"I got a letter." Natalie did not want to spell out that Ann's suggestion carried a threat of unemployment. It was too embarrassing.

Teensy's left eyebrow rose. Natalie handed her the paper.

Teensy scanned it, then read it again. She put it down and gave Natalie an incredulous look. "Oh my God. Your mom died. Wow, Nat. I'm sorry. And you're getting the house?"

Natalie shook her head; she was still trying to process it too. "I know."

"This says you have you to be in Santa Cruz to inherit. Within three months."

"Yeah."

"That's…kind of huge."

Natalie nodded. "I know."

"And Lynn and Jake aren't at the house?"

"The lawyer said he hasn't heard from them yet."

"Have you told Paul?"

Natalie sighed. "It's weird with him right now, Teense. We have to figure out how to navigate this new dynamic." She twisted her lips. "He says he's buying a condo."

"Uh-huh," Teensy said, cautious in a way Natalie recognized as her being a supportive best friend.

"He wants me to move in with him."

"Well, that's good news," Teensy said. "Isn't it?"

"In the big picture, yes. But right now, I'm hurt."

"You're allowed to be." Teensy straightened her stance and lost her smile. In its place was a frown that usually said she was morphing into Business Teensy. Natalie could almost see PLAN written in her eyes. "But you can't wallow forever. Listen. Here's what you'll do. You haven't been back to Santa Cruz since you were a teenager. And space is what you need from Paul and work. Ann is giving you the time off to deal with this and fly out there."

"I can't fly," Natalie said quickly.

"Right, you can't fly because you have some deep fear of flying that you won't even tell me about. So you should drive."

"Drive?"

"Yeah. Drive out there. Do whatever you need to do and come back. The trip will cool you off."

"Drive across the country in my beat-up, ten-year-old car? Such a good idea. And I have Penguin. You've made it clear you won't be responsible for feeding him or changing his litter box."

"Take that stupid cat *with* you."

"Yeah, cats are super known for loving car rides."

"Penguin is not a normal cat," Teensy said. "He is a demented hell beast, and he most certainly would enjoy a car ride with you more than staying here with me. And believe me, it's mutual."

Having heard this, Penguin headed into the nearest bedroom, which happened to be Teensy's. He was not unknown for voiding his bowels next to her bed in times of stress.

"Don't go in there, you rat cat!" Teensy shouted, and Penguin diverted to Natalie's room. Teensy turned back to Natalie. "I think this is a very healthy thing. If you can see your brother and sister, maybe you guys can make amends."

"That will never happen."

"And you can talk to your stepfather—"

"My mom's boyfriend."

"—and find out what happened. Seriously, I think this will help chip away at the years of hurt. What if you go back and inherit the house and you're able to confront the past? It might help you heal a bit."

"I don't need to heal."

Teensy nodded gently, as though she heard Natalie's declaration for what it was: a denial of the truth. "Okay, but what if you took care of this business, and maybe the time away will help clear your head on how you feel about work and Paul?"

Natalie breathed in through her nose. "Teense, our agreement is that you're not supposed to analyze me."

Teensy only raised her eyebrows in response. "I'm being real with you. As a friend. Not as a therapist."

Natalie knew Teensy was right. And driving might not actually cost that much, if she was careful. She could return to Boston with a renewed direction for her life.

"I don't think there will be amends with Lynn and Jake," Natalie said.

"They may not even show up."

Natalie nodded, waffling.

"I think you should go," Teensy said.

"I could start a travel blog."

"Let's not get out of hand."

Natalie sighed and looked at her best friend and saw a face she loved and respected. They'd spent so much time laughing together. She sensed that their friendship might be on the brink of changing no matter what choice she made, especially if things didn't work out with Paul. "I'll think about it."

"Natalie." Teensy handed her a cheese sandwich. "I can tell you're all muddled about things right now. The job thing is weird, and you don't know where you stand. You wish you could draw for a living. Things with Paul might be up in the air. And your mom just *died*, man. That's a lot. That's heavy stuff. You're allowed to be uncertain. But there is one thing you are."

"What's that?"

"You are your mother's child and one of her beneficiaries. So go be that for now."

This struck Natalie as true, even it wasn't necessarily who she wanted to be at the moment. It was the clearest thing she'd heard in a while, anyway, and it felt comforting. She nodded. "Yeah."

Teensy thankfully let the subject rest, and Natalie went back to bed to watch a rom-com and clear her head. She'd just settled under the covers with Penguin at her side when her phone pinged with a text. Paul.

Natalie, I'm gonna say it: I love you. I'll support you in anything you want to do. Please call me.

She sighed and stared off into space for a moment. He loved her.

Settling down with Paul and marrying him eventually would mean her future would be secured with Teensy as her sister-in-law and Natalie's entry into the Sorensen family complete. She'd have a whole new family who loved her, one she hadn't screwed over.

She steeled herself and called him. "Hey."

"Hey," he answered. "You got my text?"

"I did."

"And?"

"And…" She took a deep breath. "I'll admit: I was upset that you got the promotion and I didn't."

"I totally understand."

"But I'll also tell you: I got some news that my mother died—"

Paul started to interrupt her with condolences, but she cut him off. "No, I know, thanks. But I'm inheriting her house—our house—in Santa Cruz."

"The mansion you told me about?"

"Yeah. I spoke to Ann about it. She's going to give me time off to go out there and deal with it." Natalie felt, as she had when telling Teensy about the time off, emotionally unequipped to delve into the fact that it was an order from Ann, not a request.

Silence. "So you're going out there? You haven't been back to California since you left for college, right?" He sounded incredulous.

"Right." She waited a beat, very much hoping he didn't have an opinion, which he often did.

"So that sounds like a big deal, going out there and stirring up old issues."

"My mom died, Paul."

"I understand—and I'm sorry, of course. But think this through.

Going back there could open a lot of things from your past that you may not want to deal with. And I talked to Ann at length this morning about our relationship, and I assured her that it wouldn't get in the way of me managing you. I said we need time working together to show her how well it could go. If you leave for California, that whole process gets stalled." His voice was smooth, that professional tone he used when he was in an argument or negotiation with a planning committee. He and his sister were a lot alike in that regard. "I want you to move in with me, and my promotion changes nothing about how I feel about you."

She narrowed her eyes. "Are you suggesting that I not go to California because you want your promotion to go more smoothly?"

"No, of *course* not." His words were fast and had a tinge of indignation, as though she were the one being outrageous. "You've told me yourself that you have zero salvageable relationship with your family. Me and Teensy, we're your family now. And my parents. My parents love you!"

Natalie thought back to Teensy's earlier words. Maybe she was right: a road trip to California would give Natalie the space she needed from him, and she wanted that space very much right now. "Paul. This is big. I need to go. I need to…" She breathed in, choosing her next words carefully. She wanted to go out there and think. "Maybe we should take a break while I'm gone." There. The words were out.

"A break? What kind of break? Yes, of course, being on two different coasts is a physical break. Sure. Yes, I agree."

She pursed her lips. "A break from us. A relationship break."

"What, like, see other people? Natalie, that's crazy. No. I love you. I don't want to see anyone else. Sweetheart, this is you being really upset about some shocking news. Trust me. I've been through my share of shocking news in life, and this is a blip. It will pass."

She hated it when he did that—used his ten years on her to suggest he'd been through everything already and she was just young and immature.

"Not seeing other people," she said. "But you could, because that's allowed on a break. To be clear, I have no plans to see other people. This is just…a break from our relationship. So I can work through some stuff in my own head." The more she talked, the more appealing it sounded. It was surprising, but also not. She'd have to examine that later.

"No." Paul breathed in audibly, and Natalie could picture him shaking his head. "I don't want a break. I don't need one."

She said quietly, "I need it. I'm taking the break."

"Look, I get that you want to go to California. I hear you. Okay? I hear you. Of course I support you in anything you want to do. Go, see what the deal with your mom's house is. But no break. I'm very much in this. You and I are in a great thing, Natalie. We're collaboratively creating our lives."

"Paul." She closed her eyes. His unilateral decisions about their relationship had been an issue since they'd started dating. At first she'd chalked it up to something she could call out when it happened, since it was usually small, like ordering her ice cream for her instead of letting her decide, which was bad enough. But this was next level. "I'm—I have to pack. I'm leaving tomorrow. I'll talk to you from the road."

"Natalie—"

"I do love you. But the break starts now. I'll talk to you soon. Bye." She ended the call amid further spluttering from him. She didn't necessarily feel good about this, but she felt she'd done the right thing.

Natalie pictured herself driving across the country, wheat fields on her right, the Grand Canyon on her left, Penguin relaxing on the passenger seat, rocking a little pair of sunglasses on his furry face. If Lynn and

Jake had not responded to the lawyer yet, maybe they weren't going to. Natalie could fulfill her part of the trust, at least, and see what happened afterward. The time away would be restorative.

That decision made, she opened up the maps app on her phone and began plotting her cross-country road trip.

CHAPTER 3

Natalie opened her window to let some air in after the curvy descent down the mountains on Highway 17 into Santa Cruz. As she came to a stoplight off the highway, she realized she was sniffing out the tang of the sea. It wasn't for everyone. The scent held notes of rotten sea kelp with a bouquet of salt, but to Natalie it was overwhelmingly home.

As the light turned green, she heard a distant, clattery rumble followed by joy-filled screams. She recognized it instantly: the Giant Dipper roller coaster, an ancient wooden behemoth, echoing up from the Boardwalk, the city's seaside amusement park. It was a sound ingrained in her psyche, one she associated so much with Santa Cruz that when she heard roller coasters elsewhere or on TV, she was hit with a wave of homesickness.

She drove slowly through town, checking on old businesses, noting new ones. There was disorientation as her brain tried to reconcile the memory with the reality—a reality that had ticked on by without her for fifteen years. The old feel of Santa Cruz's lazy beach culture with a hint of dirt was still there, despite the amount of wealth that had moved into the area. She drove up the hill past Santa Cruz High, remembering all the times she and her best friend Michelle had skipped class to go to the beach. Michelle now owned a successful boutique in the downtown mall area. When Natalie had texted her from somewhere around Iowa to say she was coming back, Michelle had been thrilled. A little buzz of excitement slid down Natalie's spine at the thought of seeing her soon.

She passed the wharf and drove up the hill to West Cliff Drive, drinking in the impossible blues of ocean and sky, her excitement growing. The trip across the country had taken longer than expected—a whole seven days—mostly due to losing Penguin a few times in national parks after he'd taken off after a chipmunk, followed by hours of shaking his treat can and him pretending he'd never heard of treats until he got hungry enough to come back. It was hard to believe she was really here. The road hugged the cliffs, winding along affluent neighborhoods and enormous homes. Surfers in the water below caught whatever little swell they could, out today as they were every day year-round. The only thing marring the scene was Penguin's tiresome meowing from his cat carrier. He started up a volley of complaints every time he sensed the car slowing.

Now her old street appeared in front of her, and she saw her house's enormous roof looming large, rising above the rest of the rooflines on the block. She drove up the steep driveway and onto the pea gravel on the side of the house, the familiar crunch of her tires almost Pavlovian. The sound of home.

She got out of the car, ignoring Penguin's outraged screeches, and stretched. The sea air blew in her face, and she gulped a deep breath of it, feeling a strange mixture of pleasure mingled with guilt. This delicious and slightly rotten sea air wasn't hers to enjoy anymore, and yet here she was.

The house's dilapidation was worse than she had imagined. Her eyes traveled up the dirty siding and the cracked, broken lattice of the veranda and second story. It was still magnificent, a perfect Victorian, but it looked as though it had stood empty and alone for a long time. A gust of wind blew, and a window somewhere on the house rattled. It wasn't as though she hadn't known it was in bad shape, but seeing it in person was like visiting someone in the hospital and seeing their shrunken and withered body for the first time. The once-fine front garden was a mess of tangled thorns. Gone were the carefully designed flower beds, obliterated by weeds and the thick ropes of blackberry vines. The painted facade was grimy and pockmarked with dry rot. A surge of emotion filled her chest for this old home, for its sad, neglected state.

She pulled out her phone and called Teensy.

"Teense," she said. "I'm here."

"Thank God," Teensy said in an overdramatic voice. "I was worried we would lose you in some seedy trucker bar in Nevada."

"I almost did stay in one, but they didn't have any stripper outfits that fit my butt. Anyway, the house looks terrible."

"Well, that's why you're there."

"Yeah." Natalie kicked a piece of gravel. Her mother had moved to a small mountain community above Santa Cruz with Buck years ago. It was not clear what she'd been doing with the house. The idea of it having sat alone, cold and unloved all these years, was too much.

"Paul's been calling me," Teensy said. "He said he hasn't talked to you since you left. He's worried."

Natalie sighed. She'd ignored his calls during her drive, knowing he wanted to discuss the break—multiple text messages from him saying he was *not* on a break had made that clear. "I'm sorry."

"He wants to give you space, but can you at least call him?"

Natalie had set herself a goal of calling him when she passed through the Midwest to talk things through with him like an adult, but with every state she passed that qualified as the middle of the country, she had talked herself out of it. She owed him nothing. Well, she owed him—no, she didn't. And on and on. "I will, soon. I promise."

Penguin began howling, sensing he'd been forgotten in the car.

"I can hear that wretched animal all the way across the country," Teensy said.

Natalie laughed. "I can put him on the phone if you'd like."

"Ugh, do not. Go do your thing. I'll enjoy the cat-free quiet."

"I'm sorry about Paul, Teense." Natalie looked up at the gingerbread gables on the second story, now hanging loose.

"It's fine. We're still friends." Teensy laughed, presumably to show Natalie that she was being lighthearted. Teensy had merely raised her eyebrows and agreed it was not a bad idea when Natalie had told her about the break. But Natalie knew Teensy was worried. A full breakup with Paul would inevitably affect their friendship, even though they'd both sworn up and down when she had started dating Paul that nothing would change between them.

Natalie said an upbeat goodbye and grabbed Penguin's carrier and a bag before stepping over the line of ants making their way along the cracked cement walkway, shaking off the few who had climbed onto her shoe. Eager to be out and exploring, the cat thumped around in his carrier, upsetting the balance and causing her to nearly drop him. The huge wooden front door—redwood, hand carved by her great-grandfather with four-inch-thick tenons and a complementary Palladian arch over it—looked dry but sturdy and reliable.

Natalie allowed herself a moment to fantasize about opening the door and seeing her mother and Lynn and Jake. Older, but still recognizable. Their faces would light up when they saw her, and they would pull her inside.

"Sweetie!" her mother would call, her voice full of warmth.

"We forgive you," Jake would say. "Of course we do. It's been fifteen years. You're our baby sister. This is how family is!"

"I mean, I won't *forget* it—it was three years of prison, after all—but I do *forgive* you," Lynn would say.

She felt a surge of love for the old place and for the memories of what it used to be. It had been a long time since she last wished things had been different with Jake and Lynn. What life would have been like if she hadn't called the police that night and they hadn't gone to prison. What her mother would have been like if she hadn't shut down and retreated from them. All of them coming back here for holidays and visits. Did her brother and sister have children and spouses now? She didn't even know. Regardless, this place would be in better shape and a part of all their lives.

A pair of crows flew down to sit on low bushes near the front steps, turning their heads and eyeing her and, probably with great interest, the cat carrier.

"Signs of death," she told them. One gave a soft *qwuak*. It seemed to be expecting something, she thought. Food? Crows were supposed to be extraordinarily intelligent. She reached into her coat pocket for the packet of almonds she'd gotten at a gas station and tossed a few on the ground in front of the bush. The crows waited a moment, as though trying to discern whether it was a trap. Then the first flew back and the second one flew down. She itched for her sketchbook to draw them, but it was in the car, and the goblin noises Penguin was making probably wouldn't improve if she stepped away.

The crow grabbed the nut and eyed her, not flying away immediately. Her mother had always kept a bird feeder in the backyard. For the first time, a sharp prick of loss hit her. Her mother was not going to come back and fill the bird feeder. She was gone.

Natalie went down the steps and poured the rest of the almonds on the ground. "There. See? I'm not horrible." She wasn't sure whether she was telling this to the crows or to her mother. Thinking about her mother's death was a hornet's nest of confusion, and she'd mostly avoided it during her long hours of cross-country driving. She didn't intend to unpack it right now.

Penguin hissed and yowled in his carrier, suggesting that she hurry it up. The crows flew away.

She climbed back up the steps to the front door, pulled out her key, and fit it into the lock, relieved and a little surprised when it turned. The key was one of those things she'd taken with her from apartment to apartment even though she hadn't expected to ever use it again. Every time she thought about tossing it, she reasoned that it didn't take up much room and it was kind of a relic. It was the only thing she had from this house.

The big door swung open into a wide foyer with the grand main stairs beyond. A musty, closed-up smell greeted her, but there were no signs of transient use or vermin. The small table was still there, nestled next to the hand-carved redwood banister, but the silver tray they had used to hold mail was gone.

She reached over to flick the switch for the overhead light, and to her surprise, it went on. The trust had kept the power on, anyway. A chill had settled in the house, but that was nothing out of the ordinary. Growing up, they had lit the fireplaces in their rooms behind beautiful wrought-iron grates because central heat cost too much in a house of this size. She closed the front door and bent over to let Penguin out of his carrier, who emerged with an air of authority that Natalie certainly didn't feel. He stalked across the foyer and into the living room, exploring his new territory.

She worried that going in the living room—called the parlor when the house had been built in the late nineteenth century—would unleash difficult memories, but it was easier to follow an insouciant cat. In here, the old sofas were covered with dust sheets. The familiar old hutch still stood across from the entry, dusty and unloved. The only difference was the addition of finely illustrated bird prints on the walls. No ghosts. She peeked under a sheet and saw the old sofa from her childhood, in remarkably good condition. She pulled it away and instantly the room felt more alive, warmer.

The difficult room done, she walked through an arched doorway to the dining room. It brought back instant memories like film reels. It was an octagonal room with built-in shelving for china, now scattered with mouse droppings, but the severe oak table she had played hide-and-seek under with Lynn and Jake still sat in the middle of the room like a monarch on its throne, waiting to be adored. She trailed a hand along its edge, picturing Jake sulking at dinner as a teenager. She could see him, thin and handsome with his black hair, doing his homework there and blasting Weezer from his boom box. Her mother, standing over there, introducing Buck to them even though they'd known him for years as their married neighbor. Saying she loved him, and Buck smiling that goofy smile and saying that he loved their mother too. Jake asking what Buck's wife thought about that. Buck's face darkening with anger at Jake's impertinence. Years later, the police detective sitting in a chair over there, telling her mother exactly how serious the charges were. Her mother crying, looking very small in her own chair. Days after that, her mother sitting Natalie down and suggesting she accept the offer to a college that was far away in Massachusetts.

Penguin had gone ahead, peering cautiously around corners at first but was out of sight now. The silence in the house was deafening. In the kitchen, the exposed brick wall was cheery and comfortingly familiar despite the grime.

The old light shade was still hanging over the breakfast nook, the one her father had installed. It had been right before Christmas, and Natalie had hung out with him as he worked, squatting on her haunches and trying to look serious about holding the screwdriver. She had been looking forward to winter break. The break was two weeks long, but at age seven, this felt like an eternity, nearly as good as the endless summer months. Somehow, after the break, you'd come back to school in the new year different, changed. Older. Silly to think that now, since it was only two weeks. But in her case, that year the change had been real. Her father had left them the day after Christmas, driven out by one final catastrophic fight between him and her mother. The silence in his wake had been palpable, and then he'd died one day later in a small airplane accident, doubly devastating everyone. This was the root of Natalie's fear of flying, which she had told no one, not even Teensy.

Everything had gotten difficult after that. Their mother had disappeared for more than a month. When people had asked where Patricia was, Jake had lied and said she was staying somewhere nearby or was coming back soon or was only away for a moment. When she had returned, things had gone on as before, but they had all been wary of their mother's moods, which could change at lightning speed.

Something creaked on one of the upper levels. The old house shifting, surely.

"Penguin!" Natalie called, as though cats gave a damn when you called for them. She turned out of the kitchen and into the back hall to the dark set of servants' stairs. They never had housekeepers or cooks or anything of the sort—in fact, after her father had died, her mother had taken in a series of renters on the third floor. The back stairs were from an old era when staff existed and were not expected to use the grand front stairs. Natalie had played Lady of the Manor with Lynn when they were little, where Lynn was always the lady, and Natalie always had to be the servant. She hated the back stairs because they were so dark (so of course Lynn made her use them), but later when they were teenagers, it was useful to sneak up them when they came in late. Because he was the oldest, Jake had used them liberally and then shown Lynn and Natalie where all the squeaks and creaks were so they could avoid them and get upstairs undetected.

"Cat!" Natalie called again. She thought she heard his bell tinkling on the second level. She went up the stairs, initially hesitant because of the ingrained sense of childhood fear, then laughed at herself. The stairs were smaller and not as dark as she remembered, but she was pleased to see that her feet automatically went to the parts that didn't squeak with admirable muscle memory.

Upstairs, all four of the bedroom doors stood open. It would have been creepy, except it felt so fondly like home, well-worn and comforting.

Another creak. Natalie thought she saw Penguin's tail disappearing into what had been Jake's room. Last she'd seen it, Jake's room had been oppressively black: black paint, blackout curtains in the windows, even a black light in his ceiling lamp. She could see his en suite bathroom beyond. Lynn had coveted Jake's private bathroom with the heat of a thousand white-hot suns, trying every trick she could think of to get him to switch rooms with her. Once when he was away at a weekend track meet, she had switched the entire contents of their bedrooms. Jake had arrived home, taken one look, and calmly ordered Lynn to switch them back. He had told her it was that or she would find her room on the front lawn when she got home from school. Lynn had cut her last class the next day to get home before him, but he had already been there, throwing piles of her clothes outside. She had switched the rooms back after that.

Penguin's bell tinkled behind Natalie, and she turned to see him stalk out of Lynn's room as though he were done with it now, thank you very much. He turned and walked into the big bedroom, her parents' bedroom, empty and dusty looking. Natalie went to the last room on the floor: hers. It was at the front of the house next to the master bedroom and included one of the turrets, although on this level and the ground level they were bay windows. She wanted to call to Penguin and tell him to come look, but calling one's cat to show him your childhood bedroom was slightly higher up the crazy scale than taking him on a cross-country road trip.

A single bare mattress sat in her room, which was somehow worse than nothing. It was as though instead of voluntarily moving out, she'd been kicked out. She looked around at the walls, not painted white but still her old mint green. She had hated the green.

The cat's bell jingled. Natalie saw him running up the steep single flight of stairs to the third floor.

"All right," she muttered, following him up. "The full tour it is."

On the third level were an additional three bedrooms and a bathroom, all smaller than the ones on the second floor and built into the roof line of the house. They had not been built with comfort in mind, but Natalie had always thought them quaint with their sloped ceilings and cozier footprint.

She heard little paws on the hard wood, running into the turret room opposite the stairs.

The turret was a small, perfectly round room that had been one of their favorite spaces as kids. As with most three-story Victorians, the turret began on the first floor and reached up to the third. This room, located directly above hers, was half-size with rectangular windows and a vaulted, pointed roof. The perfect height for kids.

Now all three of the windows were broken. The little space was filthy. Spiders and their eggs sacs had taken over every corner, and four sleeping bats were nestled on the pointed ceiling. Natalie wanted to sketch them so badly that she nearly turned and ran for the car. The floor was littered with dirt, grime, and various animal refuse. Incongruously, a child-size broom leaned against the wall. No one had used it in a very long time.

Penguin had found a hole in the plaster through which he had squirmed and was now inside the wall.

"Get out of there," Natalie scolded, making a grab for him. The cat swiped at her playfully and scooted out of reach. "Penguin! Get out of there! Now. Penguin!" She grabbed the broom and tried enlarging the hole with the stick end, but he only swatted at that too.

"Who is Penguin?"

Natalie jumped so forcefully that she hit her head on the sloped ceiling. Heart pounding so hard it hurt, she turned around and saw a boy of about twelve or thirteen. And the spitting image of Jake.

CHAPTER 4

"Who are you?" the boy asked. He was tall and thin and had recently sprouted in height if his too-short jeans were any indication.

Natalie stared at him, unable to unsee her big brother from when he was thirteen. This boy even had the same haircut: straight dark hair tapered up the sides of his head, swept over from a side part.

"Who are *you*?" she asked. Jake must be dead, and this was how his ghost had decided to present itself.

The boy frowned almost imperceptibly. It wasn't only his face or hair. It was his body type and the way he held himself: slightly stooped and always wary. This was absolutely Jake.

If he *was* a ghost, then she'd like to have that out in the open right now. "Jake?"

The boy laughed, and she felt stupid. "No one calls me that."

Her head ached where she'd smashed it into the low ceiling. "What's your name, then?" If he was real, where the hell had he come from?

"Jacob. But no one calls me that either."

She closed her eyes. "I don't understand. Do you remember me? Natalie?"

At this, the boy's eyes went wide, as though she were the ghost. "Seriously? As in Natalie Walker?"

"Yes." Ghosts weren't supposed to ask these kinds of questions.

"My mom's going to freak." He turned. "Mom! Mom! I know whose car that is!"

Natalie felt very uncomfortable in the small space. This boy, who looked like Jake and had his same name and yet wasn't called either of those things and was too familiar when he shouldn't be, was talking to someone else. And as footsteps came pounding up the stairs, Natalie sensed she'd know exactly who they belonged to. Sure enough, an older, wider Lynn appeared.

Natalie gaped, speechless.

"Oh, wow," Lynn said. "You're here."

Natalie tried to take in all the changes in her sister. Lynn looked unkempt, dressed in baggy, stained jeans that were two sizes too big for her and an old, faded maroon shirt that had seen better days. It wasn't as though Natalie hadn't thought they would age, but Lynn's flyblown and tangled formerly black hair was faded into gray and she had put on weight—but then, who hadn't? The last time Natalie had seen her, she was eighteen, and Lynn was a slim twenty-year-old. Natalie had grown up seeing her sister paint layers of toughness over her worries. Now Lynn had an air of slumping weariness that was shocking.

"You're my nephew," Natalie told the kid. He even had the same pattern of freckles that Jake did.

"She was talking to something or someone called Penguin," Not-Jake told his mother.

Lynn frowned and looked behind Natalie into the turret. "Who is Penguin?"

"My cat," Natalie said. "He's in the wall."

"Your cat is in the…wall."

"Yes."

Lynn shook her head. "Okay…"

This was such a Lynn thing to say that Natalie grinned but tried to hide it. This conversation was a newborn chick, wet and unsteady and awkward.

Penguin poked his head out of the wall, perhaps curious about the conversation, and Natalie took the opportunity to try and grab him, but he dodged her.

"So bad," she murmured.

"You *did* have a cat in the wall." Not-Jake stepped forward and grabbed at the cat.

"Wait—" Natalie began, because Penguin would surely deliver one of his patented flesh-ripping claw swipes that had so terrorized Teensy, but she didn't finish, because the boy had grabbed Penguin by the scruff and pulled him out of the wall like a boss. An altogether professional move. Penguin's legs dangled helplessly as the boy pulled him against his chest and smoothed down the top of his head. Amazingly, Penguin did not yowl and attempt to remove the boy's eyeballs. Instead, he closed his eyes in pleasure at the petting.

"Ah, wow," Natalie said.

"Okay," Lynn said, eyes on the cat. "Kit, put that cat down. This place is filthy." She glanced at Natalie. "We're exhausted. Drove here from New York. We're setting up sleeping bags downstairs. Where are you staying?"

Natalie had not been sure what she would find when she got to the house, but barring wreckage or the inability to get past the foyer because of bad memories, she had planned to stay at the house. "Here. In my old bedroom."

Lynn squinted. "I wasn't really prepared to find you here—or stay in the same house with you."

A flush crawled up Natalie's body. Here it was. Lynn still hated her and couldn't stand to be in the same house as her. "I'm here because Mr. Garcia notified me. I'm sure we can sort out the house stuff and… I'll get out of your way."

Lynn grunted, which Natalie knew meant tacit agreement. "At least the power and water are on."

"No Wi-Fi," Kit said, still cuddling Penguin.

There was so much Natalie wanted to know. She'd always outwardly pretended she did not care what her siblings were up to, but that was a complete lie.

"You're living in New York?" she asked. "I'm just outside of Boston. So close. Who knew."

"Who knew." Lynn's tone was slightly sarcastic, and it held that note of finality to it that Natalie recognized as a warning: she did not want to discuss this. It was thrilling that Natalie could still read her sister.

Lynn turned and headed for the stairs, Kit following. Natalie followed too, dying to bombard Lynn with questions: What were her plans regarding the house? Had she known when their mother had died? What did she do for a living? Was Kit's father around? Why wasn't he here?

"Lynn." She knew she would sound plaintive but risked it anyway.

"We're really tired," Lynn said, her voice floating up the stairs. Again, perfectly pleasant yet final.

But the lure of talking to her sister for the first time since the sentencing was too great. Natalie followed them down the stairs. "Can we talk for a minute?"

Lynn stopped on the landing to the second floor and turned to her, hands on her hips. Kit waited behind his mother, watching them. "I'm not trying to be mean, but this is a lot. I don't know you anymore. It's a weird situation and kinda cute that Mom tried to make us all play nice with the house. But we're different people now. We're strangers."

Lynn turned, her back ramrod straight, and she and Kit went down to the main level, leaving Natalie behind.

— — —

The sound of the front door shutting was followed by the noise of a raggedy engine moments later. Natalie could tell by the way the car crunched on the gravel that it was backing up, and then a moment later she heard it recede down the street. She waited until she couldn't hear it anymore before going downstairs.

Penguin sat licking his haunches at the bottom of the main staircase. Natalie sighed and went out to the car to get his litter box, Patrick the lizard, and the rest of her stuff. Overwhelmingly, she wanted to talk to Lynn more. And she was incredibly curious about her nephew.

She unloaded her things in the house and then got back in the car and went to get groceries and a sleeping bag that didn't cost thousands of dollars and wasn't made only for sleeping on the side of a mountain at high altitude. By the time she got back, it was dark. There was no car and no sign of Lynn or her son.

There was no sign of Penguin either, but all it took was the sound of a pull-top can of cat food opening for him to appear out of nowhere. With the cat fed and her own dinner, a premade sandwich, consumed, Natalie was at a loss as to what to do next. Her mind drifted to her mother, wondering about her final days. Natalie supposed she would have to find Buck and ask him. She didn't want to. She might have to hear why her mother had not wanted to see or talk to her, especially at the end of her life.

The house popped and shifted, which it had always done, but was otherwise quiet. The only thing missing was the soft tick of the grandfather clock, which needed to be wound. Again she felt that familiar push-pull of deserving to feel out of touch, yet resenting the space of years and distance that had kept her away.

She remembered the one room she hadn't visited yet: the library. Her favorite room in the house.

As she walked down the long hall lined with framed illustrations of intricately drawn birds, Natalie wondered if she could produce something frame-worthy like that. God, she'd love to be able to do that professionally.

At the end of the hall, she paused in the doorway. This room held all her deepest and best memories, and also the saddest; it was where she used to picture her father the most. She pushed open the door and flipped on the light, the old Tiffany lamp on the enormous desk lighting up. Her eyes flitted over the familiar floor-to-ceiling shelves filled with wondrous volumes of history and fairy tales and classics. It had not changed at all. Even her grandfather's old metal half-moon chair still sat neatly behind the desk made of redwood, from the days when the coastal redwoods were still being carelessly logged in the Santa Cruz Mountains. She stepped closer to the shelves, her face falling as she saw that the books had not aged well. The spines of most of them were peeling or split, and some had mold spots. She reached over to open the single window behind the desk for some fresh air, but it wouldn't budge. The wood casing cracked ominously when she pulled.

She ran an eye up the shelves again. A book spine caught her eye near the desk by dint of still having color and lacking mold. She bent down and pulled it out. A hardcover on birds, titled *An Exploration of the Shore Birds of the Monterey Basin*. Her eye flicked back to the shelf, and she saw more reference books on birds—at least two shelves full of them. She looked at the one in her hand, and before she even saw the author's name, she felt recognition dawning: Jacob Walker, PhD.

An enormous swell of longing for her big brother filled her chest. Where was this brilliant professor brother of hers? Would he appear here like Lynn had? The thought gave her a shiver of anticipation.

The soft swish of a feline tail fluttered against her legs, and a strange clicking sound followed. When she turned, Penguin wasn't there. Strange. Moving to the doorway of the library, she called for the cat, listening into the silence for the ting of his bell. She thought she heard it faintly, far away. Her eyes moved up the wall to see framed degrees—all Jake's. She looked around and out into the hall, noticing again the framed illustrated bird prints. More of Jake's influence.

She reached out and touched one of the walls, her fingertips brushing across the wallpaper. It was faded in several places, and some spots had been worn through to the plaster behind it. When Natalie was little, her mother had been fanatical about replacing and repairing the wallpaper with the last remaining swatches left in the attic. It was obvious that her mother had wanted them to keep the house in their possession and restore it to its former glory.

She called again for Penguin, louder, longer. Nothing. Had Lynn or Kit accidentally left a door open when they left?

"What are you yelling about?"

Natalie turned to see Lynn coming in through the front door, her arms full of groceries.

"I can't find my cat. Did you or Kit let him out?"

Lynn rolled her eyes. "No. Keep a closer eye on your animal." A bag teetered precariously in her arm, and Natalie moved forward to help. Lynn, unbalanced, accepted the help but then righted herself immediately and shrugged Natalie's hand off. Typical Lynn. She'd never needed anyone's help, but for a second it was something.

Natalie followed her toward the kitchen. "Can we talk?"

Lynn dumped the bag on the counter. "Do you want to have a long, emotional talk about my time in prison?"

Natalie cringed. "No, I—"

"Good, 'cause we're not doing that. Life's been hard, Natalie. I have an amazing son, but apart from him, there's not much more to know." Lynn's ragged appearance and quick movements suggested she was on her guard and possibly worried about something.

"I mean, sure there's more, like where you live, what you do—"

"Three years, Natalie. Three years in prison. Because of you." Lynn leaned against one of the grocery bags on the counter. "We've moved on, Jake and I."

Natalie licked her suddenly dry lips, feeling nervous. "I know you've moved on. He's a professor now, with his own lab. He's got a PhD in ornithology. I mean, the guy got out and became a scientist. No, he's not the same person who went in, but—"

"I know all that." Lynn rolled her eyes. "Just because he got out of prison and educated himself doesn't erase the past. He has scars."

Natalie stared at her sister, trying to decipher what she meant. "Literal scars?"

Lynn's eyes narrowed. "What, like he was shanked in prison? Is that your idea of his time there? They're psychological scars, Natalie."

Natalie studied the chipped and faded linoleum on the kitchen floor. She'd sailed through college with ease. Her biggest issue then had been dealing with what she'd done to Lynn and Jake. She'd gotten counseling, which had helped some, but it probably hadn't gone far enough. So she'd punished herself in small ways, like forcing herself to major in architecture and environmental science even though she had wanted to study art and biology, as though denying herself what she really wanted was a way to atone for ruining Lynn and Jake's futures. Ten years on and she could see how ridiculous that was, but standing here with Lynn, the feelings were still there, strong as ever. She badly wanted Lynn to forgive her but had no idea how to go about it.

"Jake has had to fight for everything he has," Lynn said. "They nearly denied him the degree even after he presented and passed his dissertation. Even after all the research he'd done, some of it the only of its kind in the world, and after all the years of studying and research. Anyone who found out he was an ex-con questioned his integrity. Can you imagine what that's like—being one of the top people in your field yet someone always questioning whether you should be there because of a stupid mistake from your past?"

Natalie winced. "I didn't know."

"How could you know? You were thousands of miles away, and you never had to think about us again."

"I'm sorry," Natalie said, feeling that familiar old pull of shame. "That doesn't convey it adequately, I know. But I did miss you both and think about you. I tried to find you online."

Lynn shrugged, as though to say she didn't care about Natalie's attempts. "I don't do social media. You want to know about my life? Sure. Okay. I married Kit's father as soon as I got out of prison, and he turned out to be a complete shit. We never stopped fighting. I went to mortuary school. It was the only schooling he would allow me to do. I sewed the mouths of dead people shut. Even now, he enjoys telling me how worthless I am. He says I'm only good enough for the dead."

Natalie stared at her sister, horrified but trying not to show it because she sensed Lynn, who prided herself on being tough and capable, would not want her pity. She couldn't imagine any man foolish enough to argue with her strong, bullheaded sister, but of course that was stupid to think. She didn't know the first thing about their relationship.

"I'm so sorry," Natalie whispered. "Did you—did you leave him?"

"Yep." Lynn busied herself with the groceries, probably so she didn't have to see Natalie's sympathy. "The day I got that letter from the lawyer, we got in the car and drove away."

Natalie felt like a tool. Her own problems seemed ridiculously small by comparison. "Does he know where you went?"

Lynn didn't answer.

Pushing Lynn had historically invited explosions, and Natalie didn't want this fragile contact to break. She decided to try a different tack. "Any idea where Jake is? The lawyer said he lives in Santa Cruz."

A flicker of worry passed over Lynn's face. "He does live in Santa Cruz, but I don't know where he is. I haven't been able to get in touch with him. We don't talk much."

That was sad to hear. "Do you—"

The muscles in Lynn's jaw clenched as she looked at her with a clear, level gaze that made Natalie shrink a little. "Once he gets here, I expect we'll talk about options. I don't think we'll want you to stay."

Natalie opened her mouth to tell her sister that she didn't have to worry, that she was headed back to Boston once they secured the house, but a wash of pain dried her words. This was the shunning she'd always feared. The sensible part of her brain said that Lynn had had a long drive and was tired. She should leave her alone. She probably wanted to go to bed and not be interrogated by a sister she greatly disliked. But Natalie was like a kid with ice cream: talking to Lynn was an urge she couldn't leave alone.

"Night, Natalie," Lynn said, her tone pointed. She gave Natalie a stern look and left her to the quiet of the kitchen, punctuated by periodic clunking sounds from the old refrigerator.

Natalie tapped a fingernail on the counter. On the whole, the conversation hadn't been the wreckage she'd feared over the years. It could have gone a lot worse. Lynn hadn't screamed at her or refused to talk at all. While it was clear she didn't like Natalie, maybe she no longer *hated* her. But Lynn had said she didn't think she and Jake would expect Natalie to stay here. They hadn't forgotten or forgiven her for That Night, then. Natalie wasn't surprised. In the years since it had happened, she had tried all kinds of ways to justify her part in it, but the result had never changed: she was largely at fault. She, too, had never forgotten That Night.

CHAPTER 5

Eighteen-year-old Natalie was supposed to be sleeping over at her best friend Michelle's house. It was early June, two weeks until her high school graduation, and summer had officially arrived in Santa Cruz: blue skies dotted with V-shaped echelons of pelicans, the Boardwalk open every day, and crowded beaches. The perfect setting for losing one's virginity before heading off to college.

And crucially, their mother was in Portland on a weekend away with Buck. Lynn and Jake, still living at home despite being in their early twenties, had taken advantage of the freedom to plan a party.

But Natalie didn't care about the party. She had big plans with smoking-hot Alex Hernandez that night. A pitcher for their high school baseball team, number twelve. Doz, they called him, short for Dozen, the number on his uniform. She was in stupid love after three dates, only one of which had been an actual invitation as opposed to "I'm hanging out here if you want to come by."

"Are you off to have sex with that boy you've been chasing?" Lynn asked as Natalie left the house that night.

She scoffed. "I'm staying the night at Michelle's."

"Right." Lynn's throaty, knowing click said she wasn't buying it. "Stay at Michelle's, and don't make any stupid decisions. And you're not to come home tonight under any circumstances. We're having a party, and you're too young for it."

That meant drugs. Lynn and Jake could have their party. Like Natalie cared. She would be tossing her virginity out the window with Doz. He was the sole focal point of her attention, not whatever drain scum Jake and Lynn had coming over that night to toke up and play their terrible ragey music. Natalie and Michelle had decided that going off to college without their virginity was the key to beginning their adult lives. Michelle had beaten Natalie by sleeping with her boyfriend the previous weekend, so Natalie was determined to get things going.

She met Doz at a pizza place downtown. It wasn't her choice—she'd wanted something fancier to set up the momentous evening—but Doz could put away pizza like a beast, and she was willing to make concessions to smooth the way.

"Do you know when you're leaving for Arizona?" she asked. Doz had been scouted to play baseball for Arizona State and had a full scholarship waiting for him.

"Yah." He had jammed a whole slice in his mouth and spoke through the dough. His scholarship was such a big deal, and it was disheartening that he didn't want to talk about it with her. She and Michelle had spent hours talking about the different universities they had been accepted to, which included far-off ones in Boston (Natalie) and even Europe (Michelle).

"That's good," she said. "Really good."

His eyes were elsewhere, watching someone across the restaurant. Natalie pretended to fiddle with her shoe so she could execute a half turn and surreptitiously see who it was. A spike of irritation shot through her when she saw Brandi Charleston, a fellow senior and a surfer with perfect boobs and killer legs. Brandi was wearing her gym shorts from school, which were entirely too short. Natalie might wear them too, if she had legs like that. She was nothing like Brandi, and this worried her, because if Doz had a type, it might not be Natalie's.

"Where do you want to go after this?" she asked, trying to keep his attention.

He shrugged and folded another slice into his mouth.

"The beach?" she asked.

His eyes finally met hers. "Yeah. Sounds good."

Relief. Natalie had packed a colorful sarape that Jake had brought back from Mexico a few months ago when he'd gone on a marijuana run. It was perfect for spreading out on the sand and losing one's virginity. Michelle had given her a condom. She was all set.

"Hey, Doz."

Natalie looked up from her own pizza to see Brandi standing at their table.

"Hey," Doz said, his mouth miraculously empty and his voice a markedly softer, more delighted tone than the grunts he'd been giving Natalie.

"And Natalie," Brandi added, a clear afterthought.

"Hey." Alarm bells clanged in Natalie's head, and she tried to think of a reason Brandi would have for standing here talking to Doz other than that she liked him and she wanted him—and Natalie—to know it.

"A group of us are having a bonfire on the beach tonight," Brandi said, directing this to Doz. "At Twin Lakes. If you want to join us."

Natalie suspected this didn't include her. Doz's eyes snapped to hers once, quickly, as though he was trying to decide if it did too.

"We're actually going to the beach later," Natalie said, thinking that maybe they'd pick a different one on the west side. "So—"

"Sounds good," Doz said to Brandi.

"Cool. See you later." Brandi gave Doz a lingering look as she moved away, and Doz, the idiot, followed her perfect butt with his eyes. He turned back around and crammed another giant slice in his mouth.

Natalie stifled a sigh. All right, so this was not a romantic love story here, but that didn't mean all was lost.

"I was actually thinking of Its Beach," she said. "You know, by the lighthouse?"

"I know where it is." Doz wiped his mouth and attacked another slice. "Twin Lakes might be better."

Natalie's plan was falling apart. They had not exactly discussed that they would have sex, but the previous weekend they had made out in his car in front of his house, and it had gotten steamy. He'd let out a little moan and asked if she wanted to "do more," which she hadn't at the time because they were parked under a streetlight and Natalie had seen curtains in Doz's house flicker several times. So Natalie had said on Friday at school that maybe they could go to the beach this weekend and see where things went, and Doz had raised his eyebrows suggestively and said that sounded great.

"I brought a blanket," Natalie said now, hoping he'd get the hint. "And some other stuff."

Doz's eyes lit up. "Stuff from your brother?"

Stuff meant weed, of course, which Doz seemed to think was on a ready tap from Jake. This assumption was built on the legend of Jake that was still told at Santa Cruz High, in which his glory days as a supplier and partier were woven in with the fact that he was an academic superstar, excelling in all his classes, graduating as the valedictorian, and giving a rousing speech—entirely while high. Doz was possibly seeing Natalie with the hope this would prove fruitful, but she didn't know and preferred not to think about it.

"Let's go to Its Beach." Natalie chose to ignore his question about the existence—or not—of weed. She'd never smoked it and never had any inclination to try it. Lynn and Jake weren't fun when they were high. Natalie didn't want to be like that.

"Okay." Doz stuffed the last piece of pizza in his mouth and wiped his greasy fingers on an inadequately absorbent napkin. He grabbed four more from the dispenser, balled them up, and threw them down on the table before walking away. Natalie picked up the napkins and brought them to the trash can nearby. She'd dreamed, in her more fantasy-prone moments, of marrying Doz once they were out of high school with a few years of college under their belts. He'd be a promising baseball star, drafted into the minors out of college, and she'd move around with him and support him in his dream. Probably cleaning up after him wherever he went.

Yeah, no. Not exactly the stuff of great love.

But sex now: yes.

He strode ahead out of the restaurant, leaving Natalie to scurry after him, resenting that she had to scurry, resenting that she was in fact scurrying after anyone to have sex but still determined to go forward with the plan.

"Wait for me," she called, hoping that by commanding him, she could pull back a bit of the power she'd lost. Much, much later, after everything else that happened that night, she realized she'd *handed* the social power over to him, not lost it. Gifted it to him without a second thought. It was something she would resolve never to do again.

But it worked, and he slowed and waited for her to catch up. He slung an arm around her shoulders, and the weight of it felt good. His pitching arm.

He kissed the top of her head. "You ready?"

She didn't know what he was referring to, so she applied her own definition to it. "Absolutely. I have everything." She patted her beach tote.

"Cool." He squeezed her against him, and she felt better, better about the Brandi distraction and the animal-like eating and the napkin mess. He was a nice guy, and he liked her, and she could forgive the obliviousness of teenage boys. She'd watched Jake work his way through every stage of stupidity, so she knew.

In the car, he headed to Ocean Street, in the direction of Twin Lakes beach.

"Its Beach is the other direction," she said.

"Thought we'd start at Twin Lakes and then end up at Its." He reached over and rubbed her knee. A promise.

It was early dusk, and the bonfire was already blazing when they trudged through the sand to the party, in the middle of which Brandi was dancing. She had removed her shirt and wore only a sports bra—looking excellent, Natalie had to admit. Chairs and coolers sat around the bonfire, filled with kids from school. Someone handed Doz a beer, which he accepted, but no one handed Natalie anything, unless you counted the look of resentment from Brandi. As the sky deepened into orange-black, it was clear that Its Beach was not in the cards. Doz didn't speak to Natalie the rest of the night. He stood on the other side of the metal bonfire pit, talking about baseball with some of his friends. Every now and then, he grinned at Brandi.

And when Brandi danced over to him and wound her arms around his neck like a serpent and he laughed and moved his body against hers, Natalie, feeling physically sick with rejection, decided she'd had enough. She wished she could be angrier, but she'd only been using Doz anyway. Instead, she just felt lonely and stupid.

She worked her way around the pit to leave, looking one last time at Doz. He met her eyes across the swirls of firelight in the hot air above the bonfire, his smile dropping. She waited a moment, not breathing, for him to run over to her and apologize for ignoring her all night. But then he turned back to Brandi, his smile reinstated.

Natalie made her way to the road. It was three miles to walk home—so bad. The hour it took was fueled by the sharp slap of hurt, even though a part of her couldn't blame Doz for not being as into her as he was into Brandi. She hadn't given him much opportunity to know her, and she didn't have Brandi's measurements to cover for a personality. She was using him, after all, wasn't she? But this was an inconvenient truth, and she was allowed to feel hurt and betrayed.

Everyone—Brandi included—knew they were going out. Natalie really hated that part; Brandi enjoyed a solid status as Hottest Girl in School, so most of the guys drooled over her. She didn't need to take Doz. She could have any guy. Michelle's boyfriend, Dave, freely admitted to finding Brandi hot but always quickly qualified it by telling Michelle that she was beautiful and amazing and he couldn't imagine dating anyone else. (This turned out to be false, as Natalie would later learn. That very night, he was sitting on a cliff overlooking the ocean with Michelle and having a talk about their future, which was code for "I'm going to college, and I want to screw everyone there, so I'm breaking up with you." Which he did. He got chlamydia.)

By the time Natalie arrived home, her feet ached and the hurt had hardened into a throbbing anger. Music blasted from the downstairs windows. Their mother would be livid if she knew. Natalie pushed open the door to find a cloud of smoke and a glazed-eyed Lynn in the foyer. In the living room were Jake and his best friend, Carlos, and what looked like actual drug things on the coffee table, beyond the typical bongs and joints. Serious stuff.

"Come on, Natalie, we told you to stay away tonight!" Lynn yelled.

Natalie watched as Carlos bent over what looked like a hypodermic needle in his hand. She was outraged by this, fueled by her anger at Doz. "Seriously? Needles? You guys are insane. That's so dangerous."

"What did I say?" Lynn snarled. "If you don't like what you see, get out. Aren't you supposed to be out with that jock boyfriend of yours? What, he didn't want to help you lose your virginity before graduation?"

How the hell— Natalie did a quick calculation of how Lynn could possibly know.

Lynn gave her most evil grin, which was a feat considering how high she was. "You think I can't hear you and Michelle giggling through the wall? That's what it is, isn't it? You were going to go off and have cute teenage sex with him, and he turned you down." She threw her head back and howled with laughter.

From the living room, Jake raised a not-unbrotherly eyebrow and looked at Natalie through his haze. "Really?"

"No," Natalie said.

Lynn snort-laughed. "How did that go down? You asked for sex and he left?" Her eyes went wide in mock shock. "Did you beg?"

Natalie shook her head in disgust and started up the stairs, but Lynn grabbed her arm and prevented her from going. "Come on, little sister. Tell me how it went." She had that nasty glint in her eye that was a telltale sign that she was high. It was one of the reasons Natalie hated when Lynn and Jake did drugs. It turned them into ogres.

"Fuck off," Natalie said.

"We told you to stay away tonight," Lynn hissed, her smile disappearing. "This is not the place for you right now."

"It's my house too!" Natalie yelled. The anger that had hardened as she arrived home burned out of control now. She felt like she might snap.

"Go stay at your friend's house," Lynn said, still holding Natalie's arm on the stairs. "Or is she off having actual sex with her actual boyfriend?"

That was it. The evening crashed around Natalie in a heap. The knowledge that Doz wasn't right for her, his grossness with the pizza, and his base inability to roll his tongue back into his mouth over Brandi was too much. And the sex thing—Natalie didn't even care, not really, because she knew it wouldn't be great with someone who cared so little for her, but she'd set it in her mind as a milestone for college, for adult life. Going off course and not being able to close the deal was humiliating.

"I said fuck *off*," Natalie said, pushing her sister back with strength that was powered by anger and humiliation and exhaustion. Lynn fell backward down two steps, and Natalie had time to think that this was fine—it was only two steps—but Lynn was stoned out of her mind and had lost her most basic motor skills. Lynn kept falling, stumbling backward, before hitting her head on the foyer wall with a disturbingly solid crack. She slumped down, and her eyes closed. Natalie stared at her in shock, noting that the wall behind Lynn's head had a wet red mark.

"This is—" Natalie wanted to yell that it was out of control, but no one was listening. She ran down the stairs to her sister and tried to lift Lynn's head, but it was as though her sister weighed four thousand pounds. "Your head. Lynn. Your head. Jake!"

In the living room, Jake had a rubber tie around his arm and sank back into the sofa cushions, blissed on his high.

Natalie scrambled for her cell phone to call the police. "I'm calling for help." Her voice was thin and high.

"Nuh-uh," Lynn murmured, eyes open a slit, her voice strange and draggy. "No ambulance."

"I have to," Natalie said. "Your head is bleeding, and Jake's doing *heroin* or whatever."

"You can't," Lynn mumbled.

"I am," Natalie said, desperate to do something right in an evening full of wrong, which now included her big brother tying off and doing danger-ous drugs while the rest of them cracked their skulls open. Maybe Jake would get a wake-up call and straighten up. Lynn tugged on her arm. She didn't want Natalie to call. But Natalie was tired of being pushed around.

She dialed 9-1-1. A dispatcher's voice came on the line.

"No," Lynn said, her voice stronger now, less groggy.

"What's your emergency?" the dispatcher repeated in her ear.

Natalie looked at the scene in the living room. Jake, glassy-eyed, smiling. Carlos tying his arm off. She and Lynn held eye contact as Natalie told the dispatcher, "We need help. It's—it's out of control. Please come quick. My sister hit her head badly, and my brother's high. There are, like, really illegal drugs."

She gave the address, and the dispatcher said help was on the way, that there was patrol in the neighborhood now, and that she was also sending an ambulance. They'd be there in seconds. Lynn struggled to sit up and lunged for her, but Natalie had a non-inebriated and uncracked head, so she was able to move out of the way in time.

"You're a fucking monster!" Lynn yelled. "How could do you that? How could you call the police?"

"You called the cops?" Carlos called from the living room.

Natalie stared at them all, resenting that she had to be the adult here instead of the actual adults in the room.

"Idiot!" Carlos flew into action. Good, now he would put all that mess away. He began preparing things, loading up a syringe. Wait. That wasn't putting it away. What was he doing?

Carlos plunged the needle into his arm.

Time seemed to slow. Natalie heard sirens in the distance and watched as Carlos inserted the needle all the way in, a long, full push, and then his face went slack and happy. And then the sirens were closer, and she could see the blue-and-red lights reflected on the white glossy molding of the foyer and through the stained glass of the front door. The sirens ceased. Carlos collapsed against the sofa cushions before rolling off onto the rug facedown.

The next moments were a blur: Carlos convulsing with what looked like a seizure; his eyes rolling back in his head; unsuccessful CPR; a shot of adrenaline delivered to his heart that was too late; wide, shocked eyes from the paramedics; and lastly, his limp body. With nothing left to do for Carlos, the paramedics tended to Lynn's head.

The police put Lynn and Jake in handcuffs. They remained silent as they were read their Miranda rights. Natalie sat on a chair, shivering under a blanket the police gave her to wrap around her shoulders. Right before they were led out the door, Lynn turned toward Natalie and gave her a look she would never forget: hurt, disbelief, and betrayal.

Lynn and Jake were charged with third-degree manslaughter for Carlos's death. Jake for purchasing, and Lynn for providing it, which in California carried a sentence of up to twenty-five years. They both got three each. It was considered lucky.

CHAPTER 6

The morning brought sweet, pale sunshine with bountiful birdsong, and the promise of a hot afternoon through the window of Natalie's old bedroom. Although she'd never been one of those people who experienced confusion upon waking in a new place, it took her time to come to grips with where she was and what she was doing there.

But there was something else. After a full fifteen minutes of lying in her sleeping bag, which she'd unrolled on the old but otherwise clean and intact mattress, and staring out the grimy window, she realized the feeling that was shooting through her: hope. Hope was not a luxury she had indulged in for any of the time she'd been away—essentially her entire adulthood. Hope was the color of midnight blue with a thousand new stars standing out in relief, despite the years of Natalie carefully tending the mental barricade against it. The hope seeped rather than burst, warm and lush after locking it away from the light so long. It worried her, because hopes could so easily be crushed, and she could be opening herself up to years of more hurt if they rejected her again.

But lying in bed wouldn't bring about reconciliation. She had things to do.

As she pulled her legs out of the sleeping bag, Penguin roused himself from where he'd been curled up in the divot between her legs on top of the bag, stretching his forelegs luxuriantly. She picked up her phone and brushed off a small spider from the screen, hoping very much that its siblings were not in her hair. She'd have to do another sweep for spiders before bed tonight. There was a text from Michelle asking if she had arrived in Santa Cruz safely. To this, Natalie typed: Yes, I'm here and I can't wait to see you.

Yay! Michelle's reply was almost immediate. Come by my shop anytime.

Tomorrow? Natalie replied. She wanted to ease in slowly to the reality that she was here.

Yes. I'll pick up a box of croissants from the little French bakery down the street.

Ah. Michelle remembered that croissants were one of Natalie's greatest loves in life. They still joked about it. Natalie always said she would do anything or go anywhere for a truly good croissant—she had tried them all, from Santa Cruz to Watsonville—and Michelle always said silly things to see how far Natalie would go, like, "What if the croissant was at the bottom of a garbage dumpster that was filled with rotten fish heads and dirty socks worn by old men who never cut their toenails?" and Natalie would still say yes.

There were also four text messages from Paul asking to talk, still insisting he was not on a break. Natalie typed a quick Talk soon and got up.

She strode over to her bedroom door, squinting at something small and red on the floor. A dead mouse lay inside the room, in a not-insignificant puddle of blood with its innards trailing out next to it. Penguin gave a little *prrrrt* behind her, suggesting praise was in order.

"Thanks, man," she told Penguin, whom she swore grinned in response. "Super sweet of you." It wasn't his first mouse in their time together, but she supposed it was important for him to christen the house.

In the hall, the house felt as still and unused as it had upon her arrival yesterday. Penguin followed her out, tail up, assuming his breakfast would be forthcoming despite his rodent snack.

She crept downstairs and headed for the kitchen, which was empty but bright with morning sun streaming in through the windows. Dust motes filled the cast of the sun and caught the curl of steam from a French press filled with coffee on the counter. Natalie's whole being wanted that coffee like it was the elixir of life.

Dilemma.

Lynn used to fly into a tremendous rage if Natalie ever touched her things, but they were adults now. Sisters could make coffee for each other; it didn't mean they had to be best friends. Or friends at all, in their case. It was fresh, and the smell made her faint with want, especially after five days on the road drinking foul gas station coffee. There was at least a cup left in the press.

Natalie grabbed her travel mug from a small cooler she'd left by the sink and filled it with the coffee. She didn't even think before it went down her gullet. Delicious.

"My mom said you would drink that."

Natalie spilled what was in her mouth down her front. Kit stood behind her on the other side of the counter. Somehow he looked even taller in the morning sun. "Did she?"

"Yeah, and I said no one would *take* someone else's coffee." He didn't sound nasty or sassy, just curious.

"How old are you?" she asked.

"Thirteen."

Lynn would have had him, then, when she got out of prison at age twenty-three. Natalie was surprised he didn't have a phone glued to his hand. One of her friends, Angela, had a thirteen-year-old son, and he barely knew how to speak in anything but emojis and eye rolls.

"Where *is* your mom?" she asked.

"She went to see if she could get a job at the mortuary." He sat on the edge of the cracked wooden breakfast table.

Natalie frowned, surprised that Lynn was out getting a job so soon. That would suggest she was planning on staying in Santa Cruz. Then she remembered Lynn mentioning mortuary school last night. "The mortuary?"

"Yeah. She ran the cremation ovens at the one at…home." He said the word *home* carefully, as though unsure whether she could be trusted with knowing where home was.

"That's gross."

Kit shrugged. "They're called retorts."

"What are?"

"The ovens."

Natalie swallowed hard. It was actually a fitting profession for Lynn, who had always been so dark that she could have been molded from the fibers of demons.

"And, um, does she enjoy her work?" Natalie asked.

Now Kit met her eyes, and there was a hint of a smile there. "Yeah, she likes it. It's kind of weird, but kind of cool too. She always has these crazy stories. I don't tell a lot of people, because they get weirded out by the fact that she likes doing it. But you're her sister."

"I guess I am." Natalie felt a ridiculous pleasure. She *was* Lynn's sister.

She reached into a bag on the counter for a can of Penguin's food. Instantly, the cat wound around her ankles and made a nuisance of himself. Out of the corner of her eye, she saw Kit watching him.

"Want to feed this idiot his breakfast?" she asked.

Kit's eyes lit up, betraying his noncommittal grunt. He scooted off the table and came around to Natalie's side of the counter. Penguin threaded himself around Kit's feet too, since everyone was his best friend when it came to food delivery. Natalie pushed Penguin's bowl over to Kit and handed him the can of food. He peeled open the lid, the sound triggering loud meows from the cat, and dumped it in the bowl. He set it down on the floor, and Penguin fell on it as though he hadn't been fed in days.

"He's starving," Kit said.

"No, he's a good liar." Natalie smiled. "Ask him again in an hour, and he'll pretend he never had breakfast. He caught a mouse last night and ate most of that too."

This got a real expression from Kit, whose open mouth looked delighted and surprised at once. "Why do you have a cat with you? Did he come with you from Massachusetts?" He looked down quickly, as though embarrassed to have shown interest in her, a betrayal of his mom. Natalie wondered what Lynn had told Kit about her and their past.

"Yep." Natalie turned to the sink to rinse out the can. "My roommate can't stand him, so he came with me."

"That's cool. I want to get a pet, but…" He looked down. "I can't."

"Do you live in a place where pets aren't allowed?" She kept her tone light. She wanted to know about him, whether they were safe, whether his father was after them.

"Yeah." A short, final answer.

She pointed to Penguin. "Do me a favor and keep him inside the house. He doesn't know the area and won't know where to go if he gets out."

"Yeah, sure." Kit reached down and stroked Penguin with such tenderness that Natalie decided to chance it.

"Are you okay, Kit?"

Kit stood up and looked at her, his face carefully blank. It was the same closed expression Jake used to give their mother when she asked him where he'd been and what he'd been doing. Natalie suspected that asking if he was okay was not the right question, but she didn't know how to show him that she cared, that she could be a strong auntie for him. If he wanted that.

"I get it," she said. "You don't need to tell me if you don't want to."

Kit pulled out his phone and pretended to look at it. Her heart did a little achy thump for this boy who was trying so hard not to be interested and yet clearly was. This was followed by a thrill at the fact that he wanted to know about her, the aunt he'd never met. Had Lynn talked about her? She must have.

Natalie left him and went into the library, plopping down in her grandfather's ancient chair, which creaked in protest under her weight. Her first order of the day was to call the lawyer and let him know she was there. She was also hoping he would tell her that Jake had been in touch.

"Miss Walker, hello," Jorge Garcia said after his assistant put him through.

"Hello, yes. I'm here in Santa Cruz. At the house."

"Aha. Great news."

She waited, but he seemed to be waiting for her to say more. "And my sister, Lynn, is here too."

"Wonderful."

Again she waited, but there was nothing further. "So, we're here. Does that satisfy my mother's trust?"

"We need to have all three of you there at the house."

She twirled a curl around a finger. "And have you heard from Jake, my brother?"

"You are the only one to have called. I sent the letter to his address on record. Maybe you can reach out to him directly?"

At least she knew where Jake worked. "All right. I guess I can."

"Excellent!" Mr. Garcia sounded far more upbeat, making Natalie think he had been waiting for her to make that move. "I look forward to hearing from all three of you when you're together at the house."

"Does it have to be at the house? Isn't me being here enough?"

"All three of you together. Those are the terms of the trust."

This was what she was afraid of.

"It was good to hear from you, Miss Walker. Please call again once your brother and sister are both there."

She hung up and went back to the kitchen, where Kit sat still. She took a deep breath, butterflies zipping all over her stomach.

"Hey, kid," she said. "Apparently I need to track down your uncle. I'm going to his office to see if he's there. Interested in coming along?"

The immediate raise of his eyebrows indicated a resounding yes, but he kept his face neutral. "My mom might not like if I took off with you."

"True. But I'm hardly a stranger." Although she was. "We'll leave her a note."

"You could be a child abuser." Kit still affected nonchalance.

"Or I could be the awesome aunt you never had."

"My dad has a sister. She lives in Syracuse."

"But is she awesome?"

"What makes *you* awesome?"

Natalie thought for a moment. "I can draw." She pulled her sketchbook from her tote sitting on the floor and flipped to the second page, where there was an old sketch of a raven. It was one of her favorites because she had managed to capture the dark glossiness of his feathers in pencil.

"That is pretty awesome." Kit took the pad and turned the pages almost reverently, which made her instantly adore him. All the sketches were of creatures: birds, small mammals, beetles, Penguin. And then his decision, delivered casually: "Can we stop and get a doughnut?"

"Definitely. Let's hit it."

Natalie went to grab her bag, pushing away the small feeling of unease that Lynn would not like her taking Kit out without permission. Kit had accepted the idea of leaving a note, but Natalie knew Lynn better. She could ask Kit for his mom's number but suspected that calling would result in an unpleasant refusal on Lynn's part, simply because it was Natalie doing the asking. So she scribbled out a note, had Kit send Lynn a text, and hoped she could talk about it with Lynn later.

In moments, they were driving along West Cliff Drive, Natalie pointing out the surfer statue, the lighthouse, Seal Rock, the eroding cliffs. Kit was talkative and seemed interested in her tour. Maybe Lynn hadn't told Kit how much she hated Natalie.

"When you saw me yesterday at the house," Natalie said, "you knew who I was. Your mom has talked about me?"

Kit played his fingers along the windowsill. "She talks about you a little sometimes."

Natalie didn't want to make him feel like he was betraying his mom's confidence, so she withheld her follow-up questions, which were all variations on *And did she say she hated me?*

But Kit seemed to understand. "She said you did something that sent her and Uncle Jake to prison. She didn't have easy teenage years, I guess."

"No. No, she didn't." Lynn and Jake had both bowed under the weight of their mother's inattention, especially when Buck had come on the scene.

Kit shrugged. "But, like, you're not outwardly evil, so you're okay for now."

She thought she caught another smirk from him. "I could be inwardly evil."

"Like, spiders in your soul, that kind of thing?"

"Yeah, an absolute demon plotting the world's destruction."

Kit laughed. "Nah. My mom would have taken you down already."

She grinned. Lynn was fierce and protective and would not have left her son alone in the house with Natalie if she didn't have a modicum of trust in her. Natalie didn't know what to make of that. It suggested that Lynn might not hate her entirely.

It was a small point of hope.

She turned onto Delaware and headed toward the Long Marine Lab at UC Santa Cruz. Natalie remembered from her childhood that the lab, located on a picturesque piece of cliffside property on the west side of town, had a small visitor center with touch tanks where you could dip your hands in icy water and run your fingers through the soft, sticky tentacles of a sea anemone or feel the rough knobs on a jewel starfish. The lab studied dolphins and sea lions and had an enormous blue whale skeleton, and it was all free for visitors. She and Lynn and Jake used to ride their bikes all the way out there to look at the fish a few times a month. Now it seemed the small visitor center had moved out of the collection of portable buildings Natalie remembered. It had a proper parking lot and a fancy welcome center called the Seymour Marine Center and looked as though it charged admission.

The Walker Lab was located on the research side of the campus. On its website, which Natalie had checked out earlier, there was a smiling headshot of Jake, looking older and amazingly sober and sane. His web page was littered with his quotes on conservation and how humans and birds could positively interact. He had a staff too—two colleagues: a man and a woman. The man was named Dr. Asier Casillas, who looked like he was in his thirties and who, according to his short biography, had done his undergraduate and then graduate work in marine sciences at the Universitat de Barcelona in Spain. Very good-looking for a personnel photo, Natalie had thought. The other colleague, Dr. Emily Lawrence, was a slim woman with neat shoes and a tidy bun who looked to be in her fifties. Jake and his crew were very glamorous.

Maybe Jake was too wrapped up in running his own lab to have time to respond to the lawyer's letter. Being busy and studying seabirds and being awesome.

Natalie parked the car and turned off the engine but made no effort to get out. "I'm kind of nervous. I haven't seen him in a long time." This was momentous. What would he say? The same thing Lynn had said, which was *Oh, wow, you're here?* It was certainly better than outright disgust and rejection. Would he yell at her? Chase her out? Or worst of all, turn away in silence?

Kit glanced at her. "Only thing you can do is go inside and see. Pop."

She looked at him. "What? What is 'pop'?"

"It means, pop, here we are, let's go."

She glanced at him, impressed by his insight. "Okay. Let's do it. Let's go see Jake. Pop."

CHAPTER 7

"Is that him?" Kit asked. "That guy in there? Uncle Jake?"

It took some doing, wandering around in at least three circles of the hallways before they'd found a lab with huge windows and WALKER LAB OF MARINE ORNITHOLOGY etched on the glass. Kit and Natalie watched two white-coated people moving around the lab, handling specimens and talking—the two people from Jake's website: his research assistants, Dr. Casillas and Dr. Lawrence. Jake was nowhere in sight.

"No. But let's go in and see if they know where he is." She pointed to the etching on the glass. "See this? His name's right on the lab."

She pushed the door open, and a red light above it began to blink. Both of the people in lab coats turned toward the door.

"Can we help you?" the woman asked in a clipped, unwelcoming tone. "This is a working wet lab."

Natalie shut the door behind them. "Sorry. We're looking for Jake. Walker. Dr. Walker. My brother. Dr. Jake—Jacob...um...Walker."

Beside her, Kit muttered, "Smooth."

"Shut it," she whispered back. He smothered a grin.

Dr. Casillas raised his eyebrows. His website photo did not do him justice, Natalie decided. He had dark hair, short on the sides, with the hair on top either cut or mussed to stick up. High cheekbones in a heart-shaped face. There was an alert intelligence in his eyes, but also a sense of wariness. She realized that her cheeks had gone warm.

"Hi," he said.

"Hi," Natalie said. His eyes killed her. Absolutely murdered her. They were deep brown with wrinkles at the sides that hinted of kindness.

"We're looking for my Uncle Jake," Kit said loudly.

"He is not here," Dr. Casillas said, looking down at a tray in front of him full of unsavory moist things. His voice was beautiful: smooth, fluent English with a hint of a Spanish accent.

"We don't know where he is." Dr. Lawrence said. "He's gone."

"Gone?" Natalie asked.

The researchers exchanged a meaningful look. Dr. Casillas looked at Natalie again and then quickly away. "You said you're his sister? And nephew?"

"Yes," Natalie said. "Our mother recently died, and I'm back in town. My sister and brother need to be—"

Dr. Casillas jolted as though something had occurred to him. "Oh—that must be it. There's New Zealand, but that's not for another month." He looked at Dr. Lawrence, whose eyes widened at whatever unspoken discussion passed between them.

Natalie and Kit exchanged a look of their own. "Ah, okay?"

"Your mother passing away," Dr. Lawrence said. "He's due to leave for New Zealand in a few weeks. We thought maybe he had left early, but now I see it was because of a family situation. I'm sorry about your mother, by the way."

"Thank you." Natalie still felt removed from the fact that her mother was gone. The lack of grief was disturbing, surely. "Why is he going to New Zealand?"

"He's going for a year as a visiting faculty member at the University of Auckland," Dr. Casillas said. Natalie felt that warmth again when she met his eyes.

"A year," Natalie said. That was a long time. "And you think he would go without telling you?"

The researchers exchanged another look, this time uncomfortable.

"He hasn't answered his phone. And he's not home," Dr. Lawrence said.

"Where does he live?"

Natalie must have sounded too eager, because Dr. Casillas said, "You're his sister, you said?"

"Yes. Natalie Walker."

"Ah, not Lynn, then." Again his eyes met Natalie's, but he quickly looked down at his tray of things.

"Lynn's my mom," Kit added helpfully.

"Yes." Dr. Casillas nodded to himself.

"I'm Emily Lawrence," the woman said, peeling off a glove and offering her hand to shake. Natalie took it, but Dr. Lawrence's hand was like a piece of wet lettuce. "Dr. Walker's assistant."

"I am Asier Casillas," Dr. Casillas said, pronouncing his name *Ash-e-air*. "I would shake your hand but"—he looked down at his gloved hand, which had gunk all over it—"I have been handling fish innards."

"Thanks, that's fine," Natalie said. "Do you think I could get his number and home address from you? It's important that we track him down. And it seems like you two would probably like to know where he is."

Dr. Casillas glanced at Dr. Lawrence—a quick look, but it was as though he was checking to see how she was taking this request.

"Absolutely not." Dr. Lawrence seemed far more clipped now. Her arms were crossed in front of her chest in a classic pose of not having it. "I can't give out his personal information. That would be a human resources violation."

"What *can* you do?" Natalie asked.

"Nothing," Dr. Lawrence said. "He texted two weeks ago to say he was going to be out, but since then we've heard nothing. We're waiting to hear more."

Natalie sighed. "Look, if you're worried, and you work with him every day, then I'm worried too. If you could give me his address—"

Dr. Lawrence shook her head. "He would not like that. No."

"He's not at his house," Dr. Casillas said quickly. "I knocked on his door this morning. His car is gone. No lights on."

"Where would he be?" A sliver of worry snaked its way up the back of Natalie's neck. "Where can we look?"

"I think he's grieving," Dr. Lawrence said with an air of finality. "That would explain it. It's normal to take time off for that."

"Well." Dr. Casillas shot his colleague a look. "There was that time he broke up with his girlfriend and he—"

"I think what's important here," Dr. Lawrence said loudly, seemingly for Natalie and Kit's benefit, "is that Jake is the type to take time off when upsetting events happen. He'll be fine."

Natalie eyed the older woman, trying to decipher whether she believed that. "Are you saying Jake usually takes off when he's upset?" She directed this at Dr. Casillas.

But Dr. Casillas seemed wary of her questions. He fiddled with the wet things on his tray. "He will be back before his departure to New Zealand. I am sure of it."

Natalie hoped so. "Is there any place around Santa Cruz where I might look for him? It's urgent that we see him before he leaves." For a *year*. Sheesh. "There's an issue with how we're supposed to inherit our mother's house."

"He surfs a lot," Dr. Casillas said. "I keep hoping he's taken some time off to think and surf."

"He *surfs*?" Natalie couldn't imagine her brother being remotely athletic or putting on a wet suit, but then, she couldn't imagine Jake as a scientist with his own lab either. "Does he go to Steamer Lane or Pleasure Point?" Steamer Lane was a block from the house, so she hoped for the former.

"Usually Steamer Lane," Dr. Casillas said.

"Okay." That gave her a starting place.

"I've already checked there," Dr. Lawrence said. She seemed a little annoyed, as though Natalie were suggesting she hadn't looked for him hard enough.

"Yes, but you looked last week," Dr. Casillas said.

"This is weird," Kit whispered to Natalie. She opened her eyes wide in response.

Natalie pulled out her phone. "Can I give you my number, and you can text or call if you hear from him?"

Dr. Casillas peeled off his gloves and dropped them on the lab table with a wet *smack*. He pulled out his phone and stood next to Natalie. An intense heat radiated off him, and she was aware that he smelled good—a combination of cedar and something else. He gave her his number, and she sent him a text so he had hers before stepping away. The whole thing took less than thirty seconds, and yet she could not think straight afterward.

"Three weeks before he leaves, you said?" Natalie asked.

"Well, a month," Dr. Lawrence said.

"He goes for a whole year?"

"A whole year."

Something occurred to Natalie with a jolt. "You didn't call the police, did you?" That would be bad. He was an ex-con, after all.

"No," Dr. Casillas said. "We have…hesitated to do that."

"Good." She looked up and met Dr. Casillas's eyes. She thought she could see some understanding there, like he might know about Jake's past. "Thank you. I'm sorry to have bothered your process here."

"Not at all," Dr. Casillas said, sounding so pleasant that one would think they'd dropped by for tea. Dr. Lawrence, for her part, turned away and said nothing.

Natalie and Kit waved and left. They were quiet all the way out of the building.

"That was weird," Kit repeated when they reached the car.

"Yeah, it was." Natalie didn't know how to feel about the news that Jake had disappeared.

"Why is he missing? Where would he have gone?"

"I don't know. Let me talk to your mom about it." Lynn would have the right answer.

"And then he's leaving for a year in New Zealand," Kit said.

"I know. Maybe our mother's death freaked him out." The Jake she remembered was not a freaker-outer. Then again, she didn't know him anymore. All she had to go on was the professional, confident-looking photo on his lab's website. He could be a successful scientist but also someone for whom a major life event like a parent's death (or a breakup with a girlfriend) would be emotionally disastrous. It wasn't much of a stretch, given how he'd acted when their father had died. He'd been furious, fighting with everyone, both physically and with words. When Buck had moved in a full three years later, Jake had used him as a scapegoat for his anger. Natalie remembered one catastrophic fight when Jake and their mother had been yelling at each other and Jake had said something horrible, probably that she should fuck off. Buck, who had only recently begun spending the night, had stood up and thrown his fork down, startling all of them. *How dare you talk to your mother that way.*

How dare, Jake had mocked him. *How about, how dare you leave your wife three doors down and screw my mom?*

Buck hadn't known how to let it go. He had screamed at Jake, grounded him, told him he was worthless and on his way to being a degenerate failure in life. Jake had run away, but their mother had found him two days later down in the mall area on the sidewalk with a homeless guy named Pike, who had taken pity on Jake and let him sleep in his camp. Jake had come home, but he was silent and permanently furious after that.

Yeah, Jake definitely had a history of leaving when things got bad.

As she drove back along West Cliff, Natalie did not want to dissect the combination of relief and disappointment she felt at not seeing him. They passed Steamer Lane, and she wondered if one of the surfers down in the cold water was Jake. She drove through the roundabout past the wharf, pointing out old buildings to Kit, telling him which businesses had changed. At the Boardwalk, its summer operation was in full swing. The wooden roller coaster roared by on its seemingly rickety wooden track as they drove past.

"See that?" she asked. "That's the Boardwalk. We all had jobs there when we were teenagers."

"It looks like a wannabe Coney Island."

"It is *not*." She was indignant in the way only a Santa Cruzer can be. That was, if she even qualified as one anymore. It was home, yet home was also three thousand miles away.

"Where do you think Uncle Jake went?" Kit asked.

"I don't know. It sounds like his colleagues have looked everywhere he usually goes." Natalie worked to keep the worry out of her voice, like disappearing from your own lab was normal.

"You all got a letter?" Kit asked.

"Yeah."

"My mom told me her mother had died and that we were going to her childhood home in Santa Cruz, but she didn't say much more than that. We left in the middle of the night. I didn't say goodbye to my dad."

Natalie's heart hurt for him. "Wow. I'm really sorry. That's awful."

"No." Kit shook his head. "It isn't. That's how we had to leave. My dad would have been angry otherwise." His voice had turned defiant, daring her, almost, to tell him otherwise.

"Kit, oh no. I'm so sorry." Natalie couldn't imagine the fear involved in knowing you had to go in secret to be safe.

"It's fine." He stared out the side window of the car.

She wanted to reach out, tell him she was there for him, but they barely knew each other, and anyway she knew that words couldn't take away the past. She turned back up the hill toward the house.

"Seems like there should be another way to get in touch with Uncle Jake," Kit said.

Natalie glanced at this astute nephew of hers, changing the subject and trying to solve the puzzle of his missing uncle. "The trustee sent a letter. And he's been called."

"Did they try a telegram?"

"Should have tried a carrier pigeon." Natalie smirked.

Kit's face broke into a smile. "Or Morse code."

"Or semaphores."

He laughed now. "Or smoke signals."

She laughed too. "I don't know what comes after that." The easy laughter felt like a balm after the weirdness of the lab.

He grinned and let his head rest against his seat. "I win."

"Well," Natalie said, unwilling to concede.

"I do. I win."

"Hmm. New game." Natalie frowned. "Name five marine mammals."

"Whale! Otter! Sea hippo!"

"What! Sea hippo?" Natalie yelled.

"A walrus," Kit said.

Natalie laughed. "Fine, fine."

"And a shark—"

"No!" Natalie hollered in triumph. "Not a mammal!" She pushed her voice into a high-pitched wail and sang, "I winnn!"

Kit's eyes went wide, and they both burst into laughter. When it died down, they fell into silence for several streets until Kit said, "Fine. Five types of things Penguin might catch and eat," and then they were off.

CHAPTER 8

"You did what?" Lynn stood in the kitchen, her fingers gripping the bags in her arms too tightly.

"I left a note," Natalie said, pointing to the unread piece of paper on the counter. "And Kit texted you."

Lynn eyed her, and Natalie recognized her assessing look—Lynn was trying to decide how angry to be.

"I didn't see the text." Lynn set down the bags. "Ask me first before you take my son anywhere. Don't leave a note. I'm going to ask him if he was okay."

"Ask him!" Natalie said. "I'm happy to call or text you next time, but I didn't want to bother you. Assuming there's a next time. I mean, just in case."

Lynn raised an eyebrow as though it were a lot to ask. "You can text me."

Natalie hid a smile at this small concession from her sister. "Anyway, as I was saying, Jake isn't at his lab. His colleagues don't know where he is, and he's apparently leaving for New Zealand for a year to be a visiting professor or something. He's leaving in a few weeks."

"It does seem odd," Lynn said. "He'll turn up eventually though."

Natalie attempted to help Lynn unpack the bags, but Lynn shooed her away like she was a gnat. She retreated to one of the bar stools at the kitchen counter.

"Do you think he's in trouble?" Natalie asked.

"I think he's fine. He's probably off sorting out feelings around Mom's death. Or preparing for his trip. There are lots of reasons he might need time to himself right now."

Natalie frowned. "I guess. We all grieve differently."

Lynn turned to her. "And are *you* grieving?"

Natalie didn't know how to answer that without sounding like a callous troll. "I'm still sorting that out. Mom and I didn't have a good relationship. She didn't really want to see me or talk to me after I moved to Boston."

"I don't believe that."

"Why would I lie?"

Lynn shoved things around in the refrigerator to make room. "Because. She always gave glowing reports about you. 'Natalie is doing so well at her job!' That kind of bullshit. And then she'd ask, 'How is it working with dead bodies?'"

"First of all, she didn't know how I was doing at my job," Natalie said, shocked and indignant at this news, at the fact that their mother had been in touch with Lynn and had lied about having spoken to Natalie. Had her mother been trying to play her daughters against each other, or had she simply been covering her own failure at having relationships with them? A wink of hurt, followed by a note of grief, appeared somewhere inside her. "We barely talked, and when we did, she certainly never asked about my job. And second of all, it was fucked up to say that to you."

Lynn rolled her eyes. "Maybe she didn't mean it as bad as it sounded. I do, after all, work with dead bodies. She was kind of horrified by my profession."

"I mean…" Natalie said. "Did you get the job, by the way? Kit said you had an interview at the mortuary."

"The crematory. They need someone right away, so I'm starting tomorrow."

Natalie punched down a little spark of envy that Lynn had gotten a job so quickly. Not that Natalie didn't have a job. Although with her boyfriend as her boss, it wasn't fun to think about.

"So you'll be pushing bodies into ovens?" Natalie asked.

"Retorts, not ovens, and yes."

"Do you use a big pizza paddle or what?"

"While I stoke the fire, like a brick oven kind of thing?" Lynn asked sarcastically.

Natalie was unable to keep the grin from her face. "Yeah. Soot everywhere?"

"No. It's all stainless steel and computerized." Lynn turned away, but Natalie thought she saw her sister's face soften from the set frown she usually wore, a frown she'd had since high school. Now the lines had deepened in her face from it.

"Do you like it?" Natalie asked.

"Yes." Again Lynn gave her a warning look, probably in case Natalie was going to insult her for it—something Natalie wouldn't dream of. "It's not that I *like* dead bodies, but it's an interesting field. There's a peacefulness in knowing that I'm the last person to handle these people. And I guess it helps me confront the idea of death."

Lynn cracked open a large package of pork chops and plopped two in an old and battered pan, its paint faded, which Natalie recognized from her childhood. The kitchen was stocked, albeit with old and cast-off tools. Yet another weird thing about the house. Her mother had kept the power on, the water running, and the kitchen stocked with basics, but for whom? Her stomach growled as she thought about this. It was obvious that Natalie was not part of the dinner plan here. It wasn't Lynn's fault. Natalie did not expect her to make her dinner.

"I wonder who the last person was to handle Mom," Natalie said. "Or if she's buried."

"I'm more concerned that I can't ask her why she refused to see us, and we can't tell her that it was messed up to play us against each other." Lynn's tone had hardened.

Natalie frowned, surprised that her mother had refused to see Lynn too. "That's—huh. Even if we could ask, I don't think I would. I don't need to know the reasons why she made those terrible decisions." She wasn't sure that was true. She wanted to know, but she'd gone so long refusing to ask that it seemed easier to keep up the pretense.

Lynn turned to look at her fully. "I guess. At least she talked to me a little over the years."

Natalie wondered if their mother had spoken to Jake too. Or was it only Natalie she'd shunned?

"But they weren't good talks," Lynn added, perhaps seeing the hurt on Natalie's face. "Mom definitely screwed up our relationship. All she had to do was be supportive, but for whatever reason, she couldn't get past the disappointment of me and Jake going to prison."

Or me for putting you there, Natalie thought. Their mother had made mistakes with all three of them. That much was clear.

Natalie very much wanted to ask about prison, but she didn't know how to start such a conversation. For years she'd fantasized about how it might go: *Do you forgive me for calling the police?* But getting to that point of directness was scary.

"It is weird being back?" she asked instead. For Natalie, it was not as weird as she'd thought. It was surprisingly comforting seeing the shaggy outlines of the coastal cypress trees, the blue of the ocean, the gentle curves of the coast.

Lynn shrugged. "Haven't been back long enough to know." She watched the pork chops sizzling in the pan. Natalie was beginning to think that was the end of the conversation when Lynn said, "What do you do, then? In Boston?"

"I work for an architecture firm. We specialize in historic houses like this one."

"Are you an architect?"

Natalie felt a flush of embarrassment rise to her cheeks. Being an architect would have some gravitas. "No. I help with our projects. Writing reports on houses like these, like who owned them, their history, where the materials came from. But actually I'm really an illustrator," she heard her mouth say. "I draw animals. Scientific drawings." Wow, apparently her brain was calling her an illustrator now.

Lynn's eyebrows rose. "Art, huh? You were always drawing as a kid."

Natalie considered this. She rolled Lynn's words around in her head, the idea that she'd always drawn and had long had the identity of being an illustrator. It wasn't the first time she'd tried out the idea but invariably told herself that it was too late, that she had no formal training.

"When are you going back?" Lynn asked.

"After Jake gets here and we satisfy the trust." Natalie studied her fingers. Lynn was staying here and had already gotten a job. How nice it must be to start over, start fresh.

There must have been something in Natalie's tone, because Lynn's eyebrows went up in a way that made her look condescending—a look Natalie knew well. Her way of suggesting that Natalie was being a dope.

"You're holding something back," Lynn said.

Natalie didn't know what to say, because she certainly hadn't intended any unspoken subtext. "I'm not hiding anything."

"Yes, you are."

"No. Honestly."

Lynn narrowed her eyes. "You are. Something at home, maybe?"

Natalie remembered, far too late, Lynn's dark talent of extracting her truths like a pin-headed pair of tweezers. "It's nothing. My boyfriend recently got a promotion I wanted at work, and now he's my boss." God, it was like she'd ingested truth serum or something. What the hell was wrong with her mouth? Lynn didn't need to know any of that.

"That sounds problematic." Lynn slid two perfectly cooked pork chops onto a plate and turned her attention to some broccoli.

"It's fine," Natalie said too quickly.

"Well, I'm sure you'll figure it out." Lynn sounded dismissive, and Natalie worried she had tucked away the detail about Paul in order to haul it out later and use it against her somehow, like she'd done with Doz all those years ago. "Anyway, Jake will show up. He'll have to if we want to keep this house."

"So we should just wait for him to show up?"

"Do you have a better idea?"

Natalie did not. Then she remembered Dr. Casillas mentioning surfing. "Apparently he surfs now. Maybe we can check the surf spots."

"Why don't you walk down to Steamer Lane and see if he's surfing now." Lynn turned away and muttered, "It's better than you standing here yammering at me."

Natalie left the kitchen and went up to her room so as not to give Lynn the satisfaction of knowing that that was exactly what she had been planning to do. It was clear Lynn would prefer that she left. And when Natalie returned to Boston, she probably wouldn't come back here. It was a horrible thing to think, and she really hoped she was wrong. But she suspected she wasn't.

— — —

Natalie walked down to the cliffs, enjoying the refreshing coolness of early evening. Some of the older surfers would be taking advantage of the calm to get a wave in, but fewer of them would be out this late in the day. She trailed a hand along the safety fence, looking over the cliff at the water below, thinking about her conversation with Lynn and why she had let slip her dream of being an illustrator. Obviously she wanted it to be true.

What was true was that she was here, talking to Lynn, which was amazing in itself. It was interesting that their mother had not been close with Lynn. Patricia Walker had done a number on all three of them, withdrawing and making them feel like she wasn't on anyone's side. If her mother's way of apologizing for this poor maternal display was to give all three of them the house—but by making them come together first—then Natalie had to say that it was too little too late.

And yet, Natalie realized with some annoyance, it was working. If only Jake would show up.

Natalie leaned over and stared at the water. Five wet suit–clad surfers paddled in the increasingly calm water, waiting for one last decent wave. A sodden surfer jogged up the access stairs, dripping wet, board under his arm.

In fact, he looked familiar. Slimmer, maybe, out of a lab coat, but just as arresting.

The surfer stopped.

"Natalie Walker," Dr. Casillas said. "Hello again. Twice in a day."

She tried to look anywhere other than at his body in the wet suit, which was very formfitting and showed that he was in great shape. Weird things happened to her. Her scalp tingled, and the feeling of droplets of cold seawater materialized on her skin. She was mesmerized by his eyes.

"Ah, hi," she said, looking out over the water to stop herself from gawking at him. "I thought I would come check to see if Jake was here, after you mentioned he liked to surf."

"Yeah, we're usually here together," he said, resting his board against the fence. "He taught me, actually. Now I surf as much as possible."

She shook her head. "That's so strange. He was never like that as a teenager. The complete opposite, in fact."

Dr. Casillas raised an eyebrow. "He's changed, then. We often go after work and a lot on the weekends. It's crowded, but I like how you might see a sea otter or a sea lion pop up next to you."

She grinned. "This is definitely their cove."

He leaned against his board, and she tried not to focus on the way his hair looked, slicked back and wet, or the slight freckling on the bridge of his nose. Everything about his posture said confidence: no slouching, no fidgeting (as she was doing, trying and failing to appear relaxed). Natalie was old enough to know that few people ever actually felt as confident as she ascribed them, but it never failed to catch her attention when someone looked sure of their place on earth.

"Have you recently come to Santa Cruz?" he asked.

"Yes, a few days ago. I live in Boston. My sister and I are back because of my mom dying. It's…big. We've been apart for a long time."

"I have known Jake for years. He told me you had all scattered in different directions."

A pang of hope hit her. Had Jake Googled her too? "That's true. I haven't spoken to him in years. I wish I could say I knew what my brother is like now."

"He is an amazing scientist," Dr. Casillas said, his tone slightly reverent. "He inspires me daily to reach further, to uncover more. It has been a pleasure to work with him."

Natalie tried to imagine a thoughtful, inspiring version of Jake. Apart from being a big brother whom she'd looked up to as a matter of course, there had sure been a lot of anger and sass in him. "I don't know him that way."

"I think maybe he regrets not knowing you now too."

"How do you know?"

He shrugged. "He is older and wiser. You have not been in touch for a long time."

"No." She thought about the years that had passed. She'd assumed that someday she would have contact with Lynn and Jake again but had not pictured it happening this way.

"What do you do there, in Boston?"

Ah, that question again. "I work for a small architecture firm that specializes in historic houses."

"Oh, are you an engineer?"

"I'm a scientific illustrator, actually." Again. Mouth. What was it *doing*? "I mean, I want to be one. Animals. I like to draw small animals and insects." Maybe if she said it out loud three times, it would be real.

"Ah," he said. "That is very noble."

It wasn't noble, because all she had to show for it were notebooks filled with her drawings. It was a hobby. "What I mean to say is, I write property reports for work, but it's my secret dream to be a scientific illustrator." She laughed a little to suggest this was silly and then berated herself because drawing wasn't silly.

He didn't laugh. "That is great work. One of the researchers at the lab works with sea lions. He is always looking for someone to help illustrate his specimens. He says photographs are too graphic."

Too graphic? What on earth could be too graphic to photograph? Interesting. "I like to draw details, though I can't say I've drawn any gore." She thought of all the insects she'd captured in jars over the years so she could sketch them. Every time she fed Patrick a cricket, she tried to draw it first.

He raised his eyebrows. "Did you get a degree in it? The drawing?"

"I don't have a degree in it, no, but I would love to get a certification or something." She'd always wanted formal schooling in the more specialized field of scientific illustration, going so far as to explore a program at the Rhode Island School of Design, but it had been too much of a commute and too much money. This guy was like a snake charmer, getting her to say all this and reveal her secret dreams. She hadn't even told Teensy these things.

Dr. Casillas looked thoughtful. "I think there is a program at CSU Monterey. The students often illustrate the annual reports for the Long Marine Lab and some of our publicity materials."

Natalie felt every cell in her body perk up. "Wow. That's very cool. I'm always looking to see if a school has programs for it."

"You should do it."

"Oh—well. I'm not here long enough for something like that." Maybe she'd look into the Rhode Island program again when she was back in Boston.

He tapped his surfboard and looked out at the ocean. She realized he was probably cold, yet he was standing here casually talking to her. Beads of seawater dripped down his head.

"I've been hoping Jake would show up here every afternoon," he said.

"If he's not at home and he hasn't shown up to work, where would he go?"

He shrugged. "Surfing. Although he isn't."

"Should we be worried? Are *you* worried?"

He put his hands on his hips and sighed. "A little, yes. He is wasting precious time to sort things out here before he goes. We have needs at the lab."

She sighed. "I have so many questions about him."

"Can I help answer any?"

"Apart from this obvious issue of him going off without telling anyone, is he happy?"

Dr. Casillas seemed surprised, as though that wasn't what he expected her to ask. "I think he enjoys what he has."

A safe answer. But that was her primary question. She wanted to know that Jake was okay and happy, that his time in prison hadn't screwed up everything for him. Professionally, he seemed to be doing well.

"I miss him," she said. She closed her eyes in the waning sun, letting its last rays warm her face. She didn't miss only him—she had missed all of this, she realized. Her hometown, her family, the sense of security they used to have when they were young and the three of them would play games and laugh and look out for each other. She had worked hard to get over her homesickness in college, and after graduating, she had considered herself a committed Bostonian. That hadn't changed, but there was something to be said about your childhood home, especially if the early memories were warm and good.

She opened her eyes. Dr. Casillas tucked the board tether into his suit, shifting it and grimacing.

"You need to get that wet suit off," she said, then turned away so he wouldn't see her face explode into a blush at the innuendo. "I mean, it's getting cold."

He smiled. "I do, yes," he said, but didn't make a move.

She wanted to know more about him. "I hope you don't think I'm nosy, but I was reading the lab's website, and I saw you on it. You're from Spain?"

"Yes. Barcelona. Like you, I left home young, right after university, and came to San Diego to study the Pacific snapper. I met your brother when I worked with him on a paper. He asked me if I was interested in joining his lab here at UC Santa Cruz. It was an easy yes."

"Do you miss home?"

"I miss my family, yes," Dr. Casillas said. "And my country, but there is not as much professional opportunity for me there as there is here. And I love Santa Cruz. It's a great community. What's not to love with this ocean at my feet?"

"It's an unforgettable place for sure." She badly wanted to keep him talking.

"How about you?" he asked.

"I moved to Boston for college and stayed. This is the first time I've been back here."

His eyebrows rose. "And how is it?"

She wasn't sure if he meant Boston or being back. Boston was fine. But the East Coast was different, and it occurred to Natalie that part of her, while trying hard to thoroughly love the East Coast, had always reserved herself for California. For Northern California. For Santa Cruz. "It's weird being back. I seem to notice sights and smells more. I want to see old places. I want to take a drive down the coast to Monterey." She sighed.

"I don't blame you." He grinned that lovely smile, the one that lit his face so beautifully. "Sometimes I get too wrapped up in small things. Too much time with fish. I should take more drives."

"What fish do you study?"

"I am examining anchovies and working on kelp forest ecology, which has an effect on so many different species, from abalone all the way to sea otters." He looked out at the royal blue of the ocean. "It's an unending job but a fascinating one."

He crossed his feet and gave a small shake.

"You should go," she said. "You're cold. I'm sorry to have kept you."

He looked as though he were going to deny it, but then he laughed. "It is a little cold. Okay. But you didn't keep me. It was nice to talk with you."

"Yes. Same." She watched as he grappled with his board and ignored the zings of attraction pinging all over her body. "Please call me if my brother shows up, Dr. Casillas?"

"Absolutely. Of course. And please, call me Asier."

She smiled. He smiled back—a tiny, flirty smirk. It was the cutest thing Natalie had ever seen. Cute and sexy, actually. They held eye contact for a moment longer than was strictly cordial.

He walked over to a sporty black car and leaned his surfboard against it. He began peeling off his wet suit. She tried not to look but couldn't help sneaking a few peeks at his lean, muscled body. And that smirk! Yeah, Dr. Casillas—Asier—was a very attractive man.

Her stomach rumbled, and she realized she was still starving. Watching Lynn make pork chops had not helped. She headed toward home, thinking she'd have to go get herself an unappetizing but affordable sandwich for dinner again. The sun had officially sunk below the horizon, and the sky was one of those impossible shades of lavender. She kept thinking about Asier's smirk. It was interesting that such a small thing could hook her, and then she realized it had been a long time since she'd felt that intrigued. She tried to remember what it was about Paul that had interested her. He wasn't a smirker or much of a flirter. It was probably his enigmatic status as the handsome and worldly older brother of her best friend.

But he hadn't come close to sparking that instant attraction the way Asier had.

She slumped in through the kitchen door and dropped her bag on the counter, noticing a plate with a second plate covering it. A sticky note was on it. *Natalie. Here's my number. Call me next time.* Her breath caught. Lynn was giving her her number. Carefully, she lifted up the plate and found a beautiful pork chop, cooked the way their mother used to make them, with steamed broccolini and rice on the side, slick with butter.

Natalie wiped away the tears that had appeared in her eyes. Her stomach rumbled again. And she dug in.

CHAPTER 9

Asier climbed up the stairs to the cliff above Steamer Lane in his tight wet suit. He rubbed the back of his wet hair, sending drops over her. He began to peel off the wet suit, slowly, tantalizingly. She stared at his beautiful, well-defined chest, wanting to run her hands over it. He continued to roll down the wet suit. She couldn't look away, transfixed by every bit of skin he revealed, following the trail of dark hair down from his navel. Her eyes landed on his face, where she found those warm brown eyes on her—intense, deep—and there was the naughty hint of a smile on his lips. When he got to his waist, he paused, and then he continued rolling the wet suit down, taking it all the way off.

He flung it aside and pulled her to him, leaving no doubt about his interest. Somehow she was naked too, and the feel of her softness pressed against his hardness was…a lot. It didn't matter that they were in the parking lot. He ran his hands over her shoulders, down her back, over her butt. He lifted her up so she was straddling him, and then he—

Natalie awoke, deeply turned on. Also embarrassed. She lay for some time staring at her old ceiling, enveloped in the tendrils of the scene. It had been a long time since she'd had a sex dream like that about someone. Even Paul rarely made an appearance.

She climbed out of her sleeping bag, taking a moment to stretch. There was no Penguin or mouse guts to step in this morning, which was good, and Paul had not texted her during the night, which was even better. Downstairs, no one was around, but there was a decent mug's worth of coffee in the pot and this time, after the pork chop gift, she was sure it had been left for her. She wondered how to thank her sister for this small gesture. Lynn had never wanted effusive displays of gratitude, but Natalie wanted to acknowledge the kindness somehow.

"Hey," Kit said, coming in quietly behind her.

"Hey yourself," Natalie said. "What's up?"

"Nothing. My mom's at work." He flopped down on a stool, clearly bored.

"I'm going downtown today. Wanna come?"

She could tell from his expression that "downtown" didn't sound all that appealing. "Downtown Santa Cruz is amazing. It has a bunch of good shops and pedestrian-only streets. There are skate shops and other cool things. Cookie shops. The best bookstore ever."

He perked up. "Okay."

Natalie washed out her coffee mug and then remembered she needed to feed Penguin. Usually he did the reminding, winding around her legs and tripping her. She opened a can of cat food, but the snick of the lid peeling off did not result in his appearance.

"Have you seen Penguin today?" she asked Kit. He shook his head. "Last night, then? When you were having dinner?" Penguin rarely missed an opportunity to discuss how he might enjoy some handouts at the table. Again Kit shook his head.

Weird. She dumped the food into his bowl and went upstairs to get ready. The last time she'd seen him was yesterday morning. She figured he was probably exploring the attic. The house was massive, after all, and held many secrets. She texted Lynn that she was going downtown and would she mind if she took Kit with her, thrilling at the fact that she could now text her sister.

And thank you for dinner, she added.

Don't get used to it, Lynn replied within seconds.

The pork chop or taking Kit downtown? Natalie asked.

Yes, Lynn replied. Natalie grinned at the fact that her sister had managed to digitize her grunts and went to get her shoes.

— — —

Natalie parked on Pacific Avenue in front of Michelle's store. The street had wide sidewalks, and music from street performers playing a steel drum a block down made it feel beachy and festive. She pointed out Bookshop Santa Cruz to Kit, a few doors down.

"My favorite bookstore in the world," she said, vowing to hit it up that day herself before they left. "Walk back down the other way and you'll find the skate shops. There's a cool paper store too."

"Okay." Kit didn't linger, taking off for the bookstore.

Michelle's shop was on a new part of the street—new, that was, comparatively. Natalie had been a baby when the 1989 Loma Prieta earthquake had obliterated much of the downtown area and its old buildings, like the original yellow Cooper House building that had housed fun shops and bars, but when she was a little older, she remembered her parents talking about the rebuild and how it was never quite the same. Michelle's shop was in a nice stretch of storefronts, her window filled with pretty dresses and interesting pottery and eclectic local artwork, all of which was a perfect reflection of Michelle's artistic flair.

A ball of excitement sat in Natalie's stomach. Art was one of the things that had kept their bond intact over the years despite the distance between them. They'd stayed in communication with letters, emails, phone calls, and texts and had been fairly good about it, but Natalie worried that seeing each other in person would strain their casual text-based communication, art or no art. She'd missed Michelle, missed the laughs they'd shared, missed the closeness and secret language they'd had as teenagers. Teensy had taken on that role in college, but people—and friendship— were never that simple. Michelle had a tougher edge than Teensy, had faced harder battles in life, and pushed Natalie in different—and not unpleasant—ways.

Looking at Michelle's storefront and the successful business she had built, Natalie was both impressed and nervous, feeling inadequate that she hadn't done much in ten years with her own career.

She took a deep breath, taking in the unique scent of Santa Cruz—a mixture of salt and sunshine, with a faint hint of the patchouli oil the street kids wore. It was funny how the smells of childhood cut through adulthood to remind you of how things used to be. Natalie opened the door to Michelle's shop and went in.

Inside the store, colorful racks of clothes and fabrics greeted Natalie's eyes. The shop was the kind of wonderland that made you want to look everywhere at once, with its chic distressed floorboards and some kind of delicious smell, a mixture of citrus and basil that resulted in a green, herbaceous, soapy scent that reminded her somehow of Asier. Mmm. Anyway, it worked well here, and Natalie loved that Michelle was so attuned to every part of the shopper's experience. No wonder she was so successful.

A body popped up from behind a rack. "NATALIE!"

The scream propelled Natalie backward into another rack, sending it and her toppling over and splaying fine shirts everywhere. Michelle rushed over and pulled her up.

"Oh my God." Michelle crushed her in a hug. "It is so amazing to see you. Look at you! You've got pasty skin from those New England winters!"

"I'm not that pasty." Natalie extricated herself from Michelle's embrace. "Look at *you*, with this store and everything!"

"I know," Michelle said, the glint of pride clear as she surveyed her domain. "You like?"

"You know I do. I'm so happy for you."

"Come on back. I have the promised croissants."

Natalie made a slurping sound and followed her friend to the back room, where a cozy pink love seat and club chair made it look like less of a stock room and more of a lounge. Natalie took in her friend. Michelle was as beautiful as when Natalie had last seen her, which had been in the waning days of the summer after high school graduation, after Lynn and Jake had been sentenced but before Natalie had retreated to Boston. Michelle had aged gorgeously; she had a magnificent Afro now and visible muscles in her arms, and she seemed to float rather than walk. Natalie was envious. Her short, pear-shaped body was never going to look anything like Michelle's willowy frame, thanks to Walker family genetics.

Michelle plopped down on the love seat and gestured toward a pink bakery box full of pastries. "Okay, tell me everything. How was it coming home? Were you all *ughh-uhh-uhh*?"

Natalie sat opposite her friend, taking a moment to catch up with the reality of being here in front of her after so many years apart.

Michelle caught her look and laughed. "I know it's been a minute. We're old now, girl."

"I mean, thirty-two isn't old."

"It is when you're childless and not married."

"Only if you want those things."

Michelle gave a belly laugh. "Fair. Although my boy is about to propose any day now."

"Really? That's fantastic! Is it fantastic?"

Michelle smiled. "It is. We're going to have a big wedding and ten babies."

Natalie almost choked on her croissant. She couldn't fathom such a thing for herself.

"And you?" Michelle asked. "You still seeing your friend's brother?"

"Yeah. For now." Natalie picked at a nail and tried to shove the tangle of feelings Paul's name brought deep down, where she'd shoved them since leaving Boston. There was more there than just the promotion, but examining it all would take time and work, and there was too much else going on. "He got the promotion I wanted at work. I'm having a hard time getting over it."

Michelle's nostrils flared. "What! Nope. Did he just…steal it right out from under you?"

"No. I don't think so. But it means he's my boss now."

"Can I kill him for you? He is *trash*."

Natalie laughed, pleased by her friend's fierce loyalty even after all these years. "Well. Maybe don't kill him yet."

"Okay," Michelle said. "All right. You can be conflicted. Are you in love with this guy?"

Natalie tried to find the words to say that she thought she was, or at least she was close, but she took too long. "Not yet. I don't know. We're on a break."

"A break. Did he ask for that or did you?"

"I did. It's my break. He was against it. I need time to figure out what I want. And if what I want fits with what he wants." Natalie licked her lips, hoping Michelle would not do that thing where she saw right through Natalie's statements to what she was afraid of. Teensy and Michelle had that annoying trait in common—or maybe it was called being a close friend.

Michelle gave her a knowing look, and Natalie feared the worst. "I think you already *know* what he wants. Just gotta decide if you want to give it."

"Yeah." Natalie sighed. She did not think Michelle meant Paul's desire to marry her. Rather, it was about whether Natalie wanted to conform to Paul's vision. Three months ago, she'd had no problem with the idea. Well, maybe a few misgivings about it being *his* vision of happiness, but his vision had been her vision too: living together, then marriage. A complete family. "He's—I think he wants a perfect package for himself, you know? The job, a house, a wife. That kind of thing."

Michelle gave her another side-eye. "Mmm. Are you waiting for him to change and see you for you? You've always been like that. Remember Doz in high school? You wanted him to be this awesome guy, the funny person he was with his friends, but when you got him alone, he was completely different and had a bad case of attention deficit disorder with girls. And that guy you dated in college, Derek or something? He wanted you to be this cool hippie chick from California, and you kept waiting for him to realize you weren't like that."

Natalie laughed, both embarrassed and pleased at her friend's perceptiveness. "Hey, I'm cool and I'm from California! Anyway, I don't wait around for men to change. I've known Paul for years. He knows my flaws by now." All of which he had, in his irritating big brother way, coached her on during their time together.

So he wasn't perfect. She knew that. But neither was she. Maybe there had been a little bit of waiting to see if Paul would change over the five months they'd been together. Surely that was normal, though.

As though Michelle had read her mind, she said, "Well, you get back to me when he admits you're perfect as you are."

Natalie breathed out a laugh. "Man, I missed you."

Michelle grinned wide, a beautiful thing. "I missed you too, you goose. And how is the house? Is it as bad inside as it looks outside? I've driven by it."

"It's not in great shape, but the lights are on and the plumbing works."

"Any chance you'll stay?"

Natalie looked up, feeling dreamy—because even the barest idea of staying in the house was lovely. "I have a job and friends and maybe a man waiting for me in Boston."

"I hear you. Hard to leave all that. So, what about Lynn and Jake? Are they around?"

Natalie described arriving in Santa Cruz, meeting Lynn and Kit, and her visit to Jake's lab with the news that Jake was nowhere to be found.

Michelle's eyes went big and round as she considered this. She, like most of Natalie and Lynn's friends, had been in love with Jake when they were in high school. His nonchalance had seemed charming and cool, and her friends had nearly swooned when he would pull up to the high school to give Natalie a surprise ride home. He was seen as a sweet and caring older brother, and Natalie admitted that he'd generally made her feel loved and safe—except when he was doing drugs.

"Have you seen him?" Michelle said. "I wonder if he's still hot."

"I'm not qualified to remark on my brother's hotness or lack thereof. But there's a photo on his lab's website. I don't know how recent it is."

Michelle grabbed her phone and started jabbing the screen. "Wow, yeah, he's still really yummy. God, your brother was always a heartbreaker."

Natalie rolled her eyes. "Wish the heartbreaker would come home."

"Why do you think he bugged out?"

Natalie shrugged. "His colleagues at the lab think it's because of our mom's death."

"We're all allowed a little freak-out," Michelle said. "I guess you better work on finding him while you're here."

"That's my plan." Natalie sighed. Beyond checking Steamer Lane on the very off chance that he might be surfing, she didn't know where to look. "Speaking of hotness, his lab colleague is on fire. Dr. Casillas. Wow. I—wow."

Michelle grinned and poked her phone, clicking around Jake's lab website. Her eyebrows rose. "Oh yes, yes, yes. Dr. Casillas, if you please. Damn."

"And he looks good in a wet suit." Natalie felt her face flame with a mad blush at this admission, and she mentally stamped down the memory of the dream she'd had that morning before telling Michelle about seeing him the previous evening at Steamer Lane.

"A romantic sunset tête-à-tête while he was dripping seawater all over you—" Michelle hooted.

"Not quite—"

Michelle laughed. "Gets that jerk job-stealing boyfriend out of your head, anyway."

Natalie's phone rang. She looked at the screen to see Asier Casillas's name. "Speak of the devil."

"The boyfriend or the hot researcher?" Michelle demanded.

Natalie couldn't help the grin that spread across her face.

Michelle laughed and went to the door. "Take your *time*," she said before shutting it behind her.

"Hi, this is Natalie," Natalie said in her best professional voice.

"Hi, yes, this is Asier. Um. Casillas. Dr. Casill—Asier."

She smiled. He was cute in his awkwardness. "Yes, hi, Asier."

"First of all, I am *not* calling to say that Jake is back. But I am calling with an idea of when we might see him."

"I'm all ears." She covered her face, now warm. The seawater dripping from his body onto hers in the dream had felt so *real*.

"There is a gala coming at the end of July. To benefit the facility. An annual event, more like an awards ceremony. They like all the researchers to go, you know, plus our grant donors. It is a very big thing, held at the visitor center."

Natalie held her breath, her head swirling. He was asking her out. He had not found her overly silly and anxious yesterday. Of course, yes, she'd love to, yes, she would go! But wait, hello. Slow down. She was not here to date people, even though she and Paul were on a break. Should she even say yes to Asier's invitation? She could if she wanted. All of these thoughts occurred in less than a second.

"As it happens, your brother is up for a major award this year," Asier went on, which did not sound like *So, I was wondering if you'd like to go*. "He was notified shortly before he left. He was…very pleased. It's an honor to receive the award, and it results in exposure to more donors, which in turn means better grants."

This was great. This would be an easy way to find Jake. Excitement—and a little satisfaction at it being so simple—rippled through her. She'd have to stay here a little longer—the end of July was a week and a half away, but that would neatly wrap up her time here. "So it sounds like we may see Jake very soon," she said, even as she realized that this was the point of Asier's call. Of *course* he was not calling to ask her out. He barely knew her. He was a serious scientist, busy with fish concerns. He was probably married or otherwise unavailable. She didn't even know, and she was certainly not going to ask.

"I was thinking that if there is something he'll reappear for, it's this. He knows exactly when it is. We were discussing if we would need to rent tuxedos."

With effort, she forced the image of Asier in a tuxedo out of her head. "I agree, if it's as important to getting funding as you said, it seems like something he'd come to. Thanks for letting me know."

"My pleasure. I think we will see Jake very soon, then."

"When is the gala?"

"Saturday after next. It's here at the lab, held at the Visitor Center. They do a nightlife kind of thing. Very nice."

Natalie pictured herself in an outrageous ball gown, dancing with Asier on the patio. A tiara on her head. She mentally kicked herself for being fantastical, even if only she could see it. Unless Jake appeared before the gala, it could be her last chance to find him.

"I hope it works," she said.

"Yes, me too. Okay, I am sorry to disturb you. I wanted you to know."

"Not disturbing at all…thank you…yes."

There was a hugely awkward silence that Natalie did not know what to do with, and neither, it seemed, did Asier.

"Have a good afternoon, Natalie. Goodbye." He hung up.

Natalie blinked and realized she'd assigned far too much weight to the exchange. She got up, brushing off an embarrassing amount of croissant crumbs. Michelle would crow and tease her about Asier's call, and that was fine. Natalie needed a laugh. She realized how much she had missed Michelle's infectious smile and having an old friend to tease her about things that did not actually exist. Like attractive scientists calling to ask her to a ball, like she was some kind of Cinderella.

CHAPTER 10

Natalie was officially worried. Penguin had not been seen for four days and had not eaten the food she'd set out for him.

"Want me to make a sign to post around the neighborhood?" Kit asked.

Natalie's heart did a little dance at his sweetness. "That's a good idea. At least he's a smart cat and can fend for himself. I hope he's not trapped anywhere."

Lynn was long gone at work, having arrived home the previous evening in time to make dinner for Kit and then collapse into bed. Kit, as a result, did not bother hiding the fact that he wanted to hang around with Natalie. He was also interested in the house, slinking from room to room, examining details like the old wallpaper and the woodwork, asking her questions about the place.

"What's that jar?" he asked, looking around her room from where he stood in the doorway. "Is that a lizard?"

"That's Patrick," Natalie said. "The crickets in the jar are his food. And a little illustration study." She pointed to her sketchbook and some recent cricket profiles.

"Are they all alive?" Kit went up to Patrick's terrarium and looked in at the lizard, who blinked one green eye at him as though to say, "And how do *you* do?"

"For the most part." Natalie couldn't vouch for the health and well-being of every single cricket, but there appeared to be movement most of the time.

"They're kind of gross."

Natalie looked at the jar, trying to see it from Kit's perspective. This jar was only the travel version of the large collection she had at home. Teensy had made her get rid of most of them before she left. They did look a bit messy and gross, she had to agree. "I mean, I need them to draw."

"I didn't expect you to have jars of insects," Kit said. "It's messy and weird. But I like it. Can I look through your sketchbook again?"

She nodded and handed it over. Was she messy and weird? Maybe a little.

Her present situation was certainly messy. She couldn't stay in California forever, but she wanted to keep the house in the family. Leaving without Penguin wasn't an option. And if she left before finding Jake, he'd take off to New Zealand for a year and she would never see him. She still couldn't believe her mother was willing to let this house go because Jake was having a tantrum or whatever he was doing.

"You know what? Why don't we go to the beach today?" Natalie asked Kit.

He looked doubtfully out the window at the clouded-over sky. "It's ugly outside."

"This is normal coastal weather. The clouds will disappear by twelve. Then it'll warm up."

"What should we do until twelve?"

"Let's tackle the front yard."

With some cajoling, Natalie got him out the door with an ancient pair of pruning shears she'd found by the back door. They went at the weeds and shrubs, getting scratched in the process by blackberry vines. Natalie looked for signs of Penguin, but he wasn't napping under any of the bushes. She did manage to find a harlequin beetle and deposited it into one of her mother's old Mason jars that she found under the kitchen sink along with some dirt and a twig before going back into battle against the blackberries. She would sketch that beetle tonight.

"Gah!" Natalie straightened, arrested by a sharp prick of pain in her palm. A blackberry thorn hiding under a large leaf had gotten her good.

"What happened?" Kit asked, popping up from where he was cutting.

"Damn thorn stabbed me. I'm going to kill it now. It has no idea what's coming." Natalie mimed punching the vine.

Kit froze, the expression on his face horrified and frightened, before he bent low over his shrub and resumed clipping at a frenzied pace. Natalie watched him. Something was off.

"Kit," she said. No answer. "What happened there?"

"Nothing."

Natalie frowned. Something was obviously wrong. "Kit."

"Nothing." He abandoned his clippers and pulled out his phone. Unbelievably, he started watching a video.

"Kit. What is it?"

Another long pause as he started a new video. She'd given up hope that he would answer, accepting that she'd pushed him too far, when he said, "That was something my dad would say."

Natalie looked up, shocked, replaying her words in her head. *I'm going to kill it now. It has no idea what's coming.* "Wow. Kit, I'm so sorry. Your dad sounds…difficult." She'd wanted to say *atrocious*, but he might still love his dad, even if he did bad things.

Kit swiped a forearm across his face and gave a bitter laugh. "Yeah."

She moved to put an arm around him, but he scooted out of reach. It would have been comical if it wasn't obvious that he was hurting.

"It's fine," he said. "We're here. It's nice to be here. Away."

Natalie sat on her haunches, regarding Kit closely as he self-soothed with the video. "Kit, I have to ask you something. Are you afraid that your dad will come here?"

Kit didn't answer for a long time, his eyes glued to the screen. Then he put the phone away and picked the shears back up. "A little."

Moving away, he began clipping again with renewed vigor. Natalie would have to talk to Lynn about this, to get more of the story, but she didn't know what to do in the meantime to make Kit feel better. She bent toward a vine and pulled it up dramatically, making sure to hold it between the wicked thorns. She shook it, getting Kit's attention. "Look here, vine. You and I are going to have a conversation. You will not hurt me. I am more powerful than you. This is a safe house."

She sent the vine sailing through the air to their pile. It was silly, but she thought she saw a smile on Kit's face.

"You're weird, Auntie," he said, but he seemed cheered all the same, and his phone stayed in his pocket.

— — —

Just past noon, after the fog had lifted, Natalie and Kit parked on 30th Avenue and walked to East Cliff. They followed the meandering sidewalk above the ocean, heading south. Natalie scanned the water below for signs of Jake in the throng of surfers. It was impossible to tell them apart from that distance, especially when they all wore black wet suits and she hadn't seen him in fifteen years. The water was too calm to really surf, which was good, because it meant most of the surfers were just sitting on their boards, waiting for the slightest swell, and Natalie could study them. Kit jogged ahead, skittering down the salt-battered cement steps that led to coves covered in kelp, passing surfers with boards under their arms. Natalie went slower, Jake-spotting and people-watching.

Not far out, a skinny, tall surfer caught a small wave and rode it to its completion, and she squinted, straining to see if it was him. It was impossible to know. And if it was him, what would she do? Wave madly? Shout his name? She'd feel better, anyway, knowing he was out there.

She realized with a jolt that it was almost a relief that Jake was MIA, because then she didn't have to see if he hated her. Lynn's anger was expected and assumed, but Jake? He was her big brother. He had been her protector. Her father figure, whether he meant to be or not. A well of agonizing hurt sat deep down in her, waiting like a giant toad. She didn't look at it much, but it never really went away.

Her phone rang. She dragged her eyes away from the sea and checked the caller ID. Seeing that it was Ann, she picked right up.

"Natalie, this is Ann. Checking in on you." The CEO's voice was always abrupt, always busy, and today was no different.

"Yes! Ann. I'm here, just, um, dealing with family."

A pause. "Good. I trust the break has been good for you."

Natalie scrambled to understand why the CEO would care about her break with Paul, then realized she probably meant the time away from work. "So far, so good." It wasn't a lie.

"Good. We got several new projects in, and we could use you back at work to prepare the property profiles."

"Oh. Ah..." she stammered, her brain scrambling to wake up like a reptile after a long time in the shade. "I haven't quite wrapped things up with my mom's house yet."

"I told you I was supportive of you taking time away, and I still am. But you're coming up on two weeks already. I have a business to think about, and some people are anxious to settle into the new reporting structure."

Paul was obviously the "some people" Ann referred to. "I understand." Natalie pursed her lips. "I should have the family business wrapped up in another week, by the end of July. Then I'll start driving back. Is that okay?"

Ann sighed heavily, imbuing it with disappointment. "Adding in—what? You need *another* week to drive back? That's a lot of time, Natalie. I can only pay you for three weeks of vacation time and bereavement, so wrap it up." There was a pause, as though Ann was thinking back over how that sounded, because she added in a softer tone, "Of course, we all wish you well in your time of difficulty."

"Thanks. I look forward to coming back."

The call ended with Ann's signature "Talk soon" bark. Natalie gazed at Kit leaning against the fence, looking down at the water. She tried to process the ramifications of having to leave in a little more than a week. She would have to leave the day after the gala, so Jake really needed to show up by then.

It seemed too soon.

She immediately shoved that thought away. She had always been planning to go back to Boston. That was a given. No point in allowing any pathetic hometown yearnings to sneak in.

She sighed, knowing she really should call Paul too. Paul, Paul. A decent boyfriend who, over the past five months, had been attentive and sweet. He wasn't perfect, but who was? Maybe the easy banter she'd enjoyed with Asier yesterday wasn't there with Paul, but Asier was hardly a romantic partner. Paul was real, break or not. *Ignore the Asier dream, never mind that.*

She sighed again and called Paul, the phone ringing only once before he picked up.

"Natalie," he answered, using what she thought of as his "soft voice," the one he used to telegraph that he was being romantic or serious or attentive. "So good to hear from you."

"Hey," she said, using her own soft tone to show she came in peace. "How are you?"

"Really missing you." She heard the sound of a door closing—his office door. The office she had often envisioned herself in. It had a gorgeous view of Boston Harbor, and she had always pictured herself in there with her high heels on the desk—she never wore high heels to work, but that was not the point—looking out over that view while on the phone doing very important business.

"I miss you too." She thought about the warmth of his large frame when he cuddled her. The long, lingering dinners and walks in the Public Garden together. Yes, those things were good. She missed them.

"How is California?" he asked.

"Well, I'm here with my sister and her son. Waiting for my brother to appear."

"And the house?"

"It's standing."

"Sounds like you're accomplishing what you needed to do."

"Sort of. My brother isn't here, and he needs to be for us to inherit the house."

"If your sister's there, then it's likely your brother will show up." He said this gently, in a supportive tone she appreciated.

"I'm sure you're right." Jake's arrival at the house, however, was not the same as Lynn's, in Natalie's mind. If Jake was out somewhere being upset, then once he found Natalie at the house, the full brunt of his anger from over the years could be huge. He had been quick to anger and rage, even though that was mostly during his teenage years, and it had never been directed toward Natalie. She simply didn't know her brother as an adult and certainly not as the accomplished scientist he'd become.

"And Natalie. Listen. I know we're on a break—although again, I don't want to be, but I respect that you do. I want to clear the air about work, since you haven't called me so we could talk about it. I had no idea Ann was going to promote me, okay? None."

"Okay." She struggled to keep any bitterness out of the word, but if they were going to work together, she'd have to overcome it. There was a lot to unpack in his statement, including the subtle dig about how she hadn't returned his calls.

"I want you to know that I didn't swoop in to steal anything." he said. "And I want to make this work with you, both in the office and at home. I'm in this with you. I am committed."

"Well." She swallowed. Hearing that he was committed helped. It was part of the appeal of him: an accomplished man, her best friend's brother, committed to her and being her family. It was a balm, but there was that single small thread of unease that it was not the right *kind* of commitment. That it was a commitment that furthered his interests but not necessarily hers. "We need boundaries, Paul. We need to respect when we need to take time to deal with things."

"Of course. Absolutely. I agree. But I meant it when I said I love you."

She stared out at the blue expanse of the ocean in front of her, trying, as she had done so many times before, to see across the bay to Monterey, but the horizon was often too shrouded in fog to see the land.

"I—I have a lot to sort out here," she said. "I can't say what you need me to say right now. But I hope I can very soon. Please understand."

"Of course. I do understand. Although I do think you want to be careful about protecting your emotions if your brother and sister are still angry. I'm still concerned that this trip could backfire. If at any time you feel like you need to get out of there, call me. I'll fly you back."

"Oh—thanks, yeah, I mean, I have to drive—"

"There are options, Natalie." His voice had morphed into that parental tone she disliked so much.

"Got it."

"And you have every right to feel a whole bunch of things. That's normal."

Normal. What was normal? Natalie was beginning to think she didn't understand what that word meant anymore. It certainly wasn't listening to one's boyfriend condescend about feelings.

"And I want you to know, the offer to move in with me stands. When are you headed home?"

"Another week. I'll be back at the beginning of August."

Kit waved to her from up ahead, beckoning her to join him.

Paul made a *tsk* sound that managed to sound less dismayed, like a boyfriend missing his girlfriend, and more disappointed, like a manager. "That's a long way away. Can you shorten it? Maybe start back on Monday?"

She forced her jaw muscles to unclench. "My nephew is calling me. I need to go."

"Sure. Maybe we can text more often. I miss talking with you."

She officially felt a little smothered. They'd spent every day of the past five months talking, texting, or seeing each other. She had enjoyed that, but now things were different. She could chalk it up to the whole promotion thing, but she worried it was more than that. "Maybe…a little less right now, Paul. We're on a break."

"Of course," he said. "I don't mean to push you or sound controlling." He laughed in a way that suggested that would be silly, as though the thought would never cross his mind. "Like, text whenever you want to, obviously. As you said, we're on a break."

She frowned. These were the right words, said in the right order, but it was like he was pulling them out of a bag and seeing what stuck.

"Okay, Paul. I've got to go. Talk to you later." She ended the call and threw her phone into her bag. She joined Kit, who was balancing rocks on top of other rocks on the cliff's edge, next to a bunch of other cairns.

"Here." He handed her a rock. "Can't get this one to stay."

She carefully put the rock on top, steadying it as a gust of salty wind hit them. The surf was picking up. Her hopes that Jake was in the surf were waning, and he wasn't in the parking lot across the street changing into a wet suit. She kept her hand on the rock and then carefully, assuredly let go. It stayed where it was, balancing on a point.

"Whoa," Kit said.

"We used to do this when we were kids," Natalie said. Lynn would always pack sandwiches for them, and Jake would do exactly what Kit was doing—engineer rock balancing pyramids, or they would build sandcastles down on the beach.

The bite of the day's heat was gone when they finally gave up on the pyramids. Most of the surfers had gotten out of the water. As they walked back to the car, Natalie's phone rang again. Her first instinct was to not answer it. If it was Paul again, she was not going to take it. Though maybe it was Asier with news of Jake. Natalie picked up her phone and looked at the caller ID. It was Teensy.

"I hear you talked to my brother," Teensy said. "That's good."

"That was fast."

"Oh, he called me right away. He was thrilled."

"I felt bad for ignoring him."

"Well. You're on a break."

Natalie smiled that Teensy was good with it. "We are."

"Be kind to yourself, okay? Sometimes you withdraw too much. That's what I told him, by the way. I said that big emotional events can make you hide and it was nothing to do with him."

"Right." It was a little bit to do with him, though. The promotion and the break. That wasn't a point she needed to clarify with his sister, though. Not right now.

"Is that the ocean I hear in the background?" Teensy asked.

"Yeah. I'm here with my nephew. Lynn got a job, so we're hanging out while she's at work. Trying to track down Jake. You should see this sky, Teense. It's, like, a color I don't even think there's a word for. Kit and I built a rock sculpture. And the smell of the ocean! I can hear the waves at night from my bedroom, crashing against the rocks. And the sea lions barking from Seal Rock. It's incredible."

Teensy was silent a moment.

"What?" Natalie asked. "You're doing that thing you do where you go all quiet and disapproving."

"You like it there."

"Well, sure. It was my home for eighteen years."

"You coming back to Boston?"

"Of course," Natalie scoffed.

"Okay. I was worried."

"That's ridiculous." But Natalie felt a sliver of fear. Santa Cruz was home. Its very scent was home. "I don't live here anymore."

"I know I'm biased, but I want us all to be a family. As we know, my brother is the best relationship you've had in…years. I'm not telling you that. You said that yourself last month."

"True." She had said that. Paul was the most serious relationship she'd had. "I've had other good relationships, though."

"That guy with the huge beard whose entire apartment was a hydroponic farm for weed and only wanted to have sex in the back seat of rideshares? Not viable. That guy you picked up at the bar, the one who would eat all your food off your plate while you were eating it? Not viable. That guy Dave, who seemed great otherwise but turned out to have something overly weird going on with his mother? Not—"

"Stop." Natalie's face was on fire remembering those losers. "When I get back, we'll sort it out." She shushed the little worried voice in her head asking if that was really true. Writing her (shush!) reports was still not the same as (shushhh!) illustrating animals, and that would not change (shut up!). Having Paul as her manager could present challenges that might end their relationship. "I'll be driving the first of August." She noticed Kit frown at her and turn away as they started climbing the stone stairs back up the cliff.

"Natalie."

"Teensy."

"No, I'm being serious. I'm worried."

"About what? That I'll never come back?" There was a silence, and Natalie realized that was exactly it. "Teense, come on."

"*You* come on. I just—I sense something different about you. I'm not there to see you, so I don't know what it is, but it's something."

"No analyzing," Natalie reminded her in a singsong voice that usually made her laugh.

There was no laughter now. "Be careful. Don't throw things away."

"I'm not throwing Paul away," Natalie said, taking care to sound serious.

"Okay. All right. I— Okay."

"Teense. It's fine. I'll see you in a little more than two weeks, okay?"

They said their goodbyes, both forcing a little cheer. Natalie was unable to wipe away the thought that Teensy might have a reason to worry. The conversation had been unnerving. She looked back at the sea once more for good luck, noting the peace and strength of the powerful swells and the no-nonsense sideways pull of the riptide. The ocean was a study in unwavering strength and determination. She wished she had that kind of inner strength. Because she wasn't sure who she'd been trying to convince more on that call that everything would be fine, Teensy or herself.

CHAPTER 11

"What are you thinking about?" Kit asked as they walked. Natalie realized she'd been brooding for a good two blocks about her conversation with Teensy.

"Oh, just work. Going back to Boston."

"Do you like your work?" Kit asked.

"I do, for the most part."

"Is it drawing? All the bugs and animals?"

She laughed. "God, I wish. No. That's— No. I don't draw profession-ally. I'm not trained for it."

"But I saw your sketchbook. Your animals are like what you see in books."

She glanced at him, pleased. "Thanks."

"Maybe you can get a job drawing here," he said.

She glanced at him again, hiding a smile. "I mean, I write reports on historic houses. And my life is in Boston now. I can't stay here forever."

"I think you should." He scuffed his shoe on the pavement.

"That's nice of you to say." She was touched. "I—" Her phone rang again.

"You sure get a lot of calls," Kit said.

"Yeah, I'm hoping one of them will be your uncle Jake," but it was Michelle. "Heya." She shoved away the thought that she'd hoped it was actually Asier calling with news of Jake.

"Hey," Michelle said. "Every Saturday I get together with the girls, and we have a long boozy lunch. Want to come? Cara from high school will be there—remember her? And my other friend Yasmin too. I've told you about her. All four of us with sunglasses on, giant bottomless cocktails, and endless snacks."

It was the kind of thing Natalie loved and had missed. She and Teensy used to do the same thing with a few friends on weekends, at least before she and Paul got together. He liked their weekends together, and she'd given up more time with friends as a result. She hadn't minded at the time. Except for Teensy, she wasn't particularly close with any of the other women. Michelle always talked about what a good friend Yasmin was, and it would be nice to see Cara again.

"Come on," Michelle said before she could answer. "Friends are good."

"I'd love to have a long boozy lunch with you guys," Natalie said. "I can't wait."

She ignored the little inner voice suggesting that if Teensy was right and she did want to stay here, then brunch with new friends wouldn't be such a bad thing.

Her breath caught at her mind, surfacing secrets she thought she had been doing a good job keeping buried. Even if she wanted to stay here, it wasn't possible. It was outrageous for her brain to even allow that thought to slip through. She could understand feeling nostalgic for her hometown, and she could enjoy brunch with old friends, but that was it. In a week, she'd be on the road, heading back toward her future.

— — —

Lynn's car sat in the driveway when they got home, the engine ticking as it cooled down. Kit ran ahead and burst through the front door, calling to his mom to tell her about the rock pyramids. It was such a sweet, little-boy thing to do that Natalie's heart danced as she followed Kit inside. She had never been overly interested in having children of her own, but she was sure enjoying being an aunt.

"Let me shower off," Lynn was saying as Natalie walked into the foyer, "and then tell me all about it!"

The first thing that hit Natalie was the smell. A horrible, fishy odor with undertones of excrement, laced with a hint of sharp chemicals, and it appeared to be coming from Lynn. Her khaki slacks were wet and had unseemly dark patches of…stuff on them.

"Uh," Natalie said. "Lynn."

"I know." Lynn held up a hand. "A body leaked on me at work. Wasn't expecting it. It's fine."

"Leaked…"

"There was an issue with the embalming chemicals and then, um, with the cremation process. Fluid got out."

"So it's blood?"

"No, other liquids. Unfortunately, the body wasn't in great shape, so the smell's a bit strong."

Natalie's stomach did a distinct nosedive. Even Kit looked appalled.

Lynn tried to pull off a shrug as though this was no big deal, but it was rigid and uncomfortable. "Let's say that as far as tough days at the office go, this one redefines bad. It was a slurry of sorts. A lot of it landed on me."

"Please do not speak again," Natalie begged. "Please never say the word *slurry* again."

Kit looked green.

"I need to shower." Lynn began to climb the stairs. Natalie thought she saw a drop of something dark yellow come off Lynn's pants, which made Natalie think absurdly of what their mother, who was always so particular about the way the foyer looked and had a fit about any particulate they brought in, would have said about corpse juice being flung about on her grand stairs. Natalie giggled, but it came out as a stressed, high-pitched sound.

"It's not funny, Natalie," Lynn said. "The bodies have dignity. I didn't mean to create chum out of the woman."

"I'm not laughing at that," Natalie said. "I'm laughing because I'm picturing Mom's face at the sight and smell of you."

Lynn dropped her stern look, which was, Natalie would never point out, not unlike their mother's. "She hated any speck of dirt in here."

"She would be so horrified," Natalie said.

"She'd do that thing with her mouth," Lynn said.

Natalie laughed, envisioning the wrinkles around their mother's mouth twisting and pursing into her signature frown that resembled a cat's butt. Lynn's face cracked into a smile too.

"You can laugh later, after you shower, Mom!" Kit said. *"Please."*

Still grinning, Lynn climbed the stairs.

Natalie and Kit hurried down the long hall to the back of the house, where the kitchen was and where the smell was not.

"Does she come home from work like that a lot?" Natalie asked.

He shook his head. "I've never seen *that* before."

A scant twenty minutes later, Lynn came down the back stairs, freshly showered and without the smell.

"Surely a longer shower?" Natalie said.

"It was mostly the pants that got it," Lynn said.

"I hope you threw them out," Natalie said, wrinkling her nose.

"I mean, they'll get a good scrub—what?" Lynn laughed, and Natalie knew she was teasing her. "Yes, of course I'm throwing them out." She turned to Kit. "Now, kiddo, tell me about your rock pyramid."

Lynn fixed herself a well-deserved vodka tonic as Kit recounted their afternoon at the beach. Natalie sat on one of the ancient breakfast bar stools and listened, delighting in the waning sunshine coming in through the dirty old kitchen windows, the quiet of the house, the pure voice of a kid who loved his project, enveloping her in pleasure.

"And you?" Lynn asked Natalie when Kit was done. "Did you have a good time?"

"Oh, yeah. The beaches on the East Coast aren't the same."

There was a silence before Lynn said, "Staying away was your choice."

Natalie's brain rifled through—and discarded—many possible responses, like, *I had to because of what I did*, or *Mom asked for space, and you and Jake weren't talking to me.*

Lynn began moving around the kitchen prepping dinner, so Natalie stepped out the back door and into the wilderness of the yard, which had once been home to a magnificent display of rosebushes. A pile of tattered patio chairs sat in a heap against the house, covered in cobwebs and dirt. Natalie yanked three out and hauled them over to the flagstones, brushing off the dirt and plopping down in one as she surveyed the jungle. It could be tamed with some work. This whole house could. If someone was willing to stick around and put the time in.

A pang of loss hit her. She would love to work this garden. She would love to see it restored to the way her mother had it when she was little. Sitting with the feeling for a moment, she let it engulf her rather than pushing it away like she'd been doing since she'd arrived in Santa Cruz. There was so much she'd missed here. For the first time in years, she allowed herself to feel grief over the losses she'd faced: her mother, the bond with her siblings, this house.

She clarified to herself that she missed when it was good: the way her mom had looked when she'd been gardening all day, her hair escaping from her ponytail, her cheek smudged with dirt. Or the delighted squeals from playing Pirate Ship on the stairs with Lynn and Jake. Even when things had gotten harder, like when their dad had died and their mom had taken off, Lynn and Jake had made sure things were fun and that they were taken care of. Lynn had tucked her into bed at night, Jake kissing her forehead and saying in a determined way that it would be fine, that he was old enough to look after them, even though he wasn't.

She craved that familial love again. And she wanted to feel comfortable in wanting that love.

The back door opened, and Lynn came out with her cocktail glass. "Ah. The chairs. Nice." She sat down in one and leaned back to look at the clouds. "What are you doing?"

"Sitting out here, thinking."

"And what are you thinking about?" Lynn asked.

Natalie took a breath and was about to tell her but pivoted at the last second and decided Lynn might not want to walk down memory lane. "I was thinking about how my company could restore this house. It's exactly the type of project they excel at."

Lynn nodded. "I'm surprised Mom didn't sell the place."

Natalie frowned. "I guess she was holding on to it to make us all get together."

"I guess."

"Do you think...you and Jake would want to sell?" Natalie said this with trepidation. The idea of selling this house felt like sacrilege, but with three adults doing different things with their lives, what really was their endgame? Certainly Natalie could use the money. She could do a lot with her share.

"Oh, I don't know. I have no idea what Jake is doing or what he wants."

"What will you do if we sell?" Natalie asked.

Lynn glanced at her, quick, annoyed. "What's it to you?"

"I mean, I care what happens to you. And Kit."

Lynn looked at the sky. "I don't know what we'll do. We'll cross that bridge when we come to it. My plan is to stay in Santa Cruz. I don't know more than that."

The hitch in Lynn's voice wasn't lost on Natalie. Lynn being unsure about anything was unusual. But people changed. They grew up and dealt with difficult things, and it changed them.

"Listen, Lynn. Kit and I were out in the garden this morning. I was clipping blackberry vines, and one stabbed me, and I shouted abuse at it."

Lynn gave her a withering look. "Okay. Sorry to hear that?"

Natalie ignored her sarcasm. "I said I wanted to kill the vine and pretended to punch it. Kit reacted really badly to what I said and got upset. About his dad."

Lynn was quiet.

Natalie's worry grew. "Are you guys safe?"

"We're all right."

"Only all right? What does that mean?"

"Allen is a jerk, but he's in New York."

Natalie didn't want to remind Lynn that she too had been in New York a short while ago.

"Do I seem like someone who can't handle him?" For a moment, Lynn looked like she used to—strong, stentorian Lynn. But the lines on her face and the look of deep weariness said something else.

"I think you used to be someone no one would mess with," Natalie said carefully. "But things have changed."

"A hard life will do that."

Natalie looked at her hands. "I'm sorry."

"You should concentrate on Jake showing up so we can get the house and you can go back to Boston."

Natalie felt stung. "I mean, there's so much to decide—"

"Same old Natalie. You never knew what the hell you were doing. I kind of thought you would have settled yourself a little bit as an adult."

Natalie felt stung again at this sudden viciousness. "I *am* settled. I have a job. I have a boyfriend who wants me to move in with him. Jesus. I'm *settled.*"

"You can be settled on paper but still feel unhappy and unfulfilled."

"No, that's not—"

"I had a peek in your room," Lynn said.

"What? Why?"

"You haven't even been here that long, and it's already a mess. What's with all the weird jars in there? What are they?"

"Specimens."

"Of what? Are you doing something illegal?"

Natalie barked a laugh. "Right. That's you, not me." Instantly she regretted it. "Sorry."

"What's in the jars?" Lynn's tone was tight now. Natalie sensed the opportunity for a companionable evening chat melting away.

"Bugs. To draw, mostly. Or feed my lizard, Patrick."

Lynn cringed. "They're gross. Your whole room is a trash pit. I'm afraid you've turned into someone deeply weird."

"I'm not the one who came home covered in corpse juice."

Natalie knew she was angling for a fight, but something broke. A rare grin emerged on Lynn's face. "Fair."

They sat in silence. Natalie wished she could think of something to say to her sister. It was hard being related to someone yet feeling so disconnected as adults.

"Lynn. You and Jake—"

Lynn got up and walked toward the house. "Enough for tonight. I have to be at work early tomorrow." Her voice was soft, and that was something at least. Natalie suspected her sister was trying to guard against further arguing, but she would have liked for them to try having a normal conversation, one that didn't end with them snipping at each other. But Lynn rarely allowed second chances. It was very likely that none of this would work, and the sooner Natalie accepted that, the better. A tentative feeling tugged at her, something she hadn't allowed herself to feel in a long time, but it was difficult to parse it out since it was weighed down under a whole pile of other feelings.

It wasn't until much later, while she was in bed staring out at the stars through her dormer window as she had so many times as a kid, that it hit her what that earlier feeling had been: anticipation, seasoned with a little yearning. She wanted to find Jake. She wanted to work something out with Lynn. She wanted to somehow redeem herself with them. It was not a new desire; it had been tucked down in her most hidden place for fifteen years. The idea that it might be too late was a hard one to accept. This was the reality she'd grappled with her whole adult life. The best thing she could do was find Jake, help him and Lynn secure the house, and give them the space from her that they so clearly wanted to live their lives.

Then she could go home.

CHAPTER 12

Saturday morning dawned clear and beautiful with the exact right breeze coming off the ocean. Natalie turned over in her sleeping bag, disappointed not to see Penguin. It was worrying. He had gone on three-day jaunts away from home before, but this was too long, and he didn't know the area. She made a mental note to check the house's crannies and corners and drive around the neighborhood to see if she spotted him. The signs Kit had put up had not resulted in any leads.

She picked up her phone, checking for new messages, and saw two waiting for her.

Paul: So glad we talked yesterday. Sitting here missing you, loving you. xxoo

And Asier: Happy Saturday. Making some calls around to see about Jake. Wanted to let you know I'm still actively looking.

Ignoring Paul's text for now, she tapped back a reply to Asier: Thank you. Appreciate it. You're a good friend to him.

Asier's reply came swiftly. We all care about him. I'm happy to help.

And I have heard so much about you from him, it is interesting getting to know you.

Her heart jumped. Interesting how? Good interesting? Or I-heard-you-sent-my-colleague-to-prison-and-I-want-to-see-what-kind-of-fiendish-sister-does-that interesting?

She decided to answer ambiguously, just in case. Likewise, she texted back.

The next text from Asier was a smiley face. And then a smiley face with sunglasses on. She replied with her own winky smiley face. She could stand here all day at her window texting flirty emojis back and forth with Asier. Maybe she would.

But she was meeting Michelle and her friends for brunch and didn't want to be late, despite feeling a little trepidation. Would they be nice? Would they judge her for what she had done to her brother and sister? That had happened once. Teensy had told a new friend of theirs what Natalie had done, and the friend had decided Natalie was a terrible, backstabbing sister. Which of course confirmed Natalie's fears.

Natalie sent a carefully worded text to Paul saying that she was glad they had talked yesterday too, which wasn't really true. Then she picked through her box of art materials and jars (the jars *really* needed to be emptied). She dropped a cricket into Patrick's terrarium and made a mental note to pick up some more from the pet store soon.

She got dressed, drove through town the long way, along the beach, and found that she was still smiling at the silliness of Asier's emoji texts. A little guilt accompanied this, especially with Paul's love you text mixed in this morning, but they were on a break. *She* was on a break. She could enjoy another man's emojis.

Nevertheless, guilt ate at her. Because those emojis were definitely flirty.

"Ahhh!" Michelle squealed at the sight of Natalie as she approached their table, getting out of her chair and hugging her tightly.

"Cara, you remember Natalie? And this is Yasmin, my good friend." Michelle waved a hand around the table, where Cara and Yasmin sat with mimosas in front of them. Natalie looked down at her jeans and wrinkled T-shirt that had been sitting at the bottom of her bag and felt a little embarrassed in front of these stylishly dressed women. Cara and Yasmin both wore summer dresses and managed to look both sophisticated and comfortable. Yasmin wore a magnificent wide-brimmed hat, something Audrey Hepburn would have worn. Cara was unchanged from high school somehow: a freckled redhead with an arched eyebrow that suggested the world amused her.

"It's great to see both of you," Natalie said, settling into her seat as Michelle slid a fourth glass over.

"Ordered it for you."

Natalie clinked glasses with each of them. Cara leaned forward. "All right, Nat. Been a long time! Michelle tells us you're back in town to manage your mom's estate? Sorry to hear she passed."

"Thanks. Yeah, she put the house in a trust—"

"That gorgeous old house." Cara nudged Yasmin. "It's one of the massive Victorians over on the west side. Three stories. Incredible parties. Came with a resident hottie of an older brother."

Natalie shrugged. "I mean, he was a brother."

"But then he turned into a bad boy and went to prison," Cara said.

"Both my brother and sister did," Natalie said for Yasmin's benefit. "It's...a story."

"I love a good family drama," Yasmin said.

Natalie, who did not like to talk about this at the best of times even with people she knew, could feel her defenses shoot up like iron spikes around her. This was not going to be the laid-back, enjoyable lunch she'd hoped for.

But Yasmin, apparently sensing her unease, said, "Oh God, I'm sorry. So insensitive of me! And you don't even know me. I'm sorry!"

"Ah shit, same," Cara said. "You drink your drink, and we'll tell you about ourselves, okay?"

Natalie laughed, relieved they'd caught her discomfort. "Yes. I'd like that." She was no stranger to sticking her foot in her mouth and was quick to forgive when it happened to others.

"Okay," Yasmin said. "I'm Yasmin, and I am sometimes insensitive to people I've just met. I'm thirty-two, and I'm an accountant with a tech company in San Jose." Her tone was that of a person introducing herself on a reality television show, which made Natalie smile.

"And my name is Cara," Cara said, following the same tone, "and I am also thirty-two, an assistant professor at CSU Monterey in the finance department, and also sometimes insensitive to people I haven't seen in a long time."

Natalie laughed. "It's fine, you guys. But thanks." She was impressed with how easily they whipped their professional titles out. Natalie always had to explain what she did a bit, often followed by glazed eyes as she explained the process of writing home histories and who wanted them and why. In contrast, whenever Paul introduced himself to someone and said, "I'm an architect," there seemed to be an instant brightening and nodding, with interested follow-up questions. Natalie longed for that simplicity. It might be silly—she knew—but she equated a simple title with a simpler, more complete version of herself.

"What's the status of the house?" Michelle asked Cara. She leaned toward Natalie. "Cara is buying a house."

"Congratulations," Natalie said, tamping down feelings of envy like she was extinguishing embers.

"Thanks," Cara said. "I'm upgrading from a condo, so I'm very excited."

"Did you put the condo on the market yet?" Yasmin asked.

"We didn't have to go to market, actually. My agent got a preemptive offer."

It was Cara's *second* house. Natalie did a mental whole-body smothering of her envy flames, but the embers continued to smolder.

"The sale process is stressful," Yasmin said. "Last year when we sold our cottage—you remember the place we had before our current house? We had four offers, but the one we chose fell through. Luckily the backup was great, and my Realtor ended up negotiating a higher down payment."

Natalie fiddled with the strawberry in her glass and tuned them out. Housing talk was beyond her. She couldn't afford to buy a place on her own—she couldn't afford rent as it was—and had to live with Teensy. Marrying Paul was the nearest to home ownership she would likely get unless she started making more money.

"Any luck on finding Jake?" Michelle asked her quietly.

Natalie turned to her friend, grateful that Michelle knew she would have feelings, however silly, about the house conversation. "Not yet. I guess we're waiting for him to show up at the gala next weekend."

"Is Hot Scientist helping?"

"Stop! Yes, he's helping, but not in the way you're insinuating. But I did call Paul."

"Pfft." Michelle took a long swig of her drink and plunked the glass down hard on the table. "That guy."

"He said he loves me." Natalie toyed with the paper umbrella in her glass. The feeling that she wasn't sure if she loved him back was growing, which meant she was going to have to do something about it sooner or later. He offered a future, but he'd been the one to get the promotion she'd wanted. He said the right things but had been repellent the whole time she'd been in California, ignoring her boundaries and insisting they talk when she'd told him she wanted a break. The family she could have was tied up with him. But what if…what if there was an alternative to having Paul and Teensy as her family?

"*Who* loves you?" Cara said loudly. "Sorry. Did not mean to sound like no one loves you. God! Did it again. I *may* be a little tipsy." She clapped a hand over her mouth with a *smack*.

Natalie laughed. "No, it's fine. We're talking about my boyfriend, Paul."

Yasmin rubbed her hands together. "Ooh, is it a fabulous love story?"

"Not in my opinion," Michelle said. "He stole her job from her but expects her to move in with him. Anyway, there's a hot scientist after her here in Santa Cruz."

"He is not *after me* by any stretch of the imagination," Natalie said.

"He was chatting her up while in a full wet suit after he'd gone surfing." Michelle ignored her, squinting at Cara and Yasmin with what she probably thought was a knowing look but which Natalie thought looked like she'd gotten something in her eye. Natalie's own face was lava-hot as she remembered the naked-Asier wet suit dream.

"Wet suit. Done deal," Cara said loudly. "And that job-stealing boyfriend can hoof it."

Natalie laughed. "We'll see. I'm headed home next Sunday." If she found her cat. If they found Jake. If she even *wanted* to go back. If, if, if.

"A fling before you go?" Yasmin suggested.

Natalie shook her head. "No, no."

Cara grinned. "Flings are fun. Remember right before high school graduation? Everyone was having flings."

"I was breaking up with my boyfriend," Michelle said. "No flings here."

"I wasn't having any flings," Natalie said. Doz on That Night certainly didn't count as one.

"You were! You were with that guy Doz. Remember him? Alex Hernandez." Cara closed her eyes and made a rapturous face. "He was so, so cute."

"Doz wanted to get with Brandi Charleston," Natalie said. "That's how that ended up."

"He was a fool," Michelle said. "No one ever heard from him after high school. He clearly peaked."

"There's always the hot scientist," Cara said. "You can have that fling now."

"In the wet suit." Yasmin held up a finger to remind them, and the four of them giggled. Yasmin looked worried. "We're only teasing, Natalie. I hope you don't think we're mean."

"We're not mean!" Cara said. "Have we offended you? Please tell us."

"Not at all." Natalie smiled, although she realized a part of her had been holding herself rigid. Assault-teasing was a common sport among her and Teensy's crowd of friends. But no one ever checked in and asked if she was okay. They only laughed harder. Teensy would be sympathetic later, but Teensy could be one of the loudest in the moment. Natalie didn't like that. She resolved not to put up with it when she went back home. Natalie forced herself to breathe out, relaxing her shoulders. "Anyway, everyone knows a wet suit is the way to a woman's heart."

"It is to mine for sure," Yasmin said. They laughed. Not because it was funny, but because they were here together, sharing things.

The conversation turned to another topic: Yasmin's challenges with an awful coworker. "The worst thing about this guy, apart from how he takes credit for things I do, is that he stands *wayyy* too close at the copy machine. Like, the man needs to *back off*," Yasmin said.

"Oh no," everyone yelled. "No!"

"I had this fake crow at Halloween," Yasmin said. "I stuck it on top of his monitor. As a warning."

"Crows are a sign of death," Michelle said, nodding. "Good."

Natalie took a long sip of her mimosa. It was her second drink, and she'd begun to relax into the rhythm of the conversation. "Crows are great. But speaking of signs of death, did I tell you about Lynn's job?"

She hadn't, and the three of them were a receptive audience, gasping and going wide-eyed at the right parts of the story. It felt so good to make other people laugh. By the time she stood up from the table, now littered with used plates and glasses, Natalie was both pleasantly buzzed and buoyant from the beautiful day, fresh air, and fun times with new friends.

Her phone pinged as she tottered her way through the restaurant. She grabbed for it, hoping it was Asier sending her another smiley emoji. Her stomach did a little twirl when she saw his name on the screen.

We got a call from a colleague down in Monterey who says he saw Jake there this morning.

Natalie's heart leaped, but the source of its leaping was too full of complications to sort out. She typed back: Where?

He was using their lab. Want to come with me today and check it out?

She couldn't answer fast enough. Ready when you are.

CHAPTER 13

The brunch had left Natalie too buzzed to drive to the marine lab, so she called a rideshare. They were almost at the lab when her phone sounded with a text: Asier, saying that he was wrapping up a report and could she give him ten minutes? Of course she could.

She sat outside the building, her leg jangling as she waited. The morning's tipsy brunch sat heavy in her stomach, but at least her head was clear now. She downed a bottle of water, checked the time—she still had several minutes—and decided to go inside. A black thing caught her eye inside the heavy glass doors of the lab building: a large spider with an enormous abdomen—the very scariest kind—shook in its web.

The urge to get out her sketch pad hit her, even while she gave an inward shiver of horror at being so close to the thing. Ideally, the building would have to be burned down, but first she would draw the spider. She pulled out the pad she kept in her bag and a pouch of well-sharpened pencils. This was exactly the right thing to do while waiting for Asier.

She leaned against the wall and waited for the spider to stop shaking.

It looked like a feisty kind, a black widow maybe, but then she thought all juicy black spiders were black widows. She sketched the ghastly abdomen and spent some time on the spindly points of the legs, taking care with the segmentation. She wished she had a jar to put it in so she could sketch it again in her room, at her leisure, though the idea of it in her room was intolerable. It was so mesmerizing working on the segmentation of the legs that she didn't hear the footsteps clipping down the shiny hall until they were almost next to her. She looked up, still in that pleasurable daze she always had while sketching. A man in a lab coat stopped beside her, his hands on the door, and peered at the drawing in her notebook.

"That certainly is a very fine technical rendering. Those legs are particularly impressive. Of course, this spider has to go," he said, motioning toward the spider still hanging in the doorway.

She grinned. "It's definitely going to attack the next person who goes through the door."

The man, who resembled a severe British butler with a pink forehead and a gray mustache, gave a kind of pained look that suggested he didn't quite know how to smile but wanted to. "You are very wise to draw it and wait for someone else to take the fall."

She laughed and erased a part of the leg.

"You work here?" he asked. "Drawing specimens?"

She flushed hard with pleasure that he would think she worked here, *drawing*. What a compliment. "Oh, no. I'm only visiting."

"Hmm. You draw professionally, though?"

"Ha. No." She was about to say *I wish* but then realized he was asking very pointed questions. As in, where was this leading?

"Well, we always need illustrators around here."

Asier had mentioned that a researcher at the lab was looking for an illustrator. Natalie got to her feet slowly, taking care not to disturb the spider. "I'm Natalie. Natalie Walker."

"I'm Dr. Berkhower." He shook her proffered hand. "No relation to our estimable Dr. Walker, is there?"

"He's my brother, actually."

"Ah." Dr. Berkhower looked as though he wanted to say more but thought better of it. He pointed to her notebook. "He never mentioned such a talented sister. What else do you have in there?"

"Oh. Lots." She flipped through the pages, revealing studies of Penguin in various poses: napping, licking himself with his legs sticking out in different directions, standing like a little general with his front feet primly together. But also a fox, tons of crows, some marmots, and tons of insects from her jars. And a robin with a broken foot bent backward that she'd found at a park one day.

"That one," he said, pointing at the robin's broken foot. "That right there."

She looked at him, waiting for more explanation. It had been one of her favorites to do because of the challenge of drawing a deliberately incorrect posture. Although it had been sad to draw, it was fascinating. She had liked the opportunity.

He straightened. "I study sea lion mortality. As it happens, I am in need of a good illustrator, as photographs are either too graphic or not detailed enough to show the underlying causes of death—they often need detail extrapolations and callouts. Would you be interested in taking a look at a specimen I have and possibly illustrating it? If you can capture what I'm looking for, I can offer you a job."

A deep spike of excitement shot through her, spreading into pleasure at being asked. A *job*! But the excitement quickly turned to regret. "I'm—I'm only here for a short while. I'd really love to, but I live in Boston."

He frowned. "When do you go back?"

"In a week."

"I have a dead sea lion coming in on Monday, and I have to document the necropsy. A sketch would be the best thing for it. Would you work on this as a single contract?"

"Oh, wow." To be in a real lab and see actual specimens sounded amazing, even if it would be gory. Illustrating for real? "I'd love to. Monday?"

"Yes. You're not squeamish, are you? Its head was crushed by a boat propeller. You would see some unfortunate things. If you can handle it."

"I can handle it." In general, she wasn't a fan of squished animals, but she'd sketched plenty of wildlife in nature that had been mangled or otherwise handicapped. The sea lion was only tissue, after all.

"I'm in lab 4A," he said.

She could hardly believe it. "That sounds great. I mean, not great, obviously, that the head was crushed, but great—you know what I mean."

Dr. Berkhower rocked on his heels. "I do! Natalie, it was good to meet you. Come at nine. I'll have the VapoRub and gloves ready."

VapoRub? "Yes." She shook his hand again, eyeing the spider, which was trying to sneak into the doorjamb where its ambush wouldn't be anticipated. She swallowed, wondering what was wrong with her that spending extended time with crushed sea lion skulls didn't roil her insides. Drawing complex parts of animals was part of the challenge and the intrigue though. "It was nice meeting you. Be careful through the door there."

Dr. Berkhower laughed as though being frightened of a spider was ridiculous, but all the same, he kept his eye on its hiding spot as he pushed through the doors. If she were in the habit of thanking spiders, she would have given this one a big hug for waylaying her here.

— —— —

Fifteen minutes later, Natalie and Asier were driving down Highway 1 toward Monterey, past artichoke and strawberry fields and wetlands. Seeing the agriculture combined with the smooth cones of sand dunes as the highway followed the crescent shape of Monterey Bay made Natalie ache. She had missed this so much.

As they drove, Natalie told Asier about her encounter with Dr. Berkhower.

"So he invited you to his lab to draw a sea lion?" Asier asked.

"A crushed sea lion head," she said, as though the state of it made a difference. "But yeah. I'm really excited." Normally she would never tell someone she had just met how excited she was about a job because it inevitably led to more questions about her past, and that could get sticky fast.

"Berkhower is very sought-after by undergrads who want to be his lab assistants because he always has really gory specimens. There's a kind of morbid excitement about it. But his assistants never last long. Some of the sea lions are in terrible shape."

"Surely there can't be that many mangled sea lions?" she asked.

"Boating accidents are frequent, but he also gets a lot of them that have died from eating plastic or other toxins. There's a bunch of reasons they die. Some of our work intersects." He glanced at Natalie quickly. "I don't generally handle dead things."

She laughed. "Thank you for clarifying."

"Marine death doesn't go over well with the ladies, I can tell you."

Was she a lady for whom things should go over? Did that mean he was single? Natalie's head swirled with questions. "I don't actually mind it. Animals are fascinating, and I love capturing them in an illustration. There's a kind of relationship, I guess, between me and the subject. I feel like I'm paying tribute to its form and function when I draw it, dead or alive. I'm, um, prone to collecting insects in jars for sketching. No one finds that attractive either." Not one guy she'd dated had liked it, and Paul had made several remarks over the past few months about how she was maybe a little weird for it. The subtext, of course, being that the jars would not be coming with her when she moved in with him. She'd never thought about how easily she would have done that—given up those jars, which, sure, while a little grotesque, had provided a lot of material with which she could grow and expand her skills and technique. But now, talking with Asier, she was starting to feel like she wouldn't—and shouldn't have to—give them up.

Asier gave a small laugh, one that sounded like he understood her. "Not everyone can appreciate the finer points of wildlife study and conservation. Or the interest in studying why creatures die."

"Especially when they die because of the world we create," she said.

He nodded in agreement. "Yes, and our job is to provide the proof and show the world that actions have consequences."

She smiled. Asier got it, which was refreshing. Paul did not. The annoyance on his face was clear every time she stopped to sketch something that caught her eye, like that stray dog they'd seen with mange or a worm crawling on the ground, engorged from a recent rain.

"Dr. Berkhower seems like a dedicated scientist, working on a Saturday," she said. "Exactly the type of person I like working with." She felt her cheeks heat up as she realized that Asier had also been working on a Saturday.

He glanced at her, his eyes bright with knowing, sending a little thrill down into her toes.

Natalie looked at the sand dunes on the side of the road as they approached Monterey. "I haven't been here in…wow. Probably fifteen years."

"Then I am very sorry for you, because it is a lovely place."

"I'm sorry for me too. I've always loved what the bay offers. I used to stare at the relief maps showing how deep the basin goes, how this shelf drops off into the depths right offshore."

"Oh yes, all kinds of wonderful deep-sea creatures live in that basin." He said it in a low growl that Natalie found very sexy. "I love it too. So much life to study in this amazing section of ocean. It's one of the reasons I like living here. Spain has amazing marine life too, but the California coast is incredibly rich. It was an easy choice for me, especially after I met your brother and he invited me to be part of his lab."

Natalie wondered if she would have stayed in the area if she hadn't gone away to college. The day she'd graduated, she had considered coming back. But she had a job offer from Argo & Pock, and her mother suggested that "a little more time away" would be best.

"Is it difficult living so far away from your family?" she asked Asier.

He slid her a look. "Of course. As you know."

She wondered how much Jake had told him. "Well. You're here for a good reason, for a job you love. I stayed away because I had to. Because my mom didn't want me back here."

"We all have difficult choices in life," he said. "It's about finding what makes you truly happy and what propels you. What pushes you to fulfillment."

Red taillights flashed ahead of them, and Asier put the car in a lower gear as he slowed. Natalie found herself mesmerized by his hand on the gearshift and recalled that hand on her naked hip in that unforgettable dream. She had a thing about hands; she and Teensy actively slavered over a good pair of man hands. Were they strong and full of muscles and tendons? Did they look like he knew how to work with them?

"It is so shallow of us," Natalie would say.

"It's dumb too, because the last thing we want is to marry a guy who chops wood for a living," Teensy would say. "Because you know we'd have to milk cows and bake pies all day."

"Probably wear a lot of flannel and gingham."

"Nonstop backbreaking farmwork, apparently."

"Not that there's anything wrong with farmwork," Natalie would say.

"Especially at night when Mr. Farmer runs his strong man hands over you," Teensy would cackle. Natalie was grateful that the lunch with Michelle and Yasmin and Cara had been so enjoyable, because finding friends like Teensy was hard. Then again, Michelle had been here for her all along.

Natalie shook her head at herself. She was having thoughts like she was *staying* here.

"Did you come often?" Asier asked.

"What?" All kinds of inappropriate images flitted across her mind.

"Monterey."

"Oh. Right. Not as often as I'd have liked. It can be touristy."

Asier grinned. "I don't think you will find that has gotten any better."

He downshifted again, his hand hitting his thigh. Her eyes strayed to his legs, clad in formfitting jeans, and then back to his face—and she saw that he was looking at her. Even as she felt her cheeks heating like a furnace, she wondered what it was about Asier that was so alluring. Yes, he was good-looking, and yes, it was amazing that he was a smarty-pants. But she could say the same about Paul.

Asier, however, was totally different. He radiated genuine kindness.

"Your cheeks are red."

She gave a horrified shake of the head. "What? No they're not. Normal color."

"They are definitely redder than they were." A teasing note in his voice.

She tried not to be pleased that he'd noticed she was blushing, which meant he was looking at her closely. "Okay, it's, you know, the road." The road? Jesus. Asier was so sexy with his easy smile, carefully messy hair, and unconcerned posture. Also his car smelled really good—like a combination of sandalwood and citrus, whatever personal products he used, creating a beautiful alchemy with his body chemistry. She found herself inhaling the intoxicating scent. What the hell was wrong with her?

"It is all right," he said, his voice cracking adorably.

"It's—" She tried to think of something to excuse her blush. "It's what you said. About what makes you happy and what propels you."

"Yes."

"I was thinking about how my job in Boston is fine, but I've been bored for a while." She hadn't been thinking that at that particular moment, but it was still true. "Drawing propels me. I'm really excited about sketching that sea lion for Dr. Berkhower, in a way I haven't felt in my current job in a long time."

He laughed. "Good. You should do what makes you happy. Sometimes it takes a while to figure that out."

"Did it take you a while to figure it out?"

He slowed the car as they approached a sign for CSU Monterey. "I am always amazed by how I hide what makes me happy from myself. I think I hide in my work and use it as a—a kind of shield."

That was interesting. A shield from what? Getting hurt, probably. Didn't everyone try to shield themself from pain in whatever way they could? She decided not to ask, in case he didn't like to talk about it.

"So Jake was here today," she said as Asier turned onto the road toward the college, trying to push away the worry over her flip-flopping feelings about her job and Paul and everything else.

"Apparently he was here this morning. I wish he would answer his phone and not make me drive around to find him." He glanced at her once. "Although it was a very nice drive."

Cheeks. Hot.

"If we don't find him today, then I think our best bet is the gala on Saturday," he said. "He was very excited about the award."

"I can't even picture him being excited about that. I've lost a lot of years of learning about this good version of him."

Asier shot her a sympathetic half smile. "Jake told me about the evening that led to his arrest."

A little bolt of fear tore through her. She hoped Jake hadn't painted her in a terrible light. Even if she deserved it. "What did he say?"

"That there were poor choices made. His friend died from a drug overdose. You called the police out of spite."

She nodded, staring out the side window at the huge fields of vegetables. "Maybe not spite. But I did call—and I was angry at them when I did it."

"It sounds terrible. But it also sounds like you made the only decision you could in the moment."

"Is that what Jake said?" She found herself tensing.

Asier shrugged. "It is what I got from his account."

I called because I was angry at them and wanted to hurt them was not a truth she often divulged. *I betrayed them.* She hated thinking about Lynn's bloody head (a minor concussion) and bugged, outraged eyes as they had handcuffed her. Jake hadn't even looked at her. And worst of all was the memory she tried very hard never to recall: Carlos's blank, lifeless eyes.

But if Jake had recounted it with some degree of understanding, maybe all was not lost.

Asier pulled the car into the campus parking lot across from a large building and turned it off. "Are you okay?"

"Yeah." It came out, unfortunately, as a whisper, which was the universal sign that things were not okay. "Yeah. I'm fine. I don't know whether Jake is still angry."

She badly wanted Asier, who spoke to Jake regularly and seemed aware of this history, to deliver the benediction of saying Jake was not angry anymore. But he gave her a pained smile. "I don't think he is, but I don't know. It is best left for you to see. I am sorry."

She nodded. "I understand. I don't mean to bring you into it."

"It is all right." He gave her a sympathetic look that seemed to say he knew she was not fine or okay.

They went inside the building, passing several offices and labs.

"Dr. Suko," Asier told Natalie, knocking on an office door. "Get ready."

"Why?" she asked as a sonorous timbre of a voice boomed, "Enter." Natalie snickered, and Asier flashed her a look of exaggerated eyes, which made her laugh again. They rearranged their faces and went in.

"Dr. Casillas," the owner of the deep voice said. Presumably Dr. Suko, a small balding man with Coke-bottle-thick glasses who sat behind a grand secretary desk, the kind with drawers down each side and a brass and leather pen and blotter. Ostentatious leather chairs placed at angles sat in front of the desk. Tall bookshelves of leather-bound tomes sat behind him. Dr. Suko was almost lost in it all.

"Good to see you," Asier said. "Dr. Suko, this is Natalie Walker, Dr. Walker's sister. As I mentioned on the phone, his family has been trying to find him."

Dr. Suko stroked his chin as though he had a beard, except he didn't. Natalie crammed her lips together to keep from giggling. Dr. Suko didn't seem to be doing it to amuse them. "Right, right. Dr. Walker. Yes, he was in here this morning. Using the lab space."

"He has a lab with his name on it in Santa Cruz. What was he doing here?" Natalie asked.

Dr. Suko stopped fake-stroking and shot her a look of outrage. "What was he *doing*? We have a significant investment in our inverted fluorescence compound microscope! It has a Bertrand lens with three-phase contrast! We are the *envy* of UC Santa Cruz." He sat back, hands clasped over his stomach, with a smug expression that said he thought very highly of his office and lab.

"Oh, well," Natalie said in her mildest tone. "A Bertrand lens."

Asier's mouth compressed as he stifled a laugh.

"Impertinent," Dr. Suko barked.

"Which lab was he in?" Asier asked.

"He was in 2C. No, wait." Dr. Suko stroked his imaginary beard. "4B. The microscope is in 6A, however. Although that was this morning, and you certainly took your time getting here. He could be in any of them by now."

Natalie imagined a labyrinth of labs guarded by beastly creatures, the faint snorting of a Jake-Minotaur at the end.

"Did he look okay?" she asked.

"Look…okay?" Dr. Suko frowned, confused by the question. "I don't know what you're suggesting."

"Did he look, I don't know…disheveled, upset?" Natalie asked.

"I am not in the habit of inspecting people for their emotional states, Miss Walker. I am very busy running my department. Go check the lab yourself." Dr. Suko bent over his desk, as though he had work in front of him, but the desk was empty apart from its decorations. "That's all I know."

"Thank you so much," Asier said. "Good to see you, Dr. Suko."

"And you, Dr. Casillas," Dr. Suko said, looking pointedly at him and not Natalie. They had been dismissed.

In the hall with the office door shut behind them, Natalie glanced at Asier and saw that he was stifling a laugh, which only made her laugh. "Wow. He's an odd one."

"He is." Asier began walking down the long hallway. "We've been after a compound inverted microscope for our lab. Jake was going to price them out before he left. That's probably why he's here."

"How much is something like that? A couple hundred dollars?"

"Twenty-four thousand." He smiled at her look of shock. "Dr. Berkhower also has one—you'll see it on Monday." He gave an adorable little shake of his head. "But let's go see your brother."

A zip of excitement went through her. This was it. Jake. She wasn't sure she was ready for whatever reaction he would have upon seeing her, but she hadn't been ready for Lynn's reaction either, and it had been okay.

Asier stopped at a lab door marked 2C and put his hand on the door handle.

"Wait," she said. "I—I don't—"

"He will not bite you," Asier said gently. "Come on."

He pushed open the door to a dark lab. He flicked on the light, and it was obvious no one was there.

Disappointment hit her, an almost physical feeling of impact.

"Okay, not here," Asier said.

"Not here," she whispered. Asier threw her a sympathetic smile and put a burning-hot hand on her lower back as he guided her out of the lab. They walked down the hall to another lab, 4B, and now her stomach seized in a tight ball. Again, an empty and dark lab. They went upstairs. Another dark lab. Natalie's heart banged in her chest with each door they opened. One last lab, and this time the lights were on, shining underneath the door.

Asier threw her a triumphant look and opened the door.

The room was empty.

She let out a puff of air. "He's not here, is he."

Asier looked around and shook his head. "I am sorry. There is the microscope though." He pointed to an unassuming microscope on a bench.

Natalie walked over to it. She'd been expecting something as grand as the Hubble, but this was only a regular instrument, which Jake had presumably been touching not long ago. She ran a finger down the scope. She was disappointed and a little relieved and filled with a sense of homesickness all at once, which was interesting because she had never realized her feelings of home and family were tied up in Jake.

She missed him and couldn't wait to see him. But she was terrified of what would happen. She had never felt more regret for calling the police and destroying their relationship as she did now. A sob lodged itself somewhere in her lower throat, but she stuffed it back down.

"Look at this." Asier pointed to an intricate pencil drawing of a pelican in a frame next to a taxidermied pelican in a large cloche.

She moved next to him to look at it, grateful for the distraction. "Oh, that's good," she said, losing herself in the delicate marks, in awe of the skill of whoever had drawn it.

Sensing Asier watching her, she turned to look at him. His eyes held hers. A tingle slid over Natalie's scalp as every part of her seemed to lift up and come to attention. *This was exactly how it had been in the dream!* Standing this close to Asier, Natalie noticed he hadn't shaved, and she found this wildly attractive—strange, as she usually disliked facial hair— and his attention and focus on her reached down into her core. The tingle continued to spread over her shoulders, chest, middle, and farther down.

He took a small step toward her. Every nerve ending sparked, antici- pating what would come next. Eyes on hers, he lowered his head slowly—

The door to the lab banged open. Two young men came in, laughing. "Oh! Sorry."

"Hello," Asier said, turning away from Natalie. "We're looking for Dr. Walker."

Natalie's face *burned*.

"Oh yeah. He left a few hours ago," said one of the men, setting down a heavy backpack on a table.

"You saw him?" Natalie asked. "How was he?"

The men looked curiously at Asier and Natalie. "He was…fine? Said he was going back to Santa Cruz."

"Thank you," Asier said. He put a hand on Natalie's back and steered her to the door. He rubbed his (very nice, flat) stomach. "Come on, I am starving. Let's go get something to eat."

CHAPTER 14

Natalie sat across from Asier at a small table in a sushi restaurant near the harbor, trying to ignore the prices she had seen on the menu. Sushi was expensive, and her bank account was giving her a salty side-eye these days, but Asier had insisted it was his treat.

"So Jake's making day trips to see the mighty microscope." Using chopsticks, she plucked at a fancy thing called a dragon roll. "Which means he's not missing. He's hiding out."

Asier placed a colorful roll topped with tuna in his mouth. "It does mean he's around, and he's keeping up on his predeparture tasks. He has the blessing of Dr. Suko to use his microscope, at least."

"I imagine Dr. Suko's blessing is rather like a snakebite."

"The very worst, most poisonous kind, for sure."

"A deadly taipan." Natalie nodded. She'd drawn a taipan a year or so ago after seeing one at the Franklin Park Zoo in Boston, enamored with its sleek head and the slight slant of its pit organs, giving it a permanently pissed-off look.

Asier laughed. "When people talk about venomous snakes, they like to list the obvious ones, like cobras and rattlesnakes. Not enough people talk about the taipan. I like this."

"Right? It gets no love at all, and it's the most venomous snake out there."

"We should start a taipan appreciation society."

"Well." Natalie stirred a hunk of wasabi into her soy sauce dish. "I don't appreciate them, so I can't be in the club."

"That is fair. We will start the club, and then we will run away from it."

She looked at him, but he was busy with his sushi roll. Run away together. Ha! Was he flirting with her? He was flirting with her.

"So, your brother," he said in a decidedly unflirty tone. "The fact that he was here today suggests there's a reason he is staying away from his own lab."

"The amazing, mystical, wondrous microscope isn't enough of a reason?" she asked.

"Not when you have to deal with Dr. Suko. That is about as fun as a taipan rally."

"Well," Natalie said, "I think I know. I think he's hiding from Lynn and me. Actually, I think he's hiding from only me." She stopped, the words hitting her right in the solar plexus. There it was. The ugly, goblin-headed truth. Surprise tears pricked her eyes.

Asier sat back and regarded her. His face seemed so sympathetic that her heart pulled. "No. I don't think he's afraid of seeing you. Just a sense I get."

A scenario went through her head of Jake talking over his past with his friend and colleague. Asier passionately arguing that people make mistakes, but they grow—and that maybe Natalie had grown and he should give her a chance. Jake refuting it, his brows lowering and giving him that dark, furious look he always got. Asier shaking his head and sticking up for her.

She hoped something like that had happened. She was not that angry eighteen-year-old girl anymore.

"I still think our best bet is the gala on Saturday," Asier said. "He will come. He will want the recognition. It matters to him, given how hard he's worked to be where he is. If he gets an award like that, it will be important as he takes this post in New Zealand."

"About that," Natalie said. "What happens to his lab in the meantime? Does it become the Casillas Lab instead of the Walker Lab?"

He grinned. "No. We'll just look after it for him. Keep doing our own research."

She leaned back in her chair, overwhelmed by the impossibility of locating him before he left.

"Okay," Natalie said. "I hope you're right. Because I have to leave soon."

Asier's eyes snapped to hers. She wished she hadn't said that, even though not saying it didn't make it less true. "You are returning to Boston?"

"I have to. Although Jake has to come home first, and I need my cat to show up before I can go." She grimaced. Penguin was around, she was sure of it. She had seen a disemboweled gopher in the yard as she was leaving the house today. That was a good sign—not for the gopher, obviously, but it meant Penguin was around. She would do another search of the attic later for him. "And even though I get to sketch a sea lion on Monday, there's work to get back to."

"You work for an architecture firm," Asier said. "I remember."

She sighed before she could suppress it. "It's…a complicated job right now. I was supposed to get a promotion, and it didn't work out." *Supposed to* was a stretch, and she knew that now, but it still hurt the same. She saw no reason to announce Paul's existence to Asier. They were on a break, after all.

But Asier made a sympathetic face without missing a beat. "That's difficult. Do you like your job otherwise?"

Natalie shrugged. "I like the history aspect of it. I have a lot of respect for the things houses see and experience over the years yet still remain standing. It's not illustration, but I've worked there for ten years—since college."

"You can't make the jump to illustration?"

"I don't have the experience or any education in it. Which is one of the reasons I'm excited about working in Dr. Berkhower's lab. I feel like that's real, you know?"

"I am impressed by that," he said, folding his napkin neatly and placing it on his empty plate. "You arrive here and have already charmed Dr. Berkhower. But I am sure you are good at writing reports too."

She wondered if she had charmed Asier, then felt a little guilty for the thought. Anyway, nothing was happening between them. Apart from that interesting moment back in the lab when he might have been about to kiss her (and she might have been about to kiss him back), they were simply two people becoming friends, having a nice meal. That alone reached deep down into Natalie's soul and felt lovely.

"Yeah," she said. "I'm not sure I would count drawing a crushed sea lion head as charming anyone."

"Better than a taipan." Asier smiled and then deftly took the check when the waitress brought it.

— — —

It was past three by the time they made it back to Santa Cruz and Asier pulled into the parking lot of the restaurant where Natalie had left her car after brunch.

"Our trip was not fruitful, but it was fun," he said.

"Thank you for the early dinner." She wanted to thank him for more than that—for a nice drive and good company.

"My pleasure," he said.

"I hope you're done working for the weekend," she said, unwilling to get out of his car and end it.

"Ah. Well, kelp forests don't take weekends off."

She grinned, not because what he said was funny but because he was smiling, and talking with him made *her* smile. "Kelp forests must remain vigilant."

"I wish I could give them round-the-clock guards," he said. "There are so many reasons for kelp forest failure: unsuitable substrate, urchin predation, turbidity and salinity issues from bay plume. It's the plume that particularly worries me."

She nodded. "Plume worries me too. Or it would, if I knew what it was."

Asier shot her a look and laughed. "I'm happy to—" He stopped, catching himself. She wondered what he had been about to say. "Plume typically refers to hydrothermal areas of warm, cloudy water above vent sites in cold water."

They looked at each other, Natalie wondering what he was thinking.

He gave a little shrug and said, "I wish you good luck and good drawing with the sea lions." He waved, and once she was at her car with the door open, he drove away. Very sweet. No lingering, smoldering stares or silent looks of desire. Or maybe that was her. She badly wished she had that fiery attraction with Paul, but it was different with him.

Maybe worryingly different.

It had been a fun day, and that was really all she needed. A little flirtation was enjoyable. If nothing else, Asier and his overall wonderfulness—and, come on, those dreams—would give her something to think about as she drove the long hours back across the country.

CHAPTER 15

By noon on Monday, Natalie had the beginnings of a fine sketch of a truly gruesome sea lion head.

"Now, that," Dr. Berkhower said, glancing at her work, "is exactly what I wanted. Great work. I like to see someone who's not afraid to get right up in there. You are very good."

A whole tectonic plate of relief slid into place inside her. The day had not started easily—he had handed her a pair of latex gloves and a small jar of VapoRub with the ominous instruction, "Put that under your nostrils. You'll need it."

It had turned out he was right. The smell was unspeakable.

"You're not going to vomit, are you?" Dr. Berkhower asked her straight off. "I was really hoping for someone who doesn't vomit this time."

"I'm not going to vomit." She would not do it. She visualized her stomach being lined with lead before stepping in close to sketch the damage.

The morning had gone so well that he had asked her to stay for the afternoon and sketch a headless cormorant. He took it out by its feet from an enormous freezer, reminding her of a bird popsicle. It was particularly challenging to sketch it so that it appeared thawed. But by the end of the day, she had delighted and surprised both herself and Dr. Berkhower.

"Exceptional," he said, studying the drawing. "You said you don't have any formal education in illustration?"

"No." Which she hated admitting. Saying no always made her feel uncomfortable and less-than.

"I know you said you live in Boston, but is there any chance you're thinking of staying here?"

"I—I'm going back to Boston. I'm only here to deal with some family things."

"Well." Dr. Berkhower compressed his lips and thought. "A degree in illustration is usually one of the requirements for working in the labs here. If you were staying, you could look into one of the scientific illustration programs at UC Santa Cruz or CSU Monterey, and you could work part-time for me. I've been looking for an illustrator for a long time, but the ones I've interviewed never seem to have the time to devote to it or the stomach to handle it."

She wished very much that she could transport Dr. Berkhower to Boston. "Oh, wow. That's very nice of you to offer."

"You're going back in a week?"

"Yes. On Sunday," she said, already dreading the tiresome cross-country drive. It seemed like an impossible number of things needed to happen before that occurred.

"You should come to the lab's gala on Saturday. It's our biggest event of the year. Maybe it will convince you to stay. You can meet all the scientists here. I always find it to be a good opportunity for networking. Nothing like discussing the life expectancy of a sea lion with a pulverized sagittal crest over great cocktails and food! I'll sort out the ticket for you. You just show up. Cocktail attire, I'm afraid."

"Thank you. That's very kind." While it would be good to be there when Jake appeared, she had nothing to wear and even less money with which to buy something appropriate for a fancy gala.

"Great." He clattered dirty instruments into a tray and took off his gloves. "I hope this was as interesting for you as it was for me. I received an email today from a contact at the Marine Mammal Center in Marin who says she has a specimen in advanced decomposition. Cause of death is unknown. The fins were sheared off, and she wants me to look at the method of removal so we can see if it was deliberate or accidental. It would be a great opportunity for you to draw this particular serration. If for any reason you don't leave in a week, please come back. It'll be here Monday."

The thought was horrid, but the experience sounded promising. "That, ah, sounds like a great project."

"This one will be especially repugnant." He rubbed his hands together with glee. "I had one a few months ago that was in *such* bad shape that it made the whole lab stink—on the same day my air filtration system died! That was an uncomfortable few weeks in here afterwards, I can tell you."

Natalie was not sure she could ever muster the same enthusiasm for putrefaction that Dr. Berkhower had, but nonetheless she smiled and said, "Sounds amazingly gruesome," and judging by Dr. Berkhower's pleased expression, it was the right thing to say.

Natalie packed up her sketchbook and pencils and took care to wash her hands extra thoroughly even though she had not touched the sea lion. He handed her a modest check—her first professional paycheck for illustration!—and she headed out to her car. The sky was turning pink, and her back ached pleasantly from hunching over in a long, concentrated drawing session. It had been glorious. She'd worked hard on the individual components of the animal, focusing not on the gore factor but on the muscle, the tissue, and making sure each element was clear despite much of it running together in one terrible color. She had a strong sense that sketching the animal in death had helped pay tribute to its life.

She opened her car and put her gear in, then went to the front of the car so she could stretch her arms over her head and bend at the waist to stretch her back, pushing her rear out as she did so. It was a highly effective stretch that reached from her tailbone to her shoulders, and it was luckily one of the few she remembered from a series of yoga classes Teensy had dragged her to.

She was glad Teensy had insisted on the classes. Teensy was always doing things like that, pulling Natalie out of her comfort zone but laughing with her at the same time. Natalie looked forward to seeing her best friend in a week.

Dropping her forehead against the hot metal of her car, she leaned into her butt, letting her back sink into the stretch, swaying a little.

"Are you all right?"

Natalie straightened—too fast, because things cracked—to see Asier standing behind her. She could feel her face automatically heating up again. Oh God, her butt had been hanging way out there. As poses went, it was not the one she would have chosen had she'd known he'd see it.

"Um, yeah. Yeah. Stretching my back." She cringed and then cringed some more.

He seemed embarrassed too and looked anywhere but at her. "Good. Good. I wasn't sure."

"Nope, yeah. Sorry. About, um, my butt." She pushed her shoulders back, wishing a hole would open in the asphalt so she could step into it and disappear.

Asier looked down and smiled shyly. "It—it's, ah, okay. Your butt is fine. I mean—it's fine that you—you know what, never mind. I will stop talking now."

Furious heat in her face now, her head a conflagration. He was so cute.

"Did everything go okay with Dr. Berkhower?" he asked.

"Yes! It did." She talked fast to cover for the embarrassment of a moment ago. "He said he would hire me if I was staying."

"That's good news! I was hoping to catch you, actually, before you left. I wanted to ask you about Saturday."

"Oh?" She arranged her face into what she hoped was a semblance of casual pleasantry. He was going to ask her out. She was sure of it. To dinner? Drinks? Bed? All three?

"The gala," he said. "I thought that since I was telling you how Jake is up for the award—I thought you might want to go."

"The gala!" she said too loud. "Yes. Dr. Berkhower said I should go and he would sort out a ticket for me."

"Ah, yes. Good, then. Yes."

Too late, she realized she'd swooped his invitation out from under her own feet. What was she doing?

"Are you going?" she asked, trying to cover her misstep.

"Yes, I will be there." He shoved his hands in his jeans pockets, which made him look self-conscious and adorable.

"Great. Good. I'll see you there."

He nodded and moved away, waving. She sank against her car, wishing the conversation had gone differently and feeling deeply idiotic for screwing it up. *God.* Asier. Gala. Inviting her. Butts. She watched him go, admiring him and feeling even sillier. He was just being nice. Natalie got in her car and berated herself for messing up with him again all the way home.

— — —

"So you've got a job and a ticket to the ball," Michelle said, leaning against the counter. "Now all you need is a pair of glass slippers."

Natalie rolled her eyes. "Don't be ridiculous."

"I'm glad," Michelle said. "If it gets you closer to staying here for good."

"Still planning to leave on Sunday," Natalie reminded her.

Michelle twisted her face in response. She was on Team Move Back to Santa Cruz, and Natalie couldn't blame her. The idea of falling back into their easy friendship was enormously appealing. And every time Natalie stepped outside and felt that cool sea breeze, the urge to linger longer here pulled at her.

"You could stay longer," Michelle said.

"I'll lose my job if I do. And I have to figure things out with Paul."

"Mmm." Michelle didn't sound convinced, which was annoying because Natalie wasn't either. When she got back to Boston, Paul would no doubt come up with some wily words about how easy it would be to live together and how they could try it out on a temporary basis if she wanted. Natalie knew it would not be easy. Paul would be aghast at her untidiness (his place was painfully neat), and he would speak to her like an underperforming employee about her jars. He might not enjoy Penguin's royalty, and Penguin, in turn, might retaliate with well-timed vomit on his shoes. It didn't bear thinking about.

"Anyway, a dress," Michelle said.

That had been the impetus for dropping by Michelle's shop today, but Natalie had to ensure that she could afford to feed herself with her dwindling funds, especially since she still had to make it back across the country. Already she was probably going to have to sleep in her car at rest stops rather than springing for hotel rooms.

"I'd love to wear something from your shop," Natalie said, "but I'm not going to the gala."

Michelle slapped her hands to her cheeks dramatically. "What will Prince Asier say?"

"Stop. It's not like that."

Michelle leaned across the counter with a determined look on her face. "Spill it, Walker. What's holding you back?"

Natalie hoped a customer would come take Michelle's attention away from her, but the store had emptied. She shook her head instead. She wasn't going to tell her friend that her dresses were too expensive for her. Michelle deserved every bit of revenue she made from these gorgeous clothes.

"You can't afford anything in here," Michelle said, her eyes not wavering from Natalie's face. "Oh, I know my stuff is expensive. But I stand by my prices."

"And you should."

"Which is why you're going to march over to that rack right there and pick one out."

"No, Michelle—"

"Yes. It's a loan."

"No—"

Michelle stomped around the counter and pulled Natalie over to the rack. She selected a sleek black absolute dream of a dress with a silk bodice and curved neckline and held it up to Natalie. It was ridiculously sophisticated.

Natalie glanced at the price tag: over a thousand dollars. "*No!*"

"Yes. Try it on." Michelle piled the dress into Natalie's unwilling arms and pushed her in the direction of the fitting rooms.

Natalie went in, knowing Michelle would badger her until she did. She undressed and slipped the dress on, enjoying that pleasing *shoosh* sound it made as it glided onto her body, the tulle falling into place around her.

Hope rising, Natalie turned to the mirror.

It was incredible, and she looked amazing. She felt great in it, loving the way it moved with her body. Somehow it even made her perpetually messy dark hair look good. Even better, it wasn't too loud or flamboyant, so she wouldn't be seen as someone trying to attract too much attention at the gala. It was the most perfect little black dress ever made.

She stepped out of the fitting room for Michelle's inspection.

"Oh *yes*," Michelle said. "All I ask is that you spill nothing on it. And don't have sex in it."

Natalie gave her a *come on* look.

"Only thing is that I don't have shoes that will work with it," Michelle said. "You'll have to sort those out."

Natalie could stop by a thrift shop on her way home. "But the price, Michelle."

Michelle waved her away. "It's a loan, as I said. Your scientist is going to keel over when he sees you."

"He's not my scientist. I don't know anything about him except that he works on kelp forest preservation." That wasn't true—he'd told her plenty of sweet, nerdy things about himself when they'd gone to Monterey, but she plunged on. "Maybe he's a conservative Catholic who goes to mass every week and expects his wife to take his last name and bear him fifteen children. Maybe he clips his toenails and shoves them into the drawer of his bedside table, and if anyone opens it, they'll find nothing but yellowed shards. Maybe he has incurable halitosis." Natalie knew he didn't, based on their close encounter. But he *could*.

Michelle gave her a dismissive *you're ridiculous* look.

The thought of Asier seeing her in this dress and thinking she did it for him made her uneasy. No. That settled it.

"I can't do this," she said. "The dress is too nice."

"What are you afraid of? The scientist liking you in it?"

Michelle could read her like a book. "Fine. Yes."

"That's an interesting thing we need to unpack in a moment." Michelle crossed over to the register to ring up a customer. Natalie followed.

"That dress is amazing," the customer said, looking over at Natalie. "Wow. Is that from this store?"

"Yes!" Natalie said quickly, seeing an out. "I'm only modeling it. I can take it off, and you can look at it."

"Actually," Michelle said loudly, "that particular dress is not for sale. But I can show you some others like it."

The customer looked between them, picking up on the unspoken argument, and said, "Just this scarf, please."

"So," Michelle said after the woman left the shop, "let's discuss why you don't want to walk into that gala in that dress looking the way you do. You're on a break from your boyfriend—a boyfriend who isn't all that fantastic, from what you've told me—and you have this scientist you can't stop texting flirty emojis to." Natalie regretted showing her the string of increasingly ridiculous texts she'd exchanged with Asier since yesterday's trip to Monterey: microscopes, side-eyes, puke faces, fish, a sea otter.

Natalie was about to argue that a puke-face emoji with Asier was hardly flirty, but an even better objection hit her: "I don't want Jake to think I have any ulterior motives."

"Aha!" Michelle pointed a finger at her. "That's it. But why?"

The answer was obvious, Natalie thought as she headed to the fitting room to change. She wanted her big brother to understand that he was the most important thing to her. That finding him and reconciling and inheriting the house together were the only reasons she was back in town. And that she wasn't hanging around because of some handsome scientist who'd been nice to her and who made her insides feel all warm.

Which settled it. She had to go to the gala to let Jake know how much she missed him and loved him. And to do that, she needed something to wear. She looked at the dress on its hanger and grinned as she ran a hand down the bodice. It wasn't her fault she looked good in it.

— — —

When Natalie got home, she found Kit slouched on the couch, throwing an apple up in the air like a ball.

"Hey," Natalie called. "What're you up to?"

"Nothing," Kit said. The apple went almost to the ceiling, and he caught it neatly as it came down. "Mom's at work."

"Does your mom happen to have any nice shoes that she brought with her?" Natalie asked. She had been unsuccessful in finding a pair at the thrift shop.

"Like running shoes?" Kit asked.

"No. Like high heels."

Kit shrugged.

Natalie went upstairs to put the dress away in her closet. Still no sign of Penguin. She glanced out of the window, hoping to see him picking his way across the front yard. Leaving without him seemed impossible, yet what choice did she have? He wasn't anywhere that she'd searched. It was like Jake: no matter if he or Penguin didn't show up tomorrow, she'd have to leave. Both scenarios had consequences. At least with the cat, maybe Kit could keep an eye out for him and let her know if he appeared. She was fairly confident in Penguin's resourcefulness. He was alive out there. She knew that much.

Why, then, did he not come home? It was so frustrating.

Kit poked his head around her bedroom door. "Did you want to see my mom's shoes? And I also saw two crates of clothes and shoes in the attic."

"What?"

"In the attic. I was looking for Penguin. There's all kinds of stuff up there. Clothes and stuff."

A pang hit Natalie her in the heart that Kit had been looking for Penguin. "Yes to both." Together they went down the hall to Lynn's room and peeked in her closet. There were a lot of sensible loafers and a few pairs of Dr. Martens—one ankle-high pair with flower stitching that Natalie was almost sure she remembered Lynn buying as a teenager. Nothing suitable for the dress, although she was tempted to wear the Dr. Martens.

"Will you show me what you found in the attic?" she asked.

Kit led the way to the third floor and into the last bedroom at the far end of the house, where a gnome-size door led to a set of unfinished, rickety stairs. Up those was the attic, filled with tons of plastic bins and wooden chests. Natalie had poked her head up here twice looking for Penguin but hadn't fully walked into the attic. She stepped into the dim, dusty space.

Several of the boxes closest to the stairs were marked NATALIE or LYNN or JAKE. Natalie pulled her box over and opened it, revealing her high school graduation cap and tassel and a copy of her birth certificate. The rest was old school papers and artwork from her childhood.

She pulled out Jake's box and found, right on top, a sheaf of court documents: records from his arrest and incarceration. Unable to bear reading them, she put them back and closed the lid.

"Here," Kit said, pointing at a huge, ancient metal trunk. "Check out this one."

Natalie looked inside to find an old wedding veil, browned with age, the tulle crisp to the touch. Underneath it, wrapped in a stained satin bag, was a pair of 1920s flapper-style black silk high heels with closed toes and ankle straps. They looked like something the wearer might do the jitterbug in. Pulling them out, she saw they were almost exactly the same black silk material as the dress Michelle had loaned her. No water damage, and no peeling on the silk or leather. Only a little faded. She pushed one of her feet in, and it was like they had been designed and made especially for her. The shoe hugged her foot perfectly, and when she stood up, it lifted everything, making her feel elegant.

"Oh, wow," she breathed.

"Are they your mom's?" Kit asked, holding up the old veil and putting it on his head.

Natalie looked at the veil and pictured the only photo she remembered seeing from her parents' wedding. They'd been married at Santa Cruz City Hall, and her mother had worn a maroon suit. No veil. Certainly not these shoes.

"These must be my grandmother's," she said. She took off the shoes and set them aside to take with her. Digging in the box, she uncovered a weathered, puffy photo album with MEMORIES embossed in faded gold on the cover. Sure enough, there were her grandparents on their wedding day in the first photo, looking very flapperesque, her grandmother wearing those same black shoes. Natalie paged through the album, thinking of the lives lived in this old house. Her mother had been eighteen when her parents had died, leaving her on her own to manage the house. It was one of the reasons she'd married Natalie's father so young.

Natalie knew very little about her father except that he'd been an only child too. His mother had moved into the house with them but had died shortly before Jake was born. Lots of death so early on. Natalie shook her head. Her mother had not always known how to handle the three of them. And then her father had died, leaving Patricia on her own with three kids, and they had not made it easy for her, especially Jake.

But before Jake had gotten into drugs as a teenager, he'd been the best older brother, playing horsey with Natalie and helping her with homework. He'd always had the best jokes. And he had played peace-maker between her and Lynn when they'd fought. She stroked the silk of the shoes as though they were her lucky charm. Maybe things would be different. Maybe the Jake she saw would remember their good years. She closed the trunk. The shoes would get her to the gala, at least.

CHAPTER 16

The gala was in full swing when Natalie pulled into the parking lot of the lab's visitor center. She had hoped Asier would text her once Jake arrived, but so far there had been nothing. She felt like she was arriving in a pumpkin carriage, except her gourd was an aging Hyundai with muffler issues. Multicolored lights set the center aglow. Jacketed waiters moved around inside, offering glasses of champagne to people in formal wear. She crossed her fingers that Jake was one of them.

Natalie moved as though tiptoeing on ice. Tonight was the night, and hopefully she'd have one of the missing persons back. She just needed her grandmother's heels to hold up. She was afraid they'd snap partway to the door. The dress, however, was every bit as stunning as when she'd tried it on in Michelle's shop.

"Whoa," Lynn had said when she'd come down the stairs—in a not-unkind tone. "Holy guacamole."

"I'm going so I can see Jake," Natalie had said.

"If you say so," Lynn had said. "He'll show up when he's ready though."

"Apparently he'll be ready tonight, according to his colleagues."

"As are you," Lynn had said, which Natalie hadn't been sure how to take.

She teetered to the door of the visitor center, where a bow-tied young man with an iPad was checking in guests.

"Natalie Walker," she told him, half fearing that Dr. Berkhower had forgotten to put her name in.

But the young man tapped and nodded. "Here you are. Have a wonderful time, Miss Walker."

She hesitated. "Did—has Dr. Walker checked in yet?"

The man pursed his lips as he scanned the list. "Not yet."

She passed through the doors into the lobby, which was lit up with undulating blue and green lights designed to look like light under the sea. Flutes of wine and champagne bobbed in every direction, and the chatter of voices echoed off every surface.

Natalie headed for the bar. Alcoholic fortification was necessary.

"Wine, champagne, or our signature gala cocktail?" the bartender asked.

"What's the signature gala cocktail?"

The bartender held up a sea otter–shaped glass full of blue liquid and topped with a ridiculous amount of fruit and little umbrellas.

"That, of course," Natalie said.

"I love them too," someone said beside her.

Her heart leaped out of her chest, and she turned, half expecting to see Jake, but the person at her side was no one she knew. He was a tall, gangly man with too-short bangs.

"I'm Derrick." He smiled, displaying a truly shocking mouthful of teeth.

"Natalie." She accepted the sea otter cocktail from the bartender and turned to scan the crowd, which was already considerable. The cocktail tasted like mango and lemon and mint and was lovely.

"It's really pretty in here, isn't it?" Derrick asked.

"Yep. Have you tried the food?" she asked, although she didn't really care about the food.

"Yeah. It's good. Did you see the red GTO outside? That's mine. Just bought it. Got a raise. I work with mollusks." He didn't bother hiding a gaze that dragged from her toes to her breasts, lingering a beat too long on her chest.

Derrick, she knew, was standing here because of her insane dress and unescorted state. He would talk at her without letting her get a word in, ignoring all social signals that she wanted to be elsewhere. He was, she and Teensy used to joke, a remora, attaching himself to a woman and inevitably following her around all evening unless she shook him off with the cruel truth that he had no chance. Natalie always felt bad about this and let them hang around far longer than she should.

"Great." Natalie hoped her uninterested tone would convey that she wasn't a good conversation partner, despite knowing he would not catch on.

"Yeah, I'm going to rebuild the catalytic converter, though," Derrick said. "It'll take about three months. I could have bought a new GTO, but I wanted to see what I could do with an older one, you know?" He sent her chest another appreciative glance.

Natalie scanned the bodies for Jake—and saw Asier across the crowded exhibit hall, standing by the shark pool. In a tux. A fucking, ever-loving *tux*. Her mouth actually dropped open a little. Wow. This was better than the dream she'd had the night before (making that three smoking-hot, orgasm-in-her-sleep dreams now), in which he'd been in a tux and had taken it off—oh so slowly—for her.

She found her feet moving involuntarily toward the shark pool. Derrick followed, still talking at her.

"Natalie!" Dr. Berkhower stepped into her path. "You made it!"

"I did!" she said. "Thank you for getting me the ticket."

"Always fun to dress up and come to these things," Dr. Berkhower said. "I live in a lab coat that is almost always soiled, and this is the one time a year I get to wear something that isn't horrifying. Glad to see you were able to pull together a dress on short notice. You look great."

"I was going to tell her that," Remora-Derrick said. "She's *beautiful.*" His eyes did another slow and blatant glide down her body, dissipating any sympathy she might have had for him.

"Indeed," Dr. Berkhower said, but he had the sense to look across the room to offset the remark. "Have fun. I'm going to get one of those sea otter cocktails. Natalie, good to see you. I'm still disappointed you won't be in my lab on Monday, but I'm sure we'll chat again."

"Whoa," Derrick said after Dr. Berkhower moved on, doggedly at her side again. "You're working with Dr. Berkhower? He's, like, super intense."

"I sketch his sea lions." *Sketch*, present tense, had popped out of her mouth. She turned away from Derrick, attempting to escape, but he kept up with her.

"That's, like, hard-core. You're cool."

She tried to move away from Derrick, but there were too many people between her and Asier in a tux. She bobbed her head, trying to see where he was in the sea of other tux-wearers, none of whom did the hard work Asier was doing for the tuxedo industry. No sign at all of Jake.

"Welcome to the fifth annual Long Marine Lab Sciences Gala!" a thunderous voice called over a loudspeaker. Everyone stopped and turned toward the speaker, which was fatal for Natalie, because now there was no path at all to the shark pool.

"It is wonderful to see so many people here tonight," the announcer said, who was an imposing woman in a midnight-blue dress so bedecked with sequins that she blinded Natalie every time she moved. "So many wonderful luminaries from our *wonderful* research labs, so many *wonderful* patrons, so many *wonderful* new faces this year, and of course, so many *wonderful* specimens!"

A polite titter went around the room.

"*You're* a wonderful specimen," Derrick whispered at Natalie, far too loudly. People around them heard it and turned to look, smiling at Natalie. No! God!

"In a few minutes, we'll be announcing the winner of our annual George M. Wilde Fellowship Award, which recognizes outstanding contributions from researchers here on campus. This is your warning to get those wineglasses filled and sea otter cocktails ordered! And welcome!" The woman stepped away from the microphone, and people began to move around the room again.

"Here we go," Derrick said. "The same researchers are always up for it: Dr. Walker and Dr. Casillas and Dr. Boyd. Always the same three. All rock stars."

"Dr. Casillas?" That was interesting. Asier hadn't mentioned he was up for the award too.

"Yeah, but his stuff isn't exciting. He only studies kelp forests." Derrick sounded morose. "I have a ways to go before I'll be considered for the Wilde Award."

"Mollusks can be trying," Natalie agreed in her nicest tone. "Excuse me, I—"

"Actually, they're really reliable. I find that most people misunderstand them."

Natalie glanced at Derrick's earnest face and feared he was going to launch into a detailed and lengthy account of why mollusks were misunderstood. There was something in his face that she'd seen before, regrettably on Paul. That earnest, *listen to me talk* face. She couldn't bear it. She saw her chance to dart behind a large man and did so with satisfying speed, successfully leaving Derrick behind.

Natalie's sights were set on the shark pool. Asier still lingered there, but he was walking away from it now as other people came to see the creatures. She tracked his head as it moved out the open double doors to the patio.

By the time she made her way outside, he was no longer on the patio but had followed a path through the thick clumps of purple-topped ice plant, which carpeted the cliffs of Santa Cruz. He stood at the railing looking out at the darkening sea. For a moment, she took his figure in, dark against the evening sky, which was a fluorescent blue from all the lights around the bay. Her heart pounded with surprising nerves.

"Hi," she said.

Asier turned, and in the split second he was moving, she managed to take in the sharp profile of his cheekbones and jawline, making her breath catch. She saw the moment he realized it was her; his face opened and he smiled genuinely. Warmth bloomed in her chest as she watched him take her in, eyes flicking up and down the length of her dress. Unlike the way Derrick had done it, there was nothing overt or salacious in it, which was good because she didn't think Asier was like that, and she didn't want to be proven wrong.

"You made it," he said softly.

"I did." She grinned like a fool. "Any sign of Jake yet? I haven't seen him anywhere."

"Ah, no." He turned back to look at the sea. Part of her yelled *No! Keep looking at me!*

"I heard you're up for a Wilde Award tonight," she said.

He snorted. "Yes, but your brother is almost certainly going to win it."

"What does the winner get?" She kept her tone light, in case he was unhappy about being passed over. "Riches? The adoration of the university staff? An inverted fluorescence compound microscope?"

He laughed. "No. But it helps when applying for grants, which does make it valuable."

A breeze ruffled his lightly gelled hair. She realized she had been staring at his hair for an unnaturally long time and that she was essentially drooling and tried to check herself. Something had changed between them. Maybe it was her dress. Maybe it was his tux. Maybe it was the easy conversation they'd enjoyed in Monterey, or maybe it was the memory of the charged almost-kiss. Maybe it was the fact that tomorrow, she'd be back in her car, driving away from him and whatever spark sat between them.

Without looking at her, he said, "I noticed you were talking to that young mollusk researcher."

Was that a hint of jealousy she detected? "I wouldn't call it talking."

"I am sure he wanted to keep your attention."

"He's probably shy in a crowd and singled me out because I was alone too."

"I think it is more to do with how lovely you look."

Oh my God. He'd called her lovely.

She took a breath. "I'm actually really nervous to see Jake tonight. I mean, I've been here for two weeks, and I still have no idea how he's going to react when he sees me." She glanced at Asier to see if he thought this was silly.

His face, however, was filled with kindness. "It was never going to be easy anytime you saw him, right? It's like when I go home to Spain and see my family. I try to go once a year, but it's a long time to be away, you know? I always feel anxious in here." He tapped his chest with his fist. "It never gets easier, but the only thing I can do is go home and see. Whatever happens with Jake, you will get through it, because you have that family bond that can never be broken."

She pursed her lips and swallowed, not trusting herself to speak. "I'm not sure how much of the bond is left anymore, but thank you for saying that." They stood quietly at the railing, the cool sea wind ruffling her hair.

"Are you cold?" he asked, moving as though to take off his jacket. Her mouth opened slightly of its own accord. She could almost feel the warmth from his body transferred via the jacket and wanted nothing more than to wrap herself in it. But tonight was about Jake, not lusting after Asier, and she needed to keep it together.

"I'm all right. Thank you."

He nodded and straightened his jacket. "Your dress, you know. It is—" He motioned toward her bare shoulders.

"Oh—yes. I know. It's a summer dress and not up to a Santa Cruz night." Her shoulders. He was killing her!

"Beautiful," he said, almost inaudibly.

She met his eyes. Oh, how she was getting lost in them. This was hopeless. He moved closer. She focused on his chest. God, he was quite close. Everything in her responded of its own accord. She held her breath, waiting for him to say more.

"I ran into Dr. Berkhower today," he whispered. "He said you were amazing in his lab on Monday."

She meant to say something like *Oh* or *Did he?* but managed only a small squeak.

"If you are going to work with him, then maybe we can finally get at his compound inverted microscope." A smirk played on Asier's lips.

"Maybe." At that moment, she couldn't care less about the microscope.

His smile disappeared, and now he focused his eyes on hers. Everything she needed to know about him was in his soulful brown eyes, which were alert and intense. The deep lines at the corners of his eyes spoke of laughter and good humor, heightening the impression of his genuine niceness. The space between them decreased even more, his face drawing closer to hers. She tensed, rising to meet him—

"Ladies and gentleman!" the loud lady inside boomed over the mic. "It is time!"

"Here we go," Asier whispered conspiratorially, the teasing fun returning to his voice. The tension of the moment disappeared.

"Showtime," she whispered back, forcing a playfulness to match his tone. But she was still caught up in whatever had been going to happen there.

He gave that same wide, lively grin that made her want to live in the rays of its wattage. He held an arm out, indicating that she go first, and they went inside, joining the throng of people oozing through the doors. They stood off to the side, but people jostled in from all directions, and she was pushed away from him. Regrettably.

But at least now she could focus on the moment she'd see Jake.

The woman in the blinding sparkles stood at the microphone, harrumphed, and held up a sealed envelope. She talked about the long legacy of George M. Wilde, what an honor the award was, and how every researcher at the lab was a winner even if they weren't. Natalie tuned her out, scanning the crowd to see if Jake had come in at the last moment. Where was he? Her heart was racing again. She'd see her big brother in a minute. He was probably already in the room somewhere. He had to be there. It was her last shot at finding him.

"Now." The woman struggled with the envelope. "I'm pleased to announce that the winner of this year's George M. Wilde Award for Excellence in Research in the Field of Marine Sciences, Oceanography, and Related Organisms is Dr. Jacob Walker!"

A heavy applause erupted. Natalie waited, hardly breathing. She could almost see him running in from the side, wearing a bashful smile, waving at everyone. But the moment stretched, and then veered into the territory where heads began turning, looking for him. The applause began to die, uncertain. No one appeared.

He was not here.

She found Asier, and he raised his eyebrows slightly as though to say, *I don't know either.*

The woman in the sparkly dress did not seem to know what to do. She scanned the crowd, waiting for Jake to appear.

Poor Jake. Whatever was going on with him, the Jake she knew would not want anyone speculating as to his whereabouts. Without stopping to consider it, Natalie moved to the small raised stage. It was at this moment that her grandmother's silk shoes chose to disintegrate, opening and falling apart like ribbons with every step up to the stage. Embarrassed, Natalie kicked the remaining pieces to the side of the steps. Her face burned. She padded barefoot to the mic, wishing she'd remembered to paint her toenails at least.

"Hello," she said to the crowd. "I'm, um, Dr. Walker's sister, Natalie. I'm a…scientific illustrator working here at the lab." What the hell? Where had that come from? "I, um, accept this award on behalf of my brother. He is very appreciative and grateful and—stunned."

Stunned was the word. The whole crowd was looking at her, watching, some whispering.

Luckily the presenter had regained composure. "Ah! Wonderful! Thank you so much! Congratulations to Dr. Walker!"

There was more clapping as Natalie, sweating heavily now, moved away from the mic. She gathered up the shoe scraps and scurried down the steps.

Eyes were on her as she picked her way through the crowd. Asier stood next to the woman from Jake's lab, Dr. Lawrence, and they were whispering with worried looks. Natalie debated working her way toward them, but there were too many people in her path.

"You didn't say you were Dr. Walker's sister." Derrick was back at her side. "I met him a few times. Cool guy. What happened to your shoes?"

"Um," Natalie said. Too many people were still looking at her. She hated the attention. It made her want to jump into the shark pool. Asier met her eyes and raised his eyebrows a little. Natalie felt warm and breathless. Then he looked at Derrick, who was yapping something in her ear.

"Where is he? Why didn't he show up?" Derrick was asking.

"What?" Natalie asked.

"Dr. Walker. You know, we should all have lunch or something—you, me, and Dr. Walker—"

An enormous man in a too-tight suit stepped back onto Natalie's two smallest toes. She felt something crunch and yelped.

"Watch out," the man barked.

Little sparks of light exploded behind her eyelids, and tears sprang to her eyes as her brain registered the full brunt of the pain.

"Did he step on your foot?" Derrick asked. "Ouch. Just walk it off. Did I mention I'm almost done with my postdoc work?"

"I—I have to go." Natalie limped toward the doors as fast as she could. Asier was…busy, still over on the other side of the room talking very intently with Dr. Lawrence. She shouldn't be fixating on him anyway. She had a boyfriend, break or not.

You can't help who you like, her brain whispered before a fresh wave of pain hit, her toes in agony.

She made it to the doors and walked into the parking lot, her arms breaking out in goose bumps as the chilled night air hit her. The disappointment at not seeing Jake crashed around her, and more tears filled her eyes. She'd really counted on this being the perfect rendezvous, with a crowd here as a buffer against any anger he might have upon seeing her. He would be on a high after winning an award and amenable to seeing her, maybe even reconciling.

So where *was* he? Had he somehow found out she would be at the gala and intentionally stayed away?

Natalie hobbled over to the side of the building where they had a massive blue whale skeleton on display. She tried to force the tears back into her eyes, but they kept coming, now the result of both the disappointment over Jake and the obscene pain in her toes, which may have been broken. And if she was being honest, some other emotion had spilled over too, something to do with Asier and whatever had almost happened between them out on the patio. She liked him. A lot. This was a problem.

"Natalie."

She turned to see Asier. He looked as dejected as she felt. "Wait. Please do not be disappointed." He caught up to her and put an astonishingly hot palm on her arm. "Jake will come. Soon. I am sure of it."

"I'm sure," she croaked, her voice saturated by tears.

His eyebrows lowered, and he studied her, noticing the tears. "Hey." He stepped forward and pulled her close, wrapping his arms around her and engulfing her in the furnace of his body, which she did not resist. Her heart pounded against his chest. "Natalie. It is okay."

She shuddered out a sigh, tears spilling down her cheeks. "It was going to be perfect, seeing him here. And if he didn't even show up for this, then what will bring him? Where the hell is he?"

Asier pulled back and studied her. His gaze was intense, and she almost felt him absorbing her pain, like he understood her soul. This only made more tears come. The ache in her toes surely helped them along. Her brain was a muddled pile of confusion. Jake, Asier, toes, Paul. *Paul?* Yeah, Paul. On top of everything else that was happening here, she saw it with perfect clarity: at no time, ever, had she wanted Paul like she wanted Asier. She cared for Paul, but here she was, having sex dreams about Asier and dying—absolutely being *murdered*—in his arms right now. Paul was great, Paul was nice. But there was something so genuine and attentive about Asier, like she was the only focus of his entire world when they talked. And in his arms, she could think and be anything. Even if she knew she didn't have a future with Asier, she knew now that her future wasn't with Paul either.

"We will find him," he said in a husky voice.

Her knees shook. Better go with something safe—and not untrue. "I was supposed to leave tomorrow. I—I'm torn. I don't know what to do."

He released her and sighed, running a hand through his hair. He had no idea how devastating he looked in the moonlight in that tux. She had to force her hands to stay at her sides.

He looked at her again and appeared to make some sort of decision. He reached out, running his thumb across her jawline and down her neck in an almost reverent way, completely undoing her. He moved his mouth to hers unhesitatingly, and then his lips finally met hers in a soft, controlled connection. Sensual, hot, molten magma lips. Her mouth opened and she tasted him, his slightly cocktail-flavored tongue touching hers. Her legs turned to jelly and her arms to putty. Asier was utterly confident, his other hand holding her upper arm, taking on her weight as it shifted toward him. His mouth was the sweetest thing she'd ever tasted, and she could easily have died happy if an earthquake had hit at that moment and crumbled the cliff they were standing on, or a meteor had slammed down and buried them four stories into the Earth. She would die happy if this was the last thing she did. His mouth seemed to ask, *So?* And she replied with, *Yep. Just like this.* He was an incinerator. His hand moved up her arm, pulling her close against him, and she went right with it, melting against him.

When their lips came apart, he nestled his mouth against her neck, sending chills over her shoulder and up her scalp. She'd never been kissed like that. Ever.

His mouth rested near her ear, whispering, "Stay, then."

"There you are!" Derrick ran toward them, tripping and almost going airborne but somehow managing to stay upright. "Was looking for you."

Natalie and Asier pulled away from each other, her insides quivering.

"Oh, oh, ohhh," Derrick said, finally seeing the situation for what it was. "Dr. Casillas. *Got it.*"

Asier simply looked at Derrick, one eyebrow up.

"I always say, this is a great place to get some moonlight," Derrick said, making no move to leave. He patted the jawbone of the whale. "Yep. Ol' Blue."

"Good night," Asier told Derrick, his tone final. He steered Natalie past Derrick. She hoped they were going to do some more making out away from prying eyes. Because wow. *Wow.*

"Did you want to see my car?" Derrick called.

Ignoring him, Asier continued toward her car at the other end of the lot. They said nothing, but she clung to him as he helped her limp along. When they arrived, she half hoped he would ask her if she wanted to go home with him, but she also didn't want to rush things (and she still technically hadn't broken up with Paul yet, hello), so she was relieved when he said, "Jake will show up," almost as though he was trying to convince himself too. "Don't go until he does. He will get in touch before he leaves for New Zealand." Asier gave her a chaste kiss on her nose. "I know it. Good night, Natalie."

He walked away, hands in pockets, out into the parking lot. Away from the gala. Away from her. She waited until he disappeared between the parked cars.

She was too stunned to do more than get in her car and head home.

CHAPTER 17

Sunday, Natalie woke with a heavy sense of defeat. There was no way she could start driving back now. Not only had she failed to find Jake, but there was no Penguin either. Yes, she'd pretended to herself that maybe Kit could keep an eye out for him, but she could not get in her car and leave without him. She climbed stiffly out of her sleeping bag—that thing was getting really tiresome—and did her usual morning search for the cat. He wasn't lounging in any early morning sunny spots, did not come to the kitchen for his food no matter how loudly she clanged the tin, and was not sleeping among the rosebushes in the garden. He was…gone.

The most infuriating thing was that likely neither cat nor brother was far. She could feel it in her gut. He—they—would appear eventually. It just meant she couldn't leave for Boston as she had planned. She might get fired, but it was a risk she would have to take.

Natalie poured herself a cup of coffee in the kitchen and found a note on the counter: *Kit and I went for walk. Watch out for gopher.* Natalie frowned and looked around for a rodent but saw nothing. She went through the French doors opening onto the back garden with her coffee, her customary morning routine.

Thank God she looked down before stepping outside, because a headless, mutilated gopher lay on the mat. Like a little love note. To her.

She breathed in sharply with relief. *I'm still here*, she could imagine Penguin intending to say through the gopher's bloody neck stump. *Doing what I need to do.*

She stepped over the gopher and slumped down in a deck chair, letting the events of last night wash over her.

Asier's kiss. God, that had been insane. She pulled out her phone, hoping for a text from him, and was surprised to see a whole slew of texts.

Paul: All set to start the drive back today? What time are you heading out?

Teensy: I found another jar. It was not pretty.

Paul again: Let me know when you're on the road.

Michelle: How was the gala? Better not have had sex in the dress.

Asier: 😎

Nina: Call me when u can! Need to talk!!!!!!!!

Natalie felt bad about Paul's texts. He missed her, it was clear. But it was Nina's text that required immediate attention. It was unusual for her to text on a weekend, and Natalie felt uneasy. Ignoring Paul and Teensy's texts for now, Natalie sent Asier a winky emoji and then called Nina. "Hey, Nina. How are you? I got your text."

"Oh *man*," Nina said. "I'm *so* glad you called."

The bad feeling intensified. "What's going on? Everything all right?"

"*No!* Oh my *God*, Natalie. Friday at work was *so* bad."

"What happened?"

"Okay, well, I was in the conference room. You know the small one?"

"I know it."

"After lunch I was in there sorting a bunch of reports. And I stepped into the little closet, you know the supply closet with shelves in the small conference room?"

"Yes." Natalie gritted her teeth against her desire to yell at Nina to hurry it up.

"Anyway, Paul and Ann came in and *shut the door,* and they *didn't know* I was in there!"

"Okay?" Natalie braced herself to hear that Paul and Ann had rutted like wolves on the conference room table or something. She and Asier certainly had in her latest dream.

"Ann asked Paul how he was doing without you, you know, with you being out in California?"

"What did he say?"

"And—" Nina broke off, overcome. "He said you were chasing after old family problems and that it was typical Natalie and you were always doing stupid, misguided things like that." A noise of despair came across the line. "I'm so sorry to tell you this, Natalie, but I would want to know if someone talked that way about me. Especially my boyfriend."

"Yes. I appreciate it," Natalie said. Her spine had turned to ice. "We're actually on a break."

"Okay, well, either way, it's not good. Because Ann said she agreed and that you were a *mess.* I'm so sorry! And then Paul said—oh *man.*"

"Go ahead, Nina." Natalie's fist clenched around the phone.

"He said that he could see why Ann had never considered promoting you, and when they'd discussed in his interview him taking the director position, he hadn't counted on you being so obsessed with it, and all this time he'd had to pretend like he supported you getting it but really knowing it was his. *I* didn't even know that."

Natalie found her voice, croaking out an incredulous response. "He said that?"

"Yeah." Nina sounded wretched. "I hated to text you, but I *had* to tell you."

Paul had known. Every time she had talked about the director position, every time she had mentioned wanting that job, he'd known. And he'd outright *lied* to her, saying he'd had no idea. Maybe she'd betrayed him last night by kissing Asier, but he'd betrayed her way earlier by lying to her face and shit-talking her to Ann behind Natalie's back.

"I'm *so sorry*," Nina wailed.

"No, don't be." Natalie tried to think fast, to process it all. "I'm really glad you called. It's better to know than not. Did they find out you were in the closet?"

"No, but I had to stay in there for, like, an *hour*."

"Thanks for telling me, Nina. It means a lot."

"Okay," Nina said miserably. "I'm really, really sorry. Maybe I should tell them that I heard, because I'm HR and everything. God, I'm so sorry!"

Natalie breathed in through her nose. "Don't be. And don't tell Ann. There's no point in her knowing you overheard everything and you getting in trouble."

After several more rounds of absolution, Natalie ended the call and spent a long moment quietly seething. All that talk about her moving in with him—when he'd known he had taken her job. He'd said she'd been "obsessed" with it. Who the hell had she been sleeping with for the past five months?

She knew she should probably wait until she was calm, but Lynn and Kit were on their walk, and she preferred to do this in private. She anticipated yelling. Lots of it.

With shaking fingers, she called Paul.

"Hey, babe," he said, sounding out of breath. "Great timing. I got the keys to the condo on Friday! I'm moving in today. Can you believe it? I really want you to see it. One week until you're back!"

"I'm not leaving today." Damn. Damn. That wasn't what she'd meant to say. She'd meant to grill him about talking behind her back with Ann and knowingly stealing the promotion she had wanted.

"What?" His panting slowed. "You're supposed to be back at work next week. Your drive is going to take a little time, so you have to leave today."

"Paul," she said, the burn of her rising temper scorching her tongue, "why do you want me to move in with you?"

"What?" He laughed. "What are you talking about? Because I love you. I know, I know, we're on a break, but I still want this. I'm very much invested in us."

"But *why*? Why continue with the charade when you knew damn well you were getting the promotion I wanted? And when you looked down on me for wanting it? And when you think I'm a mess?" Nina's words tasted like bitter shards in the back of Natalie's throat.

There was silence as Paul absorbed what she was saying and, she imagined, realizing that she wasn't calling to talk about moving in. "What—what are you talking about?"

"You pretended to support me. And now you want me to move in with you like nothing happened."

"I assure you—"

She sighed, loud and exhausted. "Paul. Come on. What are you doing?"

"I'm simply asking when you plan to be back. I'm not sure I can sanction extra days away—it's not fair to other employees. So if you could communicate your expected departure date—"

"You know what," she hissed, "you can take my expected departure date and shove it up your ass."

"Nat, this is crazy." He had the nerve to sound surprised. "And that's rude. I'm your boss. Okay, look. I can see that you're torn. You're out there dealing with family stuff, and it's probably stirring up a bunch of emotions. I know. I get it. I felt the same way when I was coming back home after living in Europe for so long. I missed my family so much. I understand."

Paul missing his family, especially when he flew back to them at least once a year to their warm and open arms, was not the same—not even sharing similar characteristics, not even a vague *suggestion*—as her not having seen or heard from her siblings for almost fifteen years because of what she'd done.

"First of all, no," she said, taking care to keep her voice even and controlled when all she wanted to do was scream. "Second of all, unless you can explain why you hid the fact that you were promised the promotion months ago, I'm going to have to assume it's because you're a selfish ass who thought he could have his cake and eat it too."

"Natalie, I think we've gotten off on the wrong foot here. You're upset and saying things you don't mean." His voice had picked up speed, the tone he reserved for when he was going to barrage her with words, hoping to steamroll her enough that she wouldn't protest. "Listen. Listen. This is a dual conversation, right?"

"I don't know what the hell that means." She was breathing fast, her head spinning. Things with Paul were sliding downhill fast, the damage perhaps irreversible. Which didn't bother Natalie one bit.

"One part of me is talking to you as your boss," he said in a soft voice. "And the other part of me is talking to you as your partner. I miss you a lot and want you back. I got the bed in here, and I was thinking about having you in it. Being with you. Waking up next to you."

She stifled a snort of disbelief. Then she decided she did not need to stifle anything and snorted again, loudly, because she could.

"Let me speak now as your boss." His tone hardened. "I need you to be back in the office by next Monday. That's when I hold my staff meetings, and I expect you to be there. I run a tight, motivated team, and I strive for total alignment. You're going to really love the direction I'm taking the team in. In four short months, Argo & Pock will rapidiously productivate—"

"What?"

"And in order to actualize that, we have to, as a team, interactively work to impact our channels."

"What language are you speaking?"

"Because I think you'll agree, Natalie, that Argo & Pock as an organization is ripe for growth. You've been there for ten years, so you know. My team meetings are specially formulated to facilitate that growth, to catalyze it, to synergistically redefine—"

"Stop, now." She rubbed her forehead. This was going nowhere. While making decisions in the heat of anger was never wise, she struggled to see what was worth salvaging here.

"And if you're going to be part of the team, I need you there, in your seat, next Monday. I have big plans to parallel task what I call multidisciplinary channels."

"Did you get this bullshit off a business-speak generator website?" He'd always been a pretentious ass in ways like this. She'd hidden it from herself because she'd been so desperate to make it work. "You know what? This is stupid."

"What, being a responsible adult?"

"No, you assuming that things could go on as they were. It might have worked if you hadn't hidden your promotion from me and made me feel like an idiot for wanting it. It might have worked if you hadn't assumed that it wouldn't matter to me."

"We're having a disagreement," he said, back to his boyfriend voice now, his tone careful, realizing he was on shaky ground. "What, you're going to break up with me on the phone because you went to California and soaked up some sun? Wake up, Natalie. This *is* home. You don't throw away a great relationship because we're having an argument. We are aligned in our goals, so stop acting like a child."

The anger shot up again. He'd been condescending about other things before—the news, people he considered to be idiots—but seldom her life. Actually, she'd have to think about that. He *had* spoken to her like she was a child at times. But she'd bought into it too. She'd given him credit for being older and more mature. She'd assumed that because he'd lived all over the world and had more work experience, he knew more and was better than her.

Maybe he did know more in a professional sense, but he had not learned how to be a kind and decent human being.

"Think how disappointed Teensy would be if she knew her best friend was trying to break her brother's heart," he said into her silence.

Low blow, using Teensy like that.

"Why don't you fuck all the way off," she said. "Let's start there."

"Natalie." Now he did sound patronizing—and it fit him well. "I can see that you've gone through an incredibly stressful time in Santa Cruz, being back in the family house with your sister. Let's take a day or two to calm down. Regroup. Okay? Then we'll talk."

"No more talking. Nope. We're done here. We are not…aligned. I'm done, Paul. You hear me? It's over." Instead of relief, she felt disappointment. Not in breaking up with him—*that* part was a relief—but that none of this conversation surprised her. And that was worrisome. Had she been hiding a part of herself during the months she'd spent with Paul? What other signs had she overlooked or ignored?

A long silence stretched between them. Finally, he was hearing her.

"I don't think this is done," he said quietly. "This is what we both want. I've finally got the career I want, I bought an amazing condo, and I want to marry you. Okay? This is my life too."

"You want me back so I complete some goddamn trifecta of manhood for you?"

"We need to be aligned in our goals. I love you a lot, Natalie, but we're going to have to work some things out." Then he hung up.

Natalie threw her phone down, not believing how he had just gaslighted her. But the relief at ending things was palpable. She had needed to say those things, needed to tell him to fuck off. She wasn't sorry.

And yet, she suspected this conversation was not final. One thing she knew after five months with Paul was that he was determined, and he did not like to veer off course, especially courses he'd set for himself. In any case, she was not going to leave today without Jake being here for them to claim the house and with Penguin out gallivanting around and murdering rodents.

She felt great. Strong, healthy, and in control of her life, finally coming to the realization that she did not love Paul and never would. As her boyfriend—now ex-boyfriend—he'd have to deal.

As her boss…that was something else entirely. And if she lost her job over it, well, she'd figure something out.

— — —

Jake was still missing. Penguin could not be found. Natalie was worried.

It had been almost a week since that disastrous call with Paul, and her options were dwindling if she wanted to remain employed when she got back. Every day she and Kit walked the neighborhood looking for that rat cat, and then they usually went by the two surfing spots where Jake might be. Asier had not texted that he'd seen Jake. There was nothing. Natalie had avoided Teensy's texts except to tell her she was taking a few more days before starting the drive back.

Downstairs in the big yellow kitchen, Kit sat playing some violent special ops game on his phone while slurping cereal. Lynn stood hunched over the counter, wearing a T-shirt with Siouxsie and the Banshees on it—old-school and so Lynn—while paging through *Good Times*, the Santa Cruz indie newspaper.

"Good to see that thing is still in print." Natalie's voice sounded like a bullfrog from calling Penguin's name around the neighborhood yesterday during a search.

"Amazingly so," Lynn agreed without looking up.

"Morning, Aunt Natalie," Kit said.

"Morning, you." She limp-shuffled to the French press. Every step was painful. Her two smallest toes on her left foot were red and swollen and still ached from being stepped on at the gala the previous weekend.

"You look like shit," Lynn remarked.

Natalie shrugged. "What day is it?"

"Friday."

A jolt of panic went through Natalie. "Shit." The days had melted into one another: the beach with Kit, half-heartedly checking surf spots, fretting nonstop over Jake and Penguin. Asier had texted a few times, and she had told him she needed a little space to figure things out. She was careful to tell him that it had nothing to do with him and everything to do with Jake. Asier, being a decent human being, had said that of course she should take her time and that family was a heavy thing to deal with. She hadn't wanted to tell him she needed space. She wanted no space at all from him, and she hadn't realized it had been almost a week already. She had even missed the opportunity to work with Dr. Berkhower again.

She did not reply to Paul's texts, which imperiously asked if she was on the road yet.

Lynn raised her eyebrows. "You don't look too hot, kid."

Natalie poured too much creamer in her coffee, as though that would help snap her out of her crappy attitude.

"I know I haven't done much to find Jake," Lynn said, "but I had to get a job. His colleagues still haven't heard from him?"

Natalie shrugged. "No one knows where he is."

"Hmm. I mean, I thought he'd show up, but, like…yeah." Lynn scratched her chin. "It's a little worrisome."

Natalie's eyes welled with tears. She'd cried at least once a day this past week. "What can we do? We should have gotten his address by now. I should have insisted on getting it."

"Let's first find out when he leaves for New Zealand. You visit the lab and tell his lab friends that we *have* to get his address and phone number."

"Why don't you have his number?"

"I've had to change my phone and number a few times. I lost of lot of contacts." Lynn's face went dark. Natalie suspected it might have something to do with her husband. "If we have to, we'll camp out at the airport and FaceTime the stupid lawyer so he sees all three of us together."

Natalie nearly laughed at the thought of the three of them saying cheese for a group photo. Never happening.

"I can ask As—Dr. Casillas now for Jake's number," Natalie said. She still didn't know what to say or feel about the gala. It was all a mess of feelings she couldn't untangle. But now she felt a little silly. Of course she could ask Asier for Jake's number. She should have done so days ago.

"So ask him, idiot." Lynn shook her head.

Natalie refilled her coffee cup, trying to get rid of her headache. The aged analog clock embedded in the stove said it was almost eight. Time for her to hobble the two blocks down to the cliff for her customary morning check to see if Jake was surfing. She still wore her pajamas, an old pair of incredibly comfortable sweats and a baggy shirt from some music festival she and Teensy had gone to years ago, but it was acceptable attire for Santa Cruz, so she headed for the door.

"Where are you going?" Lynn asked.

"Down to Steamer Lane to see if Jake's surfing." Walking on her swollen toes seemed ludicrous, but she had to get out of the house.

"I have some time before work. I'll come. Kit?"

Kit looked between his mother and Natalie. "I'll stay here."

This was out of character for Kit, and Natalie thought he was trying to give them time alone to talk. Perceptive, amazing kid.

Lynn came around the counter. She didn't bother with shoes either. You weren't from Santa Cruz if the soles of your feet weren't callused from walking to the beach barefoot every day. Together, coffee mugs in hand, they picked their way down the driveway and over to West Cliff. A chill generating off the coast still hung in the morning air.

"You're walking like a chimpanzee," Lynn said.

"My toes might be broken."

"God, you're a mess."

"What a lovely walk we're having."

"Sisterly." Lynn's tone wasn't nasty.

"For us."

"Ha."

Natalie braced herself and said the thing she'd been wanting to say since she'd first arrived in Santa Cruz. "I'd love to have an actual relationship with you someday." She tried to sound as casual as possible.

Lynn sighed. "I don't know, kid. It's a hard thing to forgive, the prison thing."

Natalie paused as they crossed the street to the ocean side, considering her next words carefully. "I didn't want that to happen. Trust me, I've regretted calling the police that night every day for the last fifteen years." She had spent a few years in therapy in college, twisting her guilt this way and that. Her therapist had told her that Lynn and Jake and Carlos had been adults who'd made their own decisions and that Natalie had to let it go. But letting it go meant forgetting Carlos was not alive and that Natalie had played a small role in his death.

They walked slowly, and Natalie appreciated Lynn matching her pace to Natalie's slower, limpy one. To anyone's eye, they were two poorly dressed women going for a morning stroll, enjoying a nice chat. There was no rancor, no spitting undertones.

Natalie peeked over the rail at the surf. There were only a few surfers in the water. It was still cold. "It was all bad, starting with the night you were arrested."

"God, that night." Lynn sighed.

"You were right, you know." Natalie kicked at a pebble. "About me."

"Of course I was. What are you referring to, specifically?"

"I was supposed to have sex with my boyfriend that night. It didn't happen because he wanted another girl. I was pissed off and humiliated."

Lynn grunted, a sign that she remembered.

Natalie shook her head. "I was going to give him my virginity that night, as though he deserved it or something. As though it's anything but a patriarchal concept."

Lynn gave her a side-eye. "Someone's become a feminist."

Natalie took a sip of coffee and lifted her face to the sea breeze. "So I was pissed off. At him, at you, at Jake. I wanted to lash out. When I pushed you and you hit your head, I freaked out. I didn't know what to do, and I wanted Jake to pay attention, but he was shooting up in our living room. And then Carlos died because I called the cops."

Lynn said nothing, but Natalie could see from the way her sister bit her upper lip and stared at the ground that she wasn't stewing in old resentment. Natalie had not told her or Jake about any of this. After their arrests, Lynn and Jake had not wanted to listen to her, had not welcomed excuses or explanations. Big on accepting the consequences for one's actions at the time, their mother did not want to hear Natalie's attempts to explain. Buck had been sympathetic after he'd heard Natalie try, but his power was limited in those nightmarish days, and he sided with her mother.

"Well," Lynn said softly. "There was a lot going on that night."

Natalie's eyes filled with tears at Lynn's forgiving tone. She focused on the water. Only two surfers were in the water now. One of them looked like it could be Asier, but he was too far away to be sure. Natalie leaned on the rail and let the wind blow her hair into an even messier tangle. If Lynn could forgive her—maybe she already had—then surely she could forgive herself.

"I'm really sorry," Natalie said.

"I don't think any of us would have known what to do. There is no manual for how to handle a situation like that."

They stood in silence for a long time. More surfers arrived and picked their way gingerly down the cliff face to the water. Natalie wasn't sure whether Lynn's sentiment constituted a statement of forgiveness, but it was close. Natalie wanted to say something much more than *sorry* to show how much she cared—that she loved Lynn, that she'd always loved Lynn, and that even though they'd bickered and fought as kids, she knew Lynn had looked out for her, especially in those hard years after their dad had died and their mom had checked out. But they had never been in the habit of getting too deep, and Natalie didn't want to upset this delicate truce. She cast about for something to say.

"What made you start mortuary school?" she asked. "Like, did you wake up one day and say, 'I want to work with corpses'?"

Lynn snorted a laugh. "No, honestly, it was a biography I read in high school about Eva Perón. You know, from Argentina? Evita? Don't cry for me?"

"Yeah."

"When she died, they embalmed her. Like, really well, with plasticizers and all kinds of things. The words 'loving and detailed embalming' were used in the book, I remember."

Natalie vaguely recalled the history. "Wait. Wait. Didn't someone have sex with her corpse? Please don't tell me—"

"That's an urban legend." Lynn gave her a look. "I *hope*. Anyway, they were going to build this incredible monument to her where they would entomb her body, but while they were planning that, a military junta took over and her husband, the president, Juan Perón, went into exile."

Natalie had a feeling Eva Perón's body was not going to fare well in this tale.

"So Juan fucks off to Spain and marries a lady named Isabel," Lynn continued. "Back in Argentina, the military junta hides Eva's body for fifteen years."

"That's an excessively long time to hide a corpse."

"Eventually, Juan asks where her body is, and the junta says, oh, yeah, we were going to tell you—we sent her body to Italy and buried her in someone else's grave."

Natalie frowned. "Uncool."

"Agreed. But Juan and his new wife, Isabel, have Eva's perfectly embalmed body dug up and brought to them."

"There's no way the new wife was okay with that decision."

"She was. The book said she helped clean the body up and brush her hair every day. And then—"

"How can there be an 'and then'?"

"Juan and Isabel kept her in their dining room for a few years. People could come over for dinner parties and, you know, there she'd be."

"That did not happen."

"It did. Juan had problems and he was insane, but anyway, I couldn't believe that after all those years and shenanigans, her body would hold up, like, still be preserved. I was fascinated. I thought, that's got to be quite an art. As you may remember, I'm not a squeamish person, so I applied to mortuary school."

"Did you learn how to 'lovingly embalm'?"

"Let me tell you, when you embalm a body, adoration or love really isn't a part of the proceedings. And it's a myth that embalming is forever— you have to keep refreshing the chemicals if you want to keep a corpse around for years. There are restoration specialists devoted to that. I guess in the end, I wasn't really into the preservation. I don't like to embalm. There's no need to preserve bodies or make them lifelike or slap makeup on them. And it's so awful, too, what we have to do in order to make people look like they're merely sleeping. Like the staples—"

"No." Natalie held up a hand.

"So working at the crematory works for me. Ashes to ashes, that kind of thing. And honestly, I like knowing that I'm helping families say goodbye to their loved ones. No one did that for us when Dad died. Mom just couldn't deal, so she had him cremated, and then we didn't even have a funeral."

Natalie felt surprise at this softness from her sister. Their father's death had affected them all in interesting and different ways and had probably shaped the choices they made later. She had hurt her siblings because she'd felt abandoned. Lynn had become a mortician because she didn't want other people to feel alone like she did. And maybe Jake was hiding for some related reason. "You're right."

Lynn studied her coffee cup. "I don't even know how Mom died or if she was cremated or what. That sounds harsh, a daughter not knowing how her mother died. But we weren't part of each other's lives in recent years. She sent Kit birthday cards, but she stopped calling me two years ago." She sighed. "And I blame my husband for not letting me come out and visit her."

"Not letting you?" Natalie watched her sister's face.

"As I've said, he was unpleasant."

Natalie shook her head at so much lost time, such a screwed-up family. What was the point of it all?

Lynn looked straight ahead, perhaps not meeting Natalie's eyes on purpose. "Maybe Jake has answers."

As they stood next to each other, Natalie pictured her sister reading a book on Eva Perón and getting interested in embalming and thinking about that years later. She snorted, a horrified kind of laughter, and that turned into a giggling fit she couldn't stop. She hung her head and shook it, giving herself over to the laughter. Tears streamed out of her eyes—leftover stress tears, probably—but they felt good. "You," she said to her sister's inquiring face. "You, reading all that about a corpse and going, 'Yes, I want to do that too.'"

Lynn smiled, and then it turned into a laugh. In a moment, she and Natalie were giggling together.

"I mean, was it the second wife brushing Eva's hair that did it for you?" Natalie snorted.

"It was all the world traveling Eva did with apparently little damage." Lynn's giggles turned into guffaws.

They guffawed and giggled and cackled together, half crying and clutching each other's arms as they limped back to the house.

When the house came into sight, Lynn's laughter died away. "You know, you really do look like shit."

"You said that earlier. Thanks for making a point of it."

"I mean, something's going on with you. I hesitate to ask, because I don't really care about your dramas."

Natalie hid her smile. Lynn used to say that a lot when they were teenagers: *I don't care about your dramas, kid.* But saying that was her way of asking. She considered telling Lynn everything, about how much she'd loved drawing the necrotic sea lion for Dr. Berkhower, and how she missed Santa Cruz and loved Kit and worried that Jake was a raging, festering ball of murderous fury somewhere in Santa Cruz County, waiting until he saw her so he could get her. And her surprising feelings for Asier, even though she'd met him relatively recently and didn't know him very well, but she already knew enough to know that if she could feel this way about a man, it was clear Paul wasn't it for her.

But that was all too much, so she said, "I found out my boyfriend was vying for a job I wanted at work even though he knew I wanted it."

"What an asshole," Lynn said.

"And he wants me to move in with him, even though he knew he was getting the job I wanted the whole time."

"You're still with this guy?"

"No. I broke up with him last Sunday." Natalie still had a sneaking feeling that she hadn't heard the last from Paul on the subject. But maybe he had accepted the breakup and was licking his bruised ego quietly.

Lynn checked her watch. "Well. Good. Sounds like you're coming out of that for the better. I gotta get ready for work. I suggest you clean yourself up and have someone look at those toes. And go talk to Jake's lab colleagues again."

Natalie nodded. "I'll go down to the lab today."

"Maybe it's time to, I don't know, hire an investigator or something."

Natalie gave a shocked laugh. "Jake would hate that."

"I can one hundred percent attest to the fact that he would hate it. But if he's supposed to be leaving for New Zealand soon, then time here is running out, and I don't want to lose the house." Lynn looked up at the sky. "Damn, Mom. I can't believe she pulled this shit." Lynn looked back at Natalie. "And listen, you did good dumping your boyfriend. Manipulation is never a good place to go. Those kinds of people are selfish narcissists. They'll never change either. They just jerk you around and ruin your life."

Natalie studied her sister. "Is that what your husband did?"

"Oh, Allen did far worse than emotional manipulation. I went down that slippery slope real fast."

"Is Allen still a threat to you, Lynn? Or to Kit?" Natalie kept her eyes on her sister's face.

"He's always a threat." Lynn made a *who cares* twist of her lips. "But I made it clear we were done, and I left. That's what matters." She squinted her eyes at Natalie. "I have to get to work." She turned and went up the front stairs. "I mean it about your toes. You need to get those things checked out."

CHAPTER 18

Natalie taped up her toes, which did nothing to cut down on the throbbing or make for easier walking. It was as though her body was falling apart in response to the increasing sense of despair about finding Jake before he left for New Zealand. Nevertheless, she drove down to the lab. She could have simply called Asier, but seeing him in person to ask about Jake was better, like it was more official or something, and she allowed herself to believe this lie.

She parked and limped toward the lab. The blue whale skeleton caught her eye, and she decided to visit it even though it meant extra steps, because it was an amazing and huge thing—not to mention the site of the kiss she had shared with Asier a week ago. A bird honking from the cliff pulled her away down the path, as animal sounds often did. A slow realization washed over her that everywhere, always, she had turned toward the sound of an animal, big or small, and wanted to sketch it. It was like a thread existed between them, and when it tugged, she followed. Why did she deny that she could do this for a living? Dr. Berkhower had shown her she could. In fact, maybe she would go talk to him.

But a group of cormorants kvetching and jostling for space on a rock below the cliffs caught her attention. She pulled out her sketchbook and drew the long curves of their graceful S-shaped necks, the sweep of the pencil up the paper, the continuing shape soothing in its connectedness. Maybe she'd even add watercolor later—

"Natalie."

She turned around, heart racing. It was Dr. Lawrence, huddled in a jacket against the sea wind, her face washed out and lined in the cloudy light, making the lines around her eyes more pronounced. She looked tired and annoyed, which was not promising.

"I saw you walk out here," Dr. Lawrence said. "Thought I'd come say hi." There was something in her face that felt a little insincere.

"Have you heard from Jake at all?" Natalie asked.

Dr. Lawrence shook her head. "Not a word." She met Natalie's eyes, and Natalie had the feeling she was being judged. "It's good of you to stay in Santa Cruz and wait."

Natalie squinted at the older woman. "Well, we need him for some family business."

"We need him too. To talk about the lab's microscope before he leaves for New Zealand."

"I can go by his house if you'd just give me his address. Or his number. It's really important that I speak to him."

Dr. Lawrence's face changed slightly, and she twisted her lips. "I already told you I can't give that out, I'm sorry. I know you mean well, but he would not appreciate us giving out his personal information. In fact, he asked us never to give his information out to anyone—even his family. I'm sure you can understand."

Natalie could understand. Asier had told her in Monterey that Jake had told them the whole story. "I get it."

Dr. Lawrence gave Natalie a calculating look. "Listen, I wanted to talk to you, especially since you're staying in Santa Cruz for the moment. That microscope I mentioned is extremely important to our work. It would mean we could produce levels of material that would be much more amenable for grants. You have to know that's one of Dr. Casillas's primary concerns, right?"

"Sure." Natalie didn't know. Asier had mentioned the microscope a few times, but not in terms that suggested he was worried about not getting it.

Dr. Lawrence smiled, but it didn't reach her eyes. "I heard you did illustration work for Dr. Berkhower. He has an Olympus BX50 fluores-·cence microscope with brightfield applications in his lab. It's a twenty-thousand-dollar instrument."

"That is a lot of money," Natale said, trying to look impressed in case this was the response the woman wanted. She had no idea where this conversation was going.

"Thing is, he doesn't use it that much. And if you're going to stick around, maybe you could help us transfer it to our lab."

Natalie stared at her. "You want me to steal a microscope?"

"Not *steal*. Just talk to Dr. Berkhower for us. Dr. Casillas has tried, but he doesn't listen. But Dr. Berkhower mentioned how impressed with your work he is. I know Dr. Casillas would really appreciate it if you could help. We talked about it last week, in fact."

"Asier never mentioned that." Natalie did not have a good feeling about this.

"Sweetie, listen." Dr. Lawrence grimaced, as though it pained her to explain this to a plebe like Natalie. "It's nice that you call him Asier, but I would stick to Dr. Casillas. You might have come to that gala wearing that dress and hoping to turn heads—or Dr. Casillas's head in particular—but he's very much focused on his research. At my age, I've seen all kinds of people in a lab, and Dr. Casillas is one of the most professional, sincere, and dedicated scientists I've met. I think he's been kind to you out of professional courtesy to your brother. I know that might sound a little harsh, but I know Dr. Casillas well. If you really want to leave an impression, help us with the scope. You had to have guessed that was why Dr. Casillas took you to Monterey, right? We've been after Dr. Suko's microscope for a while, and when we heard that your brother was down there to look at it, Dr. Casillas thought maybe he'd gone there to negotiate for it."

Too many thoughts lit up Natalie's head, like why Dr. Lawrence cared so much about Asier's private life that she would warn Natalie off. And the microscope—was that really all Asier cared about? She remembered Asier mentioning Dr. Berkhower's microscope at the gala. *Maybe we can finally get at Dr. Berkhower's compound inverted microscope,* he'd said. She had thought his flirty little smile had meant he was joking. Another thing: Dr. Lawrence was right. She didn't really know Asier all that well—certainly not as well as Dr. Lawrence knew him. Although in Natalie's interactions with him, he had been different from the professional scientist Dr. Lawrence was describing, it was true that Natalie might have read him wrong. She'd read Paul wrong too. Maybe it was her thing: misreading men's intentions when it came to her.

"So," Dr. Lawrence said, "if you could help us out with Dr. Berkhower, it would be important to our work, and I know your brother would appreciate it too."

"Right." Natalie closed her sketchbook. She couldn't let it show how much it hurt that Asier may have been using her—all for a microscope. Was that what the kiss had been about too?

"Thanks for listening." Dr Lawrence gave that tight, insincere smile again. Natalie didn't entirely buy the story—that kiss could have launched a rocket—but the seed of doubt had been planted. Dr. Lawrence walked away down the path toward the labs. She turned and looked back, giving Natalie a little wave, as though they'd concluded a deal. Natalie stared after her, the seed of self-doubt now growing roots.

She tucked her sketchbook into her bag and checked her watch. Almost lunchtime, and she'd accomplished nothing here. She should go speak to Dr. Berkhower, but she didn't want him—or anyone—thinking she was after his dumb microscope. Instead, she limped back to the parking lot. The doors to the lab opened as she passed, and two men emerged, deep in conversation. One of them was the enormous beast of a man who had smashed her toes at the gala. The other was Asier, talking animatedly, using his hands. The toe-stomper nodded enthusiastically at whatever Asier was saying.

Natalie allowed herself to watch them for a moment. As always, seeing him caused her heart to squeeze in her chest, but now there was a note of confusion mixed in. She didn't know him well enough to know if Dr. Lawrence was telling the truth. She lowered her head and tried to walk as fast as her crushed toes would allow to her car, but of course she was in full view of Toe-Stomper and Asier.

"Natalie!" Asier called.

She debated running, but that was foolish. Instead, she threw a resentful look at Toe-Stomper, since it was his fault she couldn't move quickly.

"Hey." Asier easily caught up with her. "Your foot—is it still bad?"

She realized she was near tears. Everything was so ridiculous and difficult, and she was tired and hurting—physically and emotionally. She wanted better things: a better job, a better boyfriend, a better living situation, and a better family. This realization, borne of exasperation, made her stop walking. Her life had turned into an epic shit show, and she was tired of it being that way.

It was time for change.

"Natalie." Asier put a hand on her arm. "Are you all right?"

She whirled to face him, hit by two things at once. One, she should have simply called him, because saying what she was going to say to his face was incredibly difficult. And two, she was in trouble here. She liked him. Too much.

"Did you—" Her voice caught. She swallowed and tried again. "Are you just trying to get a microscope?"

"What?" He smiled in surprise.

"Dr. Lawrence said you wanted me to ask Dr. Berkhower if you could have his microscope."

Asier shook his head as though clearing it. "I do not understand, Natalie."

She bit back tears. Her toes throbbed. "I just—I—" Maybe if her toes hadn't been consuming her, she would have had the presence of mind to ask if he had kissed her like a lava monster fresh out of a volcano for a microscope, but it was all too much at once. "I think my toes are broken."

Asier's eyes widened. "What? Have you been to the hospital?"

She tried to make it sound like it was nothing. "It's fine."

"It's not fine. You're hurt. Can I help you? Please?"

He looked so sincere, and those deep brown eyes stayed on hers in such an intense way, as though she was precious to him. But Natalie knew the truth about him now. This had to just be his way with everyone. It meant nothing.

"Please," he repeated. "Let me take you to the hospital. I will feel terrible if I can't do that."

"I'm *fine*—"

"Jake would never forgive me if I left his sister here with broken toes."

She rolled her eyes and allowed herself to be led to his car. Yes, fine, he was helping his friend's sister. Nothing more. After he sat her in the passenger seat, she thought he would close the door and get in the driver's side, so she was surprised when he squatted down and removed her sandal.

"No, no," she protested, realizing he was going to examine the toes. "No, really! They're fine."

"They're not fine." He peeled off the tape she'd used to bind the toes. Horrified, she tried to remember the last time she'd plucked her toe hairs or given any kind of attention to her cuticles.

"Natalie." He met her eyes, and she was sure he was going to say that her toes were heinous. "They're very swollen."

She covered her eyes, unable to meet his. "That guy you left the building with just now—he stepped on them at the gala."

"Dr. Gallen?"

She peeked at Asier to see him turned toward the lab, his body tense, as though he was going to go after the man.

"Well. Listen. Let's get these seen to." Now he did close the door, got in the driver's seat, and started the engine. She couldn't believe this was happening.

"I saw Dr. Lawrence a bit ago," Natalie said. "She said that she still hasn't seen or heard from Jake."

"No, there's been nothing from him." Asier tapped the steering wheel with a finger.

"We need to find him." Natalie let her head fall against the headrest. "Time's running out."

"I know it must be difficult," he said. "I'm sorry."

She stayed silent as he drove through town, not wanting to spill more emotion. She needed to harden herself against him. He hadn't denied wanting her to ask Dr. Berkhower for the microscope. He hadn't said anything, which made him guilty in the court of Natalie Walker.

Asier turned the car into the hospital parking lot rather than dropping her off at the entrance.

"Honestly, I can walk, it's fine," she protested, but he waved that away.

"Absolutely not." He helped her out of the car, holding onto her hand like she was made of glass. "Do you know what Dr. Gallen does in his free time?"

"Stomps grapes to make wine?"

"He trains for the annual Scottish Highland Games, at the stone put. He tells me this is like the shot put, but with heavy rocks."

She tried not to laugh and failed. "Oh my God."

"I once saw him pick up a boulder embedded in the sand that was bigger than me, by himself."

"Did it crash onto his foot?"

"No, but the next time I'm out collecting samples with him, I will suggest he drop a rock on his foot out of an honor-bound duty to avenge your toes."

She giggled and then remembered he was using her for the stupid microscope.

He insisted on seeing her into the hospital, where Natalie experienced a light-headed burst of relief when they ran her insurance and said they took it and there would be only a deductible to pay. There was no way she could afford this nonsense on top of everything else. Asier stayed with her in the waiting room until she was called to be seen.

In the exam room, the doctor uncurled each inflamed toe, making her seize in pain, followed by a professional diagnosis: "Yep, they're broken." He taped her toes, bending them several more times in the process, and sent her on her way. Her face was red from the effort of hanging on through this torture as they wheeled her out to a waiting Asier.

"You didn't have to stay," she said, swallowing back her tears.

"Of course I did. Look at you. You're in terrible pain. Did they make them worse?" He put a reassuring hand on her arm.

"Yes." She covered her face at the memory of the pain. "They're just toes! This is ridiculous."

"Lots of nerves in our extremities."

They finished up and wheeled Natalie outside, where Asier pulled his car up and packed her gently in.

"Thank you again for this," Natalie said on the drive back to the lab.

"It is of course my pleasure. Are you sure you don't want me to drive you home?"

"The lab is fine."

They drove in silence for a few minutes, and then he said, "Listen, about earlier. About the microscope thing."

"It's all right." Natalie couldn't stand hearing platitudes or excuses right now.

He frowned. "My work is very important to me."

"I understand." So Dr. Lawrence hadn't been wrong. Natalie tucked this away to examine later, when she wasn't in his company and could let her heart hurt freely.

At the lab, he helped her out and into her car even though she could walk fine in the splint.

"I will have a stern talk with Dr. Gallen about stomping on ladies' toes," he said in a jokey tone.

She didn't laugh. He hadn't denied using her to get to Dr. Berkhower. The disappointment festered, ready to rise up as soon as she was alone in her car. "Thanks for your help. I'll be fine once these painkillers set in." She held up her little pharmacy bag that held nothing stronger than extra-strength acetaminophen.

"Take care, Natalie," he said. He bit his bottom lip, and she felt that now-familiar surge of attraction. "Of course, I will continue to let you know if we hear from Jake."

"Thank you." She nodded, disappointed all over again. "I respect that he doesn't want me to have his contact information."

"What?" Asier frowned. "No. He never said that."

"Dr. Lawrence said—"

"He is a private person, but you are family. And I think I know you well enough now to give you that information."

She watched him carefully, not daring to believe. Because if Dr. Lawrence had lied about that, then everything else she had said was suspect too.

Especially the part about Asier using her.

"Let me give you his number and his address," he said. "I did go by his house the other day, and it is still empty. Trash cans not put out. Do you have something to write on?"

She thought he knew he could text his number to her but was prolonging the moment. Likewise, she had multiple pieces of stray paper in her trash-filled car, but those were out of the question when she could offer her skin and guarantee feeling the warmth of Asier's hands on her again. She dug a ballpoint pen out of her bag and held out her palm.

He took the pen, holding her arm steady as he wrote gently on her hand. God, he smelled so good. And was his finger caressing her skin? No. Well, maybe. He gave her hand a little squeeze and then capped the pen and handed it back. Had it been a squeeze or a reflex? Definitely a squeeze. Would a man who was plotting ways to get an expensive microscope squeeze her wrist?

"Thanks."

He opened his mouth as though to say something but seemed to think better of it. Did he want to kiss her again? She certainly wanted to kiss *him*. But he patted the side of her car and walked away.

CHAPTER 19

Natalie tried to shift her legs, which burned from being in a crouch for too long under the window outside what she thought was Jake's living room.

"There's no one here," Lynn yelled.

Natalie sent her sister her best ferocious scowl and pointed to her eyeballs with two fingers to show that they needed to communicate in signals.

Lynn rolled her eyes. "I'm not playing your special ops military game."

"You are no fun at all," Natalie hissed, standing up. She felt like a piece of sad origami being unfolded. "You said you would do the hand signals."

In response, Lynn rolled her eyes again. "We don't need to be covert. Nobody's going to hear us. He's not here."

Natalie had to admit this was true. Jake's house was dark. No car in the driveway. Peeking through his windows revealed nothing—no overturned chairs or other signs of kidnapping, no half-eaten meals on the table to indicate he had left in a hurry. The house was maddeningly neat, with zero clutter or photo frames. The only personal item was a surfboard propped up just inside his front door.

Kit came crashing around the corner, making a tremendous noise in the bushes. "I don't think he's here."

Natalie threw her hands up in exasperation.

"What?" he asked.

"She wants you to use her dumb hand signals," Lynn said.

"Sorry." Kit crouched and pointed at Natalie and then at himself and then made a throat-slashing motion.

"No, that means abort mission," Natalie said. "You mean this." She shook her head and crossed her hands in front of her.

"Either way," Lynn said, "we can leave now."

Natalie agreed that they could. It was clear Jake wasn't home. They piled into Lynn's car. The sun had just gone down, and Natalie gazed at the lights of the Boardwalk.

"It's so pretty," she said.

"A nice thing for an East Coaster to say," Lynn said.

"You're an East Coaster too, by that logic."

Lynn snorted as though that was very untrue. Natalie's phone rang shrilly, and Teensy's name appeared on the screen.

"Hey," Lynn said. "You were *very clear* that we turn off our phones so we could be sneaky!"

"She's right, Aunt Natalie," Kit added. "You said."

"Shh, both of you. I have to take this." Natalie couldn't help her smile as she answered the call.

"Nat," Teensy said in a rush. "I just got back from my conference in Maine, and I thought you'd be home by now. Where are you? Are you okay?"

Natalie turned toward the passenger window, as though that would give her privacy in the car with Lynn and Kit. "I told you I was going to stay here a few more days."

"Yeah, but I thought that meant two days. I thought you'd be on the road by now." Teensy whistled. "Paul's going to flip."

"Teense. I found out he knew he was taking my promotion. He actively pursued it."

"What? That can't be true."

"It is." Natalie wiped a hand over her face. "I had kind of a huge argument with him about it and broke up with him."

"Paul didn't mention anything about that. He just said you were having a hard time dealing with things out there."

Natalie shook her head. She had always known Teensy would be hurt if they broke up. "Teense. Listen."

"No, *you* listen. I'm not supposed to tell you this, but I think I have to. It's kind of huge."

"I don't know if I want to know what you're talking about."

"Paul bought a diamond ring. He was going to propose to you! I helped him pick it out last month. We were going to be sisters-in-law. We still can be." Her voice was edged with desperation. "I thought I'd come home from my conference and you'd be here and we could go back to the way things were."

"Oh, Teense." A whole slew of feelings whooshed through Natalie. Regret at hurting Teensy and Paul, a little horror at how close he'd been to proposing after just five months together, and the certainty that the ring would never be on her finger.

"He's going to be so hurt, Natalie."

"I know."

"If you just call him, I know there's a solution to all this," Teensy said. "He meant no harm with the promotion. You know how he gets—he's driven! I think he just reacted badly to a few things, but you know he's a good guy."

Natalie knew Teensy adored her brother, and her blind defense of him was a result of that. Teensy was not wrong: Paul was a good guy, for the most part, and aside from some annoying traits like occasional condescension and not respecting her boundaries, they'd had a good time together. She'd be hard-pressed to find another man who looked as good on paper as Paul did. And there was the Teensy angle; marrying Paul meant Teensy would be not only her friend but her sister, a much harder bond to break. She owed Teensy so much for taking her under her wing that first day of college and generously giving Natalie a family when she had none.

"Please give him a chance," Teensy pleaded. "You're not only getting a husband, but our future as sisters too. Living next door to each other someday. Raising our kids together—they'll just run back and forth between houses and eat whatever food is on whatever table."

Natalie smiled. It was a nice picture.

"We'll get a joint swimming pool," Teensy said. "For the cousins."

Natalie sighed. She knew Paul had not just reacted badly to a few things. This was who he was. No one wanted to admit their older brother wasn't who they thought. Natalie knew that better than anyone. Even so, she felt a small rip—a sensation of pulling away from Teensy.

Teensy emitted a huff of air, the frustration clear in her voice. "That's not going to happen, is it?"

Natalie stared at the lights of the wharf. "No."

Lynn pulled the car into their driveway.

"I have to go," Natalie told Teensy.

"You're throwing your future away because he wanted a job?" Teensy asked. "He's crazy about you. Come on."

Lynn, who had never previously cared to hide that she was listening or judging, quietly ushered Kit out of the car and into the house. Natalie stared after her. Teensy had always said that she supported Natalie no matter what happened with Paul. But this was about more than Paul, Natalie realized. This was about her leaving Massachusetts and leaving Teensy.

"I've seen you struggle for *years* over the way your family has shunned you," Teensy said, but now, as though confirming Natalie's suspicion, her tone was pleading, sad. "Paul is offering you a whole, complete life, and I just…just think you should really be careful here."

Natalie pursed her lips. It wasn't Teensy's fault that she thought Natalie had left Santa Cruz in her past. Natalie had asserted that Boston was her new home many times. But now she realized she had only been trying to convince herself—unsuccessfully—of something that wasn't meant to be.

And it wasn't Teensy's fault that she was taking her brother's side now. Blood, as they said, was thicker than water, and Natalie knew how much a younger sister could love and idolize her older brother.

"I'm sorry," Natalie said. She wouldn't go into all the shitty things Paul had said. It didn't matter now.

"It was going really well, though!" Teensy wailed.

"This is more about you and me than it is about me and your brother. The dream of us raising our kids next to each other, all one family. It's about me and you not being sisters."

"I don't want to lose you." Teensy's voice sounded sadder than any time Natalie had heard. Tears pricked her eyes. "You're my best friend."

"We'll always be friends. Always, Teense. Nothing is going to change that."

Teensy sighed. "There's been progress with your sister?"

"Yeah. There really has." Natalie thought about the crazy conversation about Eva Perón's preserved corpse and smiled. Lynn had always been dark. It felt as though she was sharing that inner part of herself again with Natalie.

"You're not coming back, are you." It wasn't a question. Teensy's tone was resigned.

Natalie looked at the house through the car window. She liked her job, but it didn't compare to the rush she'd felt drawing that mangled sea lion. What if she could stay here? What if she could reclaim the Californian part of herself? Her job at Argo & Pock wasn't a big enough draw anymore, especially now that she knew Ann and Paul had said all those things and that Paul had lied to her. There was no way she could continue working there. And her relationship with Paul was over. But things were too unsettled, too wet and new with Lynn to make declarations like that.

"I'm not sure what I'm going to do," Natalie said. It sounded insincere even to her, but Teensy didn't challenge it. They exchanged hollow platitudes about talking soon and taking care and ended the call, Natalie hoping that she hadn't just lost her best friend.

CHAPTER 20

Natalie was tired of rattling Penguin's food dish and getting no response. She'd searched the attic and spare rooms daily. She'd looked under the house through the crawl space in the backyard. It had been full of spiders and deeply unpleasant, though Natalie had managed to get one into a jar for sketching. She hoped Penguin appreciated the effort.

The cat was nowhere. More copies of the flyers they'd already put around the neighborhood sat in a stack in her hand, and now she put them on the doorsteps of the houses on the theory that the neighbors might not have walked past the utility poles where she'd originally hung them.

The light was changing now, just a smidgeon. To her eye, even though it was only August, fall was on its way. She stopped in front of a house, staring at the impossibly blue, cloudless sky.

Her phone pinged, pulling her away from the blank peace of the sky. Lazily, she reached for it and held it up, wishing she hadn't when she saw who the message was from: Paul.

I'm bummed. Real bummed.

A pang of sadness hit her, but it was only the garden-variety regret of ending a relationship. Instead of ignoring him, she decided to respond honestly. Teensy said you bought a ring.

I did. I guess it was a little premature.

In case he had ideas about salvaging things, she typed, I hope we can be friends.

Three little dots appeared again, blinking for a long time. Finally, his text appeared. That's not what I was hoping to hear. Maybe we need to see each other. Reconnect. I'll fly out. This weekend. I'll come see you.

Her stomach lurched. No. Not a good idea.

I think it would help. I will gallantly fly to you.

Gallantly? Ew! Who said something like that? Nothing would help, especially not gallant overtures. She typed: Don't fly out here. Maybe we can talk when I'm back.

But probably not.

I am offering to fly to you, he wrote. You were supposed to be in the office today. We can fix this. Maybe not the job, but us.

She had expected this. Today was Monday, and by Paul's timeline, she was supposed to be in his stupid staff meeting, proactively building performance-based imperatives or whatever nonsense he'd said. And yet, if she had no job, she had no money—and few options.

I will wait for Ann to reach out to me, she typed back, hoping that would shut him up.

His reply was swift: I'm your boss, not Ann. She waited for more typing dots, for Paul to go on a diatribe about it. But no response came, and she hoped that was the end of it.

She trudged back to the house, annoyed. Did Paul really think he could not tell her about the promotion, let her think she had a shot, fire her, and still expect a relationship?

Kit appeared in the doorway of the house, holding a beach towel.

"Hey, kid," she said.

"Can we go to the beach today?"

"You're turning into a proper beach baby. Fitting into Santa Cruz so well." She worked to keep the irritation with Paul off her face.

He shrugged as though this didn't mean anything to him, but she could see a smile on his face.

"It's August," she said, glad to think about something else. "Did your mom enroll you in school here?"

"No. Should she?"

"Um, yeah. If you're going to stay here. School will be starting soon."

Kit seemed to consider this as he stayed in the doorway.

Then, after a silence: "Aunt Natalie?" Kit's voice sounded small and uncertain. If Natalie didn't know better, she'd swear it was Lynn's worried eyes peeking back at her.

"Yeah, babes?"

He hid his head under his towel. "My dad called my mom this morning. He wants us to come back to New York." She could barely hear him, his voice a whisper.

Natalie leaned against the solid redwood of the doorframe. "What did she say?"

He pulled his head out of the towel and picked at his thumb. "She said no. He said he was going to fight her in court because she took me to California."

Natalie grimaced. "And what did she say?"

"She hung up on him."

Natalie could see the uncertainty of this conversation was doing a number on him. "I'm really sorry, Kit. You know none of this is your fault, right? You know that your mom loves you and is only trying to protect you?"

He nodded. "Yeah, I know. My dad's mean."

"I'm sorry," she said again, wishing there were something she could do.

"It's all right."

"Would it make you feel better if we took some action?" she asked.

"What action?"

Natalie thought about it. "What if you enrolled in school here? Would that feel…more permanent? More like you're staying in Santa Cruz?"

Kit's face lit up. "Yeah, actually. Yeah. Can we go do that?"

"Sure. If your mom is okay with it. We could go get you enrolled today." Natalie considered texting Lynn to ask, but Lynn couldn't always get to her phone at work, and anyway, what with working six days a week, she didn't have time to enroll Kit herself. She barely had time for grocery shopping. Lynn would appreciate the help. Two days ago she had thanked Natalie for buying groceries and taking Kit to lunch.

"Okay," Kit said.

"Your mom is building a safe life for you here," Natalie said, hoping this would reassure him. "Things are looking good."

Kit bounced on the balls of his feet. "I'm ready."

Natalie went inside the house, Kit following, to get her car keys. They were working toward something concrete and actionable. They had a plan, even if it wasn't a plan for her. She had to admit, it felt good.

"Are *you* going to stay?" Kit asked as they got into the car. It was casually offered, but Natalie could see from the kid's rigid back that this was a big question. And it *was* big.

"Stay? Oh." She sighed. "I'm not sure what I'm doing yet. I'm just focused on finding your uncle Jake so we can inherit the house."

Kit shrugged. "He'll show up, right? And now you have his number and we know where he lives. We can keep checking until we find him. But let's go see my school now."

It was easy for Kit to think Jake would simply show up. But Jake was not home and hadn't been for some time. After their failed mission at his house, they had called and texted him repeatedly. His phone had gone straight to voicemail, and texts left unreturned. But at least he knew they were looking for him. Natalie had to say, it wasn't looking good that they would catch him before he was supposed to leave. And Natalie very much wanted him to appear, because she wanted the house to stay in the family. She didn't know how it would all play out yet or what she would do, but she knew that. Staying in Santa Cruz, moving back here permanently, was an attractive idea. But there were too many questions to answer before Natalie would allow herself to fully explore the idea, like whether she could support herself with a job illustrating dead things for Dr. Berkhower, or whether Lynn and Jake—if he appeared—wanted her around, or whether she was ready to move three thousand miles away from Teensy and the life she'd built in Boston.

For the first time in—ever, really—she had no idea what she was going to do next. The cocoons of college, Teensy's friendship and built-in family, and of boring and underpaid but safe Argo & Pock were gone. She was on her own.

CHAPTER 21

Mission Hill Middle School, an old Spanish-style building with red clay roof tiles, was located a few blocks from the old Santa Cruz mission, hence the name. Natalie had attended this school, as had Lynn and Jake. She felt proud to bring her nephew there if for no other reason than tradition.

"Kristopher Jacob O'Donnell," the clerk said, reading Kit's application through bifocals and making a note of something. Natalie turned to her nephew. He resembled Jake so strongly that she hadn't considered his last name. Natalie wondered if Allen O'Donnell was a blank canvas of a person with no distinguishing physical attributes. A featureless potato of a man whose DNA, when met with Lynn's fiery Walker chromosomes, had stepped aside and said, "After you."

"We're going to need a few items," the clerk said, pushing the application back to Natalie. "Immunization records, a birth certificate, and proof of residence, like a water or power bill."

"Ah," Natalie said. She had none of those.

The clerk sighed as though she dealt with unprepared parents all day. "I'll put him through as a student pending verification, and you can bring those documents anytime in the next week before school starts. Meanwhile, I'll request his transcripts from his former school."

Natalie thanked her and ignored the shiver of conscience whispering that it was not cool that she had registered Kit for school without Lynn's consent and that it was going to all come crashing on her head when she asked Lynn for his records. She ushered Kit out of the office to the courtyard. "Let's walk around the campus." The walk was more for her. She was nervous about what she had just done despite her desire to do something positive for Kit. And also, she'd left a message for Dr. Berkhower earlier inquiring about a job in his lab, and it was taking every effort she had not to check her phone every two seconds to see if he'd responded.

As they toured, Natalie pointed out obvious things like the gym.

"Yep," Kit said, pointing to the sign that said GYMNASIUM.

"The bathrooms are in that direction," Natalie said. "And a tree. And over here you'll find a bench."

Kit laughed. "My old school didn't have a gym. There wasn't enough space." He seemed excited. Natalie was sure she'd done the right thing by registering him and giving him some sense of belonging in his new home. Lynn would have to agree when she told her.

"Your mom used to have a boyfriend named Grumpus when she went to school here," Natalie said. "They used to walk home together every day. He lived on the street behind ours."

"Grumpus?" Kit laughed.

"That's what your uncle Jake called him, because he never said much and always seemed annoyed, but that was because your mom did all his talking for him. As in, she would ask him if he wanted something to eat, and he'd be about to respond, but she would say, 'Great, you will have toast.'"

Kit howled with laughter. "What else did she do?"

"She set fire to the girls' bathroom. That got her suspended for a week."

His eyes widened. "Wow."

"She was definitely headed for worse things in high school, but Buck was in our lives by then. He always threatened to make her do community service and said he'd take her around to local businesses and make her offer to paint their storefronts or whatever."

"Was Buck nice?"

Natalie considered Kit's question. The answer wasn't easy. "Your uncle Jake hated him, but he was actually pretty nice. He made our mom happy. I'm sure he was there with her when she died."

"Why don't you ask him?"

"I've thought about it, but I haven't spoken to him in so long." Natalie missed Buck, actually. She missed his kindness and his devotion to her mother and his efforts to bond with them, even if they did go largely spurned. Natalie couldn't see the point in opening old wounds by asking Buck how her mom had died. The reason didn't matter now. Her mother wasn't coming back.

"Hmm." Kit squinted. "Maybe you'd feel better if you saw him."

Natalie shrugged. "I think the time for reconciling with him or my mother is gone, unfortunately."

Kit frowned, as though he didn't quite buy this.

Her phone rang, thankfully interrupting this uncomfortable conversation. Her heart skittered in her chest. It was Dr. Berkhower. She took a few steps away for privacy.

"Hello?" she asked, trying to sound professional and not overly eager.

"Miss Walker," Dr. Berkhower said. "I got your message."

"Yes—thank you. I'm still in Santa Cruz, and I wanted to know if the job illustrating for you is something that might still be available." She crossed her fingers.

"Hmm. I had a glorious specimen in two days ago. A harbor seal with the head sheared straight off."

"Oh, ah," she said, murmuring what she hoped was a delighted sound.

"You said you have a degree in scientific illustration, correct?"

"What? No. Unfortunately not."

"Oh." He paused long enough for a sheen of worry sweat to break out across her neck. "Well. That's usually one of the job requirements."

Natalie mentally kicked herself hard for not taking the leap and enrolling in the Rhode Island School of Design's program back when she could. She'd wasted her time at Argo & Pock.

"I see," she said, trying to keep her tone calm. "Well, I'm, um, looking into CSU Monterey's illustration program." She would now, anyway.

"Oh?" She could almost see Dr. Berkhower's eyebrows go up. "Please let me know when you've done that, will you?"

"I will. Thank you." It was something. A little something.

"And Natalie?"

"Yes?"

"Tell your brother, when you find him, that my microscope is off-limits." The call ended.

A jolt of surprise hit her. Had Jake called Dr. Berkhower? Had he been in touch? Had he asked him for his microscope? That would mean that what Dr. Lawrence had said was true.

That would mean Asier was using Natalie to get to Dr. Berkhower's microscope.

Hurt overwhelmed her. She dashed off a text to Asier even as alarm bells in her head told her not to: Sorry I couldn't help you with the microscope. I know that was important to you.

And then it hit her: the job with Dr. Berkhower was off the table. If she wanted to be a professional scientific illustrator, she needed formal education in it.

She walked back to where Kit waited.

"Aunt Natalie, what happened?" Kit asked.

Natalie felt the sudden craving for the soothing comfort of bread. "I feel like we need some croissants."

"Croissants? It's three in the afternoon."

"I know, but there's never a bad time for carbs."

Kit made a lip-smacking sound. "Yeah. Little flaky butter rolls."

"Bread dreams."

"Crescent-shaped delights."

"Buttery reveries."

"Delicious all-day snacks."

They smiled, and for a tiny moment, Natalie felt a little lighter. She'd take it.

— — —

Somehow, between procuring croissants and getting waylaid in a surf shop that Kit wanted to look in, they got home near dinnertime. Asier had not replied to her text, which she was glad about. Or not glad about, because maybe he'd recognized the petulance in it and been disgusted. She had no idea what to think anymore.

"Oh!" Natalie's heart stopped when she turned on the light in the kitchen and saw Lynn sitting alone at the kitchen table.

"You tried to enroll Kit in school?" Lynn asked in a quiet tone that historically struck a chord of terror in Natalie's heart and typically prefaced a yelling session from Lynn, possibly followed by door-slamming and sometimes kicking. "The school called me to let me know I still had to submit Kit's documents to complete enrollment."

"Well," Natalie said. "Um. I was trying to help. School starts next week." Every word sounded awful, because it was.

"You are something else," Lynn said in the same deadly calm tone. "Really. You almost had me fooled."

Kit, who had come in behind Natalie, headed up the back stairs like a rabbit diving into a warren.

"I don't really see what the problem is. You're sticking around in Santa Cruz, aren't you?" Natalie said. She threw her bag on the counter and filled a big glass with water.

"Allen is the problem. Him finding us here."

Natalie's heart began to pound. "How? Being registered for school doesn't alert the authorities or ping some database. And how does he not already know where you are? This is your childhood house."

Lynn shook her head, unable to speak. "He thinks I'm from San Francisco. I said I grew up in the Tenderloin. I never told him about this place."

Natalie eyed her. "It doesn't seem likely that he'll find out where Kit is registered. There have got to be hundreds of schools in the area."

"He'll know when transcripts are pulled. Did you tell the school he had no transcripts?"

"No, I—"

"You should've said there were no transcripts! Now Allen will find out. He'll have connected with the admin at Kit's school in Brooklyn and asked to be notified if they're pulled and where they're sent!"

"That's not—"

"I assure you. If you'd met him, you'd know."

"I'm so sorry. I didn't mean to— Is there anything I can do?"

Lynn threw her the most contemptuous of withering looks. "You can stop making assumptions about my kid and my situation."

"Did he—did he ever threaten you?"

"Of course he did." Lynn kept her voice a hiss, and her eyes darted to the door to watch for Kit. "He's always threatened me. He told me he'd kill me if I didn't marry him. He told me he'd kill me if I divorced him. He told me he'd kill me if I blew my nose one more time when I had the flu."

"Lynn. I'm so sorry." Natalie's heart dropped, hating that she might have brought danger to Lynn and Kit.

"Right, me too. But back to the issue of you only being home a few weeks and already screwing me over."

"I didn't know—"

"You didn't think. Like when you called the cops that night all those years ago. Jake and I—we can't get over that."

Natalie stared at her, stunned with hurt. She'd thought they were making progress. They'd shared some laughs and were beginning to have real conversations.

"What can I do? To make it right?"

Lynn laughed again, louder. "What have you *ever* done to make things right?"

"I tried to find you. I wrote letters. I—I came out here even though I didn't know what you would say if you saw me. I stayed away for fifteen years."

Lynn clapped slowly, sarcastically. "Hooray for you, Natalie." She shook her head. "I knew this would happen. I was waiting for this moment, honestly. I was waiting for the old Natalie to show herself. And here we are. It's all about you, isn't it? Swooping in like a savior aunt, enrolling Kit in school without my permission. Are you trying to steal the house for yourself too?"

"No!" Hot tears seeped out of Natalie's eyes, part shame, part anguish. "That's not it at all!"

"It wouldn't surprise me at all." Lynn sagged in her chair, the fight suddenly leaving her body. "There is nothing left for you here, do you understand? Just go. Somewhere else. I can't look at you right now."

This was exactly what her mother had said to her, Natalie remembered. Right after Lynn and Jake had been arrested.

"You sound like Mom," Natalie sobbed.

"Maybe she had a point. This is not working. I know you wanted to think it was." Lynn hauled herself to her feet. "I don't think Jake's coming back. I think you should really consider going back to Boston." And without a look back, Lynn clomped heavily up the back stairs, each footstep sounding like a final judgement.

CHAPTER 22

Patrick the green anole lizard had died sometime in the night.

He lay on his back, bulbous eyes closed, quite stiff. Natalie swallowed and slumped, thinking back and trying to remember where she'd failed him. He'd been fed regularly—she'd run out of crickets and hadn't remembered to get more, but he'd seemed happy enough to eat the backup processed reptile food she gave him. Had she forgotten to change his water? Maybe. Maybe he was old. Either way, it was hard not to feel like him dying was a comment on her as a human being.

Downstairs, no hot coffee awaited her. Kit wasn't around, and the kitchen was dark. Natalie leaned against the counter and realized it was Saturday again, and that meant not only had she been in Santa Cruz for four weeks but that today was brunch with Michelle and Yasmin and Cara. Natalie didn't think she could muster the cheer it would require.

Can't make brunch today, she texted Michelle. Sorry. Next time.

Even though there might not be a next time. She slunk down the hall, trailing a hand along the old wallpaper. Sunshine streamed into the foyer through the stained glass in the front door, lighting up the redwood and making it feel rich and cozy, so at odds with how Natalie felt. When she had arrived here from Boston, she hadn't thought about staying in Santa Cruz. It hadn't been an option. She'd had an entire life back in Boston.

Now she'd managed to quash her possibilities on both coasts.

Her heart ached. A deep, physical hole. She hated what she had done here, hated that she hadn't been able to overcome Lynn's wariness of her. Hated that she'd failed her family again.

Her phone buzzed with a notification, no doubt Michelle telling her that was nonsense and to come to brunch. Natalie went back upstairs and sank into her sleeping bag, missing the soothing softness of Penguin's fur, badly missing his friendship and his habit of sticking his stupid wet nose on her when he wanted more pets. She even missed the disemboweled critters he presented to her. Her phone pinged again, and then again. With a groan, she pulled it out of her pocket.

Get over yourself, Michelle's text said. We'll see you at 10.

Followed by: Don't even bother replying no.

And one from Asier: I heard from Jake! He emailed me to say his flight is on Wednesday out of SFO and he wished me well running the lab. No other info. Sorry 🙁

The text from him wasn't clipped or angry sounding, which was something. Only the thought of how pathetic it would be to wallow all day in her sleeping bag compelled Natalie to get dressed for brunch. She wrapped Patrick in a tissue and buried him in the backyard under one of her mother's desiccated rosebushes before driving to the restaurant.

There was only one space remaining in the parking lot, crammed in at the end of a row under a tree with a sizeable stain of bird guano underneath it and active twittering in the branches. Natalie got out and breathed deep. The restaurant was perched on a cliff near one of the beaches, and the smell of salt and sunscreen wafted by her. She closed her eyes against the wan sunshine and wished things were different. She wanted to stay in Santa Cruz and illustrate decomposing sea mammals. She would like to never again look up a Sanborn map or write another historic structure and cultural landscape report.

She was halfway to the door of the restaurant when she remembered she'd forgotten her phone in the car. She turned back and retraced her steps to the entrance—and the back of her neck went cold. Asier and Dr. Lawrence were at the door, going into the restaurant. What were they doing here, now, of all the restaurants in Santa Cruz? What were they doing meeting on a weekend? Didn't they see enough of each other in the lab all week?

Natalie scrambled for her phone, intent on texting Michelle and saying that she was sorry, but she absolutely could not join them, but her fingers wouldn't work, and she mistyped "absolutely" as "absolurky." She backspaced and tried again and it came out "absolutyky," and autocorrect accepted it, so she gave up, deleted it all, and put her phone away. She would go inside like an adult and ignore Asier and Dr. Lawrence.

Inside, Cara saw her and waved her over, standing and using her whole arm. Natalie ducked her head, as if that would hide her from any other diners who were now looking her way. Asier and Dr. Lawrence were not in sight.

"Girl," Michelle greeted her, pulling a straw out of her mouth, "I am so glad I didn't have to drag you out of that old mansion and pull you down here myself."

Natalie kissed her friend on the cheek. "You smell good."

"It's love." Michelle's eyes glimmered, and just as Natalie was about to ask her if she had an eye infection, she held out her hand and presented a whopper of a diamond ring.

"Oh. My. God." Natalie hugged her. "Michelle! Congratulations!"

"You see why you had to be here," Michelle said.

"Heck yeah." Natalie wiped her own glimmery eyes. Imagine moping at home, performing elaborate funeral rites for a lizard to cover for how bad she felt about the mess she'd made of things, when she needed to be here celebrating Michelle.

"I want all three of you to be my bridesmaids," Michelle said, which caused more glimmery eyes around the table, and toasts, and more squealing. Natalie did not have the heart to say that she might not be here for the bridesmaid duties and might very well not have the money to fly back for the actual wedding since she now had no job.

Michelle described how her fiancé had proposed, and then Cara talked about wedding venues around Santa Cruz and Yasmin listed off possible catering ideas. And then Michelle turned her Sauron eye on Natalie.

"So, miss," she said. "You're very quiet over there."

"Ah, you know." Natalie took a long sip of her mimosa, but this did not deter Michelle, who only stared and waited. "I was in a funk this morning. Let's not talk about it. This is your day."

Yasmin cleared her throat. "Maybe we forgot to tell you. Cara, did we forget to tell her?"

"I think we did," Cara said, and Michelle nodded.

Natalie rolled her eyes. "What?"

"Saturday morning brunch is therapy for all the week's woes no matter how good anyone else has it," Michelle said. "So out with it."

Natalie's protests were summarily waved away. She gave a quick recap of her breakup with Paul, the encounter with Dr. Lawrence, learning Asier had probably only been using her, that she'd enrolled Kit in school and pissed off Lynn—crushing the progress they'd made, although she wasn't able to articulate how much that one hurt—and that Jake was still MIA and leaving for New Zealand on Wednesday.

"And," she said, sighing, "those two are here now. In this restaurant. They came in right before me."

"Wait, what?" Cara turned her head so fast that she resembled an owl.

Yasmin stood and looked around with murder in her eyes. Natalie pulled her down. "How dare she suggest he's using you to get a microscope!"

"Is that them over there?" Michelle asked, pointing discreetly (thankfully) at a corner table.

"Stop, please," Natalie begged them. "I—I don't even know what I'm doing."

"You're staying in Santa Cruz," Michelle said.

"Let her figure it out," Cara said. "She has a whole life in Boston."

Michelle popped a piece of bread in her mouth. "You going to accost Jake at the airport?"

"I'm not sure. But at least I know where he'll be Wednesday." Natalie wasn't sure of anything. She pictured herself running down a long corridor at the airport toward his gate, shouting his name, jumping over security barriers. It felt like the finale in her own TV series, and then she'd have to get in the car and drive back to real life. A new chapter in which maybe she and Teensy weren't as close as before and she'd have to find a new job, play the dating field again, and possibly get a new place to live. Her heart sank.

"Hmm," Michelle said.

All three heads turned her way. "What, 'hmm'?" Natalie asked, suspicious.

"Did you talk to your mom's partner?"

"Buck?" Natalie frowned. "No. But he wouldn't know where Jake is. He and Jake hated each other."

Michelle's left eyebrow went up, and she made a high-pitched *I don't know about that* sound.

"Buck wouldn't know where he is," Natalie said. "Trust me."

"But you haven't seen or spoken to Buck?" Michelle asked.

"You didn't even call your mom's partner?" Cara asked.

"Where does Buck live?" Yasmin asked.

"Felton." Natalie glared at them for pushing this. Also, the urge to turn and look at the back corner table again was fierce. It was distracting knowing Asier was here, in the same room.

"That's, like, five minutes away," Yasmin pointed out. "I think you should go up there."

Natalie shrugged. She'd known in the very pit of her stomach since she'd arrived in Santa Cruz that she should go, if only to tell Buck that she was sorry her mother—his partner—had passed. But she didn't want to be *told* to go.

"Oh, your scientist is getting up," Michelle said, her gaze on the table in the corner. "He's mighty fine."

Natalie used every ounce of her willpower not to turn and look and stared at her plate instead.

Michelle giggled. "You are definitely hung up on him."

Natalie lost the fight with her willpower and looked. Asier was crossing the room, maybe heading toward the restroom. He had not seen them—or at least he wasn't reacting like he had. All four of them watched his progress.

"I mean, I get what you see in him, that's for sure," Yasmin said as Asier disappeared around a corner.

Talk turned to Cara's new home and the issues she was having with the plumbing, unforeseen in the purchase process, when the conversation hushed again. Natalie looked and saw Asier making his way back across the restaurant. This time he saw her, and there was the barest crinkle in the corners of his eyes. And then—yes. That smile. That megawatt, western seaboard–powering smile. For her.

Reluctantly, she waved. He waved back. Lifted an eyebrow. Walked toward their table. Yasmin, Cara, and Michelle sat up straight.

"Hello, Natalie," he said. "How nice to see you here."

"Hello, Asier," she said, matching his formal tone. "Likewise. Thanks for your text about Jake. Any chance you asked him to contact me? I've been leaving him messages."

"Oh, I did. He didn't reply." He shrugged and extended a little wave to the rest of her friends, and Natalie knew she should introduce them, but she was nervous. Then it occurred to her that if she didn't, he would say, "Well, great to see you" and leave, and that simply could not happen.

"These are my friends Michelle and Cara and Yasmin," Natalie said. Teensy's friendship had always been her anchor in Boston, the thing that kept her feeling safe and loved. But maybe these strong, supportive women could provide that too, just as deeply.

"Hello, friends," Asier said, stunning them with his smile.

"Hellooo," her friends answered in unison.

"Nice morning for brunch," Asier said.

"It is. I see Dr. Lawrence over there," Natalie said before she could stop herself. Now he would know she had been watching him.

"Ah. Yes. We are here to talk more about microscopes!"

"Compound fluorescence ones, I bet," Natalie said, forcing herself to sound cheery.

"Yes." He laughed as though this was a joke. "You know how it is. Polarization and pH contrast."

"Natalie's an expert in *chemical developments*," Michelle said. Natalie kicked her under the table.

Asier smiled, but his cheeks might have turned a little red. "I had better get back to my meal. Friends, nice to meet you." He gave a little bow and then departed.

There was a moment of stunned silence at the table.

"Holy fucking shit," Michelle said.

"I mean," Cara muttered.

"Microscopes," Yasmin said. "Is that what it is?"

Natalie's face burned.

"He is not using you for a microscope. I hope you know that," Michelle said.

"Oh God, no, honey. No," Yasmin agreed.

"Not unless he means something else by microscope." Cara waggled her eyebrows suggestively.

Yasmin nodded. "Oh, he means that."

"Oh my God." Natalie covered her face with her hands. The images from her dreams of naked Asier doing unspeakable things to her appeared. She did her best to shake them away. "Maybe he's just nice about it, but I think he really does want me to help him get a microscope."

Cara snorted. "No one smiles at someone like that for scientific equipment."

"He said so himself," Natalie mumbled. "Twice." She jerked of her head in the direction of Asier and Dr. Lawrence's table. "And the evidence shows the two of them are over there plotting."

"Listen," Michelle said. "Your brother is leaving on Wednesday. Focus on that right now. Focus on the fact that he has finally been in touch with someone."

Cara and Yasmin murmured their agreement.

"And go see Buck too," Michelle said. "Like, today."

Natalie nodded, but she wasn't so sure. "I mean—"

Michelle put a hand on Natalie's arm, and with the touch, Natalie's defenses fell away. Of *course* she should have reached out to Buck long ago. Of course. She'd been here four weeks, operating on the same old principles of assuming people didn't need to hear from her because of the past. But everyone had moved forward. It was time she did too.

"Fine," she muttered.

"Good." Michelle looked satisfied. "*Now* we can talk about wedding stuff."

CHAPTER 23

When Natalie was twelve, the Walkers and Buck took a family camping trip. Although her mother and Buck had been together for two years at that point and Buck had been living with them for the better part of a year, tensions ran high. Jake was a raging ball of fury.

"It's going to be fun. Hot dogs!" their mother sang. "Roasted marsh-mallows on a stick! We'll set them on fire and blow them out and make s'mores. Family time!"

"This is stupid," Jake muttered. He was sixteen, and all their mother's attempts at family time with Buck were met with hostility. Buck couldn't have known that camping was sacred to Jake. Some of his best memories of their father were of their family trips to Big Basin, a state park in the Santa Cruz Mountains.

"It may be stupid, but you're coming with us," Buck told him.

"Nope," Jake said. He had been challenging Buck all summer, and each time, Natalie had watched wide-eyed, a ball of anxiety in her stomach. She wanted to like Buck. She wanted Buck to be their dad. They needed one—their mother was dizzy, forgetful, and ungrounded without a partner, and she'd been none of these things since Buck had arrived on the scene. Natalie would never say so to Lynn and Jake, but she was vastly relieved that now, with Buck around, their mother made dinner every night, packed their lunches, and took an interest in their schoolwork— even if she was emotionally remote, especially to her. Although there was a sense that they were fine on their own, the family undeniably benefitted from Buck's gentle presence.

Jake ended up coming on the camping trip, maybe because of some threat issued behind closed doors, or maybe he'd decided not to abandon his sisters. Natalie didn't care either way. She was happy to go back to the redwoods as a family.

They camped at the same campground they'd used to when their dad was alive. It was their mother's way—however misguided—of trying to connect the present to the past.

"There's a trail near here to a waterfall," Jake told Natalie and Lynn. He glanced nervously at Buck and kept his voice low. Their mother, who had said she had a stomachache, was napping in the tent. Buck was supposed to be watching them. Jake shoved a few sandwiches in a pack and hoisted it onto his shoulders. "Let's go."

It sounded exciting. Who didn't want to see a waterfall? The trail was spectacular. They crossed a giant fallen redwood over a river, using it as a bridge. Natalie remembered being scared of the steep drop on either side of the tree, but Jake had come back and held her hand as they crossed.

"Are you sure this tree is strong enough to walk on?" Lynn asked.

"Yeah. Look how worn it is." Jake pointed at the path. "Lots of people come this way. Scout's honor."

Jake had never been a Boy Scout. Lynn stopped complaining and instead wore a sour grimace, one of her favorites, but even this disappeared when they came upon the boulders and the waterfall. It splashed down into pools between the massive piles of rock. Jake tried to help Lynn (who shrugged him off) before extending a hand to Natalie, and they climbed higher, above the pines. The path, less worn now, was a steep ascent. Without the shade of the trees, the sun beat down on them. They ate lunch on a large flat rock overlooking the forest like a balcony. They were on top of the whole Santa Cruz Mountains—on top of everything. No one could touch them up there.

"Do you think Buck noticed we're gone?" Natalie asked.

"Who cares?" Lynn said.

"Mom might care a little," Jake said. "But she's busy napping."

"Do you think she's *ever* cared about us?" Natalie asked. This was a silly question, even she knew that, but she wanted to show that she was firmly on Jake's side.

"Of course she cares about us," Lynn said. "She's just had a hard life."

"Yeah, so hard living in a Victorian mansion," Jake muttered.

"Yeah," Natalie said, again in loyal support of her big brother. She loved that they were sitting together like this with no one around them for what felt like miles. No one to correct their anger or tell them in hissed undertones to be nice. Nothing but endless trees as far as she could see, even though she knew the ocean was beyond the biggest hill.

"That's not really fair," Lynn said. "Wasn't Mom, like, eighteen when her parents died?"

Jake shrugged. He cut their mother no slack.

"Imagine being all alone in that house," Natalie said, "with no one to help."

"She told me she wanted to go to college," Lynn said. "But obviously she couldn't."

"Maybe she didn't really want to go to college," Jake said, throwing a pebble off the rock shelf.

"That's why she married Dad so young," Natalie said. "Can we stay up here forever?" Sitting up here above the tree line, they were the closest they'd been to peaceful in a long time.

"Sure. That's my plan." Jake's dream was to hide away. He often said that when he grew up, he was going to have a cabin by himself in the woods where no one could yammer at him or ask him questions or annoy him.

They lay on the boulders, warming themselves like a bunch of lazy sea lions, until a frantic crackling of twigs from below caught their attention. They sat up, glancing nervously at each other and the path, out of sight past the lowest boulder. Something was coming—too loud to be a little creature.

"Mountain lion," Lynn whispered, and a bolt of fear shot through Natalie.

"Shh," Jake said and gestured for his sisters to get behind him. They scooted away, out of view of the path.

The mountain lion turned out to be Buck. "Kids!" He stopped, wiping sweat from his brow and out of breath from the hike—he was a large man at six foot three. "Jake!"

Jake held a finger to his lips to keep Lynn and Natalie quiet.

"Natalie!" Buck shouted. "Kids! Come on! This is an emergency! Your mom is hurt!"

The three of them exchanged a glance, conceding defeat, and came out.

Buck's large frame sagged with relief to see them. "Thank God. Kids, your mom is sick. Real sick. Some campers at the next site had to take her to the hospital. We think it's her appendix."

Natalie didn't know what that meant, but the fear that zipped through her was thick and immediate.

The three of them clambered down the boulders and made their way carefully back along the path after Buck. It amazed Natalie that he'd found them. It didn't occur to her to ask him how until days later, after the drama of their mother's emergency appendectomy was over.

"I kept an eye on where you were headed," he answered simply. "Wanted to make sure you were safe."

She realized years later that Buck, instead of taking their mother to the hospital himself, had stayed behind to make sure he found them so they wouldn't be on their own. Like other small examples of his compassion and kindness over the years, Natalie had tucked them out of sight. They'd been inconvenient because they contradicted Jake's anger, which she tried to side with.

"He ruins everything," Jake muttered later. "I was going to stay in the woods forever."

She knew Jake was exaggerating, but she understood that what he meant was, he felt peace in Big Basin, maybe the kind of peace that eluded every other corner of his life.

"But he helped us out," Natalie whispered later to herself, when Jake wouldn't hear her.

— — —

After brunch, Natalie drove back to the house. She pushed open the giant front door, wondering how many more times she would touch this door before leaving. If she left.

Penguin ran down the hall toward her, tail up in greeting, as though he'd been waiting for her there the whole time.

"You little stinker!" she squealed in delight. She plunked her phone on the stair post, bent down, and opened her arms. He came to her, rubbing his cheeks on her shins and hopping into her hands. She straightened with him in her arms, sinking into his luxurious purr. "Where have you been? You had me so worried."

His white patches of fur weren't totally white, as though he'd been crawling through some dirty places. He rammed his face against hers and cuddled under her chin. She realized she was crying when she felt wetness on his fur where he'd rubbed against her cheek.

"Hey," Kit said, coming down the stairs. "Wow! Penguin! You found him!"

"He found me," she said, tucking her face into his fur.

Kit stroked Penguin's side. The cat curved into Kit's hand, showing how much he liked him. Natalie remembered the first day when Kit had managed to get Penguin out of the wall so easily. The cat certainly had his favorite people.

"You wouldn't be so love-starved if you hadn't stayed away so long," Natalie whispered. In response, Penguin gave a loud "rrrt," a clear admission of his guilt.

After a moment that was entirely filled with Penguin's loud purrs, Natalie asked Kit, "You busy? Do you want to come see Buck with me, if your mom agrees?" She would not do anything with Kit without asking Lynn from now on.

Kit's eyes went to hers, surprise on his face. "Buck? Your mom's husband?"

"Well, they weren't married, but yeah."

"You're going to see him?"

Now that Natalie had realized she needed to see Buck, she couldn't remember what her original objections had been. She told Kit, "Yeah. Now. Today."

He grinned. "I don't know why you and my mom haven't gone to see him already."

Natalie frowned. This kid with his old-man wisdom!

"I mean, we had to come around to it," she said. Penguin agreed, pushing his head under her chin again.

"Well, let's go," Kit said. "I want to know more about my grandmother."

"She picked sides against her kids," Natalie said. "She couldn't handle our flaws. She didn't want me to come home and visit. Not since I went to college. Buck won't reveal anything about her that we don't already know."

Kit rolled his eyes. "I think Buck will have different things to say."

"Have you eaten?" She checked her watch—a maneuver Penguin tried to prevent by latching on to her arm and pulling it toward his mouth—and saw that it was almost noon. "Where's your mom?"

"In the kitchen. And yes, I would like lunch."

Still carrying Penguin, Natalie went down the hall to the kitchen, where Lynn sat reading with a mug.

"Lynn?"

"Hmm?" Lynn looked up briefly, glaring. "I see you found your cat."

"I was thinking of going to see Buck today."

Lynn snapped her head back up and studied her. "With the cat?"

"Not with the cat." She put Penguin down. "But I'd like to take Kit with me, if you agree."

Lynn narrowed her eyes slightly at her, as though on the verge of yelling *absolutely not*. But she un-narrowed, took a drink from her mug, and said, to Natalie's surprise, "If he wants."

"Okay. Great. And I want you to know I'll ask you first before doing anything concerning Kit again."

Lynn rolled her eyes. "Only the important things like school enrollment, please."

"He says he'd like lunch too, so if it's okay, I'll stop and get him lunch."

"He already *ate* lunch. A half hour ago."

Natalie laughed.

Lynn made a shooing motion. "Go."

Natalie brushed cat hair off her shirt, but not too vigorously. It had been a while since she had been covered in it and realized she had kind of missed it. "Okay. Thanks."

Lynn grunted. Penguin ran ahead of Natalie back to the foyer, where Kit waited.

"We're all set," Natalie told him. "Ready?"

"Shyeah." Kit grabbed his shoes from the base of the stairs as Natalie admonished Penguin to stay in sight from now on. The cat bounded away down the hall as though to say he'd always been here, right here, if she'd only looked harder.

— — —

They were almost on the freeway when Natalie realized she'd forgotten her phone at the house. She could pictured exactly where she'd set it on the post of the stairs. They would have to go back and get it. It wouldn't hurt to stall a little more. She turned the car around, and they were almost home when Kit caught on to her delay tactics and said, "Come on, Aunt Natalie. This isn't Felton."

She laughed. "I forgot my phone is all."

In response, he made an impressive Lynn-like snort.

"I'll be quick, and we'll be on our way," she said as she turned into their driveway.

A black, newish sedan with a rental car company sticker on it was parked in front of the house.

"Oh," Kit said. "Who's that?"

Natalie's response dried in her throat. She stared at the car. Paul. It had to be Paul. He'd done exactly what she'd told him not to do. Feeling outraged, she wanted to go in there, right now, and tell him to leave and never speak to her again. She couldn't *believe* he'd flown out here.

"Aunt Natalie?" Kit prompted.

"It's Paul," she said. "My ex-boyfriend." He'd texted her earlier that morning with See you soon, which she had ignored because she wasn't going to see him soon. But now she saw what he'd meant.

Kit looked worried.

"No, he's—he's not violent," she said, and something cracked in her as Kit's face relaxed. "He's super annoying though, and I don't want to see him right now."

Kit raised his eyebrows. "We don't need your phone. I have mine. Let's go see Buck."

In answer, she put the car in reverse.

CHAPTER 24

On the windy road to Felton, Kit asked Natalie more questions about his new school and whether he should get a bike or a skateboard and if the kids would care about his Brooklyn accent.

"You don't *have* a Brooklyn accent," Natalie said. She was trying not to let Paul ruin her mood, but it was hard. He was a complete and total fuckwit, coming out here like this.

"I don't?"

"I don't notice it. Maybe a tiny one. It sounds nice. You'll be fine."

Kit went on and on about a video game shop he'd discovered in the downtown mall area, how they had a little museum of old consoles and sold used games for obsolete systems as well as new games.

"Jake had every Nintendo console," Natalie said. "When he got older and didn't play as much, your mom and I used to have Mario Kart tournaments all night."

"I actually found a box with his systems in the attic yesterday. Mom said I could take it down."

Natalie was going to say that she would love to have a Mario Kart fest with him, but the words died in her throat. She'd be gone in a matter of days.

A few minutes later, they arrived in Felton, driving past a long row of small businesses housed in buildings made to look like old-timey Wild West storefronts. It was part of Felton's logging past and small-town charm, she supposed. Kit navigated them to Russell Avenue, where he'd found a Bernard Howard on the internet.

"That's him," Natalie said. "He is a Bernard. And I'm pretty sure he and my mother lived on Russell."

"I can see why he goes by Buck," Kit said.

"Like Buck's any better."

"Name five really bad male names," Kit said.

"Easy. Bernard, Harold, Maurice, Herbert, and Humperdinck."

Kit laughed, which made Natalie press her lips together against the pain. She'd miss his laugh.

"I think it's that yellow house." He pointed across the dashboard at a run-down one-story home. Rusted machinery filled the scraggly yard, and the faded sign with a barely visible WELCOME! on it hung askew from the once-white porch posts, now a dingy gray.

Two cars filled the driveway. One was a newer Audi, but the other, a faded red Civic, looked like it didn't run anymore. Natalie took it all in. "That red car. That was my mother's."

"At least we know it's the right house."

Behind them, a rusty pickup truck idled in the street. Natalie turned her wheel and moved her car to the side of the road so it could pass, but it parked in front of the house.

"Crap," Natalie said. "That's him."

Buck started to get out of his truck, moving with the slowness of someone who ached with age. His hair was all white, and he'd put on a lot of weight. It was less of a shock to see him after all these years than Natalie thought it would be; he was still Buck. The part she couldn't wrap her head around was that her mother was not here with him anymore.

Wow.

Her mother was gone. Natalie would never be able to talk to her again. She stared, her mouth dropping open a little.

Buck slammed his truck door with effort.

"This is all wrong," Natalie said.

"Pop," Kit said.

She gave him a look meant to convey that this pop thing was tiresome when meeting people you hadn't seen in years and might not be sure of their reaction, but there was no way to say that with a look, and anyway, it was endearing.

"Pop," she said, resigned.

Kit opened the car door and stepped out, which was hugely annoying because it meant she had to get out too.

Buck stood in his driveway, a plastic bag in his hands with the clear shape of a six-pack inside, looking at Kit. His face pulled back in a mask of hope, horror, and surprise. Natalie got out of her car and came to stand next to Kit.

"Patty?" Buck said, voice uncertain, full of far too much hope.

"It's Natalie." Did she look that much like her mother? The thought sobered her.

His face dropped, but then sense seemed to clear it. "Natalie. My word. Is it really?"

She stepped forward onto his driveway. The only sounds were the distant outraged screech of a scrub jay and the truck ticking as the engine cooled. "Yeah."

"I'll be." He stared at her, taking her in. "I'd run over to you, but my legs don't move like that anymore." He held out his arms, unsteady and wobbly.

Of the three of them, Natalie had spent the most time with Buck, especially during the hazy time between Lynn and Jake going to prison and her leaving for college in Boston. Before the arrests, she had liked him—been fond of him, even—although she never would've told her siblings that. He had gotten up early to make her breakfast, and he had often given her money to go to the movies. He could be funny and nice when they weren't being jerks to him, and it was obvious he adored their mother.

And her mother had been less myopic and numb to the world with him there. Buck was the one who had taken Natalie aside and told her it was bad luck that Lynn and Jake had been sentenced, but for her own sake, she should try not to dwell on That Night. He had told her, "I know it's hard, kiddo. It's never not gonna be hard. You make mistakes, and you move on, and you try better next time. That's how you live."

Buck wasn't perfect. Their mother certainly hadn't been either. He hadn't always said or done the right things, but he had taken care of them. All of the things she held against her mother—her failure to parent Natalie in the face of Lynn and Jake going to prison, her encouragement of Natalie to move far away—were simply things her mother had not been good at. But what if her mother had known that about herself and seen that Buck had those strengths and could be the reliable fixture in her kids' lives? And that by being with Buck, she was also better?

It was that realization that made Natalie move across the driveway and into Buck's welcoming arms.

His arms were clumsy, his balance poor, but he hugged her tight. "And who's this?" he asked eventually. "I thought it was a young Jake at first, but of course that can't be true."

Natalie smiled and willed back a tear. "This is Kit. He's Lynn's son."

Buck stared at Kit with delight. "Pleased to meet you, Kit." He shook Kit's hand.

"Nice to meet you, Grandpa Buck," Kit said.

Buck threw his head back and roared with laughter. "Grandpa Buck, huh? All right. I'll take it. I'll take that just fine." He looked around. "Where's Lynn?"

"She's back at the house," Natalie said.

Buck shook his head in the manner of one who couldn't believe all these developments. "I can't believe you're here. I really can't."

"I'm sorry to show up out of the blue," Natalie said.

Buck looked at her fondly. "You're not imposing, sweetheart. Come inside." He glanced at Kit. "I've got some pop, if you want." He turned to go in, the plastic bag swinging in his hand.

"Pop," Kit mouthed at her.

"Pop," she whispered back.

— — —

Buck's house was dark, despite the open windows. Heavy yellow drapes framed what light there was. Oversize plush furniture jammed the small living room, forcing Natalie to maneuver around it all to make her way through.

Buck motioned vaguely with his hand toward the couch. "I got Coke, and I got Sprite."

"Coke, please," Kit called.

Natalie sat on the couch, falling into the cushions. Kit sat next to her.

Buck brought in a two-liter bottle of Coke with two glasses and put them on the coffee table before falling heavily into a large chair across from them and folding his wrinkled hands. His knuckles were big, arthritic, swollen knobs. It had been fifteen years since Natalie had seen Buck, but she was still surprised to see him so aged.

Natalie looked around the room, trying to picture her mother living here, moving around all the furniture. Alive. "I wish I'd spoken to her before she died."

Buck nodded, knowing immediately who she was referring to. "It was a real hard time."

"I'm sure." Natalie waited for more, but it was clear she was going to have to draw it out of him. "Was...was it fast?"

"Like lightning. It spread into other organs before we could even deal with the first thing. Wasn't pretty, but she was practical about it."

"She left the house to me and Lynn and Jake."

"I know. We were in total agreement on that."

Natalie didn't know how to manage the grief that was sparking in her like fireflies, bursting on and off in every direction, and then sinking like lead weights. "There are some silly terms of the trust, like that we all have to be there together in order to inherit the house or else it goes to the historical society."

Buck nodded slowly. "Her way of making you three get together again."

Natalie twisted her mouth. "Jake's still missing."

Buck frowned. "I wouldn't say Jake's missing. He's just not there."

"Right, true," she said. "But we don't know where he is, and that's the problem."

"He's going to come back, don't worry." Buck bobbed his head again, as though agreeing with himself.

Natalie eyed him. "Do you know something? Is he staying away because I'm here?"

Buck waved his hand. "It's not because of you, honey. Jake really took your mom's death hard. He needed some time away from everything. There was a whole bunch of stuff going on, and he needed a break."

"Okay." Natalie took a breath. "Do you know where he is?"

Kit sat up straight, as though he'd been waiting for this part.

"He's here," Buck said, tapping a bloated finger on the worn arm of the chair.

Natalie stared at him in surprise, then looked around as though Jake might jump out of the wall.

"Not currently," Buck amended. "He's gone on one of his long hikes, but he'll be back later tonight, likely. Sometimes he camps out for the night, so I'm not sure."

"Jake's been staying with you? But you hate Jake." Natalie couldn't believe Jake had been right under their noses, staying with Buck, this entire time.

"I never hated him." Buck shook his head. "He was a tough teenager, no doubt about that. But he was dealing with grief over your dad dying, and I know I didn't make it easy when I moved in. But nah, hate never figured into it. He's been helpful to me. After…you know. Patty."

She had to break eye contact and study her hands to ward off the sadness. "I'm sorry, Buck. I'm really sorry."

Buck nodded, his eyes wet. "She fought hard, you know. Talked about you three a lot at the end."

"Was she sad that Natalie and my mom never came home?" Kit

asked. Natalie threw him a look, worried that he was going too hard for the big stuff.

Buck gave a sad smile. "Direct, like your uncle. Yeah, she was sad, truth be told. She regretted how she handled things and really regretted not knowing you, Kit."

"She told me not to come back," Natalie pointed out.

"She didn't think you'd listen. Santa Cruz is your home, after all. You have to understand that she had regrets. She made a lot of assumptions—that it would all work out in the end, I guess, and that you three would come together eventually. Since she wouldn't be around to see that happen herself, she engineered it in her will."

Natalie too was a champion assumer: about work, men, her siblings, her mother—even Buck, that he wouldn't want to see her. The old adage about *making an ass out of u and me* came to mind. Natalie was going to be super pissed if she'd stayed away all these years because she'd assumed her mother meant it. But then again, maybe Natalie had needed to stay away in order to think of it as home again.

"Her dream was to see all you kids together again," Buck said, worrying the arm of his chair. "She wanted that so much. I said we ought to call you, but Patty... She felt ashamed for the way she'd acted. She died ashamed too."

Natalie didn't know what to say to that.

"Did Jake see her?" she asked.

"He did see her, yeah. At the end. You have to understand that she tried to prevent it. And he wasn't too keen either, because they'd never resolved things between them. But..." Buck's eyes went unfocused, as though he was remembering the moment. "But they spoke at the end."

Natalie found that she was glad at least one of them had seen her before she'd passed.

"I'm proud of him," Buck said in a husky voice. "Jake's a good man. He applied to college from prison, and I don't think he did anything but study his whole three years in there, and then he went on and got his degrees. He was changed though, you know. You come out of a place like Kern and you're not the same."

"What's Kern?" Kit asked.

"Kern State Prison. It's a level four. Harsh. About as maximum security as the state has. The kid didn't need that. I think he was put in there because he was mouthy at first, got in a few fights. That was beat out of him quick, though. He got through it by keeping his head down. He's a fighter, you know. He wasn't the same when he came out. Didn't talk a lot. Lynn too. They both had such a tough time of it."

"What happened to my mom?" Kit asked, all agog. "After she got out?"

Buck raised his eyebrows and smiled. "We only know what Jake told us, because your mom refused to come to the house after she got out of prison. Spent her parole time somewhere around San Francisco. Jake told us she left the state after her parole was up. Patty wanted to keep up with her, but it was hard. They were both stubborn women."

"But we always knew about you. We were so glad your mom had you."

Natalie wasn't surprised to hear that her sister had dealt with her incarceration in a different way from Jake, but she was sad for her. Lynn and Jake had been close growing up and had shared many of the same friends. She wished they had stayed that way as adults.

Buck took a deep breath, looking tired. He probably didn't talk this much anymore.

"Do you need anything?" Natalie asked.

Buck pushed himself forward in his chair, his arms shaking with the effort. "No, honey." His body had withered, but he still had such animation in his eyes. She wondered if he would make a good portrait sketch. She had never drawn humans, vastly preferring animals, but Buck was a character.

"What do you do, Natalie?" he asked. "How have you kept yourself these years?"

"I sketch," she said. "Animals. I do scientific illustration." She felt a sense of sureness as she spoke the words. She was an artist. That was how it was. She thought about how she'd realized this in Dr. Berkhower's lab, standing over the atrocious sea lion. It was who she had been all along.

"You should see her drawings," Kit said. "Can I show him, Aunt Natalie? Please?"

She began to make noises about how Buck didn't care, but Kit had already pulled her sketchbook from her tote and handed it to Buck. Buck paged through, mostly pausing in the Penguin section. He stopped at a drawing of a fox she'd been working on in Boston, which seemed like another life.

"This is incredible," Buck breathed. "You were always drawing, you know that? But when Patty said you were a little artist, you said no. You'd get so mad about it."

Natalie didn't remember her mother saying that. She did remember drawing throughout her childhood for fun and relaxation, but the drawings had been of random things. She hadn't started drawing animals until she'd taken a biology class in college with a professor who had a passion for dissecting beetles and butterflies. He had offered her access to his drawers of lepidoptera specimens, and she had gotten hooked. But there had been no path at her university then for illustration in biology—or maybe she hadn't looked hard enough or asked enough professors. So she had finished her degree in architecture with a minor in environmental studies, and it had been enough to land her the job at Argo & Pock after graduation.

"I don't know why I said no," she said now.

Buck looked at her, smiling, his eyes a little watery. "Sweetheart. You kids were hurt badly. You had to say no to everything."

So much time lost, so much unnecessary hurt. A knot of misery twisted in Natalie's gut at the thought of what they'd lost. "I would have liked to tell my mom that I was hurt by the lack of contact, but I still loved her."

Buck smiled. "She knew. I promise you."

Natalie couldn't speak.

"Natalie," he said into her silence. "Look at you. Oh, girl. You've been beating yourself raw for years, haven't you?"

To her surprise, she burst into tears. Her heart ached for the lost opportunity to work things out with her mother. And ooh—her chest squeezed when she thought that she'd have time later to work things out. There was no later now.

Buck handed her a tissue and patted her hand with his stiff, liver-spotted one. "Let it out, kiddo."

She did let it out, but only for a moment more. There was snot every-where, and Natalie didn't want to horrify Kit, who looked away.

But also—and surprisingly—now that the tears were out, she felt...better. Clean. She missed her mother. She regretted what had happened. But she didn't feel desperate or like she was carrying a whale-size weight anymore.

"Thank you for being here," she told Buck.

"Jake and Lynn didn't want to hear this back then," he said, "but you three are my kids, and that's no disrespect to your dad. Your mom's pain was my pain, and I was glad to carry it, because it meant I could support her. I admit I came into it without knowing what the heck I was doing. Your brother and sister battled me and punished me for it. And to that I say, fair enough. But kiddo, it is a pleasure having you in my life."

Natalie gritted her teeth, willing herself not to cry again. She held on to Buck's hand, and they clasped each other tight in an understood love.

"Did my mom leave you any money?" she asked. "I'm sorry if that's too personal. It would be awful if you weren't left anything. I want to know that you're taken care of."

"I have this place," Buck said. "It's paid off. Patty had some money that isn't part of the trust, and she left it to me. I'm doing all right. Thanks for asking."

"I need to use the bathroom," Kit said. "Be right back."

"Second door on the left," Buck said.

"I've been looking for Jake for a few weeks," Natalie said. "He was here all the time?"

Buck nodded. "He needed a break from life. He's been finding himself in the woods."

"Is—does he still hate me?"

"Jake does not hate you. Not one bit. You've been carrying that around too?" He huffed air out. "We need to get you to let some of that go."

Oh, goddammit. Tears slipped out of her eyes again. "I already am. Seeing you helps. I'm sorry it took so long."

"Nah." He waved that away. "I wanted to marry your mom, you know."

"I know."

"It was bad enough that I was there, she always said. She didn't want to make things worse for you kids by marrying me. I didn't understand what that meant, but it was her way of trying not to hurt you guys more. In the end, we decided not to mess with a good thing." He nodded to himself, his eyes wet. "It didn't matter. We were happy anyway. She made me laugh, and I think I made her laugh."

"Even though she wasn't very nice at times?" Natalie didn't want to offend his rosy-colored view of her mother, but it had to be said.

He nodded. "No one is perfect. Do you have someone, Nattie? Did you find someone you can't wait to come home and see, even after a long day?"

She had always known that her mother and Buck adored each other, which was partly the reason why it was so painful that her mother had told her stay away. Clearly her mother was capable of tenderness. Just not with her. Her mother and Buck had been absolutely delighted with each other's company every evening, and she wanted that too. It occurred to her that Paul sometimes sat in a funk for several hours if he'd had a bad day. He would refuse to talk to her until bedtime, and she'd hated it. She never wanted to settle for that. Ever.

Natalie had the sudden urge to see Asier's face. Although he'd probably prefer to come home to a microscope than her.

"No," she said. "I don't have someone like that."

"No one?"

"I'm not sure I'd know the right person if I saw him."

"You know how you know it's meant to be?" Buck asked. "Because when you see them, all your organs do little jumps from the adrenaline. It's not only the way they look. It's the way they move and the sound of their voice. And then they speak, and you nearly lose your mind. That's how it works for me. You love every aspect of them. You want to get inside their head and know everything about them. And the thought of losing them tears you up, right here." He pointed to his rib cage. "Like, you really get shredded, you know? Destroyed, I guess—that's not too strong a word, because that's how I felt. If it's happened to you, then you know how it feels, but anyone who hasn't been through a loss can't quite understand. It's just…" He looked at his hands. "A lot of grief. You tell yourself to move on, but you know you never really can."

He wouldn't look at her. It hurt unexpectedly hard to see him grieving. Not to mention that what he'd described was very nearly how she felt about

Asier. Almost. She didn't know him that well. But maybe—maybe if they had a chance, she might realize the full intensity of what Buck was describing.

"I never felt that way about my ex-wife," he added. "But I did about your mom. That was how I knew."

"I'm sorry she wouldn't marry you."

He waved a hand. "Nah. It didn't matter. That she let me be with her and take care of her was enough."

"Was she cremated?"

Buck nodded. "Yeah. I probably talk to the box of her ashes a little too much." He paused. "You want them? I mean, you're her daughter."

Natalie's heart twinged. "No. You keep them."

She could see the relief in his sagging shoulders.

"I'm glad you were there," she said.

"I wish I hadn't listened to her when she said not to call you."

Natalie wished he hadn't either. "She didn't really know me. As an adult."

He smiled, a sad, wistful look. "She thought giving you the house was the least she could do to bring you together to support each other."

"Yeah, that hasn't worked out so well."

Buck stared at his hands. He seemed to be falling into a reverie, perhaps over her mother. Kit reappeared.

"We should probably go," Natalie said. The inevitable meeting with Paul couldn't be put off forever. "Your mom will wonder where we are." At least she knew where Jake was now. It felt anticlimactic, since he wasn't actually here. "Can I get your number? And please have Jake call me. We need to see him before he leaves for New Zealand, especially before I—I go back to Boston."

"Of course." Buck scrabbled in a side table for paper and the stub of a pencil. He scribbled his number out and handed the paper to Natalie.

"That wasn't an easy decision for him, leaving for a year. But I'll let him know. I'll remind him of the urgency."

"Thank you." Natalie stood and kissed Buck's cheek. She didn't think she had ever thanked him or kissed him or shown him any affection.

He gripped her forearm in silent love that she felt loud and clear. "You say you're leaving, but you're a West Coast girl through and through. You can't be happy in Beantown."

She tried to refrain from answering, but he picked it right out of her head. "Oh, you're torn, aren't you? Mm. No matter what you decide, come see me again."

She wrapped her arms around him and hugged him for a long time.

He clung to her, and when the squish of the hug had petered out, he got out of his chair.

"We'll come back," she promised. "Soon."

He hugged Kit, who let him. "I want to hear more from you next time, okay, kid? Less talking from your aunt and more talking from you. I can tell you got things to say. I want to hear them."

Natalie thought Kit would shy away, but to her surprise, he smiled.

When they were back in Natalie's car, she sat for a minute before turning on the engine.

"That did not go like I expected," she said.

Kit laughed. "Really? It went exactly like I expected."

She turned to look at him. "Do you have a grandfather?"

He looked delighted as she turned on the car and they pulled away. "I do now."

CHAPTER 25

Driving down redwood-lined Highway 9 back into Santa Cruz, Natalie felt as though she'd come from a good yoga session rather than a visit to her stepfather, which was how she now referred to him in her mind. The weight of guilt and shame that had plagued her for years was gone, leaving her feeling loose and happy.

That melted away when she pulled up alongside Paul's rental car at home. Lynn's car was also now in the driveway. "I am not looking forward to this." She wished she had her phone so she could text him to get out and avoid the whole mess to begin with.

"We'll tell him to leave," Kit said.

"Yep," she said. "We will." She considered doing a runner, gunning it right out of there and not looking back, but that would just be putting off the inevitable. It was the amount of *talking* Paul would want to do. It exhausted her thinking about it.

Kit got out of the car and hurried up the front walk to the door. Fat raindrops began to fall on the car—unusual for this time of year in Santa

Cruz—splatting like bugs on the windshield. Natalie got out too and approached the house, the rain increasing in volume and speed as she went. As she turned the doorknob, she pictured Paul sitting in the parlor, legs primly crossed, telling Lynn how much he and Natalie loved each other.

But when she opened the door, she heard people in the foyer yelling. Angrily. Kit yelling. Lynn yelling. A tall man with dark hair and a black leather jacket that had seen better days, yelling. Not Paul?

And then he turned around. Definitely not Paul. The man who turned to look at her was totally different and black slicked-back hair. He was an enormous bull of a person, dwarfing Kit and Lynn, and he wore a mean look. Natalie felt ill. She knew exactly who this was: Allen.

One glance at Lynn confirmed it. Her face was red and sweaty and undone in a very un-Lynn-like way. Natalie's stomach lurched horribly, and acid roared up through her esophagus. The emotional processing she'd done at Buck's combined with the rush of horrible adrenaline from Allen's presence combined to turn her stomach around a corner. She turned, but not quite fast enough, and spewed copiously on the floor and all over the man's boots. Her throat burned. Her head sagged.

"Goddamn shit!" Allen shouted, stepping back. His cowboy boots were splattered with all sorts of unholy things, remnants from her brunch and the pizza she had eaten with Kit. Rage screwed up his face, scrunching it into a knot. The space choked with his anger. Natalie couldn't believe she'd thrown up, especially after having had her face next to a rotting sea lion's without so much as a gag. So much for her iron stomach.

Lynn moaned, her face drawn. And worse, there was palpable fear on it. Natalie didn't think she'd ever seen fear on her sister's face, not even when she had been arrested.

Natalie's brain began to reassemble.

Kit stood huddled against the foyer's curved wall, pressed against the plaster, his face a mask of unmoving horror. He looked like she'd felt right before puking.

Things happened fast after that.

Allen shook his boots, trying to get the vomit off. Natalie lunged forward, grabbed Kit's arm, and pulled him toward her, yanking him out the door and down the path. She looked back once at her sister's face, who made *leave* hand motions and mouthed, "Go!"

Natalie and Kit ran through the rain to her car, not looking back to see if Allen was coming after them. She fumbled the keys, unraveling quickly, possibly about to throw up again. She managed to unlock the car, stuff Kit inside, and slam the door. The vomit came again then, and she threw up in the gravel, not as much as before though and certainly not as satisfying. Opening the door again, she handed Kit the keys. "Lock it. If he comes out, get in the driver's seat and drive away. I don't care that you're thirteen. Do you understand me? You drive away if he takes one step outside." He nodded, white-faced.

Natalie could call the police to come and get Allen out of their house. Say there was a domestic violence dispute happening. But would Lynn hate her for it? She'd made a call to the police before, and look what had happened. Would Lynn prefer that she didn't call? A normal person would call. Right? That man in there was a beast who would likely hurt Lynn, and he was more enraged now at having been puked on.

Natalie let out an exasperated cry. She could not call.

All she wanted to do was to get in her car, throw it in reverse, and roar out of there. She wanted to get Kit as far away from that man as possible.

But she could not leave Lynn behind. The feeling was so powerful that it wasn't even a decision at all.

She would not abandon her sister. Not this time.

She hopped over the gravel and landed in the plants that ran alongside the house. The rain continued to come down hard, hitting her eyes like darts and making it difficult to see. She opened her mouth, filling it with rainwater to wash away the taste of vomit before creeping along the dead flower beds toward the back of the house. She did not chance a look back at Kit in her car, because his white, terrified face would make her falter.

With every step, she debated going back to the car and calling the police. Allen was huge and looked as though he was in shape, which likely meant he was stronger than her. But she kept moving. She creaked open the back door. The kitchen lights were on, the makings of dinner on the counter: salad, a cutting board with half a green bell pepper.

And then she heard it: horrible slamming sounds coming from the foyer, along with grunts and cries of pain. Body hitting wall. Grunt. Body moving across floorboards. Grunt.

Natalie had no fucking clue what she was going to do. Calling the police seemed like a great idea. And yet…

She grabbed one of her mother's cast-iron pans from the stove. It was so solid and heavy, she needed two hands to hold it. If she had to swing it, it would be a slow-motion thing that he would surely intercept. She put it back down even as another horrible thumping sound came, followed by a cry from Lynn. She picked up a stainless-steel saucepan with a long handle. Light and easy.

She crept over to the door facing the hallway and risked a peek. No. She would have no element of surprise there. They were still in the foyer, and Natalie could see him pushing Lynn, now pulling her back, pushing her again, throwing her. *Thump.* He didn't talk; neither did she. It was a silent, violent dance.

Natalie crept up the back stairs, glad of the darkness, avoiding all the places where the stairs creaked.

Thump. And a crack, like a head against a wall. A gasp of pain.

Natalie ran down the length of the hall on the blue carpet, grateful that her mother had chosen the thickest pile possible, dampening any sound. Leaping down the main stairs to the broad landing, which she and Lynn and Jake had always called the pirate poop deck when they played, she yelled down, "Come up here, you fucking coward!"

The thumping and grunting stopped.

Allen's face appeared at the bottom of the stairs. His hand was on the massive banister—how many times had they slid down that thing as kids? Natalie's favorite times were the ones where they all went together and rammed into each other at the end. Allen couldn't reach her from where she leaned over the railing—that was the best part about the landing.

Natalie was glad to see his face battered too. Blood trickled out of his mouth. It looked as though Lynn had gotten some kicks in.

"Come here," Natalie said. "I want to tell you something."

"Natalie," Lynn warned from out of sight. Her voice sounded wet and weak.

"What do you have to say, little one?" he asked, panting from the exertion of whatever bad things had gone on—but there was a dead calm in his eyes that Natalie recognized in every villain on-screen. "You must be the nasty little sister. You can come down here and introduce yourself properly."

"Up here is where I have to say it." She didn't know what she was going to do. She only knew she needed to get him away from Lynn. If she could divert his attention, Lynn could get out.

A thought came to Natalie: She could lure him to the third floor. Yes.

She'd hide behind a door—there were a thousand doors up there and all of them were dark—and then smash her saucepan right into his head. Knock him out. Then she could ask Lynn if she should call the police.

This all predicated on him taking the bait.

"Why, so you can stab me or something?" He laughed. "Come down here." The man spat on the stairs, on the beautiful blue carpet. He took a step back toward Lynn. Picked her up from where she was on the floor, out of Natalie's sight, and threw her. *Thump.* Lynn howled in pain.

Natalie went to the very edge of the landing, the last part of it before the stairs. Perilously close.

"Come here!" she screamed and tried to think what would enrage him enough to go after her. "So I can tell you what an impotent, weak asshole you are to your face!"

Unbelievably, it worked. He moved away from Lynn, who slumped to the floor. He came up hideously fast, two steps at a time, his reflexes like a vampire's. Maybe he *was* a vampire. There wasn't time for Natalie to go back up the stairs. She raised her arm back and threw the saucepan at his head, hard. It bounced off his forehead, and a surge of elation filled her at her excellent aim. The pan left a red, ugly divot in his head. He stumbled backward, but it was only a temporary setback because he righted himself almost immediately.

He roared.

She ran.

Natalie leaped as fast as she could up the steps and then rounded the corner with practiced ease up the straight flight to the third floor. She could hear him stumble and falter at the turn, unfamiliar with the terrain, but then he was pounding up the stairs behind her. It was unfair that he was the size of a goddamn Sasquatch while she was a mouse. Natalie made it to the third floor, turned the corner, and darted into the turret room, but not before she felt fingers on the back of her shirt.

She turned and slammed his fingers in the door. He screamed, a terrible, feral noise, and then—of *course* he did this—he pushed open the door with his other hand. He was enormous and awful and absolutely enraged. And now she was trapped in the goddamn turret room with him.

Natalie saw the kid-size broom she'd used to enlarge the hole in the wall that Penguin had climbed into the day they'd arrived. She grabbed the broom and jabbed the stick end into his crotch as hard as she could. His mouth made an O, and he doubled over.

The momentum of her stab made him stumble. Too late, she realized he was changing his weight, preparing to pitch forward at her, when Penguin ran out of the hole in the wall, right in front of the man's feet, at the same time he moved to lunge for Natalie. He tripped over Penguin's voluptuous body, and his ankle rolled. He lost his balance, grabbed for the edge of the wall, and Natalie took her chance. She used the broom end again to stab his gut, sending him backward, out into the hall. She shoved again, and he pitched straight backwards down the staircase. A flash of horror and regret came over Natalie—if she killed him...

Manslaughter. That was the verdict given to Lynn and Jake because Carlos had died. How un-hilariously ironic it would be for Natalie to end up with a similar fate.

It was too late now to reverse course. The noise was deafening. The thumps and the crashes and the tumbling on the stairs made it sound as though the house was coming down. But he landed, eventually, and then...silence.

— — —

Natalie breathed heavily as she waited, not daring to look. She didn't want to be surprised by him popping out of the stairwell like a villain in a bad movie. Penguin had the absolute cheek to rub against her legs and purr.

Eventually, she heard Lynn's reduced voice on the main stairs. "Natalie?" And then closer. "Natalie?"

Natalie decided to look down the stairs. Allen was at the bottom in a fairly twisted position, as she'd feared. Lynn kneeled on the floor next to him.

"Is he dead? Did I kill him?" she called down the stairs.

"No. He's still breathing." Lynn's voice was a thick rasp, the kind that happens when someone squeezes your windpipe, perhaps. "Is Kit safe." It was not a question. It was a plea.

"He's in my car."

Lynn sank against the wall. Natalie, the broom firmly in hand, crept down the stairs. Penguin followed, tail up, purring obscenely loudly like it was all great fun. She looked at Lynn's husband, who certainly *looked* dead. His lip was sliced open, and blood trickled from his ear—that was bad, right? That was really bad.

"Lynn?" Natalie crept over to her sister and reached out her hands but didn't touch her. Lynn's lips were bloody too, and her face had started to swell. The white of one of her eyes was red with blood. Penguin rubbed his chin on Lynn's forearm.

"I'm all right," Lynn said. The firmness in her tone reassured Natalie more than anything else. "It was only an unpleasant tussle."

"No, that was…" Natalie swallowed against a dry throat. "He looks dead."

"He's not dead. Promise. He's breathing."

Natalie nodded. "Can I call the police now?"

Lynn rolled her head against the wall and looked at Natalie. Her eye was definitely swelling shut. "You didn't call them?"

"No. For…obvious reasons."

Lynn gave a weak smile and coughed.

Natalie nodded at the man. "Allen, I'm guessing?"

"That's right, you weren't properly introduced. Natalie, meet Allen."

"A deceptively mild-mannered name."

Lynn grinned, but it was a terrible thing with her bloody gums, and Natalie looked away.

"I'm so sorry, Lynn. This is my fault." Natalie twisted her hands. "I'm so, so sorry."

Lynn waved her away. "Bound to happen sooner or later. Glad it's done."

Natalie felt horrible anyway.

"What do we do when he wakes up?" Natalie asked. "Will he keep coming after you?"

Lynn regarded her husband. "No more. I'm done. Lawyer. Divorce. Cops. Restraining order. Whatever I have to do. But never again. Not here. Not in my home."

"New York was your home too." Natalie said it gently.

"I know." Lynn sighed and closed her eyes. "We were always very physical. That's one of the reasons Kit and I are here."

"Yeah, it's called domestic violence. It's abuse."

Lynn appeared to consider that. "I could never use those words."

That she hadn't been able to use those words before was amazing, but then, Natalie had been in denial about her relationship too. While Paul was nothing like Allen, it was hard to have perspective when you were in the middle of something your gut knew wasn't right—and it was hard to accept that things weren't going to turn out the way you wanted.

"Has Kit seen this happen before?" Natalie asked.

Lynn slumped against Natalie's shoulder. "Once or twice."

"Oh, Lynn."

"I know."

They sat quietly for a long moment, resting, Lynn's head against Natalie's shoulder, Allen bleeding on the floor. There were things to do, like retrieve Kit from the car and reassure him, but for a brief moment, sitting against each other was needed. As though to punctuate the moment, Penguin crawled over their laps and purred loudly, mistaking it for a cuddle session, something he certainly didn't normally do with other people.

"When do you think he'll wake up?" Natalie asked after a long, meandering moment that felt confusingly serene.

"No idea. The fall knocked him out."

"Maybe he has a concussion."

"I hope so."

Car tires on the gravel sounded the alarm that someone had arrived.

"No police?" Lynn asked.

"No police."

"Then I guess you better help me downstairs."

In response, Natalie got up and offered her sister a hand. They took one step at a time until they reached the foyer. It was a horror show in there. Blood smeared the wallpaper in long, alarming streaks.

"That's not all mine," Lynn said. "I got him good too."

"I mean, okay," Natalie said, rolling her eyes.

"Help me to the bathroom so I can wash my face."

Natalie didn't trust that Allen wouldn't wake up and come raging at them like he'd done to her in the turret, but she had to help Lynn.

"Now," Lynn said as she positioned herself over the sink in the hallway's half bath. She spat blood into the bone-white sink, turning it a crimson mess. "Go answer the door with a smile, and don't let on that we've been in a fight." She closed the door firmly.

Natalie grimaced. That was some next-level denial there, and she vowed to support her sister in getting some psychological help. Both Lynn and Kit probably needed it.

As soon as she stepped into the hall, the front door opened. It was unmistakably Jake.

CHAPTER 26

They stared at each other for a long time.

"Hi," Natalie said from where she stood in the hall.

"Hey," Jake said. Expression unreadable.

Jake stepped inside the house and looked around, taking in the carnage in the foyer. His dark eyes landed back on Natalie, alarmed. "What happened here? What's going on?"

"Well," Natalie said, "Lynn's husband, Allen, is, ah, I don't know, unconscious upstairs on the landing. I'm still not sure he's not dead, though. Lynn's spitting blood out of her mouth in the bathroom. Kit's in my car." She realized she was shaking a little, an uncontrollable shiver of the sort you got in extreme cold. Delayed shock, maybe.

Jake ran up the stairs in a flash. Natalie stayed where she was.

In a moment, Jake came back down. "He's out, but he's breathing."

Jake strode down the hall, full of purpose. Natalie wasn't certain what he was going to do and fought her instinct to flee.

Natalie stared at her brother. She'd seen his photo on his lab website, but it hadn't prepared her for Jake in the flesh. He had long, lean limbs with sinewy muscles and noticeable tendons. Dark hair. Looking intense, whether he was or not (he usually was). His face had filled out, making him striking and handsome. When she'd last seen him, apart from his sentencing, he had been gaunt and pale. Now he looked…healthy. It was a beautiful sight.

"You said Kit's here? With Lynn?" he asked.

Natalie nodded. Was Jake furious? She couldn't tell.

"Are they safe?" he asked.

"Yes." Still she waited, knowing that she would not be able to handle it if he told her to leave. But she wouldn't argue with him.

So when he reached for her and pulled her into a hug, she went stiff.

He wrapped his arms around her and squeezed tight, as though she were a relic from a happy time in his childhood that he'd unpacked from an attic crate. She wound her own arms around him cautiously, and then, when it was clear he wasn't trying to kill her anaconda-style, she relaxed into his fierce hug.

"Wow," he said, releasing her. He moved back to get a good look at her. "It's been a while, little sister."

That did it. Tears spilled out of her eyes. Not a trickle either—a deluge. In a matter of seconds, her face was wet and her nose snotty. She heaved and sniffed and snorted and blubbered. Second dang time that day.

"Are *you* all right?" he asked.

The bathroom door flew open, and Lynn stepped out. "What did you do to her?" It was as though she was expecting someone else. Natalie's heart filled. Was Lynn being *protective* of her?

In answer, Jake took Natalie by the upper arm and pulled her with him as he dove at Lynn. The three of them mashed into a hug that Natalie could not believe was happening.

Jake gasped out a laugh, the kind of sound you make when you're sniffling back your own tears. Natalie glanced at him to confirm glassy, bright eyes. This was unbelievable.

"The foyer has seen better days," he said. "And so have you, Lynn." He lifted her chin with a forefinger. She'd washed away the blood, but she was already starting to bruise. "Allen did this?"

"We disagreed about his presence," Lynn said, a note of defiance in her tone. Natalie was glad to hear it after Allen's efforts to stomp it out.

"I can see that." Jake sighed. "Have you called the police?"

"No," Lynn and Natalie said at the same time.

And all three of them smiled at each other for the first time in years.

— — —

They did call the police. Lynn made the call. As soon as she hung up, Allen made his way down the stairs. They heard him before he appeared. His lumbering, labored progress was like that of a moose.

By this time, all three Walkers plus Kit were seated in the parlor, having snacks and drinks. Lynn had an ice pack on her face. Her other injuries were worse, but she wouldn't allow any fuss. Penguin lounged like the jewel in their crown, the tip of his tail flicking lazily, as though all of this was right and good and exactly how it should be. And Natalie supposed it was. Certainly this tableau was what she'd always dreamed of, albeit without the injuries and trauma.

"Lynn," Allen said, his voice craggy and rusty, like he'd woken after a night of drinking and was battling a hangover. Probably about the same as being jabbed with a broom handle and pushed down the stairs, Natalie thought. He looked around at all of them. "Babe. Look. Let's just talk, okay?"

Jake tensed and stood. Lynn tensed and stood. Natalie put a protective arm around Kit, and they both tensed and stood too. They looked like a mob ready to chase him down. Allen took a step back.

"No," Lynn said. "I don't think so."

"We've always talked before. Can we step outside?" Allen gave a nervous glance at Jake.

"Certainly not," Lynn replied. "We've done this too many times. I'm through."

"I'll—go to a meeting," Allen said. "A therapist. Whatever you want."

"I think you need to listen to Lynn," Jake said.

Natalie had a flashback to That Night and how different the scenario was now. Then there had been no cohesion, no united front.

"I think," Natalie said loudly, "that your best bet is to communicate with Lynn through a lawyer."

Allen fixed an unsteady eye on Natalie. "You're real mouthy, you know that? This isn't your business. I'll talk to my wife however I want."

"Through your lawyers. On paper," Natalie repeated, stepping forward. She pulled the iron fireplace poker from where it stood in a brass canister. Would they go a second round? She would do it if she had to. She absolutely would.

"Or carrier pigeon!" Kit said.

"Or smoke signal," Natalie offered.

"Or Morse code!" Kit screamed. Natalie glanced at him. The poor kid's neck tendons were standing out, and his face was red. "Leave, Dad!"

Something seemed to break in Allen's face. "Kit."

"Through lawyers would be great," Lynn said calmly. "You will not stand here and upset my family anymore. As I said, this is it. My lawyer will be in touch."

Natalie looked at Lynn. There was that immovable resolve in her sister's voice that she knew well from their teenage years. It was nice to see that back.

Allen's face worked, and his eyes filled with tears. "Lynn, I'll change. I'll get help."

"No, you won't," Lynn sighed.

The doorbell rang, startling them all from the moment. Allen, closest to the door, strode over and opened it as though it was his house and he was in control. Natalie could see from the living room that it was the police. She didn't move, and neither did Jake or Lynn.

"We don't need you here, thanks," Allen said. "You can go."

"Yes, we do," Lynn called, her voice cracking.

"He attacked my sister!" Natalie yelled. Lynn shot her a look, and Natalie froze, worried she'd overstepped. But Lynn just rolled her eyes.

The two officers stepped in the foyer. Allen, perhaps sensing defeat, foolishly tried to push around them and out the door, but the officers blocked him. Allen shoved at them, and in moments, he was in handcuffs.

"Honestly, what an idiot," Lynn said.

"Kit," Allen said, breathing hard on the floor. "Listen. Okay? Your mom's upset, but we can still go back to New York. Together. Me and you."

Kit turned his head, tears spilling down his cheeks. Natalie held a hand out to him, and he rammed into her side, burying his face against her. She looked at Lynn to check if this was all right, that she provide this comfort, and Lynn gave a slight nod of approval. It was this little movement that started Natalie's own tears.

There were statements to give and accounts to recall. Natalie insisted that Lynn get a copy of all the relevant documentation. She would need it for any potential custody challenges.

When Allen was gone courtesy of the Santa Cruz PD and the house was quiet again, they sat for a moment, each processing in their own way. Penguin flicked his tail once as if to say, *idiot humans.* Kit unfurled from Natalie and sat next to his mom on the sofa. Lynn put a tired arm around him.

"Kit, listen," Jake said. "None of this is your fault. You know that, right? He won't hurt you or your mom anymore. We'll see to it. He can't take you away. He'll do his best in his limited way to be a good dad. It'll hurt, and you'll be sad, but we'll make sure you talk to someone who will listen and offer solutions for dealing with it."

Lynn gave a snort-laugh. "Is that your fancy PhD talking or the caring uncle?"

Jake threw her a look that tried to be stern, but it cracked into a smile. So he could take being teased, Natalie thought. That was new.

"When you're an adult, you can make your own decisions about your dad," Natalie told Kit.

"Your mom will tell you that she didn't think he was that kind of man when she married him," Jake added.

"He might end up being all right in time," Natalie said, although she suspected the likelihood of this was not high.

"True," Jake said. "People change."

"People change," Natalie agreed. "Maybe not him though."

Kit nodded. His tears had dried. The tension that had filled his body when his father had stood in the room was gone now.

"Thanks," Lynn said quietly.

"We're here for you. Always," Jake said, which were not words Natalie had ever heard from her brother. But they were exactly what she wanted.

She tried to take a moment to process this family reunion and draw the inevitable conclusions: old wounds had healed, or there was work to be done, or too little too late. They'd need time to do that, though. To Jake, she said. "Buck told you I came by?"

"Yeah."

Natalie shook her head. "I've been looking for you for weeks."

Jake looked embarrassed. "I had to step away."

"Your colleagues at your lab were worried."

Jake waved a hand. "I got in touch. I told them I was fine."

"You missed your big award at the gala," Natalie said.

"I heard you accepted it for me." The corner of his mouth turned up in a smile. "Caused quite a stir."

Natalie's face went red. "Oh, um, thanks." Who had he heard *that* from?

"Anyway," Jake said, "I guessed it was probably time that I stopped hiding in the woods."

Natalie didn't know what to say.

"At least we can finally call the lawyer and get the terms of Mom's trust going," Lynn said.

"You're leaving on Wednesday?" Natalie asked Jake. She picked at a hangnail, wondering what would happen after they secured the inheritance. Where she would go. If they would ever see one another again.

"Well," he said. "That was the plan. I thought it would be a good thing to move somewhere else and do something different for a while, but the work won't be wildly different from what I'm doing now. I accepted the position before I knew we would inherit this house. And before I knew family might be around. Now I'm thinking maybe there are benefits to staying here. To moving in here."

"I want to stay here," Lynn said.

"I'll do whatever you both want," Natalie said before straightening suddenly. She would respect Lynn and Jake's wishes—but she realized with a sudden smack what she wanted. She wanted to stay here. Maybe not in the house, but in Santa Cruz. She wanted to breathe the briny scent of the city, drive the wavy coastline, and draw dead things for Dr. Berkhower. She wanted to tell Michelle her secrets, have brunch with friends, and make new ones. She wanted to build a new life here and be happy.

"There's a lot to sort out," Jake said. "Plenty of time to think about our next steps." He glanced at Natalie. "But you don't have to do what we want to atone for what happened."

"Well, let's not be hasty," Lynn said, but Natalie could tell by her lighter tone that it was a requisite grumpy Lynn remark and not meant to be serious.

"Really?" Natalie asked.

"Really." Jake smiled, which Natalie had not seen in…she couldn't remember how long.

"What happened?" Natalie asked. "With you being gone, I mean. We were looking for you. Asie—Dr. Casillas was helping me."

He flashed her a quick, searching look and sighed. "I was preparing to leave for the year in New Zealand, but Mom was sick, and…it was all kind of hard to handle. Then she died, and I—I needed time away. I needed to take a moment. I hadn't really done that since prison. I was getting degrees and working on my research and never really took time to think about where I was in life. I've been spending a lot of time hiking in the woods, just thinking. Buck was generous and let me stay with him and check in. He's been pretty adrift too. We were two old dudes in the woods, thinking about what we had lost."

"You're only thirty-six," Lynn pointed out.

"We all lost a lot," Natalie said. The guilt, that old dog, crept around her body again like a straitjacket. She looked at her siblings sitting with her here, and pushed that imaginary straitjacket off. "But now we're here together."

Kit left the room, mumbling that he needed to use the bathroom.

"Natalie," Jake said, his tone serious. He leaned forward, elbows on his knees. "I need to say something to you."

Here it was. Here was the admonishment, the big speech about how seeing her was nice and all, but things could never be the same. She would take it. She was an adult. It was time she heard the truth.

"Go ahead," she said, taking care to keep her tone steady.

"I don't hate you."

Her eyes flew to his face, looking for a sign of mockery or insincerity, but he seemed serious.

"I *did* hate you," he said. "I hated you for a long time. I hated you for calling the police. I hated you for Carlos's death. I hated you because Mom took your side."

"She didn't—"

He held up a hand to shush her. "Prison does a lot of things to a person. It ruins you in many, many ways. It's hopeless and ruthless, and nobody gives a shit if you live or die." He glanced at Lynn, who nodded. He took a breath. "The image that a lot of people have about prisoners watching cable TV all day and eating like royalty and working out—that's a lie told to the public. Prison sucks the humanity from you. But I was one of the lucky ones. I did college work when I was in there. I did college work when I was in there. I busted my ass, because I knew I wasn't getting a second chance. Look, Lynn and I purchased the heroin that killed Carlos. There was no way to take back that fact. So I did my time and survived it. I got out, got my degree. I got into a field of study I love and have been able to excel in. My employers respect me. I'm lucky." He looked at Lynn. "I've had a lot of time to think, both inside and out. You get to a certain point, and it doesn't make sense to hold on to the hate."

Natalie looked between him and Lynn. This was the kind of speech she'd never allowed herself to dream about, assuming it would never happen. Was it really happening now?

"I don't remember a lot about that night, for obvious reasons," Jake said. "I remember you were upset." He exchanged a look with Lynn. "I'm sorry for whatever it was that happened that night, Nat. I think you needed me, and I wasn't there for you. I'm really sorry about that."

Never—never!—in any permutation of imagining a reconciliation had Natalie thought *Jake* would be the one to apologize. Tears covered her cheeks.

"Guys," she said, "I wasn't the one arrested that night. They let me sit with a blanket around my shoulders. Please don't apologize to me."

Jake shook his head. "Let's not rehash it. I told the police you were eighteen and innocent."

Natalie's heart cracked. Despite everything, despite the anger and the convulsing and the flashing lights and the handcuffs, Jake *had* been looking out for her. She glanced at Lynn in wonder.

Lynn had a look of bemusement, almost boredom. "Oh, don't look at me like that. Yeah, I'm a little bitter. Why wouldn't I be? I got out of prison and didn't have the success story that Jake had. Yeah, I went to college, and yes, I like my job, but as you've seen, other things haven't been perfect."

"Kit, though," Natalie pointed out.

"Definitely Kit." Lynn's tone brooked no argument.

A moment passed, and no one spoke, maybe for the sake of seeing how it felt to sit together and simply be.

Jake looked up at the ceiling. "There's plenty of room in this house. We could easily turn the whole third floor into an apartment."

"Not a bad idea," Lynn said.

Natalie stood. "We should call Mr. Garcia as soon as possible and tell him the trust's terms are satisfied, and then I can get out of your hair."

"Well," Jake said, "It's up to you to decide if you stay or not." He glanced pointedly at Lynn, who scrunched her face in response.

"What? Whatever. Yeah, it's your house too," she told Natalie, whose heart squeezed again. For Lynn, that was as good as an engraved invitation to stay.

"Thank you," Natalie whispered.

Kit bounced into the room, his face alight with wonder. "The library is so cool. Mom, you didn't tell me about the secret door!"

"Your mom and aunt didn't show you?" Jake asked. "Tsk, tsk."

"What secret door? *I* don't even know about this," Natalie said.

"Our grandfather's secret door," Lynn said. "It leads to a crawl space. C'mon, you know about this."

"Show me." Natalie couldn't believe it. "I've never seen it."

"Maybe you forgot," Jake said as they all trooped down the hall to the library.

"I would not forget a secret door." Natalie felt outraged.

Penguin followed right on their heels, eager to be part of the crowd, as they went into the library and Jake bent down to one of the built-in shelves nearest the window. He pushed down on a small wooden lever camouflaged into the bookshelf that was 100 percent not previously known to Natalie. A click, and then a quarter of the bookshelf swung open.

"Are you kidding me?" Natalie yelled.

Like the little self-righteous feline Penguin was, he hurried into the space, tail up, like he'd been waiting for someone to open it just for him. Natalie bent over to look inside. She flicked a light switch, and a bare bulb lit the space. Old trunks lined the walls, trunks that a distant, dusty part of her brain remembered seeing at some point in her childhood, containing plans and papers about the house. The floor was littered with mouse parts. The smell was about what you'd expect given the various bits of decaying rodent. A filthy club chair sat against one wall, covered in cat fur.

"No," she said. "No."

"Unbelievable cat," Lynn said next to her.

"Those are our grandfather's trunks," Jake told Kit. "There's all this historical stuff in there, including old documents about building the house."

Penguin did a little chirpy purr as though to say, *Do you like what I've done with the place?*

"How was he opening the door?" Natalie asked.

Lynn shrugged. "How does that cat do anything?"

Fair point.

"What a to-do," Natalie said.

Natalie and Lynn and Jake had often said that in a high-pitched granny voice when they were kids. *What a to-do*, Jake would shrill at them. *Look at this to-do*, Lynn would shriek at Natalie and her inevitable mess of Barbies, the majority of which were Lynn's. Natalie remembered thinking it when Lynn and Jake were arrested, but certainly not saying it.

Kit laughed. "You sound like an old woman."

She looked at her brother and sister to see if they recognized or remembered the phrase. Jake smiled. And Lynn nodded. Smiling and nodding. With each other. What a to-do.

Penguin wound himself around Natalie's ankles, threading between her legs as though to say, *You dummy. I was here the whole time. You just didn't open your eyes to see.*

CHAPTER 27

The path was a little harder to find this time around. But they remembered the campsite they used to stay at, so at least they had a starting point.

"I'm pretty sure it's this way," Jake said. "See—there's something here."

He led the way through a tangle of ferns, away from the campsites. It was hard going. If it had been an unofficial path before, it had degenerated into a faint hint of one now. Jake stopped as they came to the stream. Luckily, it was a lot shallower than it had been when they were younger since it was the end of summer and the water had mostly dried up. Natalie breathed in the cologne of wood decay and fresh pine. Sunlight flitted between the leaves, dappling their path.

"Wasn't there a giant tree here?" Natalie had a memory of using the felled redwood as a bridge, a precarious crossing over the fast-moving water.

"I think so, but we can still get across." Jake hopped over, using stones in the water as steps. It was a lot easier when you were an adult. Natalie followed suit, and they continued up the hill, fighting through even more overgrown greenery. She waited a moment for Lynn to catch up.

"Hope none of this is poison oak."

"Nah, it's not in leaves of three." Jake surged ahead, confident. "Trust me. I've been spending a ton of time in these woods lately."

Lynn caught up, grumbling about the path and how it had changed and how ridiculous this was.

They fell silent as they scraped their way up the hill through the brush. Every so often, Natalie questioned again whether this was the right path, and Jake said yes.

Then she heard it up ahead: a waterfall.

They emerged through a particularly dense bit of trees and growth, revealing the familiar boulders. The rocks were exactly as Natalie remembered them, although with a less powerful waterfall now. Her heart began pounding. It was still beautiful—more so, because she could appreciate it better as an adult.

"Okay, this is pretty good," Lynn said.

Now, as then, Jake offered his sisters a hand to hoist them up on the first big boulder. From there, it was easy to climb up and up. Natalie didn't remember this much climbing, but then they were monkeys as kids. Finally, sweaty and red-faced, she made the final pull up to the big flat rock where they'd lain all those years ago. Lynn pulled up next to her, and they sat side by side, three in a row, legs dangling over the boulder.

The view was more stunning than Natalie remembered: the tops of coastal pines everywhere, redwoods in clusters, and nothing but lush greenery for what looked like miles, and then beyond that, the blue line of the ocean. This was Natalie's California and her coast, and she felt a profound sense of completion and belonging.

She sighed happily as Jake opened his pack and handed her a water bottle and a sandwich.

"This is so good," she said, meaning the general experience, not only the ham and cheese sandwich she had bitten into.

"It is," Jake agreed. He sat down with his elbows stretched across his knees. "I've thought about this rock for years."

"Same." Natalie breathed in deep, the clean forest air filling her lungs. "Too bad Kit's playing chess with Buck."

"They're both having a good time," Lynn said. "And it's nice to be just us three." Natalie turned to her sister to see if she was being sincere, but Lynn looked off at the trees. "I miss this."

They didn't talk for a long time—ten, fifteen minutes maybe. Natalie simply took in the view and let her body relax. Lynn scooched back and stood up, dusting her shorts off. "Enough sappy sibling silence. I'm going to see if the boulders go up farther."

Natalie and Jake watched her go. After she disappeared behind some rocks, Natalie turned to Jake. "Why did Mom's death make you disappear?"

He leaned back and closed his eyes and laughed, as though he'd been waiting for her to start in on him. "It was hard. She didn't want me there at the end. Buck felt really bad about it." He stared out at the canopy. "Apparently she felt that if all three of us couldn't be there, she didn't want me there either in case that was playing favorites."

"That's ridiculous." Natalie threw a pebble in the air. "If she wanted all three of us, we could have been there."

"You would have come if she'd asked?"

Natalie considered this. That was before the announcement of Paul's promotion. She had been in a different place then. She pictured getting a call from Buck, asking her to come to her mother's bedside. Bitterness and anger would have been her first reactions, but then? Maybe, with assurances that Lynn and Jake didn't mind her presence, she would have agreed. Although she may have been petty and said no, she liked to think that wouldn't have been the case. "I don't know, honestly."

"It wouldn't have been an automatic yes for Lynn, either. I went anyway on the day she passed. I held her hand, and she looked at me, and we said only a few things. Did a lot of communicating with our eyes when she got too tired to talk."

"Ugh. That sounds awful. I'm sorry."

"Me too. That's why I bugged out. A long look—however meaning-ful—is not enough to take away the past." He sighed. "It was all so much all at once; New Zealand was looming, and I was staying with Buck, helping him with the cremation arrangements and everything."

Natalie nodded in sympathy.

"I was a zombie," he said, still staring at the sky from behind his fancy designer sunglasses. "Going through the motions at work. But a few days went by, and I realized that in all the grief and confusion, the only person I wanted to be around was Buck, which was so weird because I'd spent so much time being angry at him."

"I thought you were going to say me," Natalie said. "If this was a movie, you'd have said me."

He laughed. Old Jake did not laugh. New Jake laughed a lot. He was so much lighter. "I did want to see you, kiddo. I've wanted to see you for years."

Her throat choked up.

Lynn appeared again, making her way back down the boulders. She found her way to where Natalie and Jake sat. "Talk about anything good?"

"We only say the good stuff when you're around to hear it," Jake said affectionately. To Natalie's surprise and delight, Lynn smiled—a real smile, not a grimace and not a fake I'm-only-smiling-because-it's-expected face.

Natalie said, "We were talking about Jake bugging out when Mom died. How come you didn't tell anyone where you were? Your colleagues didn't know anything. Asier didn't know."

There was a silence, and Natalie realized she'd said Asier and not Dr. Casillas.

Jake sat up on an elbow. "Asier, huh?"

"No." Her face flushed, and she stared intently at the tree line.

"First-name basis?" There was a teasing note in his tone. "Since when?"

"I mean, he was helping me find you."

"Oh, she's had a thing for him since day one," Lynn said, leaning back on the warm rock and closing her eyes.

"No, I haven't," Natalie lied automatically, both annoyed and pleased that her sister read her so well.

Jake continued to stare at her, and she continued to not look at him.

"Anyway," she said, clearing her throat, "I think he was only helping me because he wants a microscope for the lab. I did an illustration job for Dr. Berkhower, and apparently Asier and Dr. Lawrence want me to help get his microscope." She wasn't sure of the truth.

Jake snorted. "Why would we want that old thing? No way. I actually went down to Monterey to see a colleague there and get the specs on his microscope so I could place the order for a new one. Ours will be the best microscope on campus. Also? Nice job working for Dr. Berkhower."

Natalie's heart flipped as she took in Jake's words. "There's no way that Asier wanted me to help him get Dr. Berkhower's microscope?"

Jake frowned. "He knew full well I was planning to buy a new one."

"Huh."

"I spoke to Asier yesterday, and he told me Dr. Berkhower, apparently, was highly impressed. Not many people impress that guy, so well done."

Natalie reddened. "It was so gross, but so…amazing. The detail, and getting access to a specimen like that up close. I want to do it again."

Jake smiled at her. "You should."

She took a deep breath and let it out, trying to calm her anxiety about what to do next. "He wants someone with a degree in illustration."

Jake was quiet a moment. "I will speak with him."

"Oh, no, that's—"

"Anyway," Jake said pointedly, his tone making it clear that further arguments weren't welcome, "back to Asier."

Natalie felt her cheeks heat.

Jake laughed. "Ah, there it is. Listen, he's a really good guy. The most honest person you'll ever meet—really. No joke. He can be too reserved and he's a workaholic though. I've always told him it would take someone very special to pull him out of his tendency to cut himself off from people and bury himself in his work. Dr. Lawrence thinks he's delicate and too sweet and that she needs to protect him, but he's solid, baby girl. In case you were worried about his character, which I sense that you definitely are."

"Told you," Lynn said from where she lay.

Natalie blushed again at Jake's clear reading of her. She pictured Asier and his smart confidence. A swell of attraction rose in her at the mental image of him. "He seems pretty sure of himself."

"Seriously, that guy is one of the most brilliant people I've come across. I should have let him know where I was sooner, but I was processing and being a little selfish with that. I told him I felt bad about disappearing, and

I won't do that again. He's one of my closest friends. It's an honor and a privilege to have him share my lab."

"Maybe you should amend the name to the Walker and Casillas Lab," she said.

Jake raised an eyebrow. "Now, that's ridiculous."

She threw another pebble, trying to get her brain to re-route these truths.

Jake sat up so they were shoulder to shoulder. "I want to say something to you." He took a deep breath. "I was a shit brother. I should have been there for you, but I was too busy being pissed off and throwing myself into drugs to drown out everything. I can't say I'll ever really get over Carlos dying—he was my best friend—but man, prison set me on a course I'm grateful for. I get that few people can say that, and I get that it's not typical. Lynn, for example—prison ruined a piece of her that we'll never get back."

"True that," Lynn said.

"But the success I have today is because I had time to get over myself and focus on what I needed to do to survive and never go back there."

Natalie shook her head. "But I'll never stop feeling bad that I was the reason you were in prison in the first place."

He nodded. "I know. I'm sure you've beaten yourself up plenty over the years. You were always doing that to yourself. I hope you've stopped."

"I'm trying to," Natalie said.

Lynn sat up. "Oh, for God's sake. What a couple of saps you are. Fine. I shouldn't have been so angry at you that night either. And fine, I regret that we haven't spoken in years."

Natalie tried to reach over and touch her sister's arm, but Lynn saw it coming and moved out of the way.

"Lynn says your ex-boyfriend is a jerk and stole your job." Jake shook his head.

Natalie glanced at Lynn, who'd apparently been telling Jake about her. Lynn shrugged and rolled her eyes as though to say, *Fine, whatever, we love and care about you.*

"He didn't really steal my job," Natalie said. "I thought a lot of stupid things. I was with the guy for all the wrong reasons. And I stayed too long in that job."

"You're allowed to fuck up, Natalie," Jake said.

She rested her head against his arm, and Lynn, amazingly, rested her head against Jake's other arm.

"Guys," Jake said, "I don't know how else to say this, so I'll be blunt. I don't want either of you to go anywhere. I want to rebuild our relationship. I want to make up for all the years we pissed away thinking we couldn't forgive each other. I'm not going to New Zealand. I want to stay here."

"Can you do that? Just tell them you're not coming? Will that hurt your career?"

"I have my own lab here, if you hadn't noticed. I can go where I want. Anyway, I'll tell them I need to be here with my family. It's more important."

Natalie forced back a surge of tears. "I—" She paused, unsure how to state the sticky truth. "I'm not terribly rich at the moment. As in, I can barely feed myself. I can't rent my own apartment. I have to share one with my best friend back in Boston. I don't know that I can afford to stay here."

Lynn tsked. "Stay in the house with me, silly."

Natalie looked at her to make sure she wasn't kidding.

"Yes, really," Lynn said, faking exasperation at being questioned. "I could use the help with Kit anyway."

"Thank you," Natalie said.

"I might move in too," Jake said. "We can come to a financial arrangement regarding bills. I can rent my house out, and that money can go toward the restoration and upkeep of our house."

Natalie pursed her lips in delight at the thought of them all living together. "I'd love that."

"I'm not sharing a bathroom with you again, chump," Lynn told him.

"I would love to apply to a graduate program for scientific illustration," Natalie said.

"Do that if you want to, but not because you have to," Jake said. "I'll sort Dr. Berkhower out. Don't worry." He bumped her shoulder. "So you'll stay in Santa Cruz? I need my sisters in my life. You're my family, and I want to be that again. I hope you do too."

She stared at him, tears blurring her vision, and then laughed. "Are you kidding me?"

"You know I'm not."

She pressed her head against his arm, and he folded her into the warmth of his chest. Her tears made hot rivulets between them, binding them, keeping them.

"So gross," Lynn scoffed, but she accepted Jake's arm around her too, and together, they made a Walker sandwich.

CHAPTER 28

A week later, Natalie drove Kit to his first day of school. It was gray and overcast, making the morning feel dreary. Kit stared out the window at the busy drop-off zone.

"It'll be great," she promised as he got out of the car.

Kit smiled confidently. "I know." He shut the door and went to join the throng of kids going inside. He didn't look back, not once, and Natalie found that her eyes were a little wet.

As she sat for a moment, idling, her phone chimed with a text from Michelle. Did you do it?

Natalie typed back: I set it in motion.

Michelle replied with a thumbs-up emoji followed by a hug emoji.

A few days before, Natalie had had a long talk with Michelle, who had suggested that Natalie pull the trigger and apply to CSU Monterey's scientific illustration program. What was the worst that could happen, Michelle had asked—they'd say no? Besides, Natalie had the chops.

Yesterday she'd been all over the CSU Monterey website. The

application to the program, for admission the following year, required letters of recommendation and transcripts and an essay-length statement of purpose, which sounded daunting, but she would have her UMass transcripts by the end of the week, and her essay had nearly written itself.

That left asking Dr. Berkhower for a recommendation letter.

Michelle wasn't moving in with her fiance until after their wedding, so she said Natalie was welcome to rent a room in her house if she felt like she needed her own space outside the family home. Later, Natalie had realized her first instinct had been to call Michelle and not Teensy to talk the school thing through. She knew her friendship with Teensy was bound to change with Paul out of the picture. But it was a sign, maybe, that she could live in Santa Cruz and be all right.

She pulled onto the road and headed to the lab.

— — —

The morning fog had already yielded to a gloriously sunny day by the time she reached the lab. It was the best kind of day, where a sea breeze kept everything cool but the sky was an endless blue. The grass on each side of the long road to the lab undulated, almost as though it was waving to welcome Natalie. She decided this was a good omen. The dramas were behind her.

She pulled into the parking lot, but it was full, so she drove around to the visitor center's lot and parked next to a giant SUV that had ridiculous gold trim and a weird hood ornament that looked like a horn. A sticker on the back said SAN FRANCISCO ELITE RENTALS, and for a split second she was jolted into thinking it was Allen, but that was silly. Not every rental car in Santa Cruz was Allen's, and he, it seemed, would be tied up for some time. Things had not gone well for him following his arrest for striking an officer at the house. In an apparent tantrum, he had managed to twist himself into a pretzel on the way to the police station and fallen out of the squad car upon arrival, breaking his left leg in two places that required surgery and a metal pin. A lawyer Lynn retained for her divorce and custody filing told her that Allen also had an arrest warrant out in New York for assaulting an officer there shortly before leaving for California. As a result, he was being held without bail and had a heap of legal issues in addition to months of physical therapy ahead of him. So Allen would not be here at the lab, and certainly not in a rental car that looked like a rhinoceros beetle. She got out of her car, glad all over again that Allen had engineered his own downfall.

"Natalie."

She turned as the driver's side door of the huge SUV slammed shut. Paul walked toward her.

Surprise and disappointment hit her. She took a deep breath to regain her composure. Unfortunately, he was not a mirage.

"What are you doing here?" she asked.

"Nice to see you too, babe."

She dropped her tote bag, which contained her largest sketchbook and best pens, as well as an extra shirt in case of liquid spillage. "I don't know what you want me to say. I'm not your *babe*. I can't believe you flew out here."

"I can't believe you're surprised." He grinned widely, as though this were a happy exchange, as though she were glad to see him. "You know me better than that. You're the best thing that ever happened to me. The least I could do was come here and tell you that in person."

She looked around. "How did you know to come here? To the lab?"

"Ann told me you'd resigned. She said you had an amazing opportunity at a marine lab here with a Dr. Berkhower. I looked him up and found his office." He gave that same maddening grin, as though he wanted a pat on the head and a cookie for being so clever.

"That's not creepy at all," she said. Despite his towering height, Paul did not give off a threatening vibe, and that was something, but she was a little wary given the recent episode with Allen.

"I don't mean to be. I'm sorry if it feels that way." He had the sense to take a step back. "But I'm really glad you got a job that you love. I wish you'd given notice to me directly, since I'm your supervisor—"

"You can stop right there with that." She scowled. "If you're wondering why I broke up with you, imperious bullshit like that played a part."

"I know you said you wanted to be on a break, but this is… I mean, we're still a team, you and me." He had the gall to try and look confused. She could see it was an act, as though the robotic part of his brain had sifted through possible reactions and approved the one called *look confused by her resistance.*

"I broke up with you. I'm sorry if that wasn't clear. We are no longer together. We are broken up."

A newish Volvo pulled into the spot next to Natalie's car. The driver got out, and to Natalie's dismay, it was Dr. Lawrence.

"Natalie," she said, shooting a glance at Paul, curiosity written on her face. "Good morning."

"Morning." Natalie did not want to chat with Dr. Lawrence. She hadn't seen or spoken to her since their conversation a few weeks ago, when she had suggested Asier was only interested in a microscope. Dr. Lawrence could shove it.

"This a friend of yours?" Dr. Lawrence asked, not moving toward the lab, not minding her own business.

"Paul Sorensen," Paul said, stepping forward to shake her hand. "I'm an architect. And Natalie's fiancé."

Dr. Lawrence's eyebrows shot up, and she gave Natalie a quick look that was clear: *Oh, really? And you were calling Dr. Casillas by his first name?*

"Oh my God," Natalie seethed. "You are *not*. Paul. Stop. That's not okay to say. Please leave."

"Natalie, please," Paul said.

She shook her head. "I'm sorry you flew all the way out here, but I suggest you turn that grotesque vehicle around and go back to the airport. There's nothing to say here."

"There's everything to say," Paul said. "Natalie, come on. We had a life."

"*You* had a life."

"Is there someone else?" Paul looked around the parking lot as though Natalie had stuffed paramours between the parked cars. "Is that what it is? You met someone here?"

Natalie closed her eyes and breathed out slowly. "Please leave."

"Is it Dr. Casillas?" Dr. Lawrence said in a loud whisper. "Is he the reason?"

Natalie's eyes flew open. She could not believe this woman. "Seriously, right now?"

"Who is Dr. Casillas?" Paul asked.

"I'm done with both of you." Natalie picked up her tote bag and turned to move toward the building.

"Who is Dr. Casillas?" Paul asked louder. "Are you sleeping with him?"

Natalie threw her bag down and stomped back to him, right up to his chest. He dwarfed her, which was annoying because she had to crane her neck to look at him. "I could sleep with half of Santa Cruz if I wanted to, and you would have zero say in it. You don't own me. We were on a break. And now we're all the way broken up. We are done. Got it? I love your sister, and I love your parents, but I am not coming back, and I am not going to marry you." Paul opened his mouth to speak, and Natalie shook her head. "Nope. Don't say anything. Don't speak to me again."

Natalie took a step back, watching his shocked face absorb this. She turned to Dr. Lawrence.

"And you," she yelled. "Did you not stand out here two weeks ago and tell me all about how Asier only cares about a goddamn microscope? Which Jake says he's already ordered? Why? Why would you do that?"

Dr. Lawrence looked stricken, like a told-off child. "I—"

"You what?" Natalie was surfing through the barrel of her fury now. "I can't wait to hear it."

"Natalie, I'm so sorry," Paul said, his voice thick with emotion. Natalie glanced at him to see that his eyes were wet. A twitchy feeling started in her fingers. No tears. He was not allowed to come here and accuse her and then play the victim. She turned back to Dr. Lawrence.

"I didn't—I don't want to see him get hurt," Dr. Lawrence said, her forehead creasing with concern. "He's been hurt before. He's a very sensitive soul. And a truly good person."

"And you think I'm a monster who's going to gobble his sweet little snookums self up?" Natalie shook her head.

"Your brother told us what happened." Dr. Lawrence looked at her hands. "How he went to...prison, and your role in that. I didn't know who you were. I was trying to look out for him."

"Natalie," Paul said.

Natalie breathed in carefully. "Okay, but I was eighteen when that happened."

She could see Dr. Lawrence had not considered this fact, because she looked stricken. "Oh. I—I'm sorry."

"Natalie." Paul's voice had hardened now, and Natalie could see from his set face that he had arrived at the indignant denial phase of his emotional processing. "This is rude and frankly embarrassing."

"Yes, it is embarrassing," she yelled. "For you. We are *d-o-n-e*. Go home. Good luck with being the director. I'm sure you'll appropriately engage client-centric performance-based linkage or whatever. Do not send messages through Teensy. Move on. I have." It was the most final thing she could think of to say.

"I have to say," Dr. Lawrence said to Paul, "that it seems as though you're harassing her. You'll need to leave now and stay away from her. I'm calling campus security. I'd also advise you not to speak to Natalie again, since she's asked you several times." Natalie watched with amazement as she pulled out her phone.

Paul threw his hands up and moved toward his vehicle. "Fine. I'm going." He climbed into the driver's seat, started up the car, and backed out. Natalie and Dr. Lawrence watched him go in silence.

Natalie gave Dr. Lawrence a nod. "Thank you." Then she picked up her bag and headed into the building.

CHAPTER 29

"The thing is," Dr. Berkhower said, eyes narrowed as he appraised her, "you don't retch."

He paused, as though considering the ghosts of puke past, before continuing, "And your work is excellent. So yes, I will write you a letter of recommendation for the program at Monterey Bay."

Natalie let her face burst into the grin she'd been holding back.

He tried to look fierce but ended up squinting, which she suspected was his way of smiling. "And contingent on your application to the program, I will re-extend the offer for employment, but *only* if you accept it this time."

"Thank you," Natalie breathed. "I accept!"

"And," he added in a severe tone that didn't quite have the intended effect, "if you stay and help me with this sea lion right now."

She jumped to attention. She couldn't wait to sketch the rotted tissue, and she felt that excitement of getting to work with real specimens all over again. When she'd come into the lab, he had not moved away from the bloated animal on the stainless-steel table. They'd had their entire conversation with a dead sea lion between them.

He nodded at the box of gloves. "VapoRub's in the cabinet, there."

She moved around the table and got the gloves and ointment and her sketchbook, which was looking a little battered, every page nearly filled up. Time to do her favorite thing in the world: buy a fresh one.

"Where did this poor guy come from?" she asked.

"I'd grab a lab coat by the door too," he said. "He's a squirter. Someone brought it in from one of the beaches. Washed up overnight."

Natalie put on a lab coat and finished buttoning it in time to avoid a horrible stream of juice launching into the air as Dr. Berkhower made an incision. "I can't say I'm not glad to have you back."

She smiled. "I'm glad to be back."

The week since Allen's appearance and Jake coming home had been calm and even hopeful. She'd gone to the beach with Kit in the afternoons. Lynn's external wounds had begun to heal. Jake had moved into the mansion properly, taking their parents' bedroom. Natalie and Kit had begun a huge cleaning project of the whole house. And it had become obvious to Natalie that she was ready to be here forever, smelling the salty sea, hearing the distant screams of the roller coaster riders at the Boardwalk, watching a V-shaped cabal of pelicans fly by, and totally immersing herself in this slightly scruffy beach town she knew and loved. She wanted it so badly and couldn't believe she'd hidden it away so successfully from herself over the years.

Teensy had been supportive when Natalie had called to tell her.

"I'll miss you," Teensy had said, "but I can see that it's time. I support you."

Natalie wondered if she knew her brother had flown to California. It didn't matter. She and Teensy might take a little while to get their footing back, but Natalie was confident they could. They'd been friends for too long to let distance and a petulant brother come between them.

"And besides," Teensy had added, "I don't have to live with that wretched cat anymore, so this is the best possible outcome."

Penguin seemed happy too. He hadn't disappeared again, for one, and he alternated between sleeping all night at the foot of Natalie's newly purchased bed and Kit's.

"I hear your brother is back today too," Dr. Berkhower said.

"He is." His first day back, actually. "He's here to stay."

"Hmm." Dr. Berkhower rolled the carcass. Natalie looked away as half its skin sloughed off. He handed her his scalpel. "Can you slice that part, there? I suppose he'll try to steal you away from me."

Natalie made the slice as she took in this piece of news. "Why would he try to steal me?"

"Because Dr. Casillas already tried. I told him absolutely not."

Her head shot up. "What?"

"Mind the intestines! He asked if I could spare you to sketch some kind of rare kelp he has hold of. Ridiculous."

At a slight nudge from her scalpel, a whole snakelike piece of intestine came away and spilled open. The smell was enough to make her weep, although it was sort of funny that she didn't come close to vomiting the way she had on Allen's boots.

"It was nice of Dr. Casillas to ask about me," Natalie said, trying to remain calm. Her insides squirmed in excitement. She was fairly sure it was because of Asier and not the sea lion.

"There can be no favors given because it's your brother's lab," Dr. Berkhower said primly. "Or because someone likes you." This was said with a slyness that made Natalie's face burn. "I saw the way he was looking at you at the gala." Natalie did not reply. It was interesting that Asier had asked for her. Maybe she'd see what the deal was—but with a heavy dollop of caution.

At noon, Natalie pretended she was hungry for lunch, which was not true after working around the sea lion. "Just going to step out for a bite," she told Dr. Berkhower.

He waved her away without looking up from his precious carcass. "Can you grab another stack of absorbent cloths when you come back? Supply room is down the hall. Key's right there on the rack by the door."

She glanced at the mess on the table. "Sure thing." She took off her heavy lab coat and stepped out of the lab, wending her way down the hall toward the Walker Lab, her heart pounding.

She could see Dr. Lawrence through the window. No sign of Asier. Before Natalie could keep going, Dr. Lawrence looked up and came to open the door.

"I'm really sorry, again," Dr. Lawrence said. "I shouldn't have prejudged you like that."

"I appreciate it, and all is forgiven," Natalie said, "but I do not want to discuss or rehash any part of that parking lot nonsense. Is Asier around?"

"No, sorry, he stepped out." Dr. Lawrence pursed her lips. "But I'll tell him you came by! I'll let him know the second he steps through the door. He's getting some things from the supply room."

"Actually, I have to go there too. Can you tell me where it is?"

"Even better." Dr. Lawrence pulled off her sodden surgical gloves. "I'll show you." She pulled a key out of her lab coat pocket and moved through the door past Natalie. This niceness was over the top, but Natalie recognized it as Dr. Lawrence's attempt to apologize. "Emily, by the way. My first name. You can call me Emily."

"Okay." Natalie thought it might be a while before she called her anything, but an olive branch was always a good thing.

Dr. Lawrence led her down maddeningly identical hallways until she stopped at a door marked SUPPLY ROOM and smiled at Natalie as she unlocked the door. "There you go."

"Thanks." Natalie opened the door and was overwhelmed by the shelves, neatly stocked with every kind of lab equipment imaginable. It was, to a science-loving geek, heaven. The heavy door slammed shut behind her. No sign of Asier.

She moved between the tall shelves looking for cloths but got waylaid by stainless steel dissection tools in sterilized pouches, rolls of labels and identification tape, tubes, jars of varying sizes, and identification stickers. All full of possibility, but also slightly creepy. She rounded a row of shelves, her eyes landing on a human shape, and she gave a little scream before her brain could register that it was him.

Asier.

"Tell me you got in here with a key," he said. "Because we need a key to get out, and I don't have mine."

She stared at him dumbly, her brain still trying to catch up. She had forgotten to take the key from the rack in Dr. Berkhower's lab. "I forgot my key. Dr. Lawrence let me in."

He sighed and looked down, shaking his head with quiet laughter. "So we are trapped in here now."

"That can't be true. Isn't it against the fire code to have doors that lock from the inside?"

"I agree. If a fire breaks out in here, we are toast. Literally."

His eyes met hers, and he smiled. Not a broad one, but a glad-to-see-you smile.

"Hello," he said. "That's what I meant to say first."

"Hi," she said. "Are we really trapped in here?" She hoped it wasn't true. She hoped it *was* true.

He grinned playfully. "Yes, but Dr. Lawrence knows we are here. Presumably we will get out someday."

"Hmm." She scanned the shelf next to her. "I'm looking for absorbent cloths. For Dr. Berkhower."

"Ah, yes. He got a sea lion in over the weekend, he said."

"It's in an excellent state of putrefaction."

Asier laughed. "He was really thrilled that you were coming in." He cleared his throat. "He mentioned it this morning when I saw him in the break room."

She supposed that was when he'd asked to borrow her. "I heard you want some kelp illustrated."

His lips moved, trying to hide a smile. "I made inquiries."

Inquiries. It sounded as though he were asking her father for her hand.

"And this kelp…is it special?" She leaned against the shelf.

"Very. You wouldn't know it at first. It seems like normal kelp. But when you look a little deeper, it turns out it's very special. It has amazing potential."

She was pretty sure he wasn't talking about kelp. "I'm sure drawing the kelp would be amazing. But it's funny—sometimes I work on an illustration and it doesn't really come together. I put in the work, coming back to it to make small tweaks, and it doesn't go anywhere. It just sits there."

Asier stared at her for a long time and then laughed. "Are you talking about me?"

She laughed too, glad they could be direct with one another.

He smiled, lips closed. "I don't really need kelp illustrated. I wanted to see you. Because we haven't spoken in a while."

She saw no benefit to keeping up the pretense. "I've been busy with my family. But I've missed seeing you too."

"Listen." Asier took a step forward so they were only a foot apart, and she could feel the heat radiating off him. "Natalie." The passion of the kiss the night of the gala came back to her. The air seemed to thin. Every part of her was open, waiting. "About the microscope. What Dr. Lawrence told you. You and I have not known each other for very long, but I will make it clear that I was not, and am not, interested in you getting a microscope for me. There is something about *you* that I very much want to know more about. You—" He stopped, ran a hand through his hair. "You make me feel."

"Feel?" She was having a hard time processing his words while standing this close to him.

"When Dr. Berkhower mentioned this morning that you were coming in, I...really wanted to see you." He reached over and put a hand on hers. She sucked in a breath. The skin of his fingertips was hot—hotter than fingers should be. Or was that her? "More than anything. But I wasn't sure if you wanted to see me."

"Here I am," she said breathlessly. "Didn't Jake tell you I was coming in?"

He shook his head. "Jake doesn't want to get in between us."

Us. There was an us.

"When you came here looking for your brother weeks ago, I couldn't believe it," he said. "Jake had talked about you, of course. He was sad that you lived on the other side of the country and that you didn't speak to each other. And then I saw you here, and I was struck right away. Struck—a strange word. But that is how I felt."

She watched him to be sure he wasn't playing around. He seemed sincere, but *struck* could mean so many things. Struck by beauty, struck by lightning, struck by *something*, that indefinable quality that makes your head turn toward the person exuding it no matter what. And could he be…shy? Looking down under those long eyelashes? Shy! With her!

"It was mutual," she said, feeling her cheeks go warm.

"I mean," he said, taking a step, closing the space between them and lowering his voice to a purr, "I work with kelp. It is not very interesting to many people, but I find it fascinating. Every so often, there are hints of the amazing ecosystem around the kelp."

"Like the bay plume," she whispered.

"Yes." He grinned. "It keeps my head in science too much, right? I need to feel more often—that's why I surf. When you came here and we talked, you were so clearly feeling a lot of things and were conflicted and… I don't know how to say. It made me feel too. And I want that."

She breathed carefully. "You like it when I help you feel?"

Now he gave her a playful look. "I very much like that. And more. I like that you draw and that you're into biology. I like that you didn't want to give up on trying to find a brother you hadn't seen in years, even if you didn't know if he'd want you to find him. I like that your family means so much to you."

Now it was Natalie's turn to feel shy. "Should we call someone?" she whispered, unsure why she was whispering. "About the door?"

In answer, he leaned toward her, cupping her cheek, making her die, and lowered his face to hers. "May I?"

She could barely breathe out a "yes" before his lips touched hers, tentatively at first and then with hunger. He pulled her to him, and she reveled in the full warmth of his body. His lips told her secrets that she could only wonder at, but which she looked forward to discovering. For now, she was lost in his kiss. She sank into his arms, his face, his hands. The chemistry between them was unreal and so, so good.

When they came up for air, she said, "Wow. Is that how it is here in the supply room?"

He grinned. "Only with the right person."

She went in for another kiss, reveling in all the sensations of him and in the knowledge that something was really right and good with him. Thank God she was rid of Paul. Paul was part of what she'd tried to fool herself with, trying to deny that she could ever be okay without her family or trying to make herself settle for boyfriends who were never quite right. Thank God she'd decided to stay. Maybe she'd miss hearing people say "cah" and "wicked awesome," but maybe not.

He moved his mouth to her neck, behind her ear, sending a delicious shiver of desire down her back, around to her stomach, up to her head.

"So are you going to stay in Santa Cruz?" he whispered in her ear.

"I'm not going anywhere."

"You can't anyway, because we're trapped in here."

"This room is *such* a fire hazard."

"It's not really locked," he said.

"Let's pretend it is." She ran a hand up through his hair and pulled him toward her again. In response, he nipped her bottom lip with his teeth, and she sucked in a breath of pure anticipation. He moved his mouth away from hers and put his lips close to her ear again. He whispered something softly.

"What did you say?" she murmured.

In answer, his lips moved down her neck.

"I want to know everything about you. Your likes, your hates, your family, your childhood," she said.

"I want to tell you."

Natalie felt full, hopeful. She leaned against him, sighing. Floating. Disbelieving. Wait until Teensy heard. Wait until Michelle heard. Wait until Lynn and Jake heard. Wait until the whole world heard that Natalie Walker was home and whole again.

THERE IS HELP

If you are experiencing domestic violence, including emotional abuse, please seek safety and healing.

There is safe, secure support for you.

National Domestic Abuse Hotline (safe line)
Phone: 800–799-SAFE (7233)
Chat online: thehotline.org
Text: START to 88788

Break the Silence
Chat online: https://breakthesilencedv.org

To learn more about how to talk about domestic violence, support others going through it, or respond in the aftermath of abuse, visit the resources at wannatalkaboutit.com/sexual-violence.

READING GROUP GUIDE

1. At the beginning of the book, Natalie thinks she wants the promotion at Argo & Pock. As the story develops, it's clear that's not what she really wants deep down. Think about a time you were adamant that you wanted one thing in life only to realize you wanted something completely different. How did you react? Did you go after it?

2. Discuss why you think Natalie felt so desperate to cling to her relationship with Paul and her friendship with Teensy.

3. Natalie seems to have a reluctance to live outside her comfort zone and pursue her professional dreams. Why do you think that is? Have you ever held yourself back in life, either intentionally or unintentionally?

4. Do you think Natalie was right to have called the police on Lynn and Jake That Night? Do you think it was fair that they in turn blamed her for Carlos's death and being sent to prison?

5. Do you think Natalie ever would have reconciled with her siblings if her mother hadn't died?

6. Which sibling seemed to change the most between when they were kids and now? If you have siblings, are they more or less the same, or have they changed pretty drastically since childhood? What about you?

7. Natalie is under the impression that a lot of people still hate her for what happened That Night—Jake and Lynn, her mom and Buck—when it turns out a lot of that is in her head. Have you ever mistakenly thought someone was mad at you? How did you deal with it?

8. Natalie quickly forms a close bond with her nephew, Kit. Why do you think she was so eager to do so?

9. Beyond being a romantic interest, what other role does Asier play in helping Natalie heal from her past?

10. In what ways are each of the siblings similar? How are they different? If you have brothers or sisters, do you think your personalities or the ways you deal with things are similar or very, very different?

11. Do you now live in a different place from where you grew up? If so, when you've gone back to visit, what was it like? What memories did it conjure up?

A CONVERSATION
WITH THE AUTHOR

What inspired you to write *A Very Typical Family*?

This story went through a lot of iterations before I arrived at its final plot, but throughout them all, I kept drifting to a story of adult sibling dynamics. I didn't grow up with siblings, so watching how siblings of all ages interact and rely on each other—or don't rely on each other—is fascinating. For this story, I wanted to explore the worst possible thing a sibling could do to another, and sending someone to prison was at the top of the list. There are a number of ways hurt can play out, and I was interested in what you do with that hurt and how you go on afterward. If siblings have a strong foundation from childhood, how does that buoy their adult relationship? Most of all, I wanted to play with the idea that family in adulthood is partly about choice—and we see Natalie and her siblings make that choice both ways at different times in their lives.

Santa Cruz, California is such a great setting for this book and plays a big role throughout the story. What are some of your favorite memories of having grown up there?

Santa Cruz is on a lot of lists of top destinations in Northern California, but for me it'll always look and smell like home. It's a small city and yet captivating for so many—the beaches are great, the surfing is good, and there's this sort of shabby-chic undercurrent to life there. Even the fog and the light are special. I tend to conflate memories there with an easier time in life—when I was little, family and my world was simpler. Favorite memories for me include frequent visits to Long Marine Lab. I remember visiting the blue whale skeleton when it was sitting atop a windy hill of wildflowers, unconnected and unprotected. I was a docent at the lab when I was eleven, back when it was just a series of portables, and I was featured on an episode of *Bay Area Backroads* as a result. I was that kid telling visitors, "The arteries of a blue whale are so big that a cat could comfortably run through them." The facility helped usher in my lifelong love of marine biology. Other great memories include the Beach Boardwalk—I was too little and scared for the Giant Dipper, but I loved the log ride—and walks along West Cliff Drive and in Neary's Lagoon. There is so much to do there for such a small city. The Walkers and their Victorian mansion could be any one of the city's Victorians or Queen Annes, especially those near West Cliff Drive and over on Walnut Ave. I set their home in my head on Santa Cruz Street on the west side, but I took their home from those around Third Street on the Boardwalk hill. I visit as often as I can and build new memories with my children!

Do you see parts of yourself in any of your characters? What is the process you go through from that first idea for a character to bringing them to life on the page?

I am sure there's a part of me in every character, no matter how much I try to pretend there isn't. Natalie in particular has a very passive element to her that plays out as conflict avoidance. It's difficult for me to engage in conflict or muster up the energy required to initiate a conflict, and I think that's true for Natalie. It's one of the reasons why Paul is allowed to say what he does and stick around as long as he does. In fact, edits to the story included making sure to get that confrontation on the page—and for me, it was a major deal to write those scenes! First I wrote them very passively, with Natalie simply firmly telling Paul off without raising her voice much. But I knew she had to do it better, and finding a way to do that better was a big deal for me emotionally. Unlike me, Natalie doesn't sweat and feel anxious before a confrontation. The final confrontation with Allen was similarly difficult to write because again—conflict.

As for Lynn, I think she has chosen to approach the idea of death, which has affected her so much in life with the loss of her father at a young age, then the loss of her friend Carlos, followed by her mother's death, without resolution between them, by handling it head-on as her profession. That's not something I could do myself, but I am fascinated and drawn to the way we look at death and handle—or don't handle—our reaction to it, especially in the United States. The excellent book *Smoke Gets in Your Eyes: And Other Lessons from the Crematory* by Caitlin Doughty addresses these issues and was also an inspiration and reference for Lynn's professional funerary pursuits. It is hilarious and kind of gross, which is how I choose to look at death too.

What do you think happened to the Walker family—Natalie, Jake, Lynn, and Kit—after the book ends? Do they all stick around in Santa Cruz together?

I think they all remain in Santa Cruz, because after all those wasted years, they don't want to spend any more time apart. I like to think Natalie settles into her work with Dr. Berkhower and keeps a good set of galoshes handy for those times when they have to go out to do necropsies on dead whales and sea lions on beaches. And she takes it appropriately slow with Asier, but they are really happy together. She wants to have a healthy, lasting relationship, so she's not jumping into things too quickly, but they spend a lot of time snuggling in bed on weekend mornings with the fog creeping over the cliffs. I think Natalie and Kit continue growing a really great relationship and Natalie and Lynn get to the point where they enjoy spending time together. I envision Sunday meals in the house for them all, including Buck, overriding those bad memories of That Night in the house. Friendships are important to Natalie, so she probably spends a lot of time with Michelle and new friends she makes in her illustration program. She and Teensy keep in touch—but maybe not as much.

And Penguin sticks around these days, choosing to live at the Walker house no matter how many times Natalie brings him over to the house she eventually shares with Asier on West Cliff Drive. (Penguin splits his time between the houses and often scores two dinners out of the deal.)

You often talk about the importance of tension in stories. Why is it such an important element? What are some tips you have for writers to employ more tension in their own writing?

Tension is so much fun! Tension makes the payoff of a conflict that much more exquisite. Everyone lives off tension, in good and bad ways.

It frustrates me when I'm reading a story that gives me the resolution too soon. I want to see characters yearning for what it is they want, even if they make poor choices along the way. If we all got what we wanted right away, it wouldn't be as fun. Tension is universal in stories too. It can make a horror story incredibly scary by drawing out the dread, and it can make romantic elements sing when characters yearn for each other without getting the payoff of each other for a while. A good writer, I think, pulls that string of tension taut or loose depending on the scene, playing the reader like a musician. My advice to writers struggling with tension is to throw as many obstacles in the way of their characters as possible. Never let them get what they want; don't let them be safe, don't let them be loved, and don't let them have the final say. Until they do, of course.

What was your path to becoming a writer? Did you always know you wanted to write novels?

I have always written stories. I used to fill notebooks with stories in middle school and high school. I wrote when I was younger to make sense of emotions and situations and to play out how I thought things could go—or not go. It was my own form of therapy. In my twenties, I wrote longer stories, but it wasn't until my early thirties that I got serious about it. I began to learn about the publishing industry and genres and word counts. It took a lot of manuscripts and a lot of years, but I'm so grateful to be where I am. Writing novels, supported by such an amazing team, is the dream.

What is your writing process like in terms of your routine? When and where do you write? Are you a plotter or a pantser?

I'm a plotter first! I'm a technical writer for my day job, so having an outline and structure is absolutely key—I learned that early on in my career. For novels, I usually start with the fifteen *Save the Cat!* beats (read *Save the Cat!* by Blake Snyder if you're not familiar) and go from there. I structure stories in chapters according to the plot, and then after that it gets a bit looser. I want to allow myself space to grow the story the way it wants to be grown, so I'll allow myself to meander for the first draft. I always need to squirrel myself away from family and work in order to write, so I usually have my headphones on, a cup of tea ready, and the door closed. No distractions.

What are some of your favorite books, and what is it you think you love so much about them?

I love the old sagas by Maeve Binchy and Rosamunde Pilcher. There's incredible richness in their stories in terms of character, pain, and setting. There are elements in their books that I read when I was a kid and still think about today. They handle love, siblings, parents, and friendships very well, while often being subtle in their resolution but no less satisfying. I also love dry humor. I have loved all books by Marian Keyes because she takes really complex situations and makes them so funny. I am always drawn to stories about relationships, whether it's between families or lovers, because there's so much in them that can go wrong and so much we have to do to make it right. More currently, I love smart, wry fiction about families and relationships.

Do books have a designated place in your home? What's in your TBR (to-be-read) pile these days?

I have a lot of tall bookshelves! In fact, we recently had a whole wall of our living room converted to bookshelves. I love looking at their spines and remembering the feelings I had while reading them or what I learned from them. Books are so personal too, so for me it's a shy way of saying "Here is who I am" to the world—or anyone who comes in my house. My TBR pile is always growing, and I'm compelled these days to read new releases and books by author friends. I set a goal for myself to read a certain number of books a year, but so far my average is about thirty-five. I am always trying to pick up that pace.

ACKNOWLEDGMENTS

The Walkers have evolved through many iterations and story lines, and there are many people who were beyond generous and helpful to me along the way. A huge thanks to my agent, Melissa Edwards, who took a chance on this story and on me. I couldn't ask for a better advocate on this journey and I'm so grateful. Thank you to my incredible editor, Erin McClary, who totally gets me. I've always hoped for an editor who is as insightful, thoughtful, and on it as you, and working with you has been an absolute dream come true. I am so lucky. Thanks also to Tara Rayers, whose thorough edits got this story to where it needed to be, and the incredible Sourcebooks team who worked to make this book real: Jessica Thelander, Heather VenHuizen, Stephanie Rocha, Molly Waxman, and Cristina Arreola—what a talented bunch to have with me.

Thank you to Mike Chen, who has been there from very early on with our trademark "diplomatically brutal" critiques and for pretty much everything else too. To the fierce and brilliant Denise Logsdon, who provides moral support in every way, thanks for putting up with my nonsense and being there for me through everything from words to children to cats and coyotes. Massive thanks to the irreplaceable and much-adored Kristen Lippert-Martin, who pushed me, prodded me, and Winston Churchill-ed me and my writing over the last million years, through the brain fog of having babies and the tough love of what came after. I am honored to call you friends.

To Jessica Sinsheimer, you are a gracious, generous friend and supporter, and I can't thank you enough for being there for me. Thank you to Sarah LaPolla, who read early drafts of this novel and who I know is cheering me on. Thank you to Tom Torre, who makes me laugh and always offers encouragement no matter how much I whine. Thank you to Bryan Miller, who also makes me laugh without fail and whose in-it Santa Cruz knowledge was super helpful in correcting my memory with this story.

Thanks to Kathleen Barber, who read an early (and heinous) draft of this novel and did not say bad things, only constructive, because she is a nice human. To Adrienne Go, thank you for the concise and quick overview on trusts, for the generosity of the beach house, and for supporting me from the moment I joined the family. I'm proud to call you my cousin. A thousand thank-yous to Sisalee Leavitt, whose unconditional love is a breathtaking gift, for being so excited to read, and for everything else—what a rich, amazing life we get to have. To Erika Norro, thank you for your constant support and early reads on this book and all the others, clunkers or not. To Andrea Burnett, who always has good ideas and even better stories, thank you so much for all that you do for me and for the laughter, and thanks to Barb Cavoto for your friendship, support, and making my drink weak without even asking.

To my #TeamMelissa siblings, you are truly the best group. Every day you make me laugh and provide encouragement and wisdom—even, and especially, about dead hikers. Extremely kind, ridiculously supportive, and unbelievably hilarious, I'm proud to call you friends.

Thanks to Matthew and Tim, who could have interrupted me a bit less while I was writing this book but did pretty darn well overall with giving me the space to make my dream come true. Extra thanks to Matthew for knowing Penguin even before I did. And finally to Ken, thank you for supporting me no matter what, for only mildly complaining during all the drive-bys I did of Santa Cruz mansions, and for being open to the city because of me, including the vague suggestion that we could retire there, which we totally will do as a result.

ABOUT THE AUTHOR

© Sisalee Leavitt

Sierra Godfrey is a technical writer, graphic designer, and former credentialed sportswriter covering Spanish soccer. When she's not writing about messy families, she's taking long walks, reading, and being cozy. Originally from Santa Cruz, California, she has lived all over the world, including Santorini, Greece, but now resides in the San Francisco Bay Area with her family, which includes a dog, two cats, and a turtle, all of which seemed like a good idea at the time.